A Very Religious Man

D. M. Smith

RHAPSODY

Published 2023 • United States of America

A VERY RELIGIOUS MAN

This is a work of fiction. All of the characters and places are fictional. Any resemblance to actual persons or places is purely coincidental.

Published 2023 by Rhapsody Press, Texas, USA

Oh! I have slipped the surly bonds of Earth
And danced the skies on laughter-silvered wings;
Sunward I've climbed, and joined the tumbling mirth
Of sun-split clouds, —and done a hundred things
You have not dreamed of—

From *High Flight,* John Gillespie Magee, Jr.

Part I

Brother Tom

1

It is a good day.

Boiling surf crashes and roars up the beach, hissing into sand; then retreats, spent; then roars again. Warm sunlight falls through towering cumulus, clouds of late summer—broad white columns with blazing crowns and flat, leaden footings—falls splashing like liquid fire across heaving blue water rolling in from the horizon, endlessly; a horizon now distant, razor-thin, limitless; now obscured by a far squall, drifting, changing, fading. Gulls scream and surf thunders and the beach quivers underfoot, a shifting anvil for the pounding of the waves.

A hundred yards from shore the heavy water falls and rises with a long easy sweep, the rhythm of some final power advancing shoreward, neither slow nor fast but the embodiment of the beginning and the end, all of time gathered up into that bright, empty space between two waves, to be apprehended in a single glance, a single thought, before the glance moves on.

A head appears. Crowned with short white hair, it breaks the surface followed by shoulders surging, propelling the head shoreward, until it reaches shallow water and comes to a stop.

The old man stands. He is naked, skin reddish-brown from just days in the sun rather than a lifetime, shoulders tinged blue with the cold of the water. A wave comes up, and he stands braced while it breaks about him, shooting up spray from his lean body. As though sliced in two, it passes and re-merges, rolling to its long crash along the beach.

He begins moving, forcing his way through seething foam. Water splashes about his feet as he walks onto the beach, trickles from his fleshless face and long, muscled legs. He turns, scanning the horizon as though searching, as though gazing homeward, at distant ancestors still bright in memory, and time.

He does not linger. A tattered white cloth flapping in the afternoon breeze hangs from a tall, gnarled stick stuck upright in the sand. He ties the cloth loosely about his waist. A canteen also hangs from the stick, and he takes this, unscrews the cap, and swallows a mouthful of water. The cap screwed firmly back, he slings the canteen over his shoulder and pulls the stick from the sand.

The sloping beach is a smooth, firm plane, and the high arches of his feet leave deep impressions, to be filled in and washed away by the tide, alongside sharp holes punched by the gnarled walking stick.

———————————

Dawn.

At the top of a large, round hill, a dozen or so people kneel on bare ground, in a steady breeze, and shiver a little. Before them stands a lone figure watching the brightening horizon, arms outstretched, a robe billowing about him, thick brown hair stirring in the breeze. He waits. The breeze dies. The horizon grows brighter, and a tiny incandescence appears, growing, and the light strikes the assembled People, and night becomes a memory.

The figure turns to them and smiles.

"Brothers and sisters! Let the Word light every corner of your souls! Even as the sun lights every corner of our world!"

"And yours!" they cry.

"Now go, and bring light to those still in darkness."

"Amen," they murmur, rising from their knees.

The figure walks among them. He shakes hands, talking quietly with two or three at a time. The sun clear of the horizon, mists in the valley below blaze painfully bright, leaving the hilltop a world of its own, beneath a blue dome, caressed by the warming sun.

After a time, the People begin departing their separate ways, and the figure watches, eyes tranquil.

"Onward Christian soldiers, eh?"

Brother Tom turns at the voice. Behind him, an old man leers, but looking past him as though laughing at the sun. In the raking light, lively blue eyes like crystals sink deep into cavernous sockets beneath the sloping forehead. A long nose hooks downward toward a lantern jaw. Cheeks and jaw are stubbled black, but above the ears a mat of white flutters in the breeze. The thick lips are parted in a knowing smile.

The preacher frowns.

"Ah, Marco. To what do I owe the honor?"

"Nothing special, brother. Thought I'd get up early and watch a pro at work."

"You are a cynic, Marco. You should have stayed in bed."

Marco bows slightly.

"I mean it with the greatest respect. You are an artist. One of the best that I have seen. And I have seen many, in a long life."

Shaking his head, the preacher turns and follows his People leaving the hilltop, loose robe flapping.

Marco trails behind, slower, limping slightly, one leg seemingly shorter than the other.

He chuckles to himself.

"Bring light! Oh, yes! Bring light to those in darkness!"

2

At home in a small rectory, two miles from the hill, Brother Tom removed his robe, folded it, and put it away. The robe was a plain affair, too large, and it hung from his frame at an odd angle. It had been sewn, badly, by one of the young girls of the People, but Tom wore it unabashed. She had done her best, and it seemed fitting. They had all so much to learn.

He sat to his desk and wrote out his impressions, ideas that had come to him earlier, comments from his followers, tidbits of news they had brought him. He took his time, pausing once in a while to think back, to reflect over the reactions to the morning's sermon.

His talk had been drawn from a favorite topic, the evils of the time before, and on this morning in particular the evil of organizing men and women into armies laboring for the ease and vanity of a few, as they had once been organized into armies warring for the glory and wealth of a few. The irresistible power of those armies, driven by chiefs of reckless ambition, had destroyed the world, and he had expostulated at length on the insidiousness of leadership itself, on the divine lesson of Brotherhood.

As he sometimes did, the boy Raul had posed a thoughtful question after sermon, in his typically diffident manner. Raul had surprising insight for a boy—a young man, really—and Tom suspected that several, more pointed questions might suggest themselves. From anyone else, it might have been an invitation to address those unasked questions, even a challenge, but Raul was respectful. He had merely asked whether it was wrong to rely on the labor of others.

The wisdom of the Apocalypse was wide and deep, and one learned a step at a time. Time itself was an ally of the patient, and Brother Tom was a very patient man.

So he had begun by speaking on the meaning of Brotherhood, that it was only right to contribute in what way one could, as well as one might, and to be guided by honest conviction when it was enough. As he spoke, Raul's eyes were on his teacher. And he was not alone. The confident, even-tempered flow of words drew in the others. Their own conversations forgotten, they listened, nodding from time to time unconsciously.

When it was over, Raul thanked him.

There was the sound of the front door opening and closing, and a scraping noise, Marco moving about the other room.

"Bring the tithes, Marco," he called, without lifting his head.

The old man shuffled into the study and stood near him, watching in silence.

After a minute of it, Tom glanced up.

"Why do you do that?"

"Do what, brother?"

"Never mind. The tithes?"

A worn, flat envelope slapped quietly on the desk, and Tom slid it into a drawer. He would take care of it later, after Marco had left. Not that he had reason to mistrust the old man. Still, it was the People's money, after all.

Marco was still there.

"What about breakfast, Marco?"

"Ah, of course." Marco limped from the room. Tom went on writing.

Presently the smell of frying bacon reached him, and his stomach rumbled, and he sat back and rubbed his eyes, then frowned, recalling Marco's appearance at service this morning. It was not like the old man to hike that far, that early, for no reason. Certainly not for service. Marco was a trusted helper, but he helped because he was paid, not because he believed. Or understood. Or did he? Marco was an enigma, by turns not quite flesh and blood, then all too worldly.

Tom shook his head and put his notes away.

They sat to breakfast. Tom murmured his customary prayer, and Marco waited, patient, eyes twinkling. Tom tried not to look at him. It was enormously irritating—the old man's unrelenting sunniness. He began to eat, moodily.

Marco munched a piece of dry toast.

"The church must have quite a lot of money by now, no? You never spend it."

"It keeps bread on the table."

"Ah, bread." The old man chuckled. "You could buy a pretty farm with what you must have."

"It doesn't belong to me. You know that."

"Oh, no, of course. It belongs to the church."

"To the People, Marco. This isn't a church."

"Of course."

Marco finished his toast, lightly brushed crumbs from his fingers, and proceeded to roll a boiled egg around his plate, crackling the shell. Then he peeled it.

"What will the People do with it?"

The preacher glanced up. "With what?"

Marco held up the naked egg, grinning.

"Never mind, Brother. Eat your breakfast. Keep up your strength. You have important work."

Tom stared at him a moment, but Marco was biting into the egg, his gaze elsewhere.

Sometimes the old man made no sense. Maybe he had lived alone too long. Maybe he was becoming addled, a bit senile. It could explain the constant sunniness.

He felt his mood soften, and rose to his feet.

"Take your time, Marco. I'll clean up. You needn't bother today. Go home when you've eaten."

Macro did not look up.

"Why, thank you, Brother."

Brother Tom was a driven man.

He did not appear so. He appeared imperturbable. But in a profound, wordless way, he believed that everything happens for a reason. And this belief had nearly destroyed him.

He still remembered his childhood. He remembered joy and light and expectation, cruelly so, because the expectation had been answered by the Plague that had leveled the world, and swept away those he loved. But he had lived. And, as he approached manhood, had begun to question why.

For a long time he had examined his own life, searching for a fault that would justify his pain, as he searched the lives of others, the older ones still living, for a sign of redemption, that would justify their peace. So many could not suffer and die for nothing. There had to be guilt. There had to be a reason, a lesson, some intelligence hiding, perhaps, in plain sight.

At some point, he could not remember exactly when, he gave up. And that was when the real torment began, because he could find no reason for anything. Meaning in the world was but an illusion, and for a time he doubted whether he belonged in it. Gradually, he grew into a silent, remote, brooding presence, with a wide stare and a closed mouth. People shunned him.

One day he left his home, a small farm worked by a distant relation, and wandered to the main road. When he reached it, he continued walking, stumbling over ruts and mounds, following the muddy road all the way through the exile community, with no idea where he was going, no reason to continue, but with no reason to stop. As the sun was setting, he came to a ribbon of black pavement that wound north through the trees.

He followed the pavement.

Sometime after nightfall, something leaped from the darkness, a shadow that knocked him down and went through his pockets, taking what little he had, then fleeing. He did not resist. When it was over, he got up and went on.

When day broke, he stood in the road, enthralled by the silhouetted skyline still miles distant, the City he had heard about all his life, had imagined and feared, but never seen. He watched as the sun rose higher and the silhouettes became shapes, towers pointing at the sky.

They seemed to call to him, and the City became his home. For a time.

He had haunted streets and alleys by night, hid by day, ate whatever scraps he could find or steal, and avoided the sight of people. The memory of that time was dark, forbidding, and even now he could not say just how he had survived. Or why he had left.

Andersonville had a church of a sort, a small house in the woods that served the needs of a handful of people deeply troubled by life, what was left of life, people perhaps like Tom, but humbler, more resigned. Someone found Tom lying in the main road one day, dehydrated and delirious, and brought him to the church.

The church took him in.

Astonishingly, he lived.

He was, in fact, reborn. Because now he understood.

The Plague was not Armageddon. It was not end times, not punishment for the wicked. Nor was it mindless disaster, haphazardly inflicted on those who had done no wrong.

It was a Culling.

The logic was inescapable. He perceived what had been hidden from him: that the world had been evil. And those who remained in it had indeed been saved for a reason. To begin again.

The spared had received the divine gift of a new chance. Not because they were better, but because there was not room for more. Good and evil remained. The spared were on earth to learn to do better.

This was epiphany, the salvation of dry land in a sea madness, that led him up from the depths of ignominy. This was truth, with the certainty of revelation.

But he found something more, a deeper revelation, more difficult to perceive, but crucial. Evil had been misunderstood. It was not the old sins, of lust and envy and greed. Those were mere peccadilloes, misdemeanors, venial and pitiable. They might destroy individuals, possibly families. Not worlds.

True evil was the sin of hubris, the ravages of leadership and power, of dominance and organization, the mass insanity of mass persuasion.

True good was therefore simple, beautifully so: Brotherhood. Nothing more.

It was then that Tom began to preach. And there were people who began to listen, to experience a strange and stirring connection between a man who found such profound meaning in life and those for whom life was but a wanton absurdity, a beggar's choice between the Sisyphean ordeal of survival and the horrors of aloneness and death. It was a connection that brought ten or twenty of them weekly to the top of a forgotten hill to watch the sun rise.

Brother Tom knew this to be the beginning of his life, his true life. He knew the path would be hard. But this he did not mind. For if he could not be certain where it would lead, he knew it would lead somewhere. He was on earth for a reason.

Poverty and aloneness he bore easily enough, a badge of honor, a test of strength.

But one burden he bore behind a wall of shame that hardened into something not quite self-hatred, the tormenting weakness of flesh in his otherwise chaste existence, the unspeakable shame of waking from some lurid dream with an explosion of hot fluid in his nightclothes, when he would throw himself upright, heart pounding, then stagger to the basin to clean himself and wipe away the memory.

Easing back onto his small bed, heart settling, he would close his eyes and empty his mind.

It was all right. It was all right. He was only human. Only a man.

It would be forgotten in the morning.

Claudio Marco Marcello lived in a shack.

He had found this shack in the woods and took it, because he had to live somewhere, and because no one would bother him there.

The woods skirted the hill Brother Tom used for service, just a half-hour walk from the rectory, but Marco's shack was deep inside and not so easy to find. Even Tom was not sure where he lived. Which was as the old man preferred it.

When he found the shack, it was empty. The door had a simple latch and no lock, but Marco had no need of locks. The roof leaked, until he acquired some discarded boards and made repairs.

He acquired a small table and chair, so he would not have to sit on the ground. He acquired a cot. The cot was not very comfortable, but it was what the shack would accommodate.

Above his table, he constructed a bookshelf. The shelf held a dozen volumes that interested him. Gibbon. Herodotus. Tacitus. Montaigne. The books were old, their round spines worn and cracked, pages yellowed and stained.

He cooked over a small fire in the clearing before his door. He boiled water for tea, when he could afford the desiccated leaves.

The shack had but a single pane for light, yet this was a blessing in winter, when he must stuff old papers and rags under the door and into cracks in the walls to keep snow and blood-freezing wind from whistling through unhindered. He kept dry deadwood in a pile, and on frozen days, when he was not needed at the rectory, he would push the snow from his fire-pit and ration a stick at a time, for a little blaze and some tea.

On summer days he would sit outside in his chair, reading or whittling. He would watch the light in the trees, and think. He did not brood. He did not think about the plague, Cargo Flu, nor the two decades that followed, fallow and empty.

But of what he thought, he never spoke.

Not to anyone.

3

There was something about glass and concrete and granite towering around her, sculpting rooms and offices, even kitchens, living space for people where people had no business living, neighbors in a world of steel and air hundreds of feet high over pavement.

Some lines of poetry came to her.

Oh! I have slipped the surly bonds of earth . . .

Cantilevered beams might seem far from laughter-silvered wings, but had once laughed their own quiet laughter, had flown their own kind of flight. Sunlight cascaded from walls of polished stone and scattered from windows in a thousand directions, the air alive with a kind of shimmering energy she would find nowhere else.

Agnes stood on the sidewalk in an abandoned corner of the City, her fine pale hair tossed now behind her and now across her face by gusts of wind that swirled among the buildings and whipped around her body. Her glance traveled the empty avenue, across clouded glass and faded trim, her mind filling in all things that were missing. The sounds of motors and horns and the screech of brakes, laughter and shouts for a taxi, the smells of food and coffee and maybe a cigarette, the clipped staccato of hurrying steps.

What met her eyes were fluttering pigeons and bare pavement.

She was alone, and the buildings were dead, monuments to another time, so far removed that even the memory of it no longer troubled the living.

But it troubled her now.

They're not monuments. They're corpses. Someone I once loved, without knowing it. Bit by bit, they will crumble, until nothing remains. And they will not return.

They will not return. Something had left the world, something that no one had really understood. Something about the height . . . and she cursed that other age that had not understood, that had cast away its height, and the wind whipped her body and the shimmering blurred into tears and she turned angrily and began walking, the tops of buildings high above gazing back through space, and time.

In the evening, she sat alone in her living room, with a cold cup of coffee. She had not returned to the City. Not really. She just had to be here a while.

A stale piece of bread on the low table by her knees was a reminder that she hadn't eaten today. Or yesterday. Yesterday had been spent picking through the wreckage, the remains of Barbara's place, after they had buried her. Not too much had escaped the flames. A few pots and pans, a few utensils. A pair of kerosene lamps. Some sticks of furniture. And, against a crumbling wall of what had once been the living room, a shelf of engineering books.

That was especially hard. But she had collected it all and stacked it in the barn out of the weather. Then she had fed the animals and saddled a horse—after several embarrassing attempts—and ridden here, to her City apartment, increasingly strange to her, where she had wandered the rooms, gathering things to take with her, filing away memories. When evening came, she had sprawled on a chair while the living room darkened, until there was just the soft glow of electric light from outside, the only company she needed. Or wanted.

But this morning she had felt that sudden need, to walk, to feel pavement under her feet. To take her leave.

She thought about that now. She knew the Corporation would take her back. They needed people like her, and they knew it. But that had been a job. Her life here had been a job, plus a series of relationships, encounters really, that had served to break the monotony.

Except the last encounter. The one she could never repeat.

She sipped a little coffee. Her old drawings, still tacked to the walls, attracted her glance, and she went from one to another, feeling the pencil again in her hand. The drawings had helped. They were but abstract exercises in geometry, yet they were living, intense, like a sudden shout of laughter, or a scream.

She did not want a job. Not anymore. Not after being paid by people for something she had conceived in her own mind, and brought to life with her own hands. She and Steve Foster. That had been a revelation, like a crack of thunder, still reverberating. It was how she meant to live from now on. And it meant leaving the City.

She closed her eyes, feeling the buildings of this morning tower around her again, trying to hold on to what she felt, to keep it alive somewhere inside—for the rest of her life, if necessary.

In the morning, when she left the apartment for the last time, she locked the door, pausing with her hand on the smooth wood, wondering why it still mattered to lock out the world. It seemed futile. Yet it mattered.

She went down two flights of stairs, past her mailbox lined up with the others on one wall, and out the glass door.

Her steps along the sidewalk were sure and steady. Everything was really very simple. It was a short walk to the bus stop, no different than countless other mornings in her life. Only this time it was to ride across town to a horse park, set up by the City to stop visitors from Andersonville fouling the streets. Her receipt and a small bill changed hands, and then she was mounted again, riding south, block by block as the sun cleared the tops of buildings and shadows retreated from the street; then west for two miles or so past warehouses and low industrial buildings long quieted by the Plague. Then south again, along the old unpaved road leading out of the City, that she had learned from Max.

She did not look back.

In less than an hour she was deep in the trees and approaching the small guard shack.

On her way in, two days ago, the soldiers had stopped and questioned her. Now they just nodded as she passed.

You are free to go.

The words came to her, and seemed to follow along as the shack receded.

A canopy of green arched over the broad grassy road, that went on and on, the air still and quiet but for an occasional buzz of insects, hoof falls thudding softly. Miles from anyone, it was like being suspended between life and something else, not quite knowable. Yet it didn't matter. Because everything was so simple. So simple and so easy. Because there were no questions.

When she reached the asphalt pavement that was the North Road, she was hungry. Starving. But that was a simple thing as well. Not worth even the effort to think about.

Continuing south on the asphalt for a mile or two, she found the "main road", a band of graded dirt cutting eastward across the fields and farms of Andersonville. She turned and followed it as far as an unmarked wood building, any paint long since peeled away, where she dismounted and tied the horse.

Then she walked into the pub.

Two men were eating in a corner, the charred smell of meat a sharp reminder that she hadn't touched food since the scrap of bread yesterday. But it would wait.

She went through a doorway, into the back of the pub, around a short hallway, and found a large, burly man hoisting a bucket of water to pour into a basin.

"Bill."

The man turned to face her, putting the bucket down. He watched her, looking up and down as if searching for something out of place, like a crack in her exterior calm.

She smiled.

"It's okay, Bill. I won't blow up. I'm over it."

The reply was stolid, if dubious. The first voice she had heard in days.

"Uh huh."

"I'm okay. Really."

"Look, it's none of my business. But you don't just get over it. No one does. Not in a few days."

"Well, maybe I've found a way to keep my mind off it."

"What are you going to do?"

"Well, can I rent a room?"

Bill nodded, slowly.

"Okay, Agnes. You know you're always welcome here."

It surprised her, hearing her name in that familiar, gruff voice. But it felt right. Like throwing down an anchor.

"Thanks."

In the morning, she rode out to the Foster place, on the far eastern edge of Andersonville.

Dennis Foster grew a variety of things, none of which she knew how to recognize. But his modest farm was modestly successful, the Fosters lived modestly comfortable lives, and they enjoyed a more than modest respect around town. This much she did know.

When Dennis answered her knock, she was on the front porch in tight-fitting jeans and white tee-shirt under an open leather jacket, hair tied back, blue eyes shining with something he did not quite recognize. Or maybe he did, and did not like being reminded of it.

"Steve here?"

He frowned over his big, unkempt moustache, coughed his rattling cough, and grudgingly stepped aside. From somewhere inside the house, a woman's voice called, "Who is it, Dennis?"

"It's that City gal, Mother."

Agnes walked past him, and on impulse, patted the side of his face.

"Not anymore Dennis. In his room?"

"Ahh . . . yeah," he grumbled at her retreating back.

Stephen Foster was on his feet when she knocked on his open door.

"Agnes!"

"Hello, Steve."

"Damn! I didn't think we'd ever see you again . . . Not after what happened. You just disappeared."

"Well, I'm back. And I'm staying. Do we still have our business?"

For a few seconds he just was staring at her, and she supposed she wasn't being exactly fair. He was all of nineteen, after all. But he was a good mechanic.

Steve shook his head.

"Maybe we'd better talk about that."

There was a wood-framed chair with a wicker seat by a small desk, and she turned it around and sat on it, crossing her legs, one foot swinging a little, back and forth.

"Okay. Talk."

"Okay." He sat on the edge of the bed and blew out his cheeks. "Okay. First. They've all broken down, every generator we sold, and people are pretty pissed over money spent and no electricity. But I don't know how to fix them so they stay fixed. And after you left . . . well . . ."

"Well, go on."

"Okay. Second. I've been thinking about it, and there're only so many places we can do this. We need a stream that's big enough, but not too big. And we can only build so many dams on a stream, right? The water backs up behind each one. So suppose we sell to everyone who lives in a good spot, and suppose we figure out how to build them so they don't break down. The business will support us for . . . what? A year? If that. And then what?"

"Sounds about right. Any ideas?"

"Well, what else can you invent, Wonder Woman?"

"That the best you can do?"

He shrugged, his face reddening as he muttered, "I'm not say-ing we shouldn't do it. We make a good team, you and I. Maybe we can solve the problems. And people need it. But it doesn't seem to have much of a future, you know? You going to stay around for that?"

"Maybe we shouldn't sell generators."

"No? What, then?"

"Maybe we should sell electricity."

"Isn't that what we're doing?"

"No, that's *not* what we're doing. Look, Steve. Suppose we build a really big generator. We locate it somewhere along the river where there's plenty of hydro power. Then we sell electricity like they used to, by the month. And we sell to everyone, as far as we can run wire."

"Yeah, sure. That would be something. But . . . I don't know. Think about it. Think about my dad. People around here are pretty shrewd. Pretty bullheaded. They'd rather pay for some-thing once, and own it, and not have to owe anything to anyone else later."

"Sure, but think about this. These things are hard to build. You really need to know what you're doing. And we've learned a lot. Your dad grows oats, doesn't he? He sells to everyone, and he's had twenty years to learn the best way to do it. For us to sell a little generator is like your dad selling a little plot of land with a few oat plants on it, or bushes, or whatever they are. People would have to learn to cultivate their own oat plots and take the time to do whatever *that* takes, while their neighbors are right there beside them, doing the same. It would be a huge waste of time. It makes a lot more sense for Dennis to grow his acres of oats, and for every-one else to do what *they* do, and we all sell to each other."

Steve laughed.

"Oat bushes? Dad's right about you! You really *are* a City gal. Yeah, okay, I suppose we can also say that when they pay by the month, if times get tough they can always cut back and do with-out."

"Sure. We can come up with all kinds of good reasons."

"It's an idea. But can you make a generator like that?"

"That's what we have to find out. What about you? Can you make the turbine?"

"If I can find the materials, I don't see why not."

She stood up. "Then it's a deal?"

"Yeah. Yeah, it's a deal." He rose, extending his hand, and she clasped it, watching his face as her hand held his a moment longer than he expected.

No, really not fair at all.

"Okay, Steve. See you tomorrow."

"Uh—where?"

She answered lightly, "The usual place. Barbara's."

"But—"

"We'll have to clean it up, of course. The house is a total loss."
"But . . . it's not ours. Is it?"
"It is now."
"But . . ."
"Steve. It's what she would have wanted. And that's the way it's going to be."

She was there and waiting when Steve rode up to the wreckage of the Hutchins house the following morning. Then they went to work, tearing the place down.

It was hard. She broke down once and wept bitterly, for a long time, and Steve let her alone and continued working, until she could rejoin him.

For the next few days, stacks of salvaged lumber and pipes and brick grew in the barn, and piles of ash and rotting drywall were pushed into the trees.

Then the house was gone.

4

Max Wyse left the farmhouse where he boarded and walked to the pub, to have breakfast, and to get his horse. It was not a short walk, two miles or more, but the family he boarded with had their hands full with their farm and aging parents, were not interested in taking care of someone else's animal, and with his one arm Max was not able to do it himself. But he did not mind it, the daily walk. The time to himself, early in the morning, the feel of the main road under shoes, now graded and maintained by the Town of Andersonville— this was important. He needed it.

Andersonville. Once a nameless place in the wilderness where refugees who could not, or would not, live in the City—*Exiles*— had learned to live off the land, it had grown year by year into a town, a real one, with an elected government of its own, and no one talked about Exile anymore.

When he was young and whole he had loved this place. Even if he hadn't always realized it. He loved it still, its fields and trails and rolling hills, its peace and quiet determination, stubbornness and grace. There had been people he had loved, people he had looked up to, who were gone now, and that had been difficult, as difficult, almost, as losing an arm. Be he had learned.

This morning he walked along thinking about the oil lamp at the town office. Ali had set it up last night, in the meeting room, as the officers' meeting ran long after dark.

Why can't we get rid of it! If only the office was closer to a good stream . . . if we could get a generator . . .

He hated the lamp and its smokey yellow flame, and the memories it stirred.

At the pub, he walked into the dining area and recalled the other reason he didn't mind coming here each morning.

Agnes was sipping coffee, seated at a table by herself.

He walked over.

"Eaten yet?"

"Hi. Nope, not yet. Have a seat."

He pulled out a chair and sat down.

"How's business?"

"Oh, about the same."

She was slouched, pale hair tied up, her chin thrust forward and forming a sharp angle of resolve between the line of her shoulders and the soft down at the back of her neck. He could see she was tired, but could sense the anticipation, the preoccupation, the suppressed excitement, and he smiled.

"What's new?"

"Oh . . ." She shrugged. "Not much."

"Come on. Everyone knows you guys are working on something new. What is it?"

"We can't talk about it. Too soon."

"That's right. Keep me in suspense."

A mug of coffee was brought for him, and he ordered breakfast.

"Max, I've been thinking. Do you know what this town needs?"

"Oh, I dunno. More generators? More people."

"A market."

"A what?"

"A market. Somewhere to shop. A place to haggle. A place to mix."

He laughed.

"You know this isn't the City, right? It's not like anyone has a lot to sell. Besides, we all know where everyone lives. What'd be the point?"

"I'll bet people have a lot more than you think. For instance, the Coburns are pretty good at shoes. Did you know that? We were over there yesterday, replacing a turbine. Did you know they can make a new pair from scratch?"

"No. I did not know that."

"Well, they can. They don't do it very often. Usually just for themselves. But once in a while, someone pays them to make a pair."

"Good. What's wrong with that?"

"They could do better. Suppose we had a market, and suppose people could set up every weekend and show off their stuff. You might go because you need, oh, soap, and so-and-so has good soap. But while you're there you might see the Coburns' shoes, and decide you want a pair."

"Well, I don't need a pair."

"Says who?"

He kicked at a leg of the table. "Nothing wrong with these."

"So? Get another pair."

"Why?"

"Because you see something you like! Because you get tired of the same old thing. Because you *can.*"

"Isn't that a little frivolous?"

"You know, there are people in this town who think electricity is frivolous."

"Oh, come on! That's useful."

"Only if you have a use for it. I've been thinking about this, a lot. What matters is what people are willing to work for. Isn't that right? If you want that second pair, you'll work a little extra to get them, if you have to. And here's the thing. Bob and Alice Coburn could make two pairs of shoes in less than twice the time it takes to make one. Because they have everything set up, because they can prepare all the material at once, and because they get more practice. And maybe afford better tools."

"All that from a market, eh?"

"I'm serious! You'll want that second pair, or something else, once you see it. You and everyone else. And don't forget our City friends. They'll come, too."

"Well . . . I can't say it doesn't make sense."

5

Apparently, it made a great deal of sense.

It began as a patch of grass under some trees by the town office, and in a few weeks grew into Anderson Square, two acres of blankets and tables and people buying and selling and just milling about. And grew into a headache, with the need for latrines and water and someone to settle arguments over who had claims to which spaces, particularly the shady ones. Not to mention the melon rinds and fried potatoes left scattered about and rotting under swarms of flies the day after.

Dennis Foster, chairman of the Andersonville Town Committee, had reluctantly gone along with what he called 'the damned experiment', largely because a number of people had showed up at a Committee meeting loudly demanding it. He suspected Agnes, and went around muttering darkly to himself about 'that damned City woman'.

Now he felt vindicated.

"It's a goddamned mess! Just goes to show what goddamned *pigs* people are."

It was a Saturday afternoon. Agnes had come for the weekly Committee meeting, somehow suspecting that he would try to close down Anderson Square, once and for all.

She laughed.

"The piggier, the better, Dennis!"

He swore, trying to light an ancient cigarette with a decrepit match, but the match broke, and he jabbed the unlit tube at her, fingers trembling from a whole morning without smoke.

"Then *you* clean it up! If you think it's so damned great."

"The mess means it's working, Dennis."

"It's still a mess!"

"Then *deal* with it."

"I say we shut it down."

"You *can't* shut it down. It's working! It's the best thing to happen around here since—" He thought he heard the words *electric light* on her breath, but she went on, "Look, Dennis. Tell Max to organize it better. He's president. Isn't that his job?"

The Committee were inclined to agree. They were all going to Anderson Square each week. The thing had taken on a life of its own.

Dennis didn't bother asking for a motion, and after the meeting, rode home alone, defeated.

But it wasn't just discarded rinds and neglected latrines that troubled him. He wasn't too clear on what it was. But he knew that each weekend Anderson Square was infiltrated with young people who were much more interested in each other than in shoes or soap. They wandered about, laughing and giggling, hands straying where hands didn't belong, which often ended with a slap or sometimes a fist fight, which meant posting—and paying for— police deputies.

They just don't know. I may be sixty, and they think I'm an old man. But I've seen a few things.

It was early evening when rode past his own fields, put the horse up, and walked into his own house.

"Mother! I'm home!"

There was no answer.

He went into the kitchen and washed his hands, then went out the back way, easing the spring-loaded wooden screen door closed, and stood watching.

She was in her garden, on her knees and bent over, broad-brimmed sunhat and loose gray hair visible from behind clusters of gladiolus.

He called quietly: "Mother, I'm home."

She straightened and peered his way through the stalks.

"Oh! I didn't hear you."

"You look warm. Why don't you come in?"

"I will. Just let me finish with the weeds. They're taking over."

It was hard to see anything taking over from where he stood, but he had no doubt something foreign had found its way into the beds.

"Do you want anything? Glass of water?"

"No . . . I'm fine . . ." She was already bent over again, shoulders jerking as she routed the invaders.

He went back inside. She had her garden, and for that he was grateful.

In the evening, she made dinner. She always made dinner, even though he always offered to do it. "No, I'm fine," was her lilting reply. He set the table for just the two of them, since Steve was not around, and they ate together, and he asked about her day, and she talked about the garden and the weather, and the Flores, the older couple who lived nearby and helped around the house and farm.

After dinner, she wandered out to the front porch to sit in the evening dusk. "Don't bother with the dishes. I'll do them later." But she forgot, and disappeared after an hour into Maria's room, and Dennis washed and dried and put away the dishes, alone. In silence. As he had done for the past fifteen years.

6

Pushing to his feet against the ache in his knees, Dennis Foster, aged forty five, stood up and flung a ball of weeds to one side, then pulled a tattered rag from a back pocket and wiped the dusty sweat from his face.

The air was yet cool, but the bright sun of early May was warm above the crude furrows of the half-acre vegetable plot he was weeding.

He balled up the rag and shoved it into a pocket, then examined his hands. Brown dirt was jammed under broken nails, and calluses from months of hard labor were mixed with new blisters. But not so many blisters as last week. Or the week before.

Not the hands of a businessman.

He smiled at the thought.

For most of his adult life, Dennis Foster had been surrounded by idiots, idiots who had made his printing business such a headache to run. A few were idiots who had worked for him—for a short time—but mostly they were idiots from one official agency or other, prowling his plant and nosing around for something just a bit out of place, so they could leave behind a fancy citation full of imperious injunctions and meaningless deadlines. All for a toilet seat. Or a missing yellow line. Or a pressman smoking in the break room. And above all were the idiots who wrote these regulations and passed the laws, and had no idea how to run a business.

But the idiots were gone. All of them. And Dennis Foster, who had known nothing but machinery and paper and ink and contracts, had done what the idiots could not. He had survived. Had had kept himself alive, and his family alive, for over a year.

It had been a hard winter. The land around their new home, when they had found it, had been a desert of hard brown earth and sparse brown grass; then drifting snow and knife-like wind; then, finally, the lengthening days, and rain, and mud.

It had been especially hard on the children. Maria, smart as a whip, by rights should have been in second grade, but for the idiots who could not foresee what might be carried on billions of packages moving unhindered around the globe. Instead, she cradled and rocked her little brother Stephen, while he mewed with cold and hunger. She read to him the same stories over and over, until Dennis began to fear she would shriek and hurt someone. But Maria did not complain. She said little to Dennis, and nothing at all to her mother, but rocked and soothed and read, and sometimes stared, while the wind howled.

But Diane . . .

One night, weeks before, she had told him clearly, distinctly, and without emotion, that were it not for the children, she would end her own life.

He knew that she meant it. He suspected she was capable. And it was the one thing left on earth that could fill him with dread. That night, and many nights afterward, he had held her, stroking her beautiful auburn hair, explaining his plans, explaining how they would live, not as animals, but as human beings.

She seemed to listen. He could not be sure. But she never repeated it, and gradually he had let himself believe that she had forgotten it.

And now, after a long winter of almost nothing but venison, goat's milk, and vitamin supplements ransacked during their flight, he stood looking at rows of carrots and lettuce and beans, tiny green shoots poking through the crooked brown furrows.

He lifted his eyes.

Across acres of empty fields, laid out at the foot of the distant wall of trees, was a splash of color, brilliant blue and white. Wildflowers, spreading over the ground.

Diane Foster moved rapidly, wiping and straightening, but making no sound. This was important. Things that banged or scraped or bumped were real. She worked methodically, from one end of the room to the other, from time to time catching sight of Dennis through a window.

Poor Dennis. He tries so hard.

She wiped dust from one end of the narrow fireplace mantle, but looking at the other end, then at a table, then at a picture frame, her eyes always one step ahead of her hands moving quickly but thoroughly, feeling every corner and every nook under the cloth, ensuring no particle escaped; but like a blind person's hands, so she would not have to look at them, would not have to see them dry and chafed and cracked, like the hands of an old crone at the long end of her empty days.

Maria was in her room. Diane stopped by the door to listen. It didn't seem right that a seven year old girl should be so quiet, all the time, and she opened the door a crack.

The girl was reading. Her eyes moved across the page, left to right and downward line by line. It was a book she must know by heart, but she seemed intent, engrossed.

Diane pushed the door open a little further, thinking she should say something. But Maria only turned a page, without looking up, and Diane closed the door again.

There was work to do.

In the living room, Stephen Foster expelled a deep sigh of long-suffering boredom, slid off his chair, and toddled to the front door, reaching up with both hands to pull it open. He stepped through, onto the shaded porch, squinting at the glare of yard and fields.

It all looked very hot, and very dirty.

There was a rocking chair on the porch, and he climbed up and tried to make it rock, sliding forward to push with the tips of his toes, then back, grasping tight the arms, his short body bouncing to make it go. But it only teetered a little.

He gave up and climbed down, from the rocker and from the porch, staggering into bright sunlight, making his unsteady way over rough ground toward the large, familiar figure doing something in the dirt.

But his breath whooshed and he was hauled up by his armpits and swung round, feet flapping uselessly. Ahead loomed the porch, then the dark cave of the house. The door flew by, and he was plopped in a chair, a sharp voice ordering him to sit there and draw.

He looked up at his mother's retreating back.

The front door slammed and the house became silent. He picked up a crayon and made it go round and round, round and round, meaninglessly, over a wrinkled sheet of paper. The paper tore, and he gave up and put his head down, staring blankly and sucking at his fingers, hearing the wet sound.

Diane made her morning tea.

She sat at her breakfast table in the kitchen, cup and saucer before her, and stirred in a precious bit of sugar. Raised the cup to her lips. Blew, gently. Sipped, then carefully lowered it to the saucer again, picking up the little silver spoon and stirring absently, lapsing into daydream—a familiar one, in which a search party comes through the trees and discovers them. A search party come to rescue them.

Sometimes the deathly silence of the house, day by day, made her want to scream. But she would remember the maniacal shrieking of the wind, through the long, dark nights of winter, and she did not scream. She would whisper to herself, *There has* got *to be something left,* whisper it quietly so Dennis would not hear. But never in front of the children.

The sound of the front door intruded, slamming.

He came into the kitchen, passed by her, made clinking noises at the sink. Then his sun-browned hands appeared, and a clear bowl with a bright crown of crocuses, purple and white.

He placed the bowl at the center of the table.

"You see, Di? You see? It's spring."

She stared at it.

"Di . . . honey . . ." He was behind her, one hand on her shoulder, and she reached up to cover it with her own—her eyes transfixed by the purple and white things in her kitchen.

"Di, the vegetables are coming up."

"I know, dear."

He leaned over and picked a flower, white with a green stem, and pushed it gently into her hair. He touched his lips to her head, his fingertips at her shoulders, breathing her in.

Then he left. The front door opened and closed.

Still staring at the bowl, she reached up and took the flower from her hair, crushing it against her palm as her arm dropped to her side, fingers extended to point at the floor, where the thing fell.

Then she buried her face in her hands.

When she looked up, the bowl were still there.

"God! This is *not* how I expected my life to turn out!"

And she sat back and laughed, her mouth open in wonder.

Then she started to cry again, and shook her head angrily, wiping her cheeks with the backs of her hands.

But she saw her hands and groaned.

Mother! Oh God, Mother. If you could see me now.

She got up, shoved her chair against the table, and strode into the living room.

The room was empty, silent but for Maria's muffled voice reading to Stephen behind the closed door of her room.

She walked to a window. Outside was the emptiness she loathed, the glare of the sun, the endless dust and dirt, brambles and weeds, and in the distance that menacing wall of trees. And she knew, in her heart, that whatever lay behind that wall, it was not something that would come to their aid.

We'll never leave here. Ever. We're all going to die here, alone.

She was still staring at the trees. Something had changed. They were green. And she could feel the sun through the glass. It came to her then, it finally sank in, that the long, terrible winter was over. She placed her palm flat against the pane, smooth and warm, that seemed only yesterday enameled in ice.

The warmth was intoxicating.

The lone figure upright against the distant horizon drew her, and she watched, fascinated, watched him bend and straighten, bend and straighten, tirelessly, the sweat shining on his neck, dark on his shirt, under the armpits and across the back. She could smell him . . . recalled the taste of his skin. She had forgotten how strong he was. The sun-darkened hands ripped at weeds and flung them aside, the arms matted with dirt and hair, and she imagined those hands rough and grimy under her blouse, moving across her skin, taking her naked breasts . . . and was shocked at the warmth in her legs.

She left the window and began sweeping, forcing the old straw broom noisily against its bias across the floor, shoving furniture aside to dig furiously at baseboards, thinking they might die, and might die miserably, but they would not die in filth.

Old show tunes from the past seemed to wend their way through the air, and she hummed to herself in the kitchen, preparing lunch amid a bright clatter of dishes and the smell of outdoors drifting in through an open window and feeding the hunger inside.

That evening, after a not too meager dinner, the dishes washed and the children safely put to bed, Dennis collapsed in a chair.

He luxuriated in immobility, head thrown back, eyes closed, too tired ever to move again. He thought he had never been so tired in his life, yet so paradoxically alive. But he did not want to move.

Diane's low voice brought him awake.

"Dennis. Get out of those filthy clothes. Wash. You need rest, proper rest, not like this in a chair. There's more to do tomorrow."

He grunted, pushing himself to his feet.

In the bedroom, he pulled off shirt and shoes and socks and trousers, coughing at the stink, and kicked it all to one corner. Then he stumbled in his underwear against the stiffness in his legs to the big bathroom, candle in hand, hoping to find some water in the steel pot by the sink.

But in the bathroom, on the edge of the porcelain sink, two candles already burned, the warm glow flickering yellow across the cool black-and-white tile of the floor, fading into shadow in the corners. Something caught his eye, and he looked uncomprehendingly at the bathtub, at the shimmering plane of water clean and still.

Thick towels were folded and stacked on a stool nearby.

"Sweet Jesus," he breathed. "Is that real?"

"Get in, you fool."

He turned and in the half-light saw Diane, his Diane, closing the door behind her, barefoot and with only a thin wrap draped open throat to knees.

He tried to speak, but she quickly put a hand to his mouth, let the wrap slip from her shoulders, and prodded him toward the tub.

That day was the fifth of May. For five good years, Diane insisted it was their anniversary, their real one, and for five years they celebrated as they had that first night. By candlelight they would lie and soak, Dennis propped against the slope of the tub, head thrown back, Diane nestled in his arms, his hand on her bare back, her head at peace on his bare chest.

After the second year they had wine. And each year, crocuses.

Dennis Foster was now sixty years old.

Long ago, he had stopped wondering how his wife could sleep in Maria's bed. He could not bring himself to enter the room. Not after what happened.

For weeks he had sat by his young daughter's side while her once beautiful face was swollen, twisted, and demolished by an infection that started with a small, ugly scrape, and went on to ravage every last vestige of what had made that face hers, consuming her mind as well, first with unbearable pain, then with unrelenting fever, and in her final days she wandered her own purgatory of delirium, already lost to them.

Weeks of torture, of Diane incapacitated, of eight-year old Stephen surviving on scraps, of being devoured with rage over the criminal stupidity of a world that had left him without even a simple antibiotic.

Maria had been twelve years old.

He had buried her at the far edge of a young pine grove, away from the house. He had stood by himself looking down at the mound of fresh earth, dry-eyed and hating himself, because he could no longer remember what she looked like, because the only feeling he could summon was relief, that she was finally gone.

He walked back, cold, sick, and empty. He neared the house, and through a window his son's head was visible, tousled brown hair, thin boyish neck . . . and for the first time in his life Dennis Foster broke, bawling into his hands like a child. Unable to go on.

But he pulled his hands from his face and looked at them. His hands had never failed him. They never would. Whatever needed to be done, for Diane, for Stephen, for himself, he would do. They had the farm, they had each other, and they *would* pull through.

He straightened, wiped his face, and walked the rest of the way. He went inside, and firmly shut the door.

At first, Diane just wanted to be alone. She needed time, she said, to recover.

But in the first evenings after he buried her, he would find her in Maria's room, curled up on the bed, asleep, arms folded into herself, and he would pull a blanket over her and softly shut the door, and let her be.

Her tears stopped. The dark pockets faded from her eyes. But somehow the woman faded as well, drawn ineluctably into another world, where Dennis could not follow, and at some point he understood that she would not recover. Not completely.

He looked after her, and he looked after Stephen, and with the help of Mr. and Mrs. Flores he looked after the farm.

Diane did begin to speak again, if not so freely, would garden and clean and make dinner again. But she kept one foot in that other world, and one foot, reluctantly, in this one.

7

Dan Walsh sprawled.

One arm draped over the back of his chair. One leg stretched out. The other knee bumped up and down, nervously up and down. He chewed his lip.

Dan Walsh was on the Town Committee.

Chief of Police Bert Morrow leaned back and blew out his cheeks.

"Christ."

Walsh said nothing. He scowled.

Max Wyse got up and went to one of the double-hung windows that lined the meeting room, and lifted the sash. Every year the thicket of brambles outside the Town Office was cut down, but never defeated, and with the warm air drifted inside the smells of weeds and earth, and the hum of insects.

Bert Morrow looked at Walsh.

"*Now* what do we do?"

Walsh sucked his teeth. His knee bumped faster.

"Not much we *can* do, is there? She tossed him out empty-handed."

The previous day, Max had ridden to the City on a mission from the Committee, had ridden right up to the white office tower that was Corporate headquarters. People had stared. A few had jeered. But he had tied the horse to a lamp post and walked right into the building, where he was immediately stopped by Security.

Which was as he expected. It was not as though he could call ahead and make an appointment.

Security called someone for instructions They put him in a big conference room, where he waited for two hours with a pair of guards for company. He knew it was two hours, because there was a clock on the wall. But there was no conversation. The guards, in plain white shirts and dark slacks, kept silent, standing at ease the entire time at the end of the room with the door.

At the end of two hours, Elizabeth White, the Corporation's Chief Executive, and someone who introduced himself as Bill Baird, came into the room with a small entourage and sat down.

They listened, and he complained about troops posted on the roads into the City, turning away folks with goods to sell. They nodded when he pointed out how Andersonville had helped them, had lost good people to rogue commandos, had sent more good people to join James Dornan's march back to the City. They let him talk until he ran down, looking helplessly from face to face.

Bill Baird cleared his throat.

"Max—do you mind if I call you Max? Look, Max. We certainly understand the importance of trade. And believe me, we won't forget the role you played when the chips were down. But you have to appreciate that we don't have an easy job either. These things take time."

"What's so hard about letting people buy and sell? I mean, I get security. But we're talking about a farmer with a cart of apples to sell."

"There's a little more to it than security."

"Like what?"

"You have some idea how big the City is, don't you? Do you realize how fragile things are right now? And have you thought through the risks to your own community?"

"I don't get it. What risks?"

"All kinds of risks! Where should I begin?"

"I don't know. This isn't making much sense."

Then Elizabeth White spoke.

"Mr. Wyse. Tell us what would happen if someone showed up in your town with fifty carts of apples, at half the going price."

"What?"

"Or a hundred sides of beef. Or a thousand bushels of wheat. How would you cope with that?" When he said nothing, she rose to her feet. "Trust us, Mr. Wyse. We know what we're doing."

She left, trailed by the entourage, the meeting over.

"What are you going to tell the Committee?" Bert asked.

Max shrugged, and Walsh snapped, "Well you'd better *think* of something, Mr. Town President! A lot of people were counting on this!"

"Yeah, Dan, I know. It isn't what we expected. But we'd better figure out how we're going to manage it."

"Manage it! Manage what? Are you just thinking about the next election?"

"No. I'm worried about someone doing something stupid."

"Like what?"

"Like smuggling."

"*Smuggling!* Listen to you! Since when did *you* start worrying about a little smuggling?"

"Look, it's not going to help us to make enemies of them. She's a tough customer."

"Maybe we need a tougher negotiator!"

He pulled the window down and came back to his seat.

"Look, Dan, I didn't know what I was walking into. We have to figure this out."

"What's to figure out?"

"Give her some credit. Suppose their people *could* roll in here with piles of produce at cut prices."

"Why would they? What would be in it for them?"

"I dunno. Suppose they have a surplus. Why not unload it for whatever they can get?"

"Well then, why don't they?"

Bert scratched his chin.

"Refugees."

"What? What in hell are you talking about?"

"They don't want an invasion of refugees. They could put people here out of business. People got to live. Where would they go? The City."

"He's got a point, Dan. What if our people stopped planting something because we're buying their surplus and it's not worth growing anymore, and then they have a bad season. They're going to feed their own people first."

"So, what're you saying? That we give up? Hell, maybe smuggling *is* the answer!" Walsh got up abruptly and strode from the room, muttering something not-so-under-his-breath about tits on a boar.

The front door slammed.

Max shook his head.

"Is it me, or is he getting crabbier?"

Bert squinted at the windows across the room, leaned his chair back, and laced his fingers across his round belly.

"They keep pretty tight control over everything, your friends in the City."

"I suppose they do. Why? What are you thinking?"

"Maybe we can use that."

"How?"

"They don't want things getting out of control. We don't either."

"Come on, Bert. What're you getting at?"

"You went there to get them to open door to anybody and everybody. They said no, so you came back. I'm just thinking you came back too soon."

"All right, maybe I did. But we're going to have a lot of trouble here, if they let just a few people to trade. Everyone in town wants in on this."

"Something's better than nothing. And if you're worried about trouble, wait 'til word gets around that you came back with nothing."

"Yeah, I know. Okay, let's think about this. Maybe we *can* do it a step at a time. Get them to open the door a bit, then a little bit more. People might go for that. As long as there's progress."

"They might."

"But we'll need something concrete. They'll argue forever over a vague idea. I mean, the Committee will."

"Yup. You going back there?"

"I think maybe I'd better."

"I think maybe you're right."

───────────────

Two days later, Max rode into the City once more. Again, Security stopped him inside the headquarters building, called for instructions, and put him in a room. This time Bill Baird came in alone and sat down.

"All right, Mr. Wyse. What can I do for you?"

"I need your help."

"What sort of help?"

"Well, I haven't told anyone yet about our meeting the other day. I've been thinking about it, and I know what's going to happen."

"So?"

"I think you do, too. Times are changing, you know? Maybe Cargo Flu isn't the monster it used to be, after all."

Baird's eyes grew visibly larger.

"Are you *serious?* There's a pocket in Westboro that's attenuated, after all these years, but there may be—there certainly *are*—hundreds more where it's still highly virulent! I can't emphasize enough just how reckless it is to think otherwise!"

"Okay, maybe you know that and I know that. But after Westboro, people are starting to wonder. And not just about the Flu. The City has changed. So have we. You can put up your guard shacks, but both sides are getting awfully curious about each other."

"Tell me where this is going, Mr. Wyse."

"Smuggling."

"What about it?"

"There's always been a little of it going on. We both know that. But a lot of people stayed out of it. Fear of the unknown. And the City was a *big* unknown. But now that's changing. And the more people try it—smuggling—the more they learn about each other. And the more they learn, the less everyone is afraid, and then even more people will try it, and so on, until it's out of control."

"Look Mr. Wyse, we can handle a few curiosity-seekers here. I trust you to control your own. I suggest you make sure that everyone in your town understands that if they break the law here, they'll be prosecuted. And I'm afraid that's all the help I can give you."

"I don't think that's true."

"Then why don't you tell me just what it is you're after?"

"There's something you and I can do to give people an outlet. We can't dam the river forever. But we can channel it."

"How?"

"Licensing."

Baird sat back and looked startled.

Max went on.

"We set up a way for people to get a license to trade specific goods. If there's a legal way to do it, fewer people will take the more dangerous, illegal route. Then we know what's being traded, we keep tabs, and we can adjust and rein in when we need to."

"Well, I won't deny it's been discussed. But it doesn't solve all the problems. It's not a permanent solution."

"There's only one thing that's permanent, Bill. Everything else we have to work at."

Baird was silent a moment. Then he murmured, "How did you lose your arm?" — and shook his head. "Damn! I'm sorry. That was way out of line."

"I lost it in a gun fight. Someone died. I'm not proud of it."

"I *am* sorry."

"No need. It reminds me how lucky I am."

"Well, I can't say you don't make a good point. But if we're going to do this, we need better communication. I can't just wait around for you to ride in here when the spirit moves you."

"Any ideas?"

"Suppose we start at the beginning. Do you know what a postal service is?"

8

Dan Walsh was a single man.

This was not entirely by choice. Once he had even been engaged.

Rachael had been a fellow law student, a bright, genial girl with a wide grin, a dark mop of curls, a sharp tongue that could take the paint off a barn, a frightening capacity for hard liquor, and a sinuous carnality that reduced him to abject helplessness. At first he used to wonder how he could live without her. But, after months of chaos and death, he could only wonder what had become of her. The possibilities were too gruesome to imagine, next to the memory of her lithe body and drunken laughter, and he tried to forget.

In his first year after fleeing the City for the countryside, consumed with animal survival, forcing himself to *think* against an empty stomach and the dragging pain of backbreaking labor—in that first year, it was not hard to forget. But not entirely. Life had been cruel, but it might have been a bit less cruel, had there been someone to share it with.

Living off the land without mechanical power would never be easy. But he had learned. After his first winter, he knew he would not starve. By his second winter, the farm was getting to be positively organized, the work becoming second nature. After his third, it was hard to remember he had ever done anything else.

Still young, and modestly successful—enough to barter a portion of what he raised—Walsh began meeting fellow settlers, including a few unattached women. But somehow nothing ever worked out. He could not imagine life with any of them. Instead, he stayed on his farm and he stayed alone, a practical, amiable man who would not become bitter, because the taste of bitterness came with the taste of young death.

Now in his forties, hair receding, fumbling for a battered pair of glasses to read, his dry humor shriveling to a streak of sarcasm that left him still more alone, Dan Walsh knew what was happening to him. It was the shadow of mortality, of dwindling chances. And this clear knowledge usually silenced his outbursts, despite fine roots of early fear growing deep in his marrow.

Now he found himself thinking of the City, recalling a time when he knew its streets full of people and full of energy. A time when looking ahead was exciting, not chilling. He had not seen the City since the plague.

So he went back, a kind of pilgrimage, walking along empty, echoing streets, and streets not so empty; through great swaths abandoned by the living, and smaller areas still thriving, full of young people as well as old. The City was shrunken, but far from dead. There was a heart still beating, and as he rode home he carried with him the sights and smells and sounds of that heart.

Walsh knew that Agnes had come into several horses when she took over the Hutchins place. And he knew she needed money. So he drove a hard bargain to buy horses and tack—not so hard that she refused, but hard enough that she grumbled about it for weeks afterward.

Then he proceeded to secure the first trading license with the City. To give riding lessons.

He negotiated the terms, drafted the documents, wrote penalty clauses and requirements for effective notice, and a detailed arbitration procedure. His counterparts in the City, a pair of much too innocent twenty-somethings, gaped over the recital of parties, the specimen student waiver, the signatures of the Town Committee, all thirty-odd pages neatly written out by hand. They squinted helplessly at the tight, black cursive, so Walsh read it to them, explaining paragraph by paragraph every detail, why it was there, answering every question, countering every objection.

The young man rubbed his cheek.

"But why should we pay you a . . . what is it? . . . a penalty . . . if we suspend the license."

"If you suspend without cause, it's only fair. It helps defray expenses I incur to keep the business going. And it helps prevent future officials from abusing the license to run me out of business."

"And what is . . . um . . . that."

"Force majeure. It means that if you suspend because something happens outside your power, then of course there's no penalty. We used to call it an 'act of God'."

The two children glanced at one another, and he half expected a wink to pass between them. Then the young woman smiled, in a faintly patronizing way of trying not to look patronizing.

"Do you really think all this is necessary?"

"Look, everyone who goes into an agreement, whether it's a contract or a partnership or a marriage, hopes they never need to think about these things. But you can't predict the future. So you lay out the rules at the start. Believe me, it can save ugly arguments and bad feelings down the road. It's always better to know where you stand."

"But it's so complicated!"

"It only seems that way because it's the first one. But now you won't have to reinvent the wheel for all the licenses that come after this."

"Reinvent the wheel?" The young man smirked. "Is that what they used to say?"

The woman stacked the papers in front of her and rose to her feet.

"Well, we'll take this to our manager. I don't know what she'll say." Her tone said she thought she had a pretty good idea.

Walsh tapped the pile.

"You still have photocopiers, don't you? Please make a copy for me."

The license was approved.

That summer, Walsh and two older teenaged boys he hired in Anderson Square took over a large field and abandoned barn in a clearing at the northeast edge of town, a few miles south of the City. There they hung out a sign, which read *Walsh Stables.*

The boys helped with the horses and the money, and with clearing and marking a system of trails. Word spread. His clientele grew, mostly but not all from the City, and Walsh taught the boys to guide the less experienced riders along the easy trails while he gave instruction.

He would teach one or two or three at a time, sprinkling in stories of life as a City boy forced to live off the land, reminiscing with older clients, and recalling days as a student frequenting cafés and bars long since shuttered. He found he could talk endlessly, amusingly, as people on holiday from the City rekindled his memory, and the stories came tumbling back to him.

But he never spoke of Rachael. He would see her in the olive complexion or laughing brown eyes of a girl on horseback, in the curve of her back as she held the reins, and would sometimes grow silent, then catch himself and grin in a way that would spread to his eyes, and the girl would laugh with him—a little warmth that went a long way toward making the life of Dan Walsh worth living again.

9

As soon as the wreckage of the Hutchins house had been cleared away, Agnes started making trips into the City, once or twice a week, to scrounge and to haggle. Sometimes she made small finds, like a box of appliance motors discarded by a repair shop, or a bag of large bolts and nuts and washers no one wanted, or a half-dozen fat steel pipes that Steve helped drag back to the barn.

She tracked down big warehouses where the Corporation kept its own salvage, venturing with Steve into the industrial ruin south of the City. There they found everything imaginable, from twenty-pound spools of enameled copper wire and thirty-foot wooden utility poles, to bags of cement stacked up high, and they rode home talking of what they could do with it all. But they could afford none of it.

There was not much else to work with. Lengths of cable and lumber salvaged from the burned house. Metal scraps and a hand-ful of tools from Steve's old junk pile. Yards of magnet wire ex-tracted from starters and solenoids she found in rusted-out trucks and cars abandoned in the woods.

Steve showed her ideas for his water turbine, made sketches and diagrams and tables of calculations of power and speed at dif-ferent water flows. He labored for days at sawing a short length of steel pipe into lengthwise halves, for measuring forces in a stream. The results seemed promising. But to build a *real* tur-bine . . . he was at a loss.

Working with Steve's calculations and a one of her textbooks, Agnes sketched out concepts for the generator, calculating the flux needed from the rotor, the size of the stator coils, how large the arrangement had to be to accommodate the number of poles. But it remained a concept, existing only on paper.

And they could not escape the small generators from before, the ones she and Steve had made from automobile alternators and sold to a handful of farmers who had been able to dam a stream high enough to make one work. She would gladly have bought them all back, had she the money. Instead, they had to spend days rebuilding one whenever a farmer dumped it in front of the barn, angrily demanding a working generator.

What was left of her savings was a small packet of cash wrapped up in a rag and hidden in her room at the pub, to pay Bill the modest rent he asked, and to buy meals. She had to eat, once in a while.

But one morning she found herself anxiously counting the money as soon as she got up, after counting it the night before, and she threw it aside and stood by the only window in her room at the back of the pub, staring through it at trees dry and dusty with early autumn.

The days were growing shorter. Time was growing short, and she began wondering if the City would still take her back. But she could feel the buildings tower around her, could imagine begging for a job—and she turned away, put the money back, and went out to the dining area, where she paid for a cup of coffee. Then, only a little lightheaded, she rode to the barn, to meet up with Steve and begin another day.

That afternoon, trying to knock steel laminations from one of the electric motors she had bought, she cut her hand sprang up, viciously flinging the hammer.

It slammed against a wall.

"Goddamn it!" Steve shouted. "Let *me* do it, for chrissake! Before you *kill* someone."

"Fuck you," she moaned, crouching down and sucking blood from her hand. And thinking this was the end. A complete waste of time. She was nowhere. And the rent was due on the room . . .

She stood up. She pushed past him, retrieved the hammer, and went back to the motor.

Mouth clamped shut, she swung the hammer against the cold-chisel she grasped, swung and made the chisel ring out, swung and knocked the laminations loose, swung again and again as though it were Steve Foster's face under her chisel.

10

Agnes sat up on the edge of the her bed, and rubbed her dry eyes.

It was early, maybe an hour before dawn, and dim gray light from around the curtain was beginning to outline black shapes in her room.

She slumped over, unable to sleep, leaning heavily on her knees and thinking of one more day rebuilding an old generator, maybe for the third time, thinking of failed plans, of Steve snarling . . . if she could just close her eyes a while longer . . . But she pushed off the bed and stood up.

Then she stumbled and fell over.

The seat of a wooden chair banged her head as she went down twisting and hitting the floor on her side, and she lay still a moment, the breath knocked from her.

Then she clutched her side and started crying like a child.

After a minute, she was able to choke it back. She reached up and felt the bump on her head. Her hand came away sticky with blood.

She climbed to her feet. She steadied herself, opened her door, and carefully walked to the washroom, where she found the morning pan of hot water waiting, and washed her face and hands, cleaned the cut in her scalp, and rinsed the blood from her hair.

In her room, she dressed, wiped blood from the floor, took some bills from her packet, and went out to the dining area, where she ordered a plate of ham and eggs and toast.

The meal helped. She had a second cup of coffee. Then she paid, and rode to the barn with only a small headache throbbing.

Later in the morning, she stopped to help Steve look for more hacksaw blades. Together they rummaged around dark corners of the barn, among tangles of rakes and hoes and pitchforks, and more mysterious implements, until a floorboard moved.

The board was about a foot in width, four or five long, old and dark like the rest of the floor, but not so dusty. It rocked when Steve trod on it. She kicked at one adjacent, and it rattled.

With a hoe, Steve pried up four loose boards.

"What the hell?"

In the space beneath the floor was a wooden box.

Working together they hauled it up, navigated with it around scattered tools, and hefted it onto a workbench.

The box was over two feet long and a foot deep, the wood gray and rough, the crude cover held shut with a padlocked hasp in front and three big hinges in back, the fastenings hidden and inaccessible.

Steve knocked on it with a hammer. The sound was dull and solid.

"Do you think Barbara put it there? Or someone from before?"

There was a glint from the hasp, and she angled the lock aside, revealing the surface of the hasp scratched and shiny.

"It must've been hers."

"Yeah, you're right. She was using it."

"Open it up, Steve. Let's see what's inside."

He walked around the workbench, then tapped at the hinges.

"That's probably the best way in. If you're sure about this."

"What do you mean?"

"Well, what do we actually know about it?"

She looked at him, uncomprehending, and he added, "It doesn't belong to us."

"It belonged to *her*."

"Maybe it did and maybe it didn't. We don't know that for sure."

"Come on, Steve! What're you afraid of? Finders keepers!"

With the hammer and a screwdriver, he knocked the pins from the hinges, then threw the cover back, letting it dangle from the hasp. They leaned over and peered inside, at flat bundles tied with string, neatly stacked.

He held up a bundle, an inch thick, and she gasped, digging through layers of Corporate money before she reached the bottom.

"My God, Steve! It's a fortune!"

"Yeah. Christ, look at it . . . Did she ever say anything about this?"

"No. Not to me."

"Well, maybe you're right. Maybe it *was* hers. Those hinges weren't rusted at all."

"Steve!" She grabbed his arm. "This is the answer!"

He didn't answer. He just stood staring at the box.

"Steve—what's the matter?"

"It isn't ours."

"What? Are you *crazy?* I say it is! Who else? She didn't have any family. *I* was the closest thing."

"Look, you can't just take it. It doesn't belong to us."

"What's the matter with you? We need it! The *project* needs it."

He laughed, but it came out an ugly snarl.

"Yeah, well maybe the project's just not gonna happen."

"I don't understand you! What do you want to do? Put it back under the floor? What good will *that* do anyone?"

"I don't know! But that money isn't ours, and you can't just *take* it."

"Says who?"

"I'm not taking it!"

"Fine. Have it your way. *I'm* taking it."

"Fine! It's all yours."

She replaced the cover. The old wood was rough and warm, and she let her hand linger, thinking of the City warehouses and all that lovely wire.

"Okay. It's settled."

"Fine," he muttered. "And maybe you can find yourself a new partner, too."

"What's *that* supposed to mean? I can, if I have to. Do I?"

"You know what? *Fuck* you."

He walked away.

"Steve—wait! *Stop!* Steve, goddammit it! What do you expect *me* to do? Give up? Get married? Have *kids,* for God's sake?"

He had reached the side door, but he burst out laughing, tripping over his feet and staggering against the door, still laughing.

You little shit. She strode after him.

"So you think *that's* funny? Well, *here's* something funny! Steve Foster, Andersonville *Blacksmith!* Horseshoes! Plows! Decorative . . . fire pokers! Now, *that's* funny."

She succeeded. The laughter stopped in his throat. But he pointed at her, snarling, "Not *half* so funny as *you* suckling a couple of slimy brats! While your husband hollers for his dinner!"

Without thinking, she stepped forward. Her fist shot out, landing square on his mouth.

He rocked back a little. But his hands slammed about her waist and yanked her body against his, his mouth smothering hers, and she tasted blood and bit hard. He forced her against the wall, pinning her with his hips, his hands on her breasts, and she freed her arms and tore his shirt.

They slid to the floor, a knot of rage and sweat and hair and teeth. Then his skin was on hers, his weight was on her, something pounded, filling her ears until her muscles were shaking with it and the pounding became a roar, and then she heard him gasping for breath.

"God." She put a hand over her eyes. "That was not supposed to happen."

Steve propped himself on an elbow, looking down at her. The smirk on his face was maddening, and she snapped, "Nothing personal, sonny, but I'm not much interested in suckling *your* brat, either!"

He grinned. "Well, maybe you'll get lucky. *I* did."

She slapped him. Not very hard.

"Watch your mouth. We're not kids."

He lay back, exhaling noisily. "Yeah. Thank God for that."

The barn was quiet. It was strange. There was nothing she wanted to say. There were so many things to think about, but for the moment it was enough to stare up into those shadowy spaces between the rafters, her fingers pressed against the hard floor, its surface gritty, yet smooth . . . he nudged her awake.

"I have an idea."

"We're not doing it again. Not until I get to the City."

He laughed quietly, resting a hand on her bare thigh. She pushed it away.

"Seriously," he said. "I think there's a way."

"A way to what?"

"To finance this thing. To make it happen."

She sat up, brushing hair from her eyes.

"How?"

"Jesus. Do you have any idea how beautiful you are?"

"Come on, Steve. Business. What's your idea?"

"Okay, listen. The money's not ours—look, just get it through your thick head. But that doesn't mean we can't use it."

"How?"

"We turn it in."

"We *what?*"

"We turn it in, to the town. But we incorporate, and we get the town to make us a loan. They've got an interest in this, right? And if we're successful, they'll make money on the loan."

"And if we're not?"

"Then we've spent a lot of money around town and no one's really hurt."

"What about *us?* We'll never pay it back, if we don't succeed."

"That's why we incorporate. You're not the only one who uses the library, you know. I've read about this. If we fail, it's the corporation that goes under."

"So how do we incorporate? They're still trying to figure out how to keep people from dumping shit in the river."

"I know. They'll have to invent it. But now there's an incentive. I think we just have to sell Max on it."

She looked across the barn, at the workbench with the box of money.

"I knew there was a reason I picked you for a partner."

He moved behind her, rubbing her shoulders.

"I'm good for all kinds of things."

She let herself lean back against him as his hands worked, massaging her back. But when he cupped her breast, she stiffened.

"Steve, *stop.* I told you, we can't!"

"Oh, we can do *this.*"

She grabbed his arm as his hand slid down her belly.

"Steve! For God's sake!"

11

It was several weeks later. The big table in the meeting room at the Town Office was buried in paper. Max nodded, listening to Steve explain how he would build a turbine with blades cut from steel pipe.

"It's a cross-flow turbine." Steve tapped a diagram. "With the right setup it'll work even when the river is low."

Standing close to Steve, Agnes added, a little breathlessly, "And I've found what I need for a multi-kilowatt generator! A stock of really powerful magnets I found in a City warehouse. Neodymium. All kinds of shapes and sizes, and nobody knows what to do with them! They're so strong you have to keep them apart with spacers. See that?" She held up a finger discolored with a long, black bruise. "That's what happens when you get careless with them. And I know how to make cores that'll resist eddy currents! Coat hangers! Do you have any idea how many coat hangers there are in the City?"

He nodded as if he did. "A lot, I take it."

From under the pile of plans and diagrams, Steve pulled a map sketched on a broad sheet of butcher paper.

"Look. There used to be poles right along the main road. Most of them were cut down, for firewood I guess, and we have to replace them. Now, look here, there's a fall on the river here, and we'll dig a channel around it to feed the turbine. We'll build a gate to control the flow. Then we'll run wire to the road. See? It's a big job."

"Yeah, I can see that."

"But if it works!" Agnes exclaimed. "If it *works*, we might be able to light fifty homes. Maybe the whole town someday. And it *should* work."

"Should?"

"Well, come on! We've never done this before! My God, the bearings, the turbine blades, the channel—"

"We can do it," Steve interrupted. "But it's a big job, and we can't do it alone."

Max picked up a small sketch. It was apparently a diagram of the trajectory of water, plotted at different speeds across what looked like a cross section of the turbine. He could feel the other two watching him, and out of the corner of his eye saw Agnes reach for Steve's hand.

Steve ventured, "What do you think?"

He was thinking that this was how industry should begin, with a sketch like this. But he remembered Dan Walsh muttering something about 'tits on a boar', and he waited, examining the paper, trying to look critical, and fairly certain he was holding it right side up.

"What do I think? I think the town should get a share."

"A share of what?"

"The corporation."

"But . . . but, you'll be getting interest on the loan! Right?"

"Sure. But if you two can't pull it off, where does that leave us? You're asking us to risk a lot of money on you."

"Hell, Max, you wouldn't even *have* the money, if we hadn't turned it in."

"And it's a good thing too. It's an awful lot of money. Barbara didn't leave a will, and I can sure as hell tell you that no one around here's going to go along with looting property after someone dies. Might give certain people the wrong ideas. You did the right thing."

Steve looked at Agnes. "What do you think? Ten percent?"

Max tossed down the sketch.

"Twenty-five."

"Twenty-five!"

"Like you say, Steve, it's a big job, and you've never done this before. What are your chances? Fifty-fifty? And you want me to sell this to the Committee? To your father? You *do* know what he's going to say about a corporation, don't you? So what do you expect me to bring him?" He tapped the papers. "Besides pretty pictures."

He waited, and slowly Agnes nodded.

"All right. Twenty-five. But earn your percentage. We need to incorporate, and it has to be air tight. We need rights of way, for the channel, for our poles, and all of it has to be company property. It has to be protected. Figure out how to set that up. Do your part."

Steve's hand accidentally brushed her hip as she spoke. Neither seemed to notice.

"Okay," replied Max. "It's a deal."

12

The Town Office was in an old house built long before the plague, at the edge of a wild field near the main road. The land was rocky, no one much interested in trying to farm it, and for twenty years the house had stood empty, until a year ago the new town government had claimed it.

Two great maples stood near the house, two fat pillars crowned with darkening green peppered yellow with early autumn, rising high and seeming to stretch right into the pure blue dome above. Beneath them, a line of horses was already tied up as Max arrived on a Saturday morning a week later, still turning the problems over in his mind. The money. The loan. The corporation. And the stubborn mind of Dennis Foster.

He walked inside and found a small crowd already in the front office, which might once have served as a sitting room. They kept jostling around the open doorway to the meeting room, and Bert Morrow paced back and forth, keeping clear a path and loudly instructing his deputies to summarily eject anyone who got out of order.

Max pushed past the crowd into the meeting room. The big table had been pulled back to accommodate rows of spectators sitting and standing along one wall. A few chairs along an adjacent wall were reserved. Steve and Agnes were there, and Max crossed the room and sat down with them.

It was after ten, the Committee members taking their seats, and the place was filled with rustling and murmuring and the sounds of old double-hung windows being dragged open for air, until the town secretary smacked the table with an old book.

"Settle down! Quiet, please!"

After the murmuring died, she went through some formalities, then turned the meeting over to the chairman, Dennis Foster, whose rough voice reverberated against the bare walls.

"All right! This is how we're going to do it. Spectators will keep quiet until we open the floor to the public. Everyone will get a chance to speak his piece then. If anyone on the Committee makes a motion, we may hold a vote. Spectators do not vote, and I don't expect to hear their opinion if we do. That clear? Any questions? All right, the president has the floor."

Max stood up. He looked around the crowded room.

"Well, judging by the turnout, I'd say we all have a pretty good idea why we're here. But it's not going to be an easy thing. We have a lot to consider. So I want to start by asking Steve and Agnes to explain just what it is they're offering, and what they want in return."

Dennis nodded.

A few days before, Max had brought them both to this room and had them each deliver a talk, as though trying to convince him. And at the end of it, he took Agnes aside.

"Do what you want. But my advice is this. Steve does the talking. You help as needed."

She had opened her mouth to argue, and he had cut her off.

"Do it however you like."

Now she sat with her arms folded. Steve stood up and faced the Committee, taking in the spectators as well. From time to time she glanced up at him, but mostly she looked at the floor.

Steve began.

"You all know that Agnes and I are business partners. You know about the small generators we've set up around town. And you probably know about the problems we've had.

"There are only a few places where we can set up a generator. We need a stream that's not too small and not too big, and we have to build a dam for each turbine. And the turbines have not held up.

"The reason we're here is that we want to keep providing you with electric power. We want everyone to have it. But we've studied the problem, and we have to do it differently.

"If you're my age, you probably don't remember how it was done in the old days, when they had one generating plant for a whole community. That's how it's still done in the City. And that's how we have to do it.

"Now, the City is lucky. They still have their original hydroelectric plant. They're lucky it was well-maintained to begin with, before the plague, and that some of the people who worked on it are still around. Nothing has broken down they haven't been able to fix, so far.

"We're not so lucky. We have to make everything ourselves. But if we do it ourselves, we also don't have to worry about not knowing how to fix something when it breaks.

"By the way some of you are looking at me, you may think we're a little crazy." Laughter. "Well, maybe you're right. But we have a plan, and after I explain it you may not think we're so crazy after all.

"We've mapped the river, all the way from the road west of the pub on out to the wilds east of here. And we found a fall, twenty-five feet high, give or take. Not too many people know about it, because it's a couple of miles south in the woods, and nobody lives near there.

"We plan to cut a channel, starting above the fall, and run it parallel to the river, but dropping to accelerate the flow. We'll put our turbine at the end of it. Part of the river will go down that channel and through the turbine, bypassing the fall. We'll build a gate at the head of the channel to control it.

"I'm working on a cross-flow turbine that will handle that kind of flow. Agnes is working on a generator big enough to power a couple of electric lights in maybe fifty homes. We know where to get the wire and the poles to carry power where it needs to go.

"But it's a big project. Much too big for anyone in this room to do single-handed. I can tell you those poles are heavy. We'll have to hire a crew and build a gin-pole big enough to raise and set each one. And it's going to take some manpower to dig that channel. We've found the materials we need in the City, but they aren't going to give it away. We'll have to buy it, and it won't be cheap."

He paused.

After a moment, Dennis shifted in his chair.

"You done?"

"No." But Steve just looked around the room, as though waiting for something.

The old man shook his head and slouched back.

"Okay, son. We'll all just wait right here. All right with you? We all got nothin' but time."

"All right. This is what we're offering. We'll make it happen. We know how to do it. We've been living in a barn and eating scraps for six the last weeks, working it all out, and we'll do it for six months. We'll do it for a year.

"But we need money. To hire help and to buy material. We can do it pretty cheap, because we're good at using what we find. But we can't do it for nothing. So we want the Town to invest in us. That's what we want in return."

"Seems to me, son, you want a hell of a lot more than that."

"That's what it boils down to, *Dad.*"

The old man's face went red.

Max stood up.

"I still have the floor, right? Okay, I've seen their plans. I've listened to the story. And when you first think about it, it doesn't seem possible. Agnes told me she can make a generator with coat hangers. I would have laughed—except that I never expected anyone to light a house using parts from a junk car. I don't think anyone else here ever thought this town could generate its own power. Not in our lifetimes. They've already proved us wrong. So my technical opinion isn't worth much, and I don't think anyone else's here is, either."

There were five on the Committee, counting Dennis, and stocky, yellow-haired Amalia Hanover purred in her husky voice: "That doesn't mean we should just take their word for it. Does it?"

Max waited, knowing another shoe would drop.

"Maybe we should hire a consultant from the City, hmm?"

"We could," he agreed, and when she seemed about to pursue that thought, added, "Of course, if we do, then everything these two need will suddenly get a lot more expensive."

"You always seem to have a little answer for everything, don't you? Tell me, Max, have you been offered any . . . well, let's say, special inducement?" The smile was sweet, but the eyes glittered.

"Such as?"

"Such as anything that would have an undue influence on your conduct as an officer of this town!"

"Such as?"

"Money!"

"No."

"Sex."

Dennis exploded in a fit of coughing.

Hanover patted his back.

"You all right, honey?"

He waved her away.

"No," said Max.

"No what?"

"No sex."

She smiled again as a ripple of laughter went around the room.

"Well, I'm sure we can all trust your judgment." The eyes glittered at him once more, before moving on.

"Anything else, Amalia? All right, as I was saying, if anyone can pull this off, it's Steve and Agnes."

Hanover was looking to her left, at a third Committee member.

"Speak up, Bill. I can tell when something's on your mind."

Bill Cotter eased forward on his elbows. He a short man, a bit chunky, with thin brown hair, a long face, and a mouth that seemed perpetually turned down in distaste.

"Yeah, but like you say, he always has an answer for everything."

"Well honey, we all need to hear it."

"Okay, why don't we just buy power from the City? It would have to be a lot cheaper to run some wire up there than building our own damned power plant."

"You *know* why," replied Max. "Self-sufficiency. So they can't cut us off. So we're not at their mercy."

Cotter just shook his head, but Hanover wasn't finished.

"That sounds all well and good, my friend, but our resources are finite. Why shouldn't we put them to best use?"

"I think this way we are. Self-sufficiency means know-how. I can't put a price tag on it, but there's no telling how much it will pay off for us in the long run. Who knows? One day we might be selling electricity to the City."

"I doubt *that* very much."

"Well, we don't know how it will pay off. Or when. But you have to agree with me, Amalia, that know-how is a resource we need, and badly. And one we can grow ourselves."

"I'm not so damned sure I'm convinced we need this particular type so badly."

"Well, we have to cultivate it where we find it."

She sat back, lips compressed, and Cotter grinned, a lop-sided, knowing grin.

Dan Walsh, the fourth member, just listened. One knee bumped nervously.

"Makes sense to me." Alexander McCane was the fifth. He was a big man, with small eyes set far apart in a broad face under thick, straw-colored hair.

Hanover blew out her cheeks.

"Leave it to you, Sandy. You know what they're after, right?"

"If you mean the money, of course I know. You have a better use for it?"

"Seems to me we ought to be *talking* about that! Instead of just jumping up to give it right back to the people who found it! Something's fishy about all this, but I don't know what it is."

"Trouble with you Amalia, is you should've been a lawyer. Everybody's a crook with you."

"It's human nature, sport. And human nature ain't exactly sugar 'n spice."

"I think you trust people until they show themselves."

"Well, hon, I'm surprised you're still in one piece."

McCane didn't seem to hear. He was looking steadily at Max.

"Let's hear the rest of it."

"Wait a minute."

Agnes was leaning forward, eyes narrowed into dangerous rectangles aimed squarely at Hanover. "If you have something to say, *I'd* like to hear it."

"Well, now, Miss Agnes," she drawled. "I don't think *you* have the floor."

"Oh, I think I *do.*"

"The Chair recognizes Agnes," Dennis rumbled complacently.

Amalia aimed a sneer at him. He ignored it, and she turned back to Agnes.

"Well let's just say I'd like to know where all that money came from. And what makes you so sure you're entitled to it."

"If I thought I was entitled, you wouldn't even know about it."

"So why is this the first we've heard of it?"

"Because *no one* knew about it!"

"That's a little strange, don't you think? All that money?"

"No. I don't think it's strange. Barbara was smart. She was alone, and she made sure she had something set aside in case she was hurt, or something went badly wrong."

"Well, honey, that's an awful lot of money to have saved up selling milk and butter. Don't you think?"

"Maybe she brought it here with her! Who knows? Some things she kept to herself."

"Yeah, it seems she did."

"Well? Does that satisfy you?"

"Honey, 'satisfy' isn't the word. But we'll let it go, for now."

"Suit yourself, *honey.*"

Hanover seemed to freeze a moment. Then she glared at Dennis.

"Does this goddamned meeting of yours have a goddammed point?"

"Of course it has point! We're here to talk about a loan. And about the damned incorporation thing."

"Well, *talk* then."

"All right! I'll talk. *You* two can sit down.

"I'm going to talk about the incorporation first, because if you don't get that, there's no point in talking about the loan. And because I'm against it.

"I had a business of my own once. In the old days. I was incorporated, because I had to be. The legal system was out of control. You could get sued by anyone for anything at any time, and you were crazy if you left yourself personally exposed. You see" — he jabbed a finger at Agnes and Steve — "I *know* what this is about! You two don't want to get stuck with the bills if this thing goes south. You don't want to be on the hook if someone gets hurt."

"Dennis, it's not like we're hiding—" Agnes began.

"Wait just a damned minute! I'm not finished. We don't have an out of control legal system here. Hell, we don't have much of *any* legal system. And most of us like it that way just fine. But that'll change, just as soon as someone incorporates. Because that's where it all starts."

"Oh, come on! What does one have to do with the other?"

"Young lady, you no longer have the floor. But I'll answer you, because everyone needs to hear it.

"Right now, we're all unprotected. Legally speaking. That's the point. When everyone is vulnerable, we're all just a little more careful. We settle things without hired guns, like they used to, and we settle them without lawyers, which was just as bad, and we're all damn careful not to have anything to settle in the first place! And if someone knows a better way, I'd like to hear it."

Agnes looked at Steve.

Steve looked at Max.

Max rose to his feet, and the old man sighed.

"All right. Speak your piece."

"Dennis, I remember telling John Anderson how much I love this town. That was when I was trying to convince him that we needed to do something about Jack Ryan. Although I don't think he needed much convincing. We had to do it. Things had to change. And they did. But I still love this town.

"You may be content with what you have. And you have every right to be. I envy you. But things are going to change, for better or for worse. With you or without you. They're already changing. I can see it, and so can you. We can't stop it. But we can try to steer it.

"And that's what this really about. Steering our town. For everyone's benefit. Do as much good as we can, and as little harm.

That's why I'm here. Not because anybody is paying me, Amalia, and not because anyone is sleeping with me. But because, with all the risks and all the dangers, and all the trouble this is going to cause us, I think this is the *right* thing to do."

There was a short silence. Then the office erupted in applause.

Dennis Foster lifted frosty eyes and scanned the spectators, left to right. The noise died with the sweep of his eyes. Even the front office went quiet.

"All right, then. Let's talk. Let's *talk* about whether this is the right thing to do.

"If we pass a law that let's these two incorporate, and they fail, then a lot of innocent people will get left holding the bag. They won't get paid. And *these* two, who took the money and took what people had to sell, will wash their hands of it. Then they'll go off and make money somewhere else. No one will be able to touch them. Do you think *that's* the right thing to do?"

Max rubbed his neck.

"Yeah, it's a risk. But it's a risk people will take to get new business. Look, I know what you're saying, and I won't support a law without rules for how the corporation is to be run if there's a risk of insolvency. But the thing is, nobody will be forced to deal with them. No one will have to deal with *any* corporation. If you don't want to run the risk, then just don't do business with them."

"The trouble with you is, you don't *listen*. You don't *know*. You think it all ends there. Well, it doesn't."

"Dennis, I don't get—"

"It doesn't *end* there! Once they get incorporated, you'll have to let anyone do it! And then we *will* be forced to deal with it! Everyone will be a corporation! They'd be crazy not to. And when they run up too many bills, or do something stupid, they'll just go out of business. Bankrupt the corporation and start a new one! Where's the responsibility? *You* tell me that. And don't waffle around with your rules about insolvency. I've seen it. I *know* what happens. Where's the responsibility?"

"I don't know, Dennis. But that's what we need to figure out, because I don't know any other way to make this happen. It's too big."

"*I* do."

"How?"

"Make it public! The *town* owns it. If something goes wrong, we all decide what to do! If the thing needs more money, we can decide whether to raise taxes. If we don't like the way it's run, we can change it. If it's public, we all have a right to know. We all have a say. We're all in it together."

Steve shot to his feet.

"*Goddamn it!* That's just what I *don't* want. Either *we* run it, or you do."

"Son, what makes you think—"

"Forget it, Dad. If the rest of you want to build a power plant, fine. Go right ahead. Only leave me out. I'm not going to break my back over your public power plant. I want to do this more than anything. But not like that. It's not worth it, if it's not *mine.*" He glanced quickly at Agnes. *"Ours,* I mean."

"It's okay. I know what you mean."

Face red, Dennis Foster sat staring at his son. And after a long moment of silence, Max spoke up.

"That's what it comes down to, Dennis. And would you really want it any other way?"

The old man's eyes darted at him, his unspoken thought as clear as though he had shouted *None of your goddamned business!*

"Dennis, we need people who think like that."

Amalia sighed.

"For once, I agree with him. Sorry, Dennis."

Dan Walsh tabled a motion to begin work drafting a law of incorporation. The vote was four to one, dutifully recorded by the Town Secretary.

Dennis slammed the table to end the meeting.

It took a few minutes for the spectators to clear out. Max waited, then walked out of the office with Dan Walsh.

"Say Dan, you were a lawyer once, weren't you?"

"I went to law school. Why?"

"Just checking. Glad you're on the Committee."

"Oh hell, Max. I don't know anything about that. Never even had a chance to take the bar exam."

Max grabbed his saddle with his one hand, put a foot in the stirrup, and swung up and onto his horse in a single, practiced motion. He grinned down at Walsh.

"Well, you're all we have."

"And you think someone like Amalia's going to listen to a hack like me with a sheepskin?"

"Sheepskin?"

"A diploma. A piece of paper that says I paid too much to go to a fancy school."

"Come on, Dan. Even Amalia will listen to a well-reasoned argument!"

He kicked his horse into motion.

Agnes stayed behind.

She waited quietly while Dennis looked over the secretary's notes and signed them. The secretary stacked the pages and took them with her out of the room, and the old man pulled a cigarette from his shirt pocket and stuck it in a corner of his mouth, looking up as Agnes walked up to him.

"Dennis," she said. "It's the right thing. Give it time. You'll see."

"Already seen it."

"Give us a chance. Can't you help?"

"Help you what? Ruin everything?"

"Help *save* everything! Help us build!"

"There's nothing I have to say to you. You don't listen, anyway."

"Dennis . . . Dennis, just because we all don't do exactly as you want . . . You know, you have no idea how much Steve looks up to you."

The old man rummaged through a pocket, found a match, and lit the cigarette, holding it carefully between thumb and forefinger while he dragged on it, coughing smoke to one side.

"We're all fools."

He dragged once more, dropped the cigarette, and ground it out on the floor.

"And I'm the biggest fool of all."

13

The barn acquired a sign, hand-lettered and nailed up over the big sliding doors.

Anderson Power & Light
(Incorporated)

Steve was President. Agnes was Chief Engineer. And Treasurer. Because now there was money.

She began riding to the City warehouses towing an old cart, negotiating for epoxy glue, for bags of cement, for electrical tape and spools of wire. The workbenches in the barn were a confusion of tools and test jigs, magnets stuck to a brake rotor scavenged from a wrecked truck, coils glued to sheets of plywood, with thick bundles of steel coat-hanger wire protruding through holes cut laboriously in the wood.

She hired some teenaged boys to spin the rotor with rope and pulleys, while she loaded the coils with old lights and a toaster, swearing as the coils vibrated loose or the magnets were knocked off, or the voltage was wrong for the rate of turn.

Steve worked out a jig to crank hacksaw blades, and hired more boys for the grueling job of cutting lengthwise sections steel pipe. He hired laborers to excavate the channel. He surveyed rights of way and totaled up poles and thousands of feet of wire for distribution.

Once in a while, someone from the Committee would come out for a visit, to check on the town's investment. Or out of curiosity, because nothing like this had seen in a very long time, the barn a bright, sharp world reverberating with the sounds of hammering and the rhythmic screech of a hacksaw, and sometimes the splintering rip of plywood and the foulest obscenities from the mouth of a blond goddess silently worshiped by her young crew.

She had given up her room at the pub. They were both living in the barn. They had one table for meals, and in the back a bed screened from the main area, and late at night, still burning with the day's fever of volts and amps and poles and cement, they would strain with clenched teeth and clenched fists until the fever broke and long spasms of trembling muscles swept it away, and they could sleep.

Sometime she would awaken in the dark, with the rattle of rain above the rafters and the feel of a rough blanket against her skin, and her eyes would grow heavy with the familiar sound, and she would drift off, sleep and waking merged into something not quite dream and not quite real, until her eyes opened again to gray light, and she got up ready to begin again.

Sometimes she would awake to a gash of moonlight splashed against one wall, and run her tongue along the skin of his back, and he would awaken and she would roll atop him, pushing herself upright, while he watched the outline of her face and shoulders, stroking her thighs, until her back arched and her breasts stood out, and her lips curled back in silent agony.

14

Speaking the Word each week was not an easy thing.

There was always someone new, it seemed, someone drawn to climb the hill on a Sunday morning in search of truth. Someone who had so much to learn. But there were also the many who had come faithfully for months, or a year, and the few who had been with him since the beginning. The fervor of all was equally important, all were equally deserving, and Brother Tom would spend days poring over his notes, penning and discarding, trying to keep the Word fresh for everyone.

Not so easy at all.

A rich source of material was the City, with its many thousands of citizens regimented and monitored and directed by day and by hour, like so many children or machines, managers enforcing policy as faithfully as they would a revelation from God, organization revealed as the slavery it was, and all to support a small class living in extravagant detachment and playing dangerous games with the lives of others.

Too, Brother Tom kept magazines and newspapers from the old times, with their lurid headlines and relentless advertising, and buried within stories of people crushed by weakness or by greed, or by hatred, or the machinations of business, or the depredations of war.

But the old headlines were too remote. Year by year, fewer people had clear memories of the old times, and fewer still had personal knowledge of the City.

So he began to look closer to home. The stories that swirled around the memory of Jack Ryan were fertile enough, but making an example of such an unlikeable one, who had been dead a year or more, while useful and instructive, lacked punch. It was too safe.

Inevitably, his search turned to people he knew. For a long while, he just thought about it, and kept his thoughts to himself. Even good people can make mistakes, and he was not quite ready to single out the living. Their mistakes were small, the ones he knew of, and he had no desire to spark unnecessary enmity for so little gain.

Until news reached him one day that the Town Committee had voted to draft a law for the granting of corporate charters.

Brother Tom himself knew little of these things. But the word 'corporation' reached out to him like a cold hand from the dead past, the old madness thought safely buried risen to walk again, to trample the fragile gift of a new start.

He decided he should speak with Dennis Foster, and two young boys of the People were dispatched to convey his polite request to visit for a few words next Sunday.

They returned with his curt reply. "Suit yourself."

Tom smiled. He knew the old man could not resist deference.

The following Sunday, after service was done, the tithes safely tucked away, and the dishes cleaned and put up from breakfast, he set out, on foot. The Foster place was miles off, and it was nearing noon before he finally reached it.

"Brother Dennis!"

He trudged toward a knee-high field near a line of trees, where the figure of Dennis Foster was crouching. A short length of pipe rose up and swished down with a *thunk,* and Dennis stood up, flinging something into the trees. Tom caught a fleeting glimpse of long ears and long legs, and looked quickly away, then recovered himself and moved closer. The old man crouched down and propped a loop of thin wire in the gap of a crude fence made of sticks stuck upright in the soft earth, then stood up and brushed dirt from his hands.

"Well, well. Brother Tom, is it?"

Tom mustered an equable smile and held out his hand.

Dennis clasped it a moment, his hand heavy and leathery and warm.

"Well, Brother, what can I do for you?"

Tom looked over the small plot. "Soybeans?"

"That's right. Trying them out."

Tom nodded at the snare. "The rabbits like them, I see."

"That's right."

"You think the carcass will scare them away?"

"Or attract predators. Can't hurt. And there's only so much rabbit stew I can stomach." Dennis pulled a rag from his pocket and patted his face. "All right, Brother. I guess you want to talk."

"If it isn't too much trouble."
"None at all. We'll go to the house."

———————

"So, what's on your mind?"
Dennis asked the question slouched in a chair in the shade of the porch, gazing peaceably at the bright band of sky between eaves and fields. Diane pushed through the screen door carrying a tray of glasses sparkling with cool water, passed them around, then sat in her rocker, smiling at Tom's pleasant "Thank you".
"Well, Brother?" Dennis rumbled.
Tom cleared his throat.
"You know, Brother Dennis, I don't get into town very much. Not as I should. But I do try to keep myself informed. After all, we are each citizens of the same community, are we not?"
Dennis nodded absently.
"Perhaps I should thank you for the job you're doing. As Chairman. It can't be an easy one."
Dennis waved away the compliment. "No need."
"Well, I *am* grateful. I don't want you to think I'm criticizing."
"Don't be bashful, Brother. Spit it out."
"Yes, I should get to the point. I understand we're going to start having corporations again. Here, in Andersonville. Is that so?"
Diane's rocker settled to a stop.
The corners of Dennis's huge moustache drooped.
"Looks like it."
"But . . . why?"
"Well, that's a long story, Brother. Maybe you should've come to the meeting."
"You're right, of course. I have only myself to blame, for my ignorance. But do you mind if I ask a question? Is this something you approve of?"
"Huh! I don't think so."
"But some of the others do."
"Seems so."
"Do you mind telling me who voted in favor?"
"The rest of 'em."
"All of them? Well, I am truly surprised. I'm not so sure about Mr. Dan Walsh, but I can't understand how someone like Amalia Hanover would approve."
"Well, it seems our town president's a little shrewder'n people give him credit for."
"How do you mean?"
"I think he put those two young people up to it. Planned it. Coached 'em. Set the whole thing up so the rest of us would fall in line. Probably even used me as well. Knew I'd never go for it, but he could make me look the fool."
Diane's face clouded, and Dennis finished irritably. "So that's the story, Brother. Is that what you wanted to know?"

"Well . . . I supposed it is. What are you going to do?"

"Wait. Hope he makes a mistake."

"I suppose it's all you can do, isn't it? We're a democracy now."

At that, Dennis smirked unpleasantly, but Diane murmured, "Oh, Steve . . ." and Tom glanced at her.

"Oh, that's right. Your son is one of those 'two young people', isn't he? You're not worried about him, are you?"

"Mother is worried over the little minx he's taken up with." Diane looked stricken. "And she's right to be. Little Miss Agnes is a shrewd one herself, in her own way."

"But why do you suppose Mr. Wyse is so interested in this?"

"I can think of one or two reasons. Look, Brother, there's nothing anybody can do about it, not right now, so unless you have something else to talk about . . . ?"

Tom stood up. "Of course. You have been very generous with your time."

He bowed to Diane.

"Thank you, Mrs. Foster. I'm sorry to intrude on such a beautiful Sunday."

The Fosters rose and followed him down the steps.

"Brother Tom!" admonished Diane. "You're not walking all the way home!"

"Why, of course, Sister. As I believe they used to say, it's good for the soul. No?"

"Dennis, take him home in the wagon."

"No, Mrs. Foster. I refuse, absolutely. But thank you just the same. Will I see you next Sunday? At service?"

"Oh . . ."

"We'll see, Brother," Dennis finished for her. "We'll see."

It was indeed a long walk home. But Tom had more than a little to ponder. And it was, as they say, good for the soul.

15

He stepped across the packed dirt floor of the milking shed, barefoot and sure, whistling to lure inside a small flock of his grandfather's goats. They were brown and white, with ears standing up and out as though attuned to some call only they could hear, and they jostled him, anticipating the familiar routine and the little treats that went with it.

With a slice of apple, Raul Flores led the first doe onto the wooden stand. He closed the arm of the head-gate, carefully wiped clean udder and teats, and with deft, slender fingers commenced to squeezing alternate streams of warm milk into the pail; rhythmically, left, right, left, right; steadily, without hurrying, pacing so the teats had time to fill and each squeeze produced a satisfying squirt.

The shed was warm and quiet, illuminated by hazy splashes of light that spilled in from a multitude of cracks in the walls and slowly moved across the floor, flecks of dust sparkling as they drifted through the light.

He milked each doe in turn, always in the same order and in the same way. When he finished, he lugged shiny steel pots heavy with liquid into the house, where he helped his grandmother fill jars, for themselves and a few customers, like the Fosters.

It was a chore Raul had done, morning and evening, since he was old enough to grasp the teats and relieve his grandmother. There were other chores, to be sure, and he would go with his grandfather when he must, sometimes to help out on the Foster place. But cutting hay or digging holes for fence posts was hard, hot work, and he would tire much more quickly than the older men, or even Stephen Foster, not much older than he was.

Raul much preferred the milking.

What he actually preferred was doing nothing, and he slipped out of the house before they could give him another chore to do.

The bare yard was empty, but for a few chickens loitering in the shade by the shed, and the goats in a large pen behind. The water in the trough was low. He saw it and sighed, and picked up a plastic bucket and headed for the well-worn trail that descended through dense brush to the stream below.

The stream was a small one, a-roar in spring but now just a burble. Grandfather kept hollowed out a pool for collecting clean water, and Raul dipped his bucket, then climbed the trail to toss a gallon into the trough.

He did this a second time.

On his third descent, he sat under his favorite tree to rest. His lids grew heavy, the burbling faded, and he lapsed into pleasant if unmemorable dreaming.

Face brown and narrow, and handsome, long black hair falling to his shoulders, smooth boyish limbs under baggy trousers and shirt, Raul Flores had the lithe body of a dancer and the clean lines of a healthy youth of seventeen.

He was a good boy. Everyone told him so. But he was no longer sure this was such a good thing.

Stephen Foster, for instance, was a decent enough young man. But no one would think to call him a 'good boy', not one grown so broad-shouldered and strong, and a little cocky, with a restless look about him as though he might reach out suddenly and *seize* something, without warning. Which was very disconcerting to Raul.

It was plain that Stephen Foster chafed under his father's rough authority, was eager to strike out on his own, and Raul could admire that, even envy it, without the slightest thought that he could ever be like that. Stephen Foster was a different animal entirely.

For a time Raul had been drawn to religion. The Word was intriguing, seductive, and he listened intently to Brother Tom every Sunday, sometimes asking questions, quietly thrilled by the serious passion with which the preacher answered. There was purpose in the Word. He could not fathom what it was, but could *feel* it, during a sermon, watching as the preacher built to his climax, trying to guess how he would do it this time, then closing his eyes as it washed over and the People sighed and murmured 'amen' in a kind of stunned relief. Sometimes Tom would gaze skyward, as though in pain, then extend his arms in that all-encompassing blessing, his face taking on that familiar look of benediction, and love.

There was purpose in this. There was meaning, deep and important. But Raul could not picture himself as Brother Tom.

It seemed much more likely he would stay where he was, helping his grandparents. The thought left him indescribably weary. It was not what he wanted. But he was cursed in some way, defective, with no idea what he did want.

16

Keeping time in a place like Andersonville, that survived without running water much less electricity, was a hit and miss affair. The convenience of electric time-keeping was just a story from the old times, one of many to bore young people. Anything battery powered was long since useless and discarded. A few wind-up clocks survived, and these could be set periodically against improvised sun-dials, serving well enough to schedule Committee meetings and the like. Dennis Foster still treasured and engraved mechanical watch that Diane had given him as an anniversary gift, long before the Plague. It was large, with a beautiful dial and precision mechanism. But it was just a keepsake now. It no longer ran.

The calendar required a little ingenuity. Equinoxes could be pinned down to within a few days, because much of the main road was laid out on a long east-west line, and twice a year the sun rose and set right over it. This was good enough for spring planting, to avoid being misled by unseasonably warm weather that might in fact be followed by more weeks of hard frost, or perhaps to prod a memory grown undependable with age.

But sometimes a little more was needed. Smuggling, mainly with the City, had been going on for many years, and it helped no one to misunderstand what was meant by 'next Thursday'. So more than a few townspeople had to keep in step with whatever weekday it was in the City.

Still, there were certain dates that mattered. Andersonville needed to hold its election, for one thing, every year, on the first of June, and everyone needed to show up on the right day for the voting and counting. So the Town Secretary declared that the spring equinox fell on March 21, and counted off from there. A public calendar was kept in Andersonville's town office. That this calendar might differ from the ones in the City by a day or two was a fact noticed by almost no one.

But Brother Tom noticed.

He had discovered the City's library during his crisis of faith, but had been afraid to enter it then. Now, as summer faded and the need for more rhetorical weapons grew, he would borrow a horse and travel there openly, to read, to think, to work on his sermons. He was accepted by the library's small staff, despite his rustic clothes, and left more or less to work as he pleased. But Tom would not spend a night in the City. Late afternoons on City streets were enough to dry his mouth and shorten his breath with anxiety, and he was always on the road and riding home while the sun was still well up in the sky.

He noticed one day that the calendar in the town office said September 14, when he visited the day after September 15 had been crossed off on the calendar in the City library. He mentioned this to the secretary, and watched her make the correction.

A small thing, to be sure. But many small things were coming together into something that mattered. This was gratifying. And it was gratifying that he could enjoy these quiet pleasures, after his terrifying fall.

One of the City librarians was a Mrs. Patterson, a short woman, and a little plump, with steel-gray hair pulled up into a very librarian-like bun at the back of her head. She wore long gray shapeless dresses with faded patterns of indistinguishable flowers. Fingers swollen and bent, she labored with her head down, peering with watery eyes through thick glasses, or using both hands to stiffly push back a small book on its shelf. She would look around, startled, then smile gratefully, if a little blankly, whenever Tom stopped to say 'hello'.

The other was a large woman with cherubic blue eyes and cherubic red cheeks, red curly hair, a deep husky voice, and a loud bark of a laugh. This was Sue. Sue invariably waved whenever Tom walked in, one hand flapping gallantly at the end of a stubby arm like a pennant waving from a battlement, freckled face beaming like a sunrise. She adored Tom and flirted outrageously, barking with pleasure whenever she made him blush, which was not so difficult to do, then winking conspiratorially and nodding in the direction of Mrs. Patterson, oblivious at her desk, like a decrepit chaperone.

Sue genuinely enjoyed Tom's visits, and Tom genuinely enjoyed the attention. The library was quite an empty, echoing place during the week. Only once in a while would someone else venture in, like the tall woman with short waves of dark hair lightly streaked with silver, over a high forehead and fine, widely spaced eyes; possibly a teacher of some kind, cordial, but always distant. She would work a few hours in a corner by herself, surrounded by a half-dozen books, writing out pages of notes, then quietly return the books to their shelves and her notes to a large brown handbag, and leave before anyone noticed.

Tom was the most interesting visitor they had.

Sue had no truck with religion. Tom had his ways of probing, like recounting one time a particularly successful sermon on the topic of envy. But it was wasted. Sue just beamed at him.

"Well, I can just *imagine* what those poor young farm wives were envying, Father."

She drawled this while looking meaningfully at his belt.

"Sue, for heaven's sake! And it's 'Brother', not 'Father'."

"Well, I bet you could make 'em say *amen,* all right." Standing by his table, she closed her eyes and swayed in mock ecstasy. "A-men, Brother!"

"Sue, you're incorrigible! That's *not* what I do."

"Don't tell me you like the boys. You don't look the type."

"Damn it, Sue . . . excuse me . . ."

Sue barked merrily, and Mrs. Patterson looked up from her desk, blinking.

"*Hush,*" Sue whispered, giggling as she leaned close and clutched his arm. "We woke her."

Tom read history and psychology and social science. These were fertile topics, food for thought and for sermons. He had no use for mathematics, or science—except that he was drawn, inexplicably, to astronomy. It was a kind of guilty pleasure. There was absolutely nothing of use in it. But there was something clean about it. Divine. He could not resist it.

Sue knew everything he read, and she saw the change in his face when he opened a book on astronomy. Everything else made him look serious, thoughtful. Astronomy made him look—childlike.

She rummaged in storerooms and brought him special items. A large book with dramatic pictures of galaxies and nebulae. A small dusty volume of famous observatories. And something she found one day, in the bottom of a file drawer, a few yellowed pages stapled together.

"Look at this, Father."

He had given up trying to correct her, and accepted the papers. "What is it?"

"See? Eclipses of the sun. Starting twenty years ago, but all the way out to next century."

"I think you're right. Very interesting."

"But look here." She flipped the pages and put her finger under a listing. "See that? Next spring—a total eclipse! See the map? We should be able to see it! Right here! Wouldn't that be something?"

"I believe you're right. I wonder what it will be like?"

"I've never seen one. What do the books say?"

Sue found the books, and they read about solar eclipses, about umbras and penumbras, and coronas, Baily's Beads, and the diamond ring. For an hour or more, she bubbled and Tom forgot his sermon—until he realized the time.

"I'm sorry, Sue! But I really must be off."

"You wanna stay at my place?"

"Thank you, but I really must go."

"Come on, Father! It's Wednesday. No sermon tomorrow. What's your hurry? I have a nice, cozy place five minutes from here. I'll make us dinner."

"No, Sue, really . . ."

"Okaaay . . ." She rolled her eyes. "But you don't know what you're missing."

Tom thought he had a pretty good idea.

When he returned a week later, he asked to see the list again, then studied it intently.

"What're you thinking, Father?"

"Well, I've been thinking about something. A little festival. Something symbolic. The sun fading away, leaving everything black as night. Then—a new dawn."

"You mean like . . . like the plague?"

"Well, something like that."

"Geez, Father. That's a little morbid."

"Oh no! It wouldn't have to be. It should be a celebration."

"Hmpf. Well, it's *your* religion."

"I just wonder how accurate this is. If we held a celebration, and the eclipse didn't happen, it would be pretty embarrassing. Might even shake some people's confidence."

"It looks scientific."

"But what about the calendar?"

"What do you mean?"

"Well, you know, with everything that happened back then, it wouldn't surprise me if they lost track. The year might even be wrong."

"I never thought of that. Tell you what. I'll see what I can find out."

On his next visit, she told him, "I talked with an old guy from headquarters. He said there were so many people keeping track of dates, even all the way back then, that he'd stake his life on it."

"Well! This may work out after all."

"So, what're you going to do? Have everybody dress up in togas and drink wine and eat grapes?"

"Oh, no, nothing like that."

"Too bad. I'd like to see you in a toga. You could lie on my lap and I'd feed you a grape, or something."

———

The idea fascinated. He imagined the sun fading away, until night fell in the middle of day, the white diamond ring gleaming around the black moon like a promise, then a new dawn, high overhead, breaking right over the People. And, as something that would happen only once in a generation, it would be an appropriate symbol of everything he had come to believe.

The People were not children, of course. Tom had no illusion they would see the eclipse as anything other than a celestial shadow passing harmlessly over the land. But there was nothing mystical about a birthday, either, or an anniversary. They were days like any other. It was simply human nature to grasp at symbols, to represent an organizing principle, to serve as reminder, as focal point. As a kind of renewal in itself. Symbols were important, and he did not intend to let this one to go to waste.

But he worried about the date. He fretted about it. Something could go wrong. And if it was human nature to grasp for symbols, what kind of symbol would it be if all were invited to celebrate the Word, and the eclipse failed to appear?

He pestered Sue, and she talked with others, people in the planning department, one of whom laughed when she explained.

"Well, you can set his mind at ease. We know all about it. Totality will occur about ten-thirty. And tell him not to miss it. None of us will live to see another. Not here. Not by a long shot."

When she told him, he thanked her profusely, and she took the opportunity to celebrate, by hugging him rather enthusiastically, longer and a little more closely than friendship required.

———

Tom dubbed it Renewal Day.

It would be the third Saturday in March, to celebrate the end of both winter and the plague, to mark the start of spring and the birth of the Word. The day would become an annual reminder of who they were, of where they had come from.

Marco listened to him skeptically.

"A day of celebration? I should think the People would rather forget the plague, beginning, middle, and end. What would they celebrate?"

"We have a lot to celebrate. All of us. Including you, my cynical friend."

"Well of course, I am happy to be alive. We all are. Do we need an eclipse to remind us?"

"You still don't see, and I blame myself. Words sometimes fail me." *Not so often,* thought Marco, but said nothing. "Humanity is essentially good, my friend. Yet everything happens for a reason. Never forget that. But why should evil befall humanity?"

"A very old question, Brother."

"But not such a difficult one. The real evil was not the plague, as bad as that was. The *real* evil was what came before. Maybe that's hard for you to accept, because a few were free and comfortable. But many more were slaves. They were not free. They were organized, they were deceived, they were trained to perform for others, prancing and jumping like circus animals, subverted by lies and by helplessness. Because they *were* essentially good, they were perverted by the lies.

"They were organized without being asked, they were led without being told why, and they went along because everyone else did. They were corrupted, with no choice and no way out.

"The evil was in the way they lived. And humanity could not change that, not until the way itself was destroyed. A long, long crushing evil was purged by cataclysm. It was painful. It was heart-breaking. But see the result."

Very soberly, Marco replied, "Not so good for those who died."

"We don't know what comes after this life."

"Maybe nothing. Eh, Brother?"

"No one believes that. But whatever happens, it is for us to live in this moment, to fully experience the precious gift of life, no matter how brief—and to not lose ourselves to an artificial world of regimentation and money, run by leaders and managers who are themselves slaves. The plague shattered the chains. It gave us the gift of a new chance. That's what we celebrate. And that's what we must remember."

"Well, you'll have to polish your delivery, but it might work."

"Still the cynic, my friend. Still the cynic. Are you so afraid?"

"Me?" laughed Marco. "I am an old man. What have I to fear?"

17

"Dennis."

He looked up from his book, startled at the low voice.

Diane was by his chair, hands clasped tightly in front of her.

"What is it, Mother?"

"I think . . . I think I'd like to go to Service Hill this Sunday."

"What's Service Hill?

She looked down at the floor.

"It's what they're calling it now."

He hesitated, still baffled, and her voice dropped even further.

"Where Brother Tom preaches."

He nearly laughed, but stopped at her downcast eyes and tightly clenched hands.

"Mother! What's wrong?"

"Oh . . . I just want to try it. A little like church. Do you remember? Like the old days."

He did not like being reminded of the old days, and it must have shown in his face, because she raised her clasped hands a little and tried to explain.

"I'm sorry! I just want to hear what he has to say . . . I'm so empty . . . I don't mean *you* have to go . . . but I'm so empty . . . and I just thought . . . I thought you should know . . ."

He stood up. He took her hands.

"Of course, Mother. If that's what you want. Of course I'll go."

She quickly shook her head. "Oh no! I know what you think of him."

"Oh, he means well, I suppose. And I won't let you go alone."

"He *does* mean well. I just want to—"

"Then there's nothing to explain. We'll go together. This Sunday."

"Oh, thank you! Thank you so much, dearest." Her arms slipped around him, and he tried not to think how long it had been since their last embrace.

"Thank you so much."

Service Hill rose from a wooded area a ways south of the main road, quite a long walk for many of the People, and a long climb, especially for the very early service Tom liked to hold when the season permitted. For Dennis and Diane it meant waking two hours before dawn—quite an easy thing to do, if you knew how. A large glass of water before an early bed, and another on the night-stand. An old trick, reliable as an alarm clock.

They walked hand in hand along a cart-road maintained occasionally by the town; not as firm as the main road, but not too treacherous in the dark. They climbed the hill in dim twilight, Diane's arm wrapped tight about his arm, a chill breeze greeting them as they arrived at the top, where a dozen or more had already gathered, gray figures talking in hushed tones, or standing in quiet meditation.

Shortly, Tom came over and greeted them, heartily shaking Dennis' hand, and impulsively hugging Diane.

"I am so glad you could make it! Are you warm enough, Mrs. Foster?"

"Oh, yes!" she replied, still puffing from the climb. "*Very* warm. I'm not used to this."

"May I call you Diane?"

"I wish you would. I'm a little too old to enjoy being Mrs. Foster all the time. Oh, Dennis! You know what I mean."

He patted her hand on his arm.

"Well, Brother," Dennis rumbled, trying to be cordial. "What happens now?"

"Just a few minutes. We'll start in a few minutes."

A band of silvery light was growing in the east when Tom called everyone to assemble, and they came together in a rough semicircle, maybe three dozen strong, Tom with his back to them, watching the horizon.

Then he turned, and led them in a prayer of thanks, recalling their blessings, acknowledging their hardships, while they punctuated with quiet amen's and so-be-it's. In the gray light Dennis could see the Flores, hands folded respectfully, eyes cast downward—except for Raul, whose gaze followed Tom.

The sermon began simply enough. Humility. Brotherhood. Live close to the soil. Be of service. The kinds of things he had heard all his life, and he only half-listened. He slid a surreptitious glance at Diane, saw her eyes gleaming with the cold light of dawn, following the man slowly pacing before them. She must have felt his gaze, because she looked up at him and smiled, her hand finding his as she turned back to listen.

Tom was far from finished. His voice rose, and the words took a new turn.

Remember the Plague! Remember the web of greed and lies, spun by leaders who led the world to destruction. Depend on yourself! Stand on your own.

He reviled the great Corporation to the north, with its army of drug addicts laboring for a new generation of leaders and kept ignorant of the Word. And he spoke darkly of the unknown dangers that awaited Andersonville, if an ambitious few were allowed to gamble with half-baked plans and dangerous forces, with no responsibility for consequences.

The resonant voice filled the air: Cast a jaundiced eye on promoters of all types! They are not here to do you service. They are not to be trusted. And a raw glint of sunlight suddenly pierced the horizon, striking the hilltop like a silent *Amen*.

"Now go! And bring light to those still in darkness!"

The afternoon was briskly cold, but sunny, and after a light lunch they sat together on the porch.

Diane wanted to talk. She wanted to talk about the farm, about the new soy crop, about the rabbits, about anything, it seemed, but the sermon they had heard that morning.

But the sermon hung over them.

As the sun rose and its light spread across the top of Service Hill, Marco had appeared with loaves of bread, and the People broke it together and ate while Tom walked among them, shaking hands, stopping to talk or to listen, and Marco collected tithes, small amounts of money or promises of food, or firewood, or help around the rectory.

Together they had walked home in silence, Diane with her arms folded, her gaze straight ahead. They reached the house and crossed the porch into the empty living room, and she had patted his shoulder and thanked him for taking her.

Dennis thought that might be the end of it. But next Saturday, in the evening, she reminded him it was time for bed, that they had to rise early; he complied without a word.

They walked again to Service Hill through darkness. Again they held hands, and he tried to recapture the feeling of the week before, the feeling of quiet intimacy, as though she were returning to him after a long time away. But this time was different. A feeling nagged at him, a disturbing one that the woman beside him was in some way not really there. He squeezed her hand, gently, and she squeezed back.

Weeks later, he was no longer certain what he felt. At service, Diane would stand upright, back straight, nodding as Tom spoke; then kneel to pray, her eyes closed; then stand again to watch the sun rise with the rest of the People. He stopped thinking about it. It was what she wanted. It gave her strength. And that was enough.

18

Diane suggested it, and said she would pay. Mrs. Flores said no, no, no, it was a wonderful idea, and they would take care of it, and on a Sunday afternoon Raul Flores found himself driving the little mule-drawn cart with a bucket of goat's milk carefully tied down in back, toward the rectory, and Brother Tom.

At the rectory, he knocked and carried the bucket inside, and Tom thanked him, and Raul nodded mutely, awe-struck, avoiding Marco's ironic gaze. Tom invited him to stay for tea, but Raul stammered something about his grandmother commanding him to return home immediately.

This was a lie. He was afraid of Marco.

From then on, twice a week, Raul brought a new bucket of fresh milk and retrieved the empty, saying as little as possible and trying to avoid Marco, who watched him and smiled as though they shared a secret. Raul escaped as quickly as he could. Even when the preacher asked for his thoughts on the week's sermon, he made an excuse, and quickly drove away with the empty bucket bouncing around in the back of the cart, cowering miserably at the noise, and at the memory of Marco's knowing grin.

Instead of delivering the milk one Sunday afternoon, he fell asleep against the tree by the stream, and awoke when the sun was going down. He knew what would happen next, and he entered the house through the kitchen door and presented himself to his grandmother, who promptly and loudly scolded her lazy, unreliable, good for nothing grandson, while his grandfather sat at the kitchen table looking on in silence thick with disapproval, and fingering his leather belt. Raul bolted from the kitchen the moment he was released.

He drove to the rectory, seething. Of course they had not beaten him since he was a boy, but the memory was humiliating. He hated getting into trouble.

Tom answered his knock, looking surprised, but let him in. Raul placed the bucket in the wooden ice box in back, fetched the empty, and headed straight for the door.

"Brother Raul! May I offer you some tea?"

Raul stopped, the empty bucket knocking against his leg. He glanced about the room. They were alone. No Marco. Only the preacher, a few feet away, his face politely questioning.

Raul looked at his shoes.

"I don't think I should."

"Well, you are always welcome, Brother."

"I'm late. And they're already angry with me." He wanted Tom to tell him it was all right to stay.

"Next time, perhaps."

He nodded mournfully.

"All right, then. Good night, Brother."

"Good night."

"Drive safely."

The cool night air, the creak of the wheels, and the slow tromp of the mule, soothed his humiliation, and he began swaying easily with the cart as it rolled over the trail, and eventually saw the lamp flickering in a window of his house, and knew they had turned it up for him, burning the extra oil even though he was seventeen years old now and could find his own way home in pitch dark.

It was just what they did.

When Raul realized that Marco would be away in the evening, at home in his shack, he explained to his grandmother how much better it would be to deliver the milk later, so it would be fresher in the morning. Mrs. Flores shrugged, but nodded her approval. She suspected the truth, knowing both Marco and her grandson as she did, and did not press him.

Still, he was seventeen. His grandparents were not getting any younger, and one could wish that Raul would grow up just a bit faster. Maybe the preacher would be a good influence, maybe help the boy gain some confidence.

19

Brother Tom could see that Raul did not much like Brother Marco. This was not surprising. Neither did anyone else.

Marco was a valuable sexton, but no one would think him one of the People. No one knew just what Marco believed, or whether he believed in anything at all. Tom was fairly certain he did not. But the ultimate goodness of people could not be denied, even where the flower of goodness seemed choked by weeds of malice. And Marco, discomfiting as he was, was anything but malicious.

Each person had that spark of understanding, of self-awareness, a precious bit of the divine. Evil was not mindless, like a hurricane or an earthquake. Evil was intelligence that perverted understanding, that strove to corrupt the divine.

Whatever else he was, Marco was not evil.

And while the old man might seem addled at times, smiling pointlessly over nothing at all, he had a surprisingly sharp wit and could deflect a clever argument with a deceptively simple parry. Sermons left him unmoved. He assisted conscientiously, without complaint, if sometimes painfully slowly. But the Word would never enter his heart at the point of a verbal *coup de grace*. Tom instead tried to show him, using his own life as example, and leave Marco to come to his own conclusions.

Raul was another matter. Tom could see the boy was troubled. Almost certainly a little late adolescent awkwardness. Growing pains. But who could say? And perhaps there was something he could do to help.

So he let Raul drink his tea in silence, one evening when the boy had agreed to stay a few minutes. Tom talked about the weather and the repairs Marco had made around the rectory. He wanted to put the boy at ease.

"Well, Brother, I suppose you must know the Fosters pretty well."

Raul nodded glumly.

"I am so glad to see them at Service now. I think it does Diane a world of good. Don't you?" Raul stared at the floor, and Tom chuckled. "Of course, I have no illusions about Dennis. Now, there's a practical man. I don't think he'll ever have any use for the prattling of an idle preacher. What do you think?"

"I think . . . I wish I could be like Steve Foster."

"You do? But, why?"

"He's strong. He's not afraid of anything."

"I suppose that's true. But what are you afraid of?"

"I don't know."

"Steve *is* a strong young man. But we each have our own gifts, Raul. Try to remember that."

Raul looked at him with miserable eyes. "What are mine?"

"You know, I could say that you're intelligent, and good with animals, and a blessing to your grandparents. But I won't, because you're still growing, and each of us has to learn for himself his own gifts. Don't you think that's true?"

"I wish it wouldn't take so long."

Tom laughed out loud.

"Ah, Raul! Boys have probably been saying that since time began."

Raul flushed and looked down at the floor.

On Raul's next visit, Tom was careful to avoid using the word 'boy'.

He talked about his last sermon, and was not too surprised to see Raul follow more intently as he touched upon the old bugaboos of lust and envy, not as sins, but as failures of understanding, failures of self-awareness, not evil in itself. Real evils were things like hubris and authority, indoctrination and lies, wherein the sinner sets out to undermine his victim's understanding, to deprive him of the divine spark.

He went on talking, about Renewal Day, about his plans and ideas, the festival he would hold every year. And then he remembered the boy's presence.

"Ah—I'm sorry, Raul. It seems I was a little carried away."

"It's okay."

"Well, what do you think? An eclipse should be pretty exciting, don't you think?"

Raul shrugged. Tom sighed. "Well, we'll see."

"I'd better go."

"All right, Brother. Don't forget your bucket."

When Raul next came and knocked, Tom remained at his desk, calling out that the door was unlocked. Raul let himself in, and Tom apologized without getting up that he was too busy for tea. Raul exchanged buckets and left without a word.

When he heard the front door close, Tom got to his feet, awkwardly.

Sometimes he could work through it, until the blood subsided on its own. But not tonight. Tonight it was insistent, humiliating.

Maybe he would go for a walk. A long walk outdoors usually helped.

Maybe I should marry. Isn't that how it's done? But who would have me?

He smiled, thinking of that silly girl, Sue.

20

Raul closed the ice box.

Brother Tom was still at his desk, and Raul knew this meant they would not have tea. Sometimes the preacher had more important things to do, more important than tea with a boy.

He crossed the main room to the front door, and pulled it open, then remembered the empty bucket. It was still by the ice box. Irritably, he shoved the door shut and turned to get it, but stopped.

In the small study, Brother Tom was standing, his back turned. Then he bent over and leaned on the desk, head down, supporting himself as though ill.

Very quietly, and a little frightened, Raul walked to the study.

"Brother?"

The older man jerked upright.

"Raul! Are you still there?"

"I'm here. What's wrong?"

"Nothing's wrong. Go home."

But Raul moved closer.

"Brother . . . what's wrong?"

He placed a hand on the preacher's shoulder. Startled, Tom twisted away, keeping his back turned.

"Raul, please go!"

But Raul had glimpsed the problem, and it was one he well understood.

"Ah, poor Tom. So alone."

He was very close to the preacher, close enough to count the hairs on the back of his neck, the threads of his shirt. Close enough to smell the faint, intoxicating odor of sweat.

"Raul, did you hear? Please go."

But Raul reached around Tom with both hands and deftly slid slender fingers inside the loose trousers, quickly undone.

Tom choked a wet, strangled sound, his body suddenly rigid as with an electric shock, and as Raul moved his hands, the man started shaking, helpless as a leaf on a gale.

Then he staggered away and dropped to his knees.

"Oh, God . . ."

He moaned, but did not look around. Raul had not seen his face since he entered the room.

"I just wanted to help you, Brother. You're so alone."

No answer.

"It's not a sin, is it?"

"Oh, Raul! For God's sake."

"Is it?"

Tom was kneeling, head bowed, his face in his hands, looking like a man in prayer. Or like a man suffering, and Raul imagined cradling that tortured head, stroking the thick brown hair.

But he said, "I know what you're afraid of."

The preacher's hands fell from his face, and from his slight angle Raul could see the eyelashes widen, could sense fear like poison seeping into the room, and for the first time in his life, did not feel like a boy.

"Don't worry. I won't tell anyone. You'll see. I'll never tell anyone. They would hate me. Ha! They might even kill me. But they'll never know."

Tom did not move. Raul watched a moment longer. He wanted to put his arms around the preacher, but some instinct told him he must wait, and he left the study.

He retrieved the empty bucket and let himself out, tossing the bucket in the back of the cart, heedless of the noise. Then he drove homeward, trying to remember himself as the dutiful grandson.

It was not easy.

21

What could he do?

Raul was just a boy. A very misguided one, to be sure, growing up so isolated, the only adults in his life much too old to serve as example in this particular . . . phase of life. It wasn't Raul's fault.

But it isn't my fault either!

Yet no one would believe that. Anyone would think he had forced himself on a trusting boy. Except, perhaps, Marco. Now, *there* was one with no illusions. But the thought of Marco filled him with dread. It also ignited a sharp resentment. There was no point in telling Marco anything at all.

Yet he could not help watching for signs in the following days. Marco exhibited none. Although he did look puzzled one day, when he caught Tom staring at him . . .

It was nothing! Just a foolish, foolish mistake on the part of a very foolish boy. And if it never happened again, why, that was the proof. He would say nothing. Except a little hint, maybe, to Mr. Flores, something to the effect that the boy might need a little guidance. Something like that.

Delivery day came again. Tom did not remember until late afternoon, when his belly fluttered and his nostrils flared with a sudden intake of breath.

He steadied himself.

It's all right. It's all right. There's nothing to be afraid of. Just explain what a foolish mistake it was, that no one will hold a mistake against him, that perhaps he should talk with his grandfather about what he's feeling, about growing up to be a man, and all that.

The knock came.

He opened the door.

From one hand, Raul carried the bucket. In the other—a bunch of flowers.

Tom stared as Raul grinned and then went to put up the milk. He returned, the flowers now in a glass of water, and set them on a low table.

"You don't have a wife, Brother. No one to make your home a little brighter. See?" He picked up the empty bucket. "Good night, Brother."

The door closed. Tom just stared at it. He had not been able to utter a word.

After service on Sunday morning, as the People were breaking bread, he found Mrs. Flores and thanked her for the milk.

"But I wonder, Sister, if Raul should be driving home so late, after dark?"

"Oh, I worry sometimes, too. But he knows the way well enough. And he's almost a man now, so I keep my worries to myself. He's so good with the mule."

"Well . . . if you would prefer to send him earlier, I'm always there."

"He says it's better for the milk, to bring it later." She leaned closer. "Truthfully, I do think he's afraid of your man Marco."

Tom almost offered to send Marco away, but stopped at a quizzical look from Mrs. Flores, and nodded instead.

"Of course. Whatever you think best."

22

Raul drove to the rectory, the way so familiar that he paid little attention, even though the sun had set and the twilight in the small vales between hills was dark as night. The darkness did not bother him. Darkness was nothing to be afraid of. That was for boys, and a boy would have pretended that this was a delivery day, like any other. But today there was no bucket of milk in the back of his cart. Nothing to burden him as he walked up to the rectory door and resolutely knocked.

The door opened, and he stepped inside.

Brother Tom walked away to the middle of the room and turned to face him. He looked very serious. Stern.

Raul closed the door and waited.

"Raul, I want you to listen to me."

He glanced at the low table where he had put the flowers, and sighed.

"Oh, I knew you wouldn't keep them."

"What?"

"You didn't want Marco to know I brought them."

"Raul . . . I want you to listen."

"I know what you're going to say."

"Well, you may think—"

"But I can't help it."

"Raul, I realize you're confused."

"But I'm not."

He smiled, feeling shy again, moving slowly toward the preacher.

"I'm not confused at all."

"Aren't you?"

On impulse, he reached for Tom and kissed him on the lips, then stepped back quickly, as though he might be struck down.

Nothing happened.

"You see, Brother?"

Tom stared past him, unconsciously licking the touch from his lips.

Raul flushed. The room was sultry, the floor seeming to move under his feet, and he stepped closer, and clasped the preacher's hand.

"Please. Forgive me."

His body a scant inch from Tom's, he leaned a little and placed one hand flat on the man's belly, his head gently against the chest, listening to the heart inside, pounding.

Tom put a hand to Raul's shoulder, as though to push him away.

"Raul . . . this is not right . . ."

"Foolish man."

He slid his hand inside the trousers, and reached up to pull Tom's head down and kiss him again, full on the mouth, and with the thrill of his life felt the preacher's arms around him, crushing.

23

"Are you ill, Brother?" Mrs. Flores touched his arm.

Tom nearly jumped.

"Brother Tom! What's wrong?"

"Nothing . . . nothing. I'm just a little tired."

"You're so pale! Are you eating?"

"Yes, of course!" Tom tried to smile. "Nothing to worry about, Sister. I just didn't sleep well, that's all."

"Poor boy!" She clucked. "Living all alone like that, and working so hard! I'm sure you don't eat enough. Come have dinner with us!" Mr. Flores stopped beside her. "Oh, Del! Wouldn't it be nice to have Brother Tom to dinner?"

Mr. Flores inclined his head.

"It would be an honor. Such an important one, a man of the cloth."

"I'm sorry—but you'll have to excuse me . . ."

He made his escape, and Del's quiet voice came from behind:

"No matter, Rosie. He must have something important on his mind."

The sermon that morning had been a miserable affair. Painful. He had fumbled for words, lost his train of thought, and the People had glanced at one another, confused. But he had been able to brazen it out. Or so he thought, until Mrs. Flores . . . that woman seemed to radiate an aura, a shrewd wisdom that would not be deceived. He had escaped before that frightening gaze could penetrate his robe and discover the truth marked on his body—

God, stop it!

He looked around. Mrs. Flores was still watching him. Marco was handing out the last of the ceremonial bread. Tom strode to him quickly, as though carrying news of vital importance.

Marco turned as Tom came up and whispered, "Is there enough?"

"Enough . . . what, Brother?" Marco whispered back.

"Enough bread."

"Why, yes. Of course. There is enough bread."

"I see. I wasn't sure."

He patted Marco's shoulder and walked away, noting Mr. and Mrs. Flores engaged in conversation with another couple. No longer watching *him*.

Raul would knock at his door, and Tom was powerless to turn him away. Just the thought of Raul's mouth, of the boy's skin smooth and electric under his fingers, left his knees weak, his belly fluttering.

But afterward, lust expelled and Raul dozing on his side and turned away, Tom would stare up at the black ceiling, eyes wide with guilt—or fear—until Raul would get up, slip on his baggy clothes, and quietly let himself out. Then Tom would awaken by himself in the morning, sunlight filtering into the room, his mind clear, the thing that had transpired in the hours of darkness more dream than flesh. And no one could see a dream. A dream could do no harm.

His next sermon was better. The People seemed at ease. If not quite as inspired.

Week by week, guilt subsided, until everything was as before.

Nearly as before. With each sermon, he regained his confidence. He walked among the People as they broke the ceremonial bread, and nodded to them, smiling at their thanks—but now with a sense of apartness, of a wall, as if they were far away and their thoughts no longer mattered.

One night, instead of staring at the ceiling, he gazed at the young man's shadowy back. Slowly, tentatively, he slid a hand over the slender waist and let it rest against the belly rounded a little under his fingers.

Raul sighed deeply, peacefully, and drew Tom's arm close about him.

They slept that way until morning.

24

Diane Foster could feel herself reborn.

The preachers' words had a strange power. They soothed something deep inside, a wound long scarred over and twisted, leaving her soul bent, herself a spiritual hunchback. That was how she thought of it, as she stood on Service Hill to watch the sun rise. And so very glad to see it.

Brotherhood. It seemed to say everything. Explain everything. A word to dissolve the burdens, the unnatural claims people made upon each other. Claims that led to slaves and masters. Brotherhood meant freedom, when you thought about it, and free was what she was coming to feel.

She mused over this. Why had she asked Dennis to take her, that first time weeks ago? Something Rosa had said. That Tom spoke truth. A truth the old churches had forgotten. And coming from Rosa, that was praise indeed.

She did not argue with her husband. She knew what she knew. Perhaps he would come to see it too. Once, she actually thought he might, when she caught him listening, *really* listening. Later, though, she had to shake her head, he was such a hopeless cynic.

But devoted. She knew from Rosa he would say things to Del he would never say to her. Not disrespectful things, really. But Dennis could never take the 'brotherhood of man' seriously. To Dennis, Tom was an idler making a living selling people what they wanted to hear. Comforting things. Soothing things. Nothing to do with the real business of living.

Yet he never said this to her. She knew exactly how he felt and what he thought, yet there was never an outward sign. He was the doting husband, taking her to service, kneeling with her, standing by her side as she spoke with Brother Tom, holding her hand as they walked home again.

For thirty years his love had been like this, constant as day and night. He had stuck by her with a loyalty so complete that she had seldom noticed.

Like the sky, she thought. It would always be there.

25

South of the farms of Andersonville was a river, flowing west to east. For much of the way the water was tens of yards across and placid, moving slowly toward a choke-point at the eastern edge of town, where a great plug of boulders and tree trunks formed a heavy cascade roaring into a basin twenty feet below, and from there the river ran swiftly beyond Andersonville toward the sea.

It was here that AP&L proposed to build a power station.

For weeks a crew of hired hands labored at building a channel alongside the river, starting a ways upstream the fall and ending at a natural rim above the basin. It was difficult work, and the digging went on week after week as one young man after another quit, complaining it was too much work for too little pay. But in the end, four stuck it out and finished, then lined the channel with cement purchased at no small expense from the City. At the head of it, they erected a heavy sluice gate that could be pried up in to let water flow into the channel, or driven down to block it. With the gate firmly in place, they cut through the last few yards of earth separating the channel from the river, and finished with the dangerous job of dredging muck from swirling water.

At the end of October, the job was complete.

They celebrated by killing and roasting a pig outside the barn that was AP&L.

Agnes went white the morning Steve slammed a heavy hammer between the pig's eyes, and the animal went down like a bag of cement, hind legs kicking spasmodically. The crew hoisted the twitching carcass with a gin-pole, to drain the blood, then scald in a barrel of boiling water She recovered enough to help scrape the hair before the gutting and cleaning.

With the pig spitted over an open fire, she lugged pots of hot water into the back of the barn, and bathed, and put on clean clothes. Her arms were growing heavy and languid, and she lay down and curled up on the bed—for just a minute. It felt like the first time she had stopped in many weeks.

Steve found her an hour later, and pulled a blanket over her, then left her alone until it was time to eat.

Two months later they stood side by side at the rim of the basin, near the end of the cement-lined channel. Below them, supported above the water by heavy poles, was a wooden framework. Mounted within this framework were the generator and turbine.

Steve had obsessed over the turbine. After it was lowered and bolted into the framework and the bearings secured, he had adjusted steel plates that directed water from the channel to strike the horizontal blades near the top of the turbine, and from there the water angled down and out through the blades at the bottom, giving an extra kick as it flowed into the basin. He had obsessed over the turbine's balance, screwing on counterweights and filing edges until it would spin with a push of his hand and a silent blur of the blades.

The generator was built around its stator, a three-foot square of plywood with two dozen coils of wire arranged in a circle and set behind the steel rotor. The crew lowered it into place, then spent a day shimming under Steve's direction, until the rotor could be coupled to the turbine shaft and spin smoothly. A dozen bolts were tightened, and with one push turbine and rotor turned as one, cogging to a halt as the magnets glued to the rotor tugged at the cores fixed in the wooden stator.

Small poles were set up along the rim of the basin, and wire snaked up from the stator and drooped from pole to pole, to another, smaller wood frame set up away from the water, supporting a dozen light bulbs and a tangle of wires running from socket to socket.

Agnes hugged herself against the cold. The sluice gate was in place now, the channel empty but for a slick coating of ice. This was to be their first real test, and she tried to remember the months of work behind them, the money and the energy they had poured into it. But standing here above the basin, surrounded with the roar of water, the time and the money did not seem quite real, and she wondered why she felt so nervous.

"What do you think?" she yelled over the noise.

Steve nodded toward the frame of bulbs.

"You check that thing? It looks like a fire hazard."

"Of course I checked it! While you and the guys were going over the turbine. Everything's tight. No opens. No shorts."

"Then we're ready."

She laughed without reason, and hugged him.

Steve looked back. A little above and a couple hundred feet behind them, the crew of four lounged against the sluice gate. Steve raised his fist and made a pulling motion up and down.

They waved back, and bent to the gate.

Water began to trickle and meander down the frozen channel. The men levered with crowbars, and the water became a rush, arcing from the end of the channel and striking the blades.

The blades began to move.

The gate inched higher—until Steve frantically waved back and forth, because the turbine was spinning and the bulbs glowing, at first a barely visible yellow, now with a white incandescence.

She shrieked.

"It works!"

"Of course it works!" he laughed. "What did you expect?"

She leaped and clung to him, her legs around his waist, her arms around his neck, kissing him hungrily as cheers and catcalls went up over the roar of the water.

Then her legs unfolded, and she slipped back to earth, her eyes on the glowing lights.

26

Bright moonlight illuminated the path that ran along the foot of Service Hill, and Marco was able to follow it easily, toward the rectory. Frost was falling, tufts of dead grass sparkling as he passed, until he followed the path into the trees. A mile or so later, he came out again and stopped in deep shadows cast by the moon riding high overhead.

He pulled the old rag of a coat closer about his shoulders.

The small house that served as rectory stood out ahead, a study in silver and gray ghostly in the moon-washed clearing, the windows black, not even a candle burning. Next to the house, against one wall, stood a mule, the gray sides of the Flores cart visible beside it.

Marco leaned against a tree.

A year ago, he had thrown in his lot with a force of nature. In Brother Tom he had found a breath of inspiration for a growing and wondering People. But the force had ebbed, the inspiration gone flat, and what remained now was a mechanical presence that left the People each Sunday lost, irrelevant, feeling the world was moving on without them.

An hour later, the peace of the clearing undisturbed, Marco melted back into the trees.

"It's winter, Brother."

Munching toast, the old man watched Tom openly from across the breakfast table.

"So it is." The preacher did not look up. "Something on your mind?"

"Renewal Day."

Tom stopped eating.

"What of it?"

"You never speak of it."

"Well?"

"Well, what are we going to do?"

The preacher shifted a little, but continued looking down at his plate.

"Does it matter?"

"I think it does. Such an important day."

"Is it?"

"Of course it is!"

"Why?"

"You made it so."

"Well . . . maybe I've changed my mind."

"What a careless thing to say!"

Tom finally looked up.

"What?"

"You don't have that *right*—to change your mind."

The preacher laughed a little, his eyes uncertain. "Marco?"

"You *gave* them Renewal Day. You don't have the *right* to take it away."

"What in God's name are you talking about?"

"Ah, yes. God. You've become quite casual with God's name, haven't you?"

"Marco! What's gotten into you?"

"No, the question is what—or *who*—has gotten into *you*."

For a moment, the preacher was speechless. Then he spoke again, but the voice had grown thin.

"What are you talking about?"

"Are you frightened now?"

"Should I be?"

"If you are not a complete fool."

"Marco, I don't have to listen to this!"

"No. Of course not. I can't force you to listen. You are the more powerful. You could stop me. You might even kill me, if you chose to." Tom stared at him, and Marco smiled. "Is that what you're thinking? You could, you know."

"Marco—"

"Marco, what? Marco, don't tell anyone? I haven't."

Tom did not move. Only his eyes widened.

"There. Now you understand."

"What . . . do I understand?"

"That I know your little secret. And that I've no reason to tell it. Because who, or what, you keep in your bed does not concern me."

The preacher seemed to shrink, and Marco added, gently, "Is there a problem, Brother?"

"*God* . . ."

"Oh? Why the drama? Even Socrates — such an illustrious one! — even Socrates slept with young men."

"Do you think *that's* a comfort? My God, man! I can't even speak the *truth* to people."

"The truth?" Marco placed one hand on the table as though to hold himself steady. "The *truth?* Your job is *not* to speak 'truth'! Your job is to tell stories."

"I speak the *truth!* The Word—"

"The Word is a story. A fable. Like any other. And if it leaves behind some . . . 'truth', why, then it has done what it can."

"I don't accept that! That's the old way! It's not *my* way."

Marco rose to his feet, and Tom stared up at him.

"Then Brother Tom must learn a difficult *truth*. Do you hear? You cannot stand in front of your true believers, and be one of them! Do you understand that? *Do* you?"

Tom stared up at the crystal eyes in their cavernous sockets, gazing down from a suddenly revealed height . . . and was speechless.

The illusion passed. Marco turned and limped through the open doorway, a shrunken figure of Man stooped with age.

Raul awoke.

It was very dark. The outline of the preacher sitting upright on the edge of the bed came to him slowly, and he watched, his eyes slitted, for what seemed like a very long time.

Finally the preacher exhaled, lay back, and in a little while the sound of his breathing came slow and even.

Raul closed his eyes.

27

The rectory was a very small house at the edge of a wood, in a clearing among the hills on the eastern edge of Andersonville. Whoever might have occupied it before the plague was a mystery. It must have been abandoned a long time. When Tom found it, the floors were buckled and uneven, the roof prone to sudden leaks, and it did not appear it would stand much longer. But he began making repairs, patching the roof and levelling floors, resetting doors, finding panes for missing windows. Encroaching decay was beaten back by the life-force of a caring owner, and the place had become a home.

Now it gained the aspect of a command post.

Tom weekly leveled fire at the perversion recently instituted by the Town of Andersonville: legal corporations. He decried the release from responsibility granted the inexperienced owners of Anderson Power & Light, who proposed to unleash such a dangerous and unstable force, with no oversight and no credible assurances. He condemned the Town Committee for turning over so much money, without guarantees, and with little hope of seeing its return. And he warned darkly over the future of AP&L's young employees, that they were not learning the skills and judgment needed to make a living on their own, that if AP&L were to be unexpectedly successful, they would be wholly dependent upon it, wage-slaves with nowhere else to go.

When the season turned to winter, Service Hill was abandoned, and the People gathered in the wan light before dawn each Sunday in front of the rectory. There they listened, riveted, shaking their heads at the greedy recklessness of Steve and Agnes, speculating over the motives of the Committee—especially those members whose former vocal opposition was only too well-known, and whose silence therefore so inexplicable. Dennis would sense Diane glancing up at him when Tom made a telling point, but would say nothing, looking straight ahead. Later, as she prepared lunch in silence, he would watch her, waiting for the accusations that never came.

"Mother, do you want to talk about it?"

"About what, Dennis?"

"About what that foo— . . . about what the preacher said this morning."

"No, Dennis, I really don't. I don't want to argue with you."

"Mother, it isn't as simple as he makes it sound. It's more complicated than that."

"But isn't that just it, Dennis? Isn't that just what he's saying?"

"Mother—"

"Let's not argue, dear. I know you'll do what you think best."

Against this he was helpless.

But someone else was not so helpless, and one night, several sections of wire were cut and left dangling from newly set poles, property of Anderson Power & Light.

Dennis rode out to the rectory and confronted Tom.

"Brother, you'd better control that flock of yours! That was sabotage, the other night."

"I beg your pardon?"

"You're stirring them up. That's your right, I suppose. But not when they destroy property!"

"I have never advocated violence. I have never advocated the destruction of property. But if people feel that strongly . . . Well, perhaps you and the Committee should take notice."

"Let me put it to you this way. We'll build a jail, if we have to. We'll round up all the troublemakers and lock 'em away. If that's what you want."

"The People are not criminals!"

"Let's hope not. It would be a shame if someone went to jail because they thought *you* were encouraging them."

The preacher seemed to choke. His mouth twisted. But with a cold composure, he answered.

"All right. I shall carry your message for you."

"That's all I ask."

28

Tom began to preach Renewal Day.

There were many who found something vaguely mystical, even miraculous, at the appearance of a solar eclipse at just this place on earth, at just this moment in time, when a sign was so sorely wanted.

But Diane Foster was not vague at all. She knew the reason. The Word had been revealed to Brother Tom, and Dennis could not mistake the look of triumph on her face as they left the rectory on a frozen Sunday morning in January.

Service Hill lay under a heavy blanket of snow.

Diane had clasped the preacher's hand after sermon, eager with a thought that had occurred to her while he spoke.

"Wouldn't it be lovely, Brother, to wait and re-open Service Hill on Renewal Day? It would *mean* something, don't you think? After we've hidden away here all winter? It would mean something like . . . like being reborn. Don't you think?"

Tom had covered her hand with his.

"An excellent idea, Mrs. Foster. It will very definitely mean something."

She had smiled through tears that came like a spring shower, and as quickly dried away.

"It will be lovely indeed," Tom repeated. "Thank you."

The Fosters walked home with the Flores, Diane and Rosa walking ahead and chatting gaily despite the cold, Dennis a few steps behind with Del, and responding to Del's repeated attempts at small talk with short, grunted syllables.

They stopped by one of the fields, brown stalks poking bleakly through the snow. The women hugged, and Del waited until they parted for their respective homes.

Then he nudged Dennis.

"You must be proud! To have electric light again! From your own son. Who would have thought such a thing?" He winked. "You will get a family discount, surely? The father won't pay retail, eh?" He laughed pleasantly.

Dennis remained silent. It was all anyone talked about. Electric power, sold by the month, to one and to all. Well, almost all. He glanced at the distant house with a mordant satisfaction. It would be a long time before anyone ran a wire as far as *this* place.

"It is hard to take from your own children, Mr. Dennis. I know this. Still, we all have to, sooner or later. If we are lucky, no? One day Raul will take care of me and Mrs. Flores. You will not want us when we are old, too old to work."

Dennis grunted.

Del nodded sagely.

"You see? I am right. It is just life. It is not to be ashamed of. Your son has done a great thing, but he is still your son."

"Great, is it."

"Why of course, Mr. Dennis. You don't think so?"

"Clever is what it is, Del. Clever."

"*More* than clever, my friend! Useful! And it will make him money."

Dennis snorted, and Del shook his head.

"What has happened, with you and Steve? Why do we never see him? And his lovely lady-friend! So talented."

Dennis unbuttoned his coat, dug out a mangled cigarette, and stuck it between his lips.

"I hope it makes him money, Del. But money won't save him. It won't save any of us."

"*Save* us? My God. From what?"

He took the unlit cigarette from his mouth, jamming it irritably back in his pocket.

"From . . . from *folly!*"

He marched off.

Mr. Flores watched his retreat.

"Folly. Yes, well, you would know all about that, I suppose."

———————

Dennis marched back to his house.

Inside, he shrugged off his coat and tossed it aside, and nearly walked past Diane, waiting for him in the living room.

He stopped.

"Oh hullo, Mother. Are you all right?"

"Of course I am. What's that in your pocket? Is it one of your filthy cigarettes? You promised, Dennis."

"I haven't smoked it, Mother. I never light it."

Reluctantly, his hand extended the cigarette toward her.

She sighed.

"Please, throw it away."

He did so, lingering a moment over the mangled paper tube at the bottom of a wastebasket, then went to the kitchen to wash.

In the kitchen, his gaze remained lowered. He did not push aside the tattered curtain over the sink, did not look out the window to see the pine grove down the hill where the trees stood straight and tall. Instead, he looked at his hands, at the bony knuckles and chipped nails, the thick wrinkled skin, grimy as always, embedded with his own soil. But the tobacco stains were fading. His old cough, too, was fading.

That was just the trouble. Everything seemed to be fading.

Although his hands had not failed him. After all these years, it was a thought that gave him no small satisfaction.

Until he found himself wondering if he hadn't somehow failed his hands.

Damn. What a stupid idea.

There was a basin next to the sink, and he scooped some water and rubbed his face, then picked up the rough cake of soap and began to lather his hands.

The Word was all well and good. He wouldn't argue with it. It was the sort of thing everyone believed. Tom took it a bit too far, of course, but that's what a preacher did. You always take it a little too seriously when you're in the business.

Simplify. Live close to the soil. Be of service. Cast a jaundiced eye at organizers and promoters. They aren't there to do you service, no matter what they say. Who would argue? Wouldn't the world be a better place if everyone lived a little more like Brother Tom?

He certainly couldn't argue with what it did for Diane. For years she had kept one foot in another world. But not any longer. Now there was a peace about her. A gentle strength.

Still, one had to take the preaching with a very large grain of salt. The man seemed to believe in the literal truth of God's intervention. Which was all right for him, preaching fine stories about Creation, about a Culling, about the evils before. But Dennis's horizons were not Tom's. The metes and bounds of *his* mind had been laid down years before Tom was born, in a world expansive and complex. He had built his own printing business, with a line of four-color presses, a long list of big customers, and a shipping dock busy five and six days a week, with everything from catalogues to glossy reports, by the pallet-full.

Tom's world was smaller. Much smaller. Much more idealistic. A utopia, perhaps. But a very small one.

Dennis rubbed his hands dry with a towel, wondering if Steve could build something one day that they might all have running water.

Diane entered the kitchen.

"Lunch, dear?"

"Mm."

"Well, Father! What has *you* so lost in thought?"

"Just thinking. About Steve."

"What about him?"

"I suppose he's done something great."

"Well, I suppose he has!"

"I just can't forgive him, though."

"Forgive him—what?"

"For the way he hurt you."

Diane patted his shoulder, and proceeded to rinse her hands.

"Now, Father. I don't think he's hurt me."

"The way he left here? Took up with that . . . *woman?* Never comes to see us?"

"Well, they probably don't feel very welcome."

"Would *you* welcome them?"

"He's my son. I don't approve of everything, but he's still my son. I'll always love him."

Dennis pondered this, trying to understand just what it was *he* felt. For some reason, it was not so simple.

Diane gently took the towel from him and dried her hands.

"How could I not love him?" She smiled. "He's exactly like his father."

29

In the Town Office, a hand-printed calendar hung on the wall, with the word eclipse in bright red letters marking the third Saturday in March. Someone had also penciled in *Svc Hill*. People stopped in and asked about Renewal Day.

The Town Secretary told what she knew.

"It's open to everyone. A potluck festival. We all bring something. There's supposed to be singing and music and such. You don't have to be a member of their religion. Tom said he's not going to preach, just give a little talk to anyone who's interested. It's mainly about getting together to watch the eclipse and celebrate spring."

"No preaching? Maybe we'll come. The grandkids would like that. Where will they get music?"

"Well, Amalia Hanover plays flute."

"*Amalia?* Flute? Now *that* I have to see."

Apparently a great many people had to see it. Tom expected a crowd, and he had every intention of taking full, if covert, advantage of it, to strengthen the faith of the People, to impress upon the others the People's deep connection with reality—natural, human, and spiritual.

The Sun would be the inevitable symbol of that spiritual reality, of the divine illumination in the souls of men and women, a reality not merely of facts and logic, nor of crude emotion, but the fusion of feeling and knowledge, revealed to those who could surmount the mundane affairs of human existence and be reborn into it. For what else was Spirit? And what was Mankind without it?

Generations were born and born again, history a story of death and rebirth, none better to appreciate this than the brotherhood of gray-haired survivors who would bring their children and grandchildren to Renewal Day. The brief eclipse would illustrate that death itself was but an instant in the cycle of renewal, a momentary shadow that could never darken the eternal Spirit.

So ran the mind of Brother Tom.

The third Saturday in March dawned bright and clear over the rectory. The People listened to a short talk by their preacher, of how God and nature were conspiring to create the perfect opportunity to show their fellow survivors the power and light of the Word, not through speeches and sermons, but through *them,* through their presence and personality.

Preparations began. Chairs and tables fluttering checkered tablecloths were carried up the Hill as the Sun began its slow climb toward the appointed hour, the hour of rebirth that would open the festival and reopen Service Hill as a place of devotion. Townspeople climbed the hill with covered bowls and dishes of food, and shivering children. All helping, all eager, yet subdued. Even the children were muted, sensing the undercurrent of wonder.

By mid-morning, all was ready.

Expectant, but patient, they waited, watching for the sign from above and the time to break their fast. Amalia played quiet airs, her flute badly tarnished but still sweet-sounding, Amalia herself unusually quiet, seeming to radiate a human warmth few had expected of her.

The sun climbed.

The air warmed. Cool water and lemonade were served. People collected in knots and gossiped. Children lost their inhibitions and raced about, playing tag, parents and grandparents surrendering to the release of energy too long pent up. Tom walked among them all, smiling, introducing himself to those he did not know, thanking them for helping to celebrate.

The sun climbed.

The laughter became noisier, and Amalia put away her flute. Adults tried to hush hungry children, small hands tugging, small voices asking why it was taking so long. The People helped as they could, bumping little ones on friendly knees, urging just a bit more patience. Tom's smile became forced; his robe felt hot and clammy.

The sun climbed.

The lemonade ran out. A child burst into tears, wailing over the crowd.

The sun now high overhead, Tom stood off by himself, squinting up at the brilliant white disk, and its unblemished perfection felt like a slap to his face.

Someone guffawed, and he turned sharply, but no was one looking his way.

Marco approached, looking upward, one hand shielding his eyes.

"Well, it appears someone was mistaken, Brother."

Tom threw up his hands.

"That stupid *girl* was mistaken!"

"Girl? What girl? Someone you know?"

"Oh . . . just a silly girl who works at the library, in the City."

"Ah. Perhaps that explains it."

"Damn it all, anyway!"

Marco stepped back, surprised, and Tom rubbed his face, trying to force calm into his voice.

"Marco, we'll just have to make the best of it. Tell them it's time."

The old man nodded and left, and presently bowls and plates were uncovered, bottles of home-made wine and beer opened, and what was left of Renewal Day passed into a pleasant afternoon.

But the pleasures of the day were lost to Brother Tom.

Nor did they reach Diane Foster, distraught that the miracle had failed.

He could not understand it. He simply could not. He had seen the old papers himself. He had studied them. It was not something the stupid girl had made up.

Had she lied about the calendar? Tom searched his memory. No . . . he had seen the calendar in the library long before she unearthed the eclipse papers. She could not have lied about that.

The papers must be wrong, then. The old astronomers had made a mistake. Or—the damned bureaucrats must have lost track of the date after all! —in the chaos so long ago.

There was no other explanation.

Marco had urged him to leave the tables and chairs where they were, overnight, on the hilltop. It might be good to sit with the People after sermon tomorrow, to talk things over, to deal with any concerns, any questions, any wavering; and he had agreed, too distracted to argue.

A hand rubbed his shoulder.

"Are you finished, big boy?"

Raul grinned at him. They were alone in the rectory.

"I suppose I am. I just wish I knew what happened. I don't know what to *talk* about tomorrow . . . I was so careful . . . and I'm just out of ideas. I'm . . . I'm tired."

Raul squeezed his bicep.

"But strong. Take me to bed. I've waited so long, and I'm *hungry.*"

"Is that all you think about?"

Raul backed away. He threw down his shirt, pouting like a child, but with the lean torso of a young man. Then he dropped his trousers.

The preacher sat upright. Raul shouted, *"Take me,* you big prick! I'll make you *forget* there was ever such a thing as an eclipse!"

30

The sermon Sunday was a stumbling affair, off the cuff, trailing away without warning, leaving the People watching the horizon, wondering when the sun would rise. When it did, it was Marco who came forward to point at the tables and leftovers from Renewal Day, encouraging everyone to stay.

Tom made his usual rounds of greeting, but even Dennis Foster could see he was distracted, uncertain. This was a side to Tom he had not seen before, and he slapped the preacher's back.

"Let it go, Brother. Somebody made a mistake, that's all. It's not the end of the world."

Tom smiled, looking pathetically grateful.

"No, I suppose you're right. But I had such plans! And there won't be another in our lifetimes."

"And for that I'm truly sorry. We've never seen one, have we, Di?"

"No, Father. And I guess we won't."

Marco was standing away from the tables, by himself. People passed dishes and ceremonial bread, and the old man watched, his face unreadable. It was odd. Marco often seemed in a world of his own, but this was different. Dennis had the fleeting impression of a man studying a ploughed field, thinking about what he would plant.

Well, Marco's an odd one. Nothing new in that.

Tom touched his arm.

"You'll stay a while?"

"Of course!" exclaimed Diane, after a moment of uncomfortable silence. "Of *course* we will. Oh, there's Rosa! Excuse me, I haven't said hello to her."

Tom watched her hurry away.

"Such a wonderful woman . . . you must love her very much . . . Ah—I'm sorry. Please forgive me. I'm not myself today."

"No worries, Brother. Look, do you feel all right? Maybe you should eat something."

Tom sat at a table, Dennis joining him. The sun rose higher, and brighter, and they ate and drank with the others, and before too long Tom was leaning on his elbows, warming to the rough humor of the farmers seated around him, the failure of the eclipse apparently forgotten. He told stories of his own, of his excursions into the City, and the library, and the lewdly flirtatious Sue. He laughed with them, and seemed to lose himself for once in a brotherhood of a different kind . . .

The dishes picked clean, people were beginning to excuse themselves, those with children departing and descending the hill first. Dennis tried to catch Diane's eye, but she was deep in talk with Rosie, and he gave up and settled back in his chair, trying to listen to the conversation. But he was losing interest, thinking instead of some repairs he should work on this afternoon.

Just a handful of people were left on the hilltop. Marco strode suddenly into their midst, head high, face stern. The buzz of conversation died, and they turned to him, drawn irresistibly to a presence no longer self-effacing or clumsy.

He looked like a judge.

The hilltop seemed unnaturally cool and quiet, and Marco's crystal eyes seemed to blaze with an unearthly light, his low, insistent voice reaching them as from the bowels of the earth:

"Come with me."

They rose. They followed him, to the spot where Tom preached, and instinctively spread out in a rough semicircle. Marco looked from face to face, and his eyes settled on Raul.

Those beside the young man seemed to move away.

"Raul!" Marco's voice, profound as the voice of God, pinned the boy in place. "Raul! Look up at the sky!"

But the boy was paralyzed, staring in terror at Marco.

The old man pointed overhead. *"Look!"*

Raul looked, and all eyes followed.

Overhead was but a narrow crescent of the sun, and a sound of awe rustled through the small crowd.

"You see, Raul?" came the voice of God. "It is a sign. There is something you must tell us."

A breeze whistled across the hilltop. Raul was shaking. He stood alone as though called to Judgment, and a small, frightened voice pierced the failing light.

"Raul!" called Rosa Flores. "What does he mean?"

But Raul just stared upward, pressing his fists to his head. *"No!"*

"Brother Tom!" boomed the voice of God. "What have *you* to say?"

Tom was immobilized, his jaw slack, staring at the transformed countenance of Marco as though staring over the edge of a precipice.

The voice boomed again.

"Raul! You are just a boy! *Save* yourself! Repent, and confess!"

"I . . . I couldn't help it!"

The sun was nearly gone. Night was gathering.

The voice urged: *"Time is running out! Confess! Confess—before it is too late!"*

"Ahhh, God almighty!"

Raul shook violently. A dark stain spread on his trousers, and he screamed.

"I let him fuck me!"

A heavy sigh rustled through the crowd, and they turned to Tom, whose face was now gray as death.

Dennis looked at Raul wild with fear. He looked at Mrs. Flores, her lip quivering as she passed a hand over her eyes. He saw Diane lean forward, arms across her stomach as though physically ill.

And he saw Tom—ten yards away and staring at Raul—make one step in the boy's direction—Raul sank to his knees, arms folded over his head as though warding off a blow.

"You son of a bitch!" It was his own voice that echoed across the hilltop, shocking him, and he shouted, *"You goddamned son of a bitch!* We *trusted* you!"

The crowd murmured dangerously.

"God *damn* you," he breathed, picking up a stone without thinking and hurling it.

The missile passed harmlessly, and Tom turned to Marco, his face twisted in a mute plea. But Marco just shook his head, sadly.

"Come, Brother. Confess. There is no redemption without that."

Tom opened his mouth—but staggered as a stone found its mark. He clutched at his head, a dark trickle oozing between his fingers.

"God *damn* you!" roared Dennis in the same instant.

"Brother!" Marco held up a hand. "Brother—no!"

Dennis stared down at his own hands, but now Tom staggered, again and again, as black rocks arced and struck and spun him 'round. Then his face reappeared, one eye blinded, blood dribbling from his chin, and the crowd, feral and snarling with all the hatred and malice of a wounded animal, saw the ruined face, and the missiles slowed.

Tom staggered, wailing at the sky. *"Oh, God—!"*

One more rock struck home, and he fell.

Blackness rushed over Service Hill, cold stars burned above, and with a rustle of footsteps the People melted into the night.

Then there was silence. Until Marco spoke.

"You had better go."

Dennis stared at his hands. Marco's face loomed in front of him, and that strange, profound voice came: *"Go!"*, and he backed away, saw Diane, grabbed her arm, and fled with her down the hillside.

Marco closed his eyes. Then he walked to the figure sprawled on the ground, mewing and twitching, and he crouched down beside it.

After a long breath, he reached for the throat.

"Shh, my brother. Shh. It will be over soon."

Marco stayed in the rectory that night.

He wandered the empty rooms, picking up objects and putting them down again, randomly, without seeing them.

He sat at Tom's desk. He lit a small lamp, and it burned throughout the night while he drifted in and out of sleep.

When he could see the world outside again, he put out the lamp and got up. He walked to the door, but his step slowed. He paused. He was alone. The rectory was silent, as though waiting.

He opened the door and stepped outside.

A narrow band of dim light spread across the far horizon, slowly growing, changing, brightening from gray to white to pink, and he watched without moving, while the light grew around him.

31

Diane Foster lay in bed the whole of Monday. Dennis waited on her, shifting her pillows, urging her to eat, stroking her hair. But she would accept only sips of water. She seemed in pain, yet shook her head whenever he asked.

There was work to be done, but he let it go. He stayed inside, to be near at hand. The house had been quiet before, with just the two of them, but now the empty silence as he sat alone in the living room seemed more tangible than the house itself, and he sat thinking that this was how it would feel, at the end, when they were both gone.

Tuesday morning, she sat up and looked around the darkened bedroom.

"Is the sun out?"

"Yes, Mother. The sun is out."

"I'd like to see it."

It felt like there was a stone in his gut, as though he had heard unspoken words.

But he kept his voice steady.

"When it warms a little. It's early."

Later, he brought her outside and installed her on the porch, in the rocker, propped with pillows and wrapped in blankets. She closed her eyes and seemed to breathe in the light.

"You have work to do, Dennis. Don't you?"

He sat in another chair.

"It'll keep."

She nodded peacefully, and Dennis looked out from the porch at the faint green beginning to spread over the earth, feeling her presence, holding on to it. Holding on to their world, while it might last.

Presently, a lone figure came walking towards them, and he heard Diane's clear voice:

"Rosie!"

Mrs. Flores walked quickly to the porch.

He rose to his feet.

"Mornin', Rosa."

"Miss Diane! Are you ill?"

Diane had not moved from her rocker, but the gray had ebbed from her skin.

She smiled.

"It's nothing, dear. I feel better now. How are you?"

Rosa went to her and took her hand.

"I'm so sorry! I should come back, but . . . but I don't think this can wait."

"What can't?" Dennis rumbled.

She beckoned him closer and lowered her voice.

"You know Brother Tom is . . . gone."

A shadow seemed to pass over, and again the gray touched Diane's face. But Rosa patted her hand.

"Listen. Someone wants to talk to us."

"Who?" asked Dennis.

"I don't know. But word is going around. Someone wants to talk to us. All of us, from . . . the church. You know."

"What about?"

"About Tom, maybe. No one knows."

"When?"

"Tomorrow. At the rectory. In the morning."

Dennis was silent. But Diane asked, "How is Raul?"

Rosa's lip trembled.

"Oh, I don't *know*. He never came home!"

"You poor thing. You must be frantic."

Mrs. Flores nodded, fighting back tears.

"Dennis, will you bring Rosie a glass of water?"

Dennis grunted and went inside.

Diane squeezed her friend's hand. "Did you have any *idea?*"

"*Ohh* . . . I knew there was *something*. He was away so many nights! Mr. Flores thought he had found a girl, maybe a married one, and kept it secret . . . but . . . it didn't seem right. If you know what I mean. Raul is a good boy, Miss Diane. Just a bit different."

"He *is* a good boy. I hope he comes home soon."

Dennis returned with a glass of water.

"Oh, thank you, Mr. Dennis, but I'd better go. Mr. Flores is so worried."

Rosie kissed his cheek, patted his arm, and hurried down the steps.

32

They gathered as they were summoned, fifty strong, in the clearing in front of the rectory, the boy Raul walking among them, welcoming each, and reassuring.

When she arrived, Mrs. Flores rushed at him.

"Oh my God! Little One! What happened?"

"Don't worry, Grandmama. It's going to be better. You'll see—"

She smothered him in arms and tears, and he gently broke free and moved to greet others. Del watched, shaking his head, but satisfied for the moment.

The Fosters arrived, Diane walking with an effort, until Raul appeared again, bowing and smiling, and her face lit with recognition, and wonder.

Del extended his hand. "Well, Mr. Dennis. What do you think is going to happen now?"

"I don't know, Del. Maybe anything."

"What do you mean?"

Dennis waited until the wives were to one side, whispering together.

"Someone has to pay, Del. That's what I mean."

Delmar Flores nodded, his eyes bleakly considering.

"Yes . . . yes, of course. But who?"

"Maybe all of us."

"What a thought!"

Raul called from the door of the rectory. "Please!" he called to the crowd. "Please listen!"

They turned. Out of the rectory stepped a figure clad in a white, hooded robe. They waited. The figure stood still, head bowed as though in contemplation, then stepped forward, the arms reaching up to push back the hood and reveal the crystal blue eyes and snow-white hair of Marco.

Then he stood before them, slowly taking them in, as though searching, as though asking each a question.

"Brothers and sisters."

He looked taller than they remembered. His back no longer stooped.

"We have suffered a great tragedy. We have lost an important friend and teacher. What are we to do?"

Dennis Foster stood straight, waiting for the old man's pronouncement, ready to accept whatever it might be.

"It is hard to understand what has happened. I have spent long hours searching my own conscience." He paused. "Had I not felt compelled to bring what our teacher was doing to light, he would be with us here today. But I could not live with that knowledge. No one could."

They followed his glance to Raul, and Raul looked down, breathless, his hands folded tight, until Marco continued.

"So. What are we to do?"

They waited.

"Listen to me!" Marco's voice filled the clearing. "Listen to what I say!

"We live in a world of beauty, and of darkness. Of love, and fear, and sorrow. Of death, and birth. And we—*all of us*—are born to *see* it, and to see it clearly. Perhaps there are other creatures who feel pain, who know a kind of love. But none possess the light of knowledge that burns so brightly in each of us.

"This is who we are. At the bottom of it all, on this great world hurtling through space, this is who we are.

"But the light of knowledge can burn only so bright. It is powerful, but not boundless. It burns from the moment of birth until our eyes close for the last time. And perhaps afterward. But it can not shine through every darkness. We are, after all, only human.

"There are many kinds of darkness. There is hatred, unreasoning and blind. There is unremitting grief. There is illness beyond comfort, pain beyond enduring. Such darkness may cover us in night so deep our way is lost. The flame flickers out.

"But there is a darkness yet more evil. When the light of our own understanding is turned against us, to ensnare us and trap us, to force us to live and work, not for the sake of a tyrant we can see and hate as we should, but for the sake of something faceless. An organization. An army, of slaves that exist for no reason other than enslavement. The darkness of our minds yoked to each other's darkness, so that what makes us human becomes the tool of our destruction.

"This was civilization before the Plague. Great armies and great corporations, and great webs of lies. Rivers of corruption. A world run by masters who were themselves slaves. The poison entered the veins of humanity long before the virus. The virus only finished the work of evil begun centuries before.

"Thus the poison was purged, at last. But at what hideous cost! *This* is what we must never forget. This is what our brother tried to teach us. He tried to teach me. Now I understand.

"Of Brother Tom, there is little to say. He fell to his own darkness that he could not escape. It was not the first to torment him. It was merely the last. But it is not what we should remember.

"Remember the man who saw light, the man who showed it to us, who brought us this far. We can wish him peace for that.

"We can honor his memory by continuing the journey, with honesty, with courage, and with devotion. And perhaps, somewhere, he will be proud of us. Proud of what we do. Proud of who we are."

Part II

Marco

33

There were places in the City where people did not go. Not willingly. Not legally. Blocks of streets and neighborhoods abandoned and written off, closed up during the old plague, Cargo Flu. What had come roaring through the City like the day of final judgment was but a memory now, yet a frightening one, and there were places, like this one, where people just did not go.

Which suited Craig Olsen just fine.

He emerged from the door of an ancient hotel and stood on the empty sidewalk in his underwear, scratching blond stubble and blinking in the early morning light. Behind him, the girl came out of the hotel, pushed a tangle of bleached hair from her eyes, then walked rapidly away, high heels clicking on pavement, short pink skirt stretching tight with each stride, small breasts bouncing under a black halter. He glanced over his shoulder at her gyrating ass and wondered where she could possibly hide the money he had given her.

He yawned.

His stomach rumbled, and his bare feet shuffled back into the building, up a flight of stairs, and into his room, where two clouded windows let in a little dirty light, revealing his clothes scattered on the floor. The bed was not made, probably had not been made in twenty years. There was a nightstand, with its useless lamp and telephone, and a wallet, also useless. And some pills.

The pills were the drug *rope*. People Craig knew called them 'little pink friends'.

He knew how many were left. There was no need to count them. The girl had not taken any. Like other whores, Misty had learned early the value of *rope,* and what happened to little girls stupid enough to swipe it.

But if he could not find any food to steal, he might have to sell them. The girl had the last of his money.

Selling *rope* was not hard. Something had happened a while back—maybe a year ago—and maybe at the time he knew what it was. Now all he remembered was that the supply had dried up, for days or for weeks, he wasn't sure. It had come back, of course. But not so easy to get. It would not be any trouble to sell what he had.

A dark cloud seemed to gather in his brain, warning him to stop.

Shit. Patti.

He could see her looking up at him, on her back and under the naked, heaving bulk of Pete somebody-or-other from down the street. He had just stepped into the bedroom after returning home from . . . somewhere . . . and saw it all in a glance. Only he didn't really see it. He had thought she was being raped. But then her head turned, she had looked straight at him, and they both knew the truth.

He knew it was the *rope*. They had been without *rope* for a week. It had come back while he was away. That was why she laid Pete somebody-or-other from down the street. And it was probably why he remembered.

Pete was a big man. He got off her and knocked Craig to the floor. Then he finished with her and left. Craig was in the bathroom rinsing blood from his mouth when Patti came in, tying the sash of a dirty bathrobe.

"You okay, baby?" Her cheeks were flushed, her voice soft and high like a child's.

He was leaning over the sink, staring at the black hole of the drain.

"Did he force you?"

He did not really expect an answer.

"Shit, Patti. The place is a dump. What'd you do all week?"

He knew he should not have asked that. Not while she was high. Any other time she could have lied to him, convinced him, because he had to believe. But not on *rope*. She had stared at him with the truth in her stupid brown eyes, and in her mouth hanging open.

Sometimes Craig could remember he had been foreman at the metal shop, where steel and aluminum and copper scrap were melted and recast and hammered and machined, to make replacement parts, for tractors and cars and trucks. Even the hydroelectric plant.

The crew had been a good one. They had worked hard, and they had played hard. Parties and barbecues and softball and weekends with the wives at the shore to dig for clams and drink beer and take *rope* and fuck all night. And when he remembered, he sometimes wondered what had happened to them, after he left. But mostly he forgot.

His little pink friends helped with that. And they helped him survive on bleached hair and hard eyes and black halter tops, and whatever food he could buy or steal, working in the back of a drab café and sleeping in an ancient hotel, where he bothered no one.

34

The *rope* ran out. Again.

At least what he could afford. There were still pink pills. His dealer had them, a stash she kept hidden away, as a reserve. But where he used to buy ten with what he earned sweeping floors and washing dishes for a week, now he could buy one. Or food.

He bought the pill.

"We'll split it," he told Misty, his favorite whore, when she walked in that night and stripped off her halter.

She stared at him in confusion.

"What? That all you got? How we gonna fuck on one pill?"

"We'll split it."

"Fuck that." She wrapped the halter around herself and tied it behind her.

"Here, *you* take it."

"And do what? With you all dickless?"

She was right about that. He tried to concentrate on her nipples under the halter, on avoiding her eyes and the black and gray roots of her hair. But it wasn't working.

"Okay, *I'll* take it." He popped the pill in his mouth.

"Fuck you, dickless. I'm outta here."

"What'm I payin' you for, Misty?"

"You don't pay me enough to do it like that. Not with you."

He stood up and blocked her way.

"Don't you even think about walking out on me! You're a whore, and you're gonna do a little whorin' right here."

"And you're fucked in the head. You touch me and I have friends who'll feed you your own dick. You know that, don't you?"

He knew it, and he let her walk past him.

In the morning, he came out of the hotel early, dressed, too hungry to sleep. He went to the café where he worked. In the confusion of an argument between a waiter, a cook, and an irate customer over a missing plate of ham and eggs, someone caught Craig in the back, scooping scrambled eggs into his mouth.

They threw him out.

Later, wandering aimlessly along some random street, he remembered there was a place where he could wash cars and get paid cash under the table. But he hadn't been there in a long while. Where the hell was it? Light-headed, he roamed up one street and down another as morning passed into afternoon. But he searched without success.

The next morning, when he awoke in his room, it was still dark. He had been dreaming of food, great steaming plates of scrambled eggs and greasy bacon, and he came to his senses cold and coughing and dizzy.

But now he remembered. He could find the car wash.

He arrived long before the place opened, while the sun was just rising and the City beginning to come to life.

"Yo, Olsen! What you want?"

He looked around, and saw Pete, Pete somebody-or-other from down the street.

Pete ran the car wash.

Oh . . . Christ.

"I want to wash some cars."

Pete looked him. He seemed puzzled.

"Yeah. Okay. You can wash a few. But keep outta sight."

Later, when Pete handed him a small wad of cash and leered, Craig took it without a word and hurried away. Raucous laughter that followed.

The money carried him a few days. When it was nearly gone, he went back to the café and paid for a meal, silently daring anyone to refuse him. They left him alone, eating at a table in a corner by a large window. He took his time. When his plate was clean, he pushed it aside and sat with a final cup of coffee, staring outside, at people and cars, pigeons and buses—and a woman who crossed the street, coming toward him, her eyes briefly meeting his, then gliding away as she turned and strode along the sidewalk, clean and bright and in a hurry. In the glass he saw his own reflection: Gaunt face. Dirty blond stubble. Ragged hair.

Then it dawned. He hadn't had *rope* in a week.

It was almost like before. When he had come home from the headquarters building—that was it! James Dornan was dead. Killed, somehow. Frank Gambrell had been arrested. Elizabeth White was CEO. He and dozens of others, foremen and managers, had been given details to take back to their people, to explain what was happening, the plan to restore order.

Apparently, order had been restored. Until now, he hadn't really noticed.

At seven-thirty the next morning, a short, pudgy man with thinning hair and a bad limp unlocked the door to a windowless office and turned on the light. A familiar figure stood up from his desk, in clean jeans and white shirt, face shaven, hair brushed painfully down.

"Hello, boss."

"Olsen! For chrissake, what're you doing here?"

"Need a job, boss."

"Get lost! You got no job here. I gave your job to someone else."

"Yeah, I know. I can't be foreman. But I'll do anything. Sweep floors, clean bathrooms, I don't care. I've got to live."

"Olsen, you dumb shit. You should've thought about that a year ago. How'm I supposed to hire you? Whattaya want me to do? Pay you on the side? You know I can't do that."

Craig shook his head.

"No. Not on the side. Legitimate."

"How?"

"Give it a try, Dave. You always have room for a good man. Ask. What's the worst that can happen?"

Dave Barton went behind his desk and sank into his chair. He lit a cigarette, and extended the pack, but Craig shook his head.

"What happened to you, Olsen?"

"It's a long story."

"Yeah. I heard about Patti. The cunt."

"Don't blame her."

"Are you kidding me? After her bangin' that—"

"It was the pills, Dave. Those goddamn pills. Tell me why doesn't the Corporation do something about that? God knows how many she took, when she finally got her hands on some."

"Yeah? You goin' back to her?"

"Can't. Can't do it."

"Yeah, well, she's a cunt. Sorry, Craggy, but it's a fact. You can't take it, you might as well leave now. You know the way out."

Slowly, Craig nodded. "Just don't rub my nose in it."

"Deal."

Barton sat awhile in silence, brow furrowed, dragging on the unfiltered cigarette until it burnt down to his fingers and he ground it out on the yellowed tile floor.

"So you need a job. Well . . . maybe I *can* do something about that. But not cleaning bathrooms. You're too good with your hands. I'd rather get you something on the floor."

"When?"

"Give me a few days. How do I reach you?"

"You can't. I'll check back."

Barton studied him.

"You know what happens if you fuck up, right?"

"I won't."

"We'll see about that. Come back at the end of the week."

"Thanks, boss."

Craig stuck out his hand.

Barton ignored it.

"Just come back at the end of the week. No guarantees. I'll tell you then if there's a place for you."

"Okay, boss."

"Oh—and Craggy. Leave the goddamn key."

Craig dropped an old brass key on the desk, and left.

They let him wash dishes for meals at the café, after he persuaded them, quietly but with a dangerous insistence, that he was off *rope*. Even so, it left part of each day empty, and the nights at the hotel. He thought a lot about Patti, about the good times. But Dave had called her a cunt. Patti. A cunt. That hurt. And maybe it hurt because it was what *he* had thought, that day in the bathroom, his mouth dripping blood.

He had blamed the pills then. But the pills were inanimate objects. She had taken them. Without him. No one had held a gun to her head. Was it just that one day, or the whole week? Of course, if she hadn't taken them after all, that was even worse. But she had. Without him.

What he had thought to be real, about their short marriage, was a lie. A convenient lie. Convenient for whom, and how, he wasn't entirely clear on. But it was a lie.

But so were his nights with Misty. Those had supported a fabric of existence, what he had thought of as existence. But it was another lie, dissolving like smoke when the pills ran out.

He thought about this all week. He wasn't angry. He didn't blame these women. He himself had been in on it. He had pulled the wool over his own eyes. Only Dave Barton had spoken the truth, in his crusty way. Part of it, anyway. And he wondered why he had had to hear it from Dave Barton.

At seven thirty Friday morning, Craig followed Barton into the windowless office.

Barton sat behind his desk, lit his morning cigarette, and took a long drag.

"Okay, Craggy. Here's what I can do. I can put you on the floor for a month. One month. At the end of that month, if you're not producing the way I think you should, you're out. No questions. No argument. No second chances. And if you fuck up, just once, you're out. At the end of the month, if you make it, I'll go back and see if they want to make it permanent. No guarantees. No promises. Best I can do. Want to try it?"

"I'll do it. You'll see—"

"Don't waste your breath. I already know what's going on. You don't have a choice. Right? You hit bottom. All your friends are gone, and you got nowhere to go. So, what we're going to find out is, what do you do when you're not in the gutter. We're going to find out if that's where you really belong."

"Okay, boss."

"Just don't fool yourself thinking I'll feel sorry for you. Maybe I will." Barton shrugged. "It won't change anything."

"Okay, boss."

"You're not the first to get messed up on that stuff. I've seen plenty of others. I threw them out, too. I had to. You don't want to know what happened to them. *I* sure as hell don't."

"Right, boss. When do I start?"

"Monday. Now get the hell out. Make sure you're here on time and ready to work."

35

That spring, the City began a bus service to Walsh Stables.

Four times a day on weekends the bus carried people who came to ride, to learn, to have a picnic, to drink a few beers and take in some scenery. Dan Walsh was making money, and what he didn't spend on benches and picnic tables, or replacing the barn roof, or on the wages of the two young men he had hired, he stashed away.

People came of all kinds. Some to feel a connection with trees and fields and ponds, and they would ride for hours. Some out of curiosity, who wandered about and never came back. There were regulars, and families, and young children. Walsh acquired a few burros.

But when the woman Marta stepped off the bus on a Sunday afternoon in May, Johnny Gelpin, the older of Walsh's crew, knew immediately that this was something different. He stared from the barn, at high cheeks and a high forehead, at waves of dark hair, at fine, widely set eyes, at the easy, confident manner of walking, shoulders back, arms languid, gaze relaxed yet level.

Without taking his eyes from her, he said, "Hell's that?"

Pete Sawyer looked up from crossing off an appointment.

"Dunno, Johnny. What d'you care? You're married."

"What's she looking for?"

"Not you, Johnny. That's for damn sure."

But the woman had spotted them, was walking toward them, an ironic smile narrowing her eyes as she stopped in front of the barn.

"Where might I find the owner?"

"Ahh . . . " Johnny hedged.

"You mean Mr. Walsh," Pete supplied. "Giving lessons."

"Dan Walsh, would that be?"

Johnny hemmed. "Ahh, yeah . . . "

"And I would find him . . . ?"

Pete nodded toward a party dismounting some distance away. "Right over there."

"I see. Thank you."

She walked away.

Pete glanced at his companion.

"Better not let Jen catch you gawking like that. And hell, Johnny, that gal's fifteen, twenty years older than you."

"Yeah . . . I know. Something about her, though . . ."

"Just keep your mind on Jen. You only been married a few weeks."

"Jen's got nothing to worry about," Johnny growled. He went back to work, but could not help glancing at the receding figure, wondering what in hell a woman like that wanted out here in a place like this.

The same thought occurred to Walsh, when he turned at the cool voice pronouncing his name.

"I'm Dan Walsh. What can I do for you?"

She held out her hand.

"The name's Marta."

The hand was not small. It was strong, yet warm, and soft. Not the hand of a farm wife.

He clasped it a moment. "Marta . . . ?"

"Just Marta, I'm afraid." She seemed to be studying him. And seemed to see things.

He frowned uncomfortably.

"How do you happen to know my name?"

Stepping closer, she looked into his face and murmured, "I was told to ask for you."

He coughed, stifling an electric thrill.

"Well, what can I do for you?"

Laughing, she poked at his shoulder. "Riding lessons, if you please!"

"Riding lessons . . . ?"

"It's what you do here, isn't it? Or have I found the wrong Dan Walsh?"

"No." He blew out his cheeks. "You found the right one."

"Is there a problem?"

"No. No problem. You just didn't strike me as the type."

"Really! You'll have to tell me about that sometime. I didn't realize there was a type."

He laughed, a little. "Never mind. Have you ridden before?"

She held his eye.

"Oh, once or twice. Nothing too memorable."

"Ah . . . then. We'll start with the basics, I think."

"Yes. The basics. Let's start with that."

"Um . . . I'm booked all day."

"*All* day?"

"I'm afraid so. Right up until the last bus leaves."

"I see. That's too bad, isn't it?"

"Look, I'm sorry. If we had telephones, you could have saved a trip."

"Oh, I don't know. Sometimes there are advantages to that."

"Marta, I'm really sorry. I'd like to teach you."

"You would, would you? *When* would you like to teach me?"

"The bus only runs on weekends. Unless you have another way to get around?"

"No. It's just me."

"Ah, well, can you come next Saturday?"

"I could, I suppose."

"*Will* you come Saturday?"

"All right. I will. What time do you want me?"

"Three. The last bus to the City is at half-past four. We can ride an hour or so, if you're up to it."

"If *I'm* up to it? Well, we'll see. All right, Dan Walsh. Three o'clock Saturday. It's a date."

He whistled shrilly for Pete, and Pete came trotting.

"Petey, go tell that bus driver to wait. Shake a leg. He's about to leave."

Pete ran for the bus. Marta watched him.

"You think of everything, don't you?"

"Didn't want to see you stranded."

"There's really not much chance of that, is there? No, don't walk me to the bus. I'm a big girl. And you're a busy man."

She walked away.

"Ouch," he muttered.

A soft laugh floated back.

On the appointed afternoon, a week later, when Walsh had finished with a party of three youngsters learning to canter and was leading them towards the barn, Marta was out front, alone, atop a dark chestnut mare, reins carelessly in hand.

"My God, Marta . . . they shouldn't have left you like that."

She leveled her steady gaze at him.

"Well, it's not exactly my first time. You look good on a horse, by the way. I'm surprised."

The cool confidence took him aback. He stopped beside her as Pete and Johnny jogged up and led the others away.

"What surprises you?"

"The cowboy thing. You don't look the type."

He laughed.

"The type?"

"You look like a banker. Or a lawyer." She grinned at his look. "Sorry. Petey's been telling stories. I hope that's all right."

"I suppose it's all right. But I'm not a lawyer. Never was. Not a real one."

"Well, you don't really look like one. Not with those shoulders."

"You pretty much work with your hands out here. And I've been doing it a long time."

"Mm. But alone, apparently."

"Maybe Petey *does* talk too much."

"I thought it was all right."

"I suppose it is."

"Well, are we going to sit here on these horses talking all afternoon? Or are we going to ride?"

"Where should we begin? I see I don't need to teach you how to get on, apparently."

"It's coming back to me. Let's ride somewhere."

"Let's see a few paces first."

She glanced sideways at him. Then she kicked her horse, and the mare seemed to leap, but stepped smartly into the same canter he had been trying to teach his students.

She was heading for the tree line when he caught up with her. She glanced again at him again, then broke into a gallop, turning just before the trees and trotting along the edge of the field until he caught up once more. Then she gave the mare her head and a kick and took off flat out.

They raced across the breadth of the field, pulling up short just before the trees at the far end.

His voice cut across the melodic sound of her laughter:

"Okay, Marta. What's your game?"

"Game? What do you mean?"

"You don't need lessons. Why the story?"

"Well . . . I suppose I haven't been entirely honest with you."

"Why?"

"Why? I don't know."

"Come on."

"I really don't. I wanted to get out of the City. At least for a while. I wanted to be alone. But not completely."

"I don't see why you lied."

"I did, didn't I? I don't know. Shame, maybe."

"What of?"

The corners of her mouth turned slightly down.

"Wanting to escape. It's a little pathetic, don't you think?"

He hesitated. "A man?"

"No!" She laughed. "Nothing like that!"

"Look, Marta, if you want to ride, just say so. You can do what you like. You don't need me, and you don't need to lie. A lot of people want to get away. You're not alone."

"Ride with me, Dan. Please?"

"Well . . . if that's what you want."

"Show me around. Show me something beautiful. Can you do that?"

It was not the plea or cry for help it might have been. Not by a long shot. Whatever had brought her here, the self-possession was intact. And that was captivating.

She raised an eyebrow. "Something wrong?"

"No. Nothing's wrong. We can ride as far as you like."

He sat alone in the dim light of evening, the walls of his old house fading from awareness, and Dan Walsh relived an afternoon he would not soon forget.

He had led her along a rugged trail seldom used, through pines and meadows, then up a rocky hillside. Together, they had stopped at the top, Marta gazing at the smoke-blue shapes of the City miles distant, at sparks of sunlight glinting from the sides of buildings that looked like mingled sheets of crystalline rock, but with meaning. She dismounted and walked around the top of the hill, the breeze in her hair, following the empty horizon above fields and woods and streams.

But she came back to the City.

"I'd forgotten how beautiful it is."

"Beautiful," he answered quietly. "But sometimes ugly."

"As all beauty. Don't you think?"

"Maybe."

She raised a hand to shade her eyes, and he stood looking at her profile, at the vertical line of her forehead, the prominence of her temple, the strands of silver streaming into the darker waves standing out from her scalp.

She turned to him and smiled. "Thank you. For bringing me."

They sat on some large rocks, sipped water from canteens, and listened to the peculiar quiet achieved, not with walls, but with distance. The sun was warm, the breeze dry and steady, and he let his own gaze wander, content to feel her presence. And strangely feeling no regret.

"Daniel."

"What is it?"

"Were you ever married?"

"No."

"I didn't think so."

"Why do you ask?"

"Because I'm curious about you."

"Why?"

"You're an unusual man."

"No. Not really."

"Oh yes, you are. You just don't see it."

"Don't fool yourself, Marta. The only thing unusual about some-one like me is what I had to do to survive. We're all like that, the first generation out here."

"Talk to me about it."

"There's not much to tell. It was hard. That's all."

"Anything you regret? Anything to be ashamed of?"

"Nothing I'm ashamed of."

"But things you regret."

"Things I've missed."

She studied him, not trying to hide it. "You could have found someone, you know."

He laughed. "I did try."

"But not what you wanted."

"No."

"So you let her go?"

"Just what is it you're after?"

"You say there are things you missed. But maybe they weren't there."

"What about you?"

"Oh, no! You don't escape that easily."

"Well, what do you want me to say? That maybe you're right?"

"At least consider it."

He stood up.

"Let's go, Marta."

She rose and stepped in front of him, as if to block his way, nearly as tall and looking directly into his eyes.

"What is it you're afraid of, Dan Walsh?"

"Maybe you."

"I'm a dangerous woman."
"I'll bet you are."
"Don't fool yourself."
 He hesitated.
"It's good advice, isn't it."
"It ought to be. I heard it from someone who should know."
"Sometimes I wonder if it's the right advice."
"It's the right advice. Trust me."
 And she turned away.
 They mounted up and picked their way down the hillside, riding back through the meadows and woods in silence. When they reached the Stables, the bus was already picking up the last passengers of the day. Pete took the horses, and Walsh walked with her to the bus.
 They stopped, and she reached up, put a hand behind his neck, and kissed his lips.
 Then she stepped back, grinning.
 "That was for today."
 Her fingers brushed his cheek. Then she turned and climbed aboard.
 The bus still idling, he walked back to the barn.

 The room came back to him.
 He sat very still, feeling again the touch of this woman he could not have imagined.

36

 When it rained, there was no business, and it rained for days.
 Johnny Gelpin and Pete Sawyer sat in the barn at Walsh Stables, whittling aimlessly. The horses were fed, watered, and in their stalls. A noisy stream dribbled and gushed off the roof, splashing into the mud outside the big sliding door.
 They had the stable to themselves. Most weekdays the boss spent on his farm, leaving them to deal with the horses and the occasional customer, like some big shot from the City who might drive out in his own car. But not today.
 Johnny yawned.
 If this had been last summer, there would have been jars of beer stashed for days like this. But Johnny's recent marriage to Jen Sawyer had in some ways made a new man out of him. It was only a matter of time before she was pregnant, if she wasn't already, and Johnny had a pretty fair idea what old Mr. Sawyer would do, should his daughter and infant grandchild show up on his doorstep because Johnny Gelpin was fired for drunkenness.

Mr. Sawyer had made that plain, on their wedding day, using words that Johnny would not only understand but remember very clearly. The law and Chief of Police Bert Morrow notwithstanding.

The air in the barn was cool, and damp, and a hot cup of coffee would have gone down almost as well, but the boss had been equally clear what would happen if he found someone had lit a fire inside the barn. Johnny sighed, glancing around at dry hay and wooden stalls.

Petey's knife slipped from his hand and dropped to the ground. Johnny got up and stretched. Petey snored.

He walked to the big door, opened just a foot or so, and peered outside. The rain had stopped, leaden clouds hung low, and the ground in front of the barn was a glistening expanse of mud and puddles. There ought to be a better way to drain it, he thought. Something to work on later.

He wandered over to a workbench, and mused over a small pile of envelopes.

There was mail now, dropped off and picked up at the town office by someone from the City, and once a week Johnny or Pete would ride in because there was always mail for the Stables, which they would leave stacked on the workbench. The boss liked to read the thank-you's and compliments, even the occasional complaint, and sometimes tack up a crayon picture of horses done by a very young hand. This week's mail had been on the workbench since yesterday, when Johnny happened to notice the return address on a small, square envelope lying on top the pile: A single, black, cursive 'M'.

It was none of his business. But Johnny would have given a lot to know just what was in that letter. No damn crayon picture, for sure.

37

Rain rattled against the window of his rented room at the back of a farmhouse, rain that might go on for days, relentlessly soaking. Not like the sudden, chill reminders in late autumn of coming winter, but the cool, steady promise of spring, and rebirth.

Max Wyse sat on a wooden chair and watched.

There had been a time, not too long ago, when the walls of this room had seemed to close in on him, driving him to things he would rather forget; but that was behind him. Now he glanced around the room—at the bed, the small dresser, the piles of books, the plain trappings of his plain existence—with something like affection. Because his days here were numbered.

They were throwing him out.

His landlord, an accountant who had escaped the Plague to become a vegetable farmer, had passed away this winter, and the two sons were planning families of their own, dividing the house between them, as well as the responsibility of caring for their aging mother. They no longer had need of, or room for, a boarder. So they had informed him. Besides, they implied, why didn't a grown man, who was president of Andersonville, have a home of his own?

Thunder rumbled. The window rattled, and he got up and leaned against the sill.

It was a reasonable question.

He had plenty of time to think about it. AP&L was on its way. Dan Walsh and a few others were doing business with the City. The Committee had even written some laws. There was less and less for a president to do.

But Andersonville did not have much in the way of housing, and what land was cleared was mostly farmed. Max would never be a farmer, and he wasn't alone. Farming was not for everyone, even if you weren't crippled with one arm. Still, everyone had to live somewhere, and lately he had been thinking about this as well.

And he thought about the Anderson ranch, still watched over by the town since John and May Anderson passed away, more than a year ago. The town had no use for it, of course, and the house was falling ever further into disrepair. But it might be a good place for him. And he could rent out a room or two.

But what was really intriguing was another idea he had started kicking around, of carving out a few acres and building new houses, small ones, using his modest savings to finance one at a time, sell it, make a little profit, and finance the next.

It might be a good business.

He peered out at the dirty weather, and decided he should brave it and ride to the town office. He could look over the survey and think about how much of the ranch he might afford.

He had nothing better to do.

Bert Morrow, Joe Dryden, and Ben Keller loitered in the town office, drinking stale coffee while it rained outside the old double-hung windows.

Keller stretched his arms and groaned in mock fatigue.

"Yeah," muttered Dryden. "Wish this shit would end."

Leaning back in his chair, his feet propped on a table, Bert Morrow said nothing.

"Ali!" Keller called. "You make any new coffee yet?"

"Make it yourself," retorted Ali Knight, not at all impressed with the fact that these were grown men while she herself was not yet nineteen. "I'm *Town* Secretary, not *your* secretary. Don't you have work to do?"

Keller laughed unpleasantly.

"Don't expect anybody to report a fire today, Miss Ali."

"You can call me 'Miss Knight', if you want. Otherwise, it's just 'Ali' to you." She caught Dryden grinning. "What're *you* lookin' at, Joe Dryden? You're no better, sittin' around here like there wasn't a road to tend to in this town."

The front door opened, and Ali's face suddenly brightened.

"Join the party, Max!" She waved him in. "Don't drink that," she added, grabbing the steel pot. "I'll put some on fresh."

"Thanks, Ali."

Keller shook his head. "What makes *him* so special?"

"He's our *president,*" intoned Dryden.

"He ain't a bum," she laughed, tossing old coffee out the door.

Dryden snorted.

"So what brings you out in this rotten weather? Nothing better to do?"

"Wanted to look at the survey."

"What'd I say?" muttered Ali. "What'd I say?"

"Yeah?" Keller drawled, without any real interest. "What's so important about that survey's worth ridin' through all this shit for?"

"Watch your mouth, Ben Keller."

"Hush up, Ali. You act like you didn't grow up on your daddy's farm."

Max shrugged out of his wet coat and kicked off his shoes. "Been thinking about the Anderson place."

"You involved with that church?"

"What?"

"Brother Tom's church. Although I gather he's not around anymore."

"I don't have anything to do with them." He retrieved the rolled up survey from a cabinet. "Why?"

"There was someone from the church out here the other day, looking at the survey. Seemed interested in the same thing."

"Who?"

"The one that took over. Old guy."

"Know what he was after?"

"Nope. Just happened to be here."

"So you didn't talk to him."

"Nah. No reason. He's a strange one, though."

Ali walked over, set a steaming mug by Max, and helped him spread the survey out.

Keller scowled, got up, and went to pour himself a cup.

"You gonna to buy it, Max?" she asked.

"Thinking about it. Some of it, anyway. I don't think I can buy it all."

"You know that church has money."

"Yeah, I suppose they do."

"Well, I'd rather see you get it." She patted his good shoulder. "You'd put it to better use."

"Maybe. I just wonder what Marco's up to."

"I dunno," she sniffed. "But I don't like him."

Max chuckled at her look of distaste.

"You know, Ali, you can't just deal with people you like."

"I still don't like him."

Leaning over the survey, he pondered the extent of the ranch, the house, the pasturage, the orchard—an awful lot of good land doing nothing, going to waste. The town was watching over it and keeping the animals fed, having buried John and May Anderson, and in the absence of any next of kin, but he knew the orchard was carpeted with rotten apples, the vegetable plot was overgrown with weeds, and the roof had started leaking. A few people had expressed some interest in maybe, possibly, acquiring an acre or two, if the Town was inclined to dispose of it and the price was right. But it was a good distance from the main road, and more than a year had come and gone and nothing had come of it. Truth was, most people had their hands full as it was.

Max did not have his hands full.

Committee meetings were held weekly, coming to order each Saturday morning, as Anderson Square was filling up, which did nothing to improve Chairman Foster's disposition. The meetings were open to the public, although the public generally took no interest, the meeting that decided on incorporation being an exception. Occasionally, one or two citizens would show up and sit more or less patiently until given the opportunity to bring up for consideration whatever was on their minds, usually a complaint, generally about a neighbor, sometimes referred over to the chief of police.

Max arrived next Saturday as the Members were taking their seats around the big meeting table.

Ali set out her paper and pencils, Dennis Foster opened his mouth to call the meeting to order, and there was a loud rap at the meeting-room door. Sitting with his back to the door, Max saw the look of surprise in the Chairman's face, and he turned.

Into the room strode Marco, young Raul a step behind.

Dennis frowned and cleared his throat.

"Can we help you?"

"Well, Chairman Foster, that is what I came to find out."

"You have a matter for the Committee?"

"I do. Have I come to the right place?"

Dennis pointed to a handful of chairs along one wall.

"This is it. Take a seat. When I open the meeting, we'll deal with any business on the agenda. You'll be expected to remain silent, unless you want to ask to be recognized. I may or may not do so. After we finish, I will recognize any members of the public here, such as yourselves, and you'll be given an opportunity to talk. Any questions?"

"None at all. The rules seem clear."

"Well, take your seats, then, and we'll get on with it."

The main item of business was to approve another release of money to Anderson Power & Light, so Steve could buy more cement from the City, to make secure footings for the poles his crews were setting. The price of cement had gone up, and rumor had it that some planner in the City had found out there was a demand for it.

Dennis grumbled but voted in favor, as did the others. There was little chance of rejection. Too much had been invested already. But it irked him that they should take the town's money, and approval, for granted, and not even bother to attend.

He was still grumbling when he remembered Marco.

"Ah . . . right. I suppose we'd better get to you." He glanced at the others. "Anything else? All right, the Chair recognizes Marco. Are you here on behalf of . . . ?"

Marco stood up.

"The Church of the Word."

"Church of the Word. I see. Didn't know it had a name."

"I hope to leave here with more than a name, Chairman Foster."

"And how's that?"

"I hope to leave with your approval to incorporate our little church."

The Chair broke into a hacking cough.

"A church! Why in God's name incorporate a church?"

Marco smiled, patiently.

"I'm afraid God has very little to do with it. The Church is an organization of men and women, and not a little money, who come together in the name of God, but must do his work with the tools of men."

Watching Dennis confounded and angry seemed a special joy to Amalia Hanover, and she burst into laughter.

"Seems you were right, sweetie! What do you think, Dan? Would that be legal?"

"Well, there's nothing in the law excluding religious organizations. So not only would it be legal, but as long as they agree to meet the requirements, which are mostly formalities, I don't see how we can refuse."

Alexander McCane was eyeing Marco.

"Maybe. But I'd like to know what you're after."

If Marco took offense, there was no sign of it. He answered easily. "Meaning?"

"Meaning, what's the point? I know what Steve and Agnes were after. They're taking some pretty big risks with a lot of money that isn't theirs. What about you? What risks are *you* taking?"

"Now, Sandy," observed Amalia, a lilting drawl in her gravelly voice. "That's a damned astute question. How'd you get to be so smart? What about it, Marco? You afraid of something? Just what're you getting up to?"

The old man continued smiling pleasantly.

"Are these official questions? As I recall, we may incorporate for any lawful purpose. But no matter. Your curiosity would be satisfied soon enough. We have a growing congregation. Some have a troubled past. A few do not have real homes, and others must live in homes they would prefer to leave. They need peace, a release from fear, a guiding hand. In short, Ms. Hanover, the Church of the Word intends to establish a retreat, with land we can work on, and build on, for ourselves. We do not wish to seem . . . antisocial, let us say. But it would be best for us to establish a certain amount of self-sufficiency, a certain isolation. Meaningful work, fellowship, and undisturbed contemplation are often the best medicine for a troubled soul. Don't you agree?"

She nodded slowly. "You taking applications?"

Marco acknowledged the quiet laughter with a brief smile and glanced at Max, who was not laughing.

Amalia scratched her chin.

"I still don't get it. Why do you have to incorporate to start a retreat?"

"For the Church to use congregation money and buy land for itself, I think it advisable."

The room was silent a moment, until Walsh mused out loud, "But where? What do they think they can buy?"

Max sighed.

"The Anderson ranch. What else?"

He tried to argue, but nothing he could say matched a cash offer for the entire property—enough cash to spur the Committee to quickly sort out in what way the town was legitimate owner, with rights to sell.

"Sorry, Maxie," Amalia told him later. "But sometimes money talks."

"Yeah, I know. Probably would've done the same, in your shoes."

"Sure, hon. Don't you think I know that?"

Bill let him have a room at the pub for the same rent he was paying at the farmhouse. The room was not large, and he wanted the feeling of space, so he donated his remaining books to the Town Library. They were beginning to feel a burden, anyway.

He was bored, and edgy, and as the weeks of spring drifted toward summer, he toyed with the idea of not running for election again. But he came to his senses in time. There weren't so many ways for a one-armed politician to make a living. So he ran, unopposed, and it was another year as Town President.

But there was a bright spot. Anderson Power & Light.

The novelty had worn off the poles set up alongside the main road, and people were awaiting the big day, when electric power would actually be switched on, even people who were not in line to be wired anytime soon. Nothing said *progress* like electrification, and the sheer expectancy was like a storm brewing. It was all anyone seemed to talk about.

Except, possibly, Dan Walsh. Dan Walsh went around talking about expanding the Stables. He also went around smiling a lot. This caused more than a little gossip, mainly about a mysterious woman from the City. Johnny Gelpin saw to that. People would ask Dan if it was true, and he would wink. "Why not? I'm not that old, am I?" His famous streak of sarcasm faded, and in its place people felt something remarkably like benevolence. They felt it when he walked into a room, and found themselves smiling for no reason at all.

Even Max. Even as his restlessness grew, even as the town felt increasingly small and increasingly remote, he felt relief around his friend Dan Walsh. It was impossible not to feel happy for the man. And a little envious, though he had not yet met the woman.

38

The last pole had gone up weeks ago in April, near a farmhouse a little ways south of the main road. The last wire was dropped from the pole and spliced into the old service connection at the side of the house.

In May, after checking the entire power line from one end to the other, for the second time, Steve finally let half his crew go. The rest he kept on two days a week, to jockey the generator and lever the sluice gate when needed, because Agnes was still working. She was trying to get the generator to deliver a stable voltage. It kept fluctuating, up and down, at random.

In June, with the generator still not ready, he let the rest of the crew go, except one young man willing to work a while longer on a promise of shares in the company.

One evening at the end of June, Anderson Power & Light held an emergency meeting of its board of directors. All three of them. They had been forced to accept Bill Cotter, as a condition for the Town to extend its investment beyond the original loan. Cotter was no fan of AP&L, and made no secret of it, his presence at monthly meetings held in the barn for his benefit like a dark cloud.

But tonight he was in rare humor.

"Looks like you two've screwed the pooch!"

Cotter's mouth always looked as though he were sucking a lemon. Tonight it was his voice that smirked, and Steve could only imagine a rope around that short neck compressed under the long horse-face. But he could not answer. The generator still did not work, and Agnes still could not explain why.

But she answered calmly, "Bill, I haven't figured it out. But I will."

"You've been at it for weeks. Months. That about says it all, doesn't it?"

Steve exploded.

"Come on! Give her time! She's smart! She'll get to the bottom of it."

"I *know* she's smart! That's just the point! She's *had* time. And all that time tells me the problem isn't a simple one. She can't solve it with an adjustment or a repair, or she'd've done it by now." Cotter turned round, hard eyes on Agnes. "Right? It's a fundamental design problem. And *you* don't have the money to start over, to invent a new one."

"I don't think we *need* a new one."

"With all due respect, you don't know *what* you need. *Do* you."

"For chrissake, she's working on it!" Steve wasn't sure which was worse, their failure or Cotter's pleasure in it. "Give us a break!"

"A break? Oh, no no no no no! You two better listen. This is *not* the time to start whining about a break. You two've spent a lot of money that wasn't yours. A lot of people were counting on you. They *trusted* you—far more than they should have, in my opinion, but I'm just one vote. They actually thought you could deliver. But we know you can't, don't we? It's a flop! So you'd better belly up and deliver the news. It won't be pretty. You might even have to leave town. But you *owe* it to people. And the longer you put it off, the worse it'll be." He paused, and the round eyes narrowed with contempt. "And don't even *think* about asking for more. Ain't gonna happen! Not with what *I* know. You two've run this thing into the ground. I haven't told anybody yet just how bad it is. But I *will,* if you don't, and damned soon, too."

Stave had known this was coming. He had known the Committee was asking questions. But despite all the weeks of frustration and his hatred for Cotter, all he could do was glare at him in helpless silence.

Cotter's eyes met his, fish-cold.

"You're done, pal. Time to do the right thing. The only thing left. Admit it, and stop the bleeding."

When Bill Cotter left, Agnes sank to the floor, her face against her knees, and wept openly.

Steve watched her. There was nothing he could say.

39

At one end of the conference room, two young men stood at ease, in identical dark slacks and white shirts open at the collar. They did not appear armed, but their incurious eyes and muscular builds left little doubt as to why they were there.

Raul, who accompanied Marco almost everywhere now, occupied a chair at the end of the long table, nearest to them.

At the middle of the table, Elizabeth White and Bill Baird, along with two assistants, sat on one side. On the other side stood Marco. Neither the guards, nor the lack of refreshment, nor the seating arrangement, escaped his notice.

He did not sit down. He stood waiting.

Stiffly, White nodded to him.

"Please sit, Mr. Marco. Tell us what we can do for you."

Her impatience was palpable. The corners of her eyes were creased with fatigue, and her hands folded on the table actually seemed to be supporting her.

This might be harder than he expected.

"Madam White. Please excuse me, this is plainly a bad time."

"Madam?" She frowned, looking irritated.

"You are effectively a head of state, no? With all due respect, the form seemed appropriate. Please accept my apology if it wasn't." He inclined his head. "I suppose I am something of the country bumpkin to you."

He waited, giving her time.

"Why don't you sit down, Mr. Marco?"

"Brother Marco, if you please. Or simply Marco." He pulled out a chair and sat, watching her face as he stated quietly, "I am not a head of state . . ." — and leaving the sentence unfinished.

A moment passed, and there was a barely perceptible nod of her head.

"What can I do for you?"

He smiled faintly, a gesture of encouragement.

"Let us not be hasty, Madam. This is perhaps a poor time. I should not presume too much."

"And why would you think that?"

"Rumors, Madam. I try to ignore rumors. Still . . ."

"What sort of rumors?"

"Perhaps . . . some trouble in the ranks?"

What else?

"*Christ,*" muttered Baird, and White glanced sharply at him. "Even *he's* heard about it."

She turned back to Marco, and her voice was now dismissive. "A certain unrest, Brother Marco. Unfortunate, but under control." By the way Baird slouched, fingers drumming, Marco thought this might be generous. But it was an opening.

Maybe not so hard after all.

"Well, you are not alone, of course. There was that ugly episode in Andersonville, not too long ago. I'm sure you heard."

"No, I don't think I did."

"Ah, well. You have many weighty problems to absorb you." He paused, looking at her placidly. "Something of a riot. Small, but alarming. A warning, if you like."

"A warning?"

"Of course. And not to be ignored."

The two executives waited, and Marco let them wait, as though no explanation were necessary.

Baird lifted his hands a little, gently slapping the table.

"Well? How did you deal with it?"

"How? Faith, Mr. Baird. Faith."

"Faith?"

Marco looked directly at him, but the deeper tone of his voice addressed the Corporation's Chief Executive. *Listen to me.*

"Mr. Baird, today there is a small part of Andersonville that is peaceful, productive, and faithful. Some were once among the flotsam and jetsam of our little society. Some even participated in violence, in a moment of outrage and passion. Now they live with a sense of duty. To each other. To their families, if they have them. To a higher power. You see, Mr. Baird, everything happens for a reason." He could not resist glancing at White, to ensure she was watching him. "Do you believe in God, Mr. Baird?"

"What?"

"If you believe in nothing, one should pity you." He turned to White. "I am not your enemy, Madam."

"I am not so sure that makes you my friend."

Marco smiled. "You are frank."

"Why shouldn't I be?"

"Perhaps."

"What do you want, Marco?"

"Your indulgence, Madam."

"What sort of indulgence?"

"I should like to start a small mission."

"A mission?" Her head tilted a little. "Why?"

"Those who are lost can be found. And salvaged."

"And you think *faith* will salvage them," drawled Baird.

"Truly. Nothing else."

Baird started to reply, but White cut him off.

"All right, Marco. Let's see what you can do. But not in the City proper. I will authorize your 'mission' where there are plenty of lost souls for you to salvage, and you will observe the boundaries laid down. We will review the situation periodically, and after a suitable time I shall decide whether those boundaries should change.

"You are an intelligent man. There should be no need to remind you that we remain the legitimate authority within the City. I believe the old phrase was 'Render unto Caesar'. I trust I am not being too subtle."

He inclined his head, and she stood up and walked to the door, the entourage trailing.

"Madam White."

"Yes?" She looked back.

"A suggestion. Anderson Power and Light is in serious difficulty."

"Is it?"

Marco sighed. The woman was that incurious. "It is. Perhaps your intelligence service might brief you. My suggestion is this. The City has ample electrical power for its needs. Were you to supply Andersonville, at a suitably low price, it would be very difficult for them to refuse. *Extremely* difficult. And I'm sure they would have to be correspondingly grateful."

She stared at him a moment. Then she nodded and walked out.

40

It was late.

Agnes let herself out and shut the side door.

Steve was passed out on the bed, still in his clothes, one hand outstretched over an empty wine bottle fallen to the floor beside him. No need to worry about waking him.

Months of horses and carts traveling back and forth had broadened and beaten down the path from the barn to the main road, and it was easy to follow in the dark. But the footing was rough, and it was slow, until she stumbled onto the graded surface of main road itself and started walking.

She couldn't sleep. Hadn't been able in days, since the meeting with Cotter. Steve was useless, and sinking. She knew she would have to face it all without him. Face the end. And she would. She would do what had to be done. But right now . . . right now, she just had to get away from the place, just for a little while.

Anderson Power & Light. Pretty grandiose, for a barn.

The night was unseasonably cool. She wore a light jacket, and the walk made her warm, but every minute or so, when she passed the ghostly outline of an AP&L pole, she felt a distinct chill. Because Cotter was right. The goddamn bastard was right. There was a design flaw, and she didn't know what it was, and the money would not last much longer. The bastard was right about that, too. There was no way to start over.

She kept hearing his words, "You're done, pal . . . you might have to leave town . . ." and she walked with her eyes wide and her mouth dry with the stark reality of it.

Another pole went by. She smelled the wood, the creosote, the musty fragrance of freshly turned earth and cement.

So much work. So much goddamned work.

There was something else Cotter was right about. The Committee had to be told. She was sure he had said nothing, that he was saving it to watch them crawl. Cotter had been a thorn in their sides for months, and they had treated him like dirt beneath their feet. But now the tables were turned.

At first she had thought about running away. She could leave a letter of resignation for Steve, and just leave. But she would have to go back to the City. Go back to those empty monuments. It would be worse, much worse, than facing the Committee.

She smiled through the darkness, a little grimly, because she knew what was going through Steve's mind. He could not face his father. Did not have the balls. But poor little Stevie had nowhere to run. And she remembered where she had heard that phrase before, from Jim Dornan, the original CEO, right there in Barbara's house. *"You have to have some balls, too."* She felt certain he would have understood AP&L. But Dornan had been all business. Probably would have pulled the plug, too, just like Cotter.

James Dornan had been a force of nature, but a controlled, disciplined force, and she recalled how he had immediately apologized after letting slip that earthy phrase.

Apologized! To her!

Oh, Jim. If you could see me now.

Still, there was nothing she could blame Cotter for. The man was unpleasant, but a success in his own right. They were all successful, those on the Committee. And Cotter was right about her: She was a flop. It wasn't Steve's fault. After all, Steve Foster wasn't much more than a boy.

But that's just it! What was I thinking? What in God's name was I thinking?

Through the darkness, thirty or forty yards ahead, the rough edge of another pole appeared. But as she neared it, it looked wrong. Crooked, and set too far back.

It looked, in fact, like the pub.

Sure enough. She had walked this far. Better turn around.

But she stopped in the middle of the road. Because there was nothing to go back to. Only Steve drunk in bed. Could there be a place around here to rest, maybe get some sleep? The ground looked damp. Maybe the stable . . . or . . .

She walked the rest of the way, and around to the back of the pub. It was pitch dark, but she could tell she was passing the stable by the smell of the horses, and she found the wall of the pub by feel, then the door, and rapped at it. A minute went by. She rapped again, and heard a faint thud from within.

The latch rattled. The door opened a crack, letting through a sliver of light, then opened wide. Bill's son Mike stood there with a candle, his mouth hanging open.

"Agnes!" he whispered. "What's wrong?"

"Can I stay here tonight?"

"Uh . . . sure. Okay. Sure." He stepped aside to let her in. "What happened? Are you all right?"

"I'm all right. Just don't want to sleep in the barn tonight. Is it okay?"

"Yeah. Yeah, it's okay."

He led the way down a short hallway and around a corner. To the left, an open doorway framed the dark cavern of the big dining room, the tables and chairs dimly outlined in the glow of a lamp on a table near the far wall. And sitting by the lamp, eyes gleaming in the yellow light, was Max Wyse.

She halted in mid-stride, and Mike chuckled.

"Yeah, he can't sleep either."

She put a hand on Mike's arm and gently pushed.

"Thanks, Mike. I want to talk to him."

"Okay. 'Night."

Max watched as she approached. He did not look surprised, rather strangely intent, as though expecting her. She walked up to him and looked down at the dark coat thrown over his shoulders, at the pale oval of his face, at his one hand resting on the table.

"You know?"

He raised an eyebrow, and she sighed.

"No, of course not. You couldn't."

His foot pushed out a chair, and she sat down and folded her arms.

He looked at her and waited.

"Oh . . . Max. Well, you're going to hear about it from someone. It might as well be me. I'd rather it was me . . . "

"Well?"

She told him. About the weeks of failure. The meeting. The money. Everything. But the only sign that he heard her was one finger tapping the table.

She added, "I'm sorry, Max. You don't know how sorry I am."

"Why?"

"Because it's over! Don't you get it?"

"You're giving up?"

"Max!" She fought back a burst of tears. "Weren't you *listening?* There's nothing I can *do.* And we can't hide it! Bill Cotter knows everything. Don't you get it?"

"Fuck Bill Cotter."

She choked, caught between a laugh and a sob, then slumped, drained, her elbow on the table, her head propped in her hand, and let her eyes close.

"That's right. Fuck Bill Cotter. I'm not afraid of him. But he has a point."

"What about Steve?"

Her shoulders made a small attempt at a shrug. "Drunk."

"Not much help, then."

"That's a fact."

She leaned heavily on her arm, the days of tension slowly draining from her. The shadowy quiet of the room felt strangely tangible, as though her body were being supported by it.

"Agnes. Look at me."

Her eyes opened a little.

"Sit up," he said. "You look like you're falling asleep."

"I could sleep a week." But she sat up.

"Agnes, we need this."

"I wish I could do it for you."

"That's not good enough."

She shrugged. "It's all I have."

"Bullshit."

"*God,* Max! You never give up."

"Agnes, we *need* this. All of us. You. Me. Steve. Our town. Everyone you know. Even Bill Cotter, who's too thick to see it."

"Well, there's nothing I can do."

"You can finish what you started."

"*How?* I have no *money.* I have a drunken coward for a partner—"

"Stop."

"Bill Cotter hates my guts, as he has every right to—"

"Stop it."

"What do you *want* from me?"

"Everything you have."

"Oh, God. I should never have come here. I should've gone to Dennis. And just. Get it. Over with."

"Agnes, listen to me. Just listen. I know where you are. You can't see a way out. But I'm telling you there *has* to be a way. I know it's hard. But there's too much at stake. You owe it to yourself. Don't even think about anyone else. You owe it to *yourself,* to put every ounce of strength and thought into this, until you break it or it breaks you. I know that sounds heartless. I wish I could tell you something different. But I *know* you. You're someone I can never replace. I love you, and I'm telling you what you have to hear—"

He stopped, and the shock in his face was what she felt in her own.

But he finished.

"No one else will."

The voices had died down when Mike padded into the dining area and found Max in a corner, sprawled on a bench, and Agnes curled up beside him. Both fast asleep.

He returned with a blanket, draped it over them, and went back to bed.

41

Craig Olsen squinted into bright June sun raking the street.

It was a mild evening, but he was perspiring as he walked, warmed by several beers and a big steak dinner, courtesy Dave Barton and the shop crew.

Today was his anniversary.

It had been a good year. Barton had started him on the manual brake and shear, and within in month he was turning out work as good as anyone. And as fast. Barton kept him on, moving him around to electric saws, hydraulic presses, and welding. Now he was doing lathe work. He hadn't been in the casting room yet, but that would come.

There was just one regret, and he kept it to himself. There was no opening for foreman.

He was still living at the hotel. It cost nothing, kept off the rain, and after twelve months of good pay and no rent, there was a fair amount of cash tucked away.

But it wasn't just the free rent. He had not bought *rope* in over a year—and there was no way he would ever put good money Dave Barton was paying him down that rat-hole, ever again.

The sun bright in his eyes, he bumped into someone on the sidewalk, a woman handing out flyers. They were everywhere these days, and he excused himself and stepped around her.

"Sir! Have you heard the Word?"

He shook his head, walking on. "Sorry, sister. Not interested."

"What if I could change your mind?"

Something in the voice reached him. He stopped.

"How?"

"Take a closer look."

The woman waited, the flyers in her hand dangling at her side, a plain woman with graying hair and dark lines around eyes that looked strangely familiar . . .

"It's me, Craig."

"Good God! . . . Misty—is that *you?*"

"Not what you expected, huh."

"Oh, it's not . . ."

"It's okay, honey. I don't mind."

He ran a hand over his hair.

"Jesus. It's been such a long time."

"Not that long. A year."

"A year . . ."

"That's all. But things happen. I got married, you know."

"No, I didn't know."

"Well, of course you wouldn't. And I should tell you my real name. It's Carol. Always was. But we didn't use our real names, in those days."

"Are you . . . are you happy?"

"Thank you. Yes. I am. More than I could ever tell you."

"I'm glad he makes you happy."

"He does make me happy. Very happy. His name is Gaston, by the way. Funny name, don't you think?"

"Gaston."

"That's right. But he couldn't make me happy until I learned how to *be* happy. Isn't that strange? That we'd have to learn how to be happy? I'm very lucky to have Gaston in my life. I don't deserve him. But Gaston didn't save me."

He asked before he could stop himself.

"What did?"

"This."

She pushed a flyer into his hand.

"Ah . . . Carol . . ."

"Are you afraid?"

"Well, no . . ."

"You should be. It can change you."

"I'm back at work, Carol. I *have* changed."

"Because you had to. You hit bottom, and you bounced back, and I'm glad you did. But *this*—" she tapped the flyers "—this is what it's *really* all about. Believe me, if we had known this before . . ." She shook her head fervently. "We never would have fallen like that. It's that powerful."

"I'm glad it helped."

"Promise me you'll listen. Just once! That's all I ask. Just come once. Promise?"

"Ah . . . okay . . . all right. I'll give it a shot."

"You won't be sorry."

The mission was one of those abandoned store fronts, all dust and dry rot and clouded plate glass, that lined so many City streets. But this one had been swept out, scoured and painted, and now hosted a motley collection of twenty or so chairs, stools, crates, and whatever else could be found to sit on.

It was Saturday morning, and Craig sat on an overturned wooden box, arms folded, waiting, while Misty—Carol—tried to help some farmer, who looked like he had never seen this many people in one place before, get organized. Stragglers drifted in and settled down. Carol and the rube conferred in whispers, while a dozen souls Craig had never seen before yawned and waited for something to happen.

Finally, she clapped her hands and faced them all, bright-eyed and smiling.

"Thank you all for being so patient! You won't be disappointed. We're very lucky today. Today we have a visitor all the way from Andersonville itself. Please welcome Brother Jim!"

Craig glanced at his watch. Twenty minutes late.

The rube nodded at the smattering of applause, thanking everyone for their kindness. Lanky and brown, with a thin scraggly beard, fine brown hair unevenly cut, and a deep, resonant voice, Brother Jim began some homely chatter about service to the Church, how much he enjoyed coming to the mission, how gratifying it was to see new faces.

Someone in the audience yawned. Another tapped his foot. Someone else was blinking hard, trying to stay awake. Brother

Jim droned on, the room warm and close, and Craig rubbed his neck, thinking about his latest project, a replacement flywheel, more difficult than he had expected. He had already thrown out two attempts. He recalled a shirt he had torn the other day, caught on the knife-edge corner of sheet metal he was helping to stack, and he wondered if he could sew it. Good work shirts weren't so easy to find . . .

The droning faded, into a warm, sunny afternoon on a beach somewhere, someone who looked like Patti waving to him, distant voices laughing over the roar of the waves . . . but the sun was blotted out, and the roar became a crash of thunder, and Craig opened his eyes on Brother Jim's comically stern countenance and two fingers held up, rhythmically punctuating the words:

"Everything. Happens. For. A. Reason."

He paused, taking in each of his auditors. None were fidgeting.

"That was the point of my little story, brothers and sisters. Of course, I don't mean to say every little thing that happens to you. If you stepped in something unpleasant on the way here this morning, there was probably no good reason for it. But, hey. Who knows?"

He let them have a chuckle.

"It's the *big* things in life. The *big* things happen for a reason. We don't always know what it is. We don't always know it at the time, when something happens that will turn out to be the most important thing in our lives!"

Carol raised both hands. *"A-men!"*

"So my message today is a simple one. Open your eyes. Look around. When the most important thing in your life comes along, don't be the last to know."

Carol leaped to her feet, enthusiastically applauding, and the room joined her, loud clapping interspersed with occasional *amen's.*

A little dazed, Craig went along, applauding.

Then it was over, chairs pushed and knocked aside as people threaded their way to the front to meet and shake hands, or towards the door.

Craig stood up and looked around, at a loss.

Something tugged at his arm. Carol.

"Come on, honey! I want you to meet him."

She led him to the brown man laughing loudly with a few of the local derelicts.

"Brother Jim! This is Craig Olsen. The one I told you about."

Jim stuck out his hand, and Craig took it, slowly, looking at Carol with questioning eyes.

She reddened a little.

"I just told him I ran across an old friend from before—"

"Glad to meet you, Brother Craig!" boomed the brown man.

"Just Craig for now. I'm not sure this is really for me."

"I have a big mouth, Craig, and that's why they get me to talk. But don't let that put you off."

"Sure. Okay. I'll give it some thought."

Suddenly serious, Jim rested a surprisingly large hand on Craig's shoulder.

"Carol's told me how far you've come. All on your own! I admire that, Brother. I admire it a lot. And she truly is happy for you. Just remember, though, you're not alone. You can come here any time. You don't have to be a member of anything. Just come and talk, whenever you feel like it."

"Yeah. Okay. Thanks."

"And come out to Service Hill! Any Sunday. You'll be surprised. There's folk there a lot like you. Solid, down to earth, reliable people."

"Like I said, I'll give it some thought."

Jim laughed again, slapping his shoulder. "That's all we ask!"

Carol walked him out.

"I'm so happy you came. Tell me what you thought."

"Oh . . . I don't know. I suppose he said some interesting things. I just feel like I'm pretty self-sufficient. You know? Always have been."

"But Craig, honey, why do you think this started in Andersonville? Can you imagine a more self-sufficient bunch of people? Every one of them lives off the land! Can you imagine them working for paychecks? For the *Corporation?*" She laughed at the thought, then looked up at him, her eyes serious. "Tell me something. What was it he said that interested you most?"

"Well . . . I suppose . . . the idea that everything happens for a reason."

"Yeah, that's a big one. But it doesn't mean we're predestined. When Gaston came along, I could've let him slip through my fingers. Before, I would have. But I was ready. I knew he was there for me. My eyes were open." Holding onto his arm, she raised herself on tip-toe to kiss his cheek. "You keep your eyes open, too, honey. Maybe I'll see you around?"

"Maybe."

" 'Bye, honey. It was great to see you."

She turned and went back inside the mission.

Craig walked to the hotel, climbed the stairs to his room, and sat on the edge of his bed, looking at the walls. They were yellow and stained with age. But comforting. They meant home, that he was safe.

Safe! From what? Brother Jim? The man was harmless. Safe from Misty? But Misty was married, happy, and had no interest in Craig Olsen. Which was a relief. Although what this said about his past . . . he winced.

Every day he went to work, saw the same people, and came back here again. On weekends he might hitch a ride out to the lake and do some fishing. There were still whores around, some were clean, and once in a while he availed himself. It was a need. But after today, it would be hard to look at one and not see Carol.

Carol. Misty. *Christ.*

He thought about how she had changed. It wasn't just bleach and makeup. It was the eyes. Misty's had been hard, hungry, until the *rope* hit, and they emptied.

Carol's eyes were peaceful. Accepting.

Nervously, Craig got up and paced the room.

That was it. The acceptance. That was the change. She was happy, she was full of acceptance—and it seemed like death, the obscure end to a long, hopeless struggle.

That was what frightened him.

But what should he expect? What was her life as Misty, but a long struggle to stave off the end, with as little suffering as possible?

The thought was terrifying.

He went out. He went to the café and had lunch. Then he was faced with the afternoon, and he walked for blocks, to the main avenues where buildings climbed to the sky, to the plaza surrounding the white building that was Corporate headquarters, and he wandered among the pools and gardens kept clean and bright and cheerful.

But he could not stop seeing her eyes.

She was happy, and he was glad for that. But whatever it was he saw her eyes, he hoped he would never feel it in his own.

42

Steve sat on a stool in the barn, elbows on the workbench, head in his hands, staring at the ledger of AP&L's cash. The bottom line matched the pile of bills and loose change stacked next to it. He had counted the money himself. Three times.

It would not be long now. Then he would have to go home. How much would he have to grovel, before they would take him back? The thought sickened, even more than the dry headache from the bottle of wine he had put away last night. But there was no choice. There was nowhere else to go.

A brilliant wedge of light sliced across the floor, piercing the stuffy haze in his head. He looked up as two figures entered through the side door

He stood up, squinting. The door slammed shut, and he could see.

Agnes—and Max Wyse.

"What the hell's *he* doing here?"

With a peremptory sweep of her arm, she cleared the top of the workbench, scattering the ledger and money.

"I asked him here. Sit down."

"What the hell! Why?"

"Because I asked you to."

He hesitated, his eyes frozen on hers, trying to think of a snappy comeback—but he caught the gleam of the empty wine bottle, left carelessly on the floor, right out in the open.

He sat.

Max Wyse took a seat opposite. Agnes sat between them, at the head of the workbench, as though presiding over a board meeting.

He looked from one to the other. They were sitting apart, looking straight at him. Yet he felt *something,* some form of communication, invisible to him, passing between them.

His scalp prickled.

"What the hell's going on?"

"You tell me," she answered. "Tell me what's going on. Tell me where we are."

"We're nowhere! As you damn well know! You and that damned—"

"What are the prospects?"

"Prospects?" He laughed, but stopped, because it hurt, and because he sounded hysterical. *"Prospects?* We're dead!"

"Is that your final, considered opinion?"

He shut his mouth. Something was going on. She sat straight, shadows prominent beneath her cheekbones, eyes cold and direct. There was something happening . . .

"Well?" she repeated. "Is that your final opinion?"

"Yeah. Unless you know something *I* don't. Unless you know how to fix it. Do you?"

"No. I think Bill Cotter is right. There's a design flaw, and I don't know what it is."

He looked at Max. "And now *he* knows. *Shit!* Does my dad know?"

Max shrugged. "When do you plan on telling him?"

"I haven't decided!"

"But it's your job, right? You're still president of AP&L, right?"

"Yeah. For what it's worth."

"Maybe it isn't worth much, but you still have responsibilities."

"Christ, I really don't need this."

They were both watching him, as though waiting to see what he would do. He just stared back at them.

Then she said, "Speaking as a director, I want to know what your plan is. Cotter won't wait much longer. You have to make a decision. What do we do?"

"Oh, sure, it's easy for *you* to sit there and tell *me* to make a decision! When this blows up, you just high-tail it back to the City! Right? Well, what am *I* supposed to do? Have you thought about that? Where do *I* go?"

"I don't care."

It was flat, unemotional, like an observation about the weather, or an unneeded scrap of wire. His face grew hot.

She turned to Max. "Is there anything you want to say?"

Max was watching him, the fingers of his one hand drumming the workbench.

"Steve, I'll make you an offer."

What the fuck? "What offer? What are you talking about?"

"I'll buy you out."

"What?"

"I'll buy you out. I'll buy your share of AP&L."

"Why?"

"That's my business."

He looked at Agnes. "You . . . and he . . ."

"Don't even go there."

"How . . . how much?"

Max gave him a figure, adding, "It'll be enough for you to live on a while."

"Needless to say," she added, "you won't be living here."

"And there's a condition, Steve. When I buy you out, you resign. From everything."

A new thought pushed its way through the fog, and he turned on Agnes.

"You . . . you know how to *fix* it!"

She shook her head, but the thought had struck like revelation. It was the only explanation.

"That's *it!* You know how to *fix* it! That's why you want me out!"

"You're wrong, Steve."

"Damn! You do!"

"All right. I'm done here." Max rose to his feet. "I'll leave it with you, Steve. Good luck with the Committee."

"You just want to scare me out cheap! Why else would you want my share?"

"You really want to know? She wanted to spare you this, but I'll tell you. I think something might possibly be salvaged from all this. Just possibly. But not with you here."

"Well, *fuck* you, Mr. President! Where're you going to find a mechanical engineer?"

"Oh, I think the new president of AP&L could hire one, if she needed to. Know anyone?"

"Jesus! Fuck you!"

"Okay, I'm done. Agnes, I'm sorry to see it go down like this. Sorry I couldn't help. It was worth a try."

She stood up as well, the triangular hollows under her cheekbones a dangerous contrast to the cold rectangles of her eyes.

"Steve, I'm not waiting any longer. I'm going to ask your father to call a meeting. Tomorrow, if he can manage it. You can come, or not. I don't care. But pack your things. You're moving out today."

She walked with Max to the side door.

The door opened, and Stephen Foster looked at the bright window of daylight opening in the long, black wall, and at the sharp silhouettes about to step through.

He leaped to his feet.
"Okay! *Okay!*"

Dennis opened his front door, and sighed.
"Ahh, son. He buy you out?"
"What? You mean you *knew?*"
The old man nodded. "They told me."
"When?"
"Yesterday."
"You knew *yesterday!* And you let them *do* it?"
"Tell me something, son. They give you a chance?"
"What?"
"Did . . . they . . . give . . . you . . . a . . . chance."
"Jesus. If you could call it that."
"Well, they said they would."
Steve shook his head, staring in wonder at his father.
"Son, if'n you hadn't been so drunk on self-pity, you would've seen it for what it was. A chance."
"They lied! And you knew!"
"They didn't lie."
"They cheated me!"
"I don't think they did. I think they did you a favor. You just don't see it yet." There was anguish in Dennis Foster's face. "Son, you weren't ready for this. You just weren't ready. That's all. Now come on in and shut the door. Your mother's been tidying your room."
Choking on something that felt dangerously like a sob, Steve stumbled inside.

43

"You *what?*" Amalia Hanover fairly spat.
"I bought Steve Foster's share of Anderson Power and Light."
"Max, for the love of . . . You ever hear of a conflict of interest?"
"Yeah, I know. I know how it looks."
"*Do* you? Why'n hell you do it, then?"
"It needed to be done."
Amalia plopped back in her chair, lifting her hands in exasperation and looking side to side.
"A little help here?"
"What's done is done," observed Dennis. He leaned back, both hands flat on the meeting table, and made two sharp little slaps. "Question is, what do you want to do about it?"
Bill Cotter chuckled.

"You know, Wyse, you're a bit sharper'n I gave you credit for. I never expected that. But it'll all work out in the end." He yawned elaborately.

Amalia blew out her cheeks.

"Christ, Bill. That's not much help. And Dennis? You knew about this?"

"Yup."

"And you didn't try to stop it."

"Nope."

"Well, why *not?* For the love of God!"

"Like the man said. It had to be done."

"*Why?* Will somebody tell me that?"

"To maybe salvage something from the wreckage."

"Oh, *I* know how to salvage something. We foreclose!"

Dennis glanced at her indifferently. "And do what with it?"

"Well, hire new management, for one thing!"

"Done. The young lady is president."

"Ha! What about your boy, then?"

"Home, licking his wounds."

"Well, I don't know that *President Agnes* constitutes a change in management!"

"The board thinks it does."

"The *board!*" She shrieked laughter. "The board! Who's the board? The two conspirators?"

"Three," said Cotter. "I voted for it."

"Have you all gone stark, raving mad?"

Cotter grinned.

"You know, Amalia, I've always had the greatest respect for you. But in this particular instance, you don't know your ass from your elbow."

"Oh, *don't* I!"

"Tell her, Dennis."

"Tell me what?"

Dennis cleared his throat and picked up the envelope lying in front of him.

"Got a letter here from the City."

The room went silent. Max stared at the envelope.

Cotter smirked.

"It's a rough game, Max, old boy."

Amalia's gravelly voice snarled, *"What'n hell're you talkin' about?"*

Dennis pulled out a piece of paper and unfolded it.

"This here's an offer to sell us electricity. Pretty damned cheap, too."

"Lemmee see that!" She snatched it away and read it, mouthing the words, then gave a long, low whistle, looking up at Max.

"You didn't know about this, I take it."

He shook his head.

"Bill's right. It *is* a rough game. I hope you didn't pay a lot for Steve's share." She tossed the letter in front of him. "I don't see how AP&L could compete with that."

He read it without touching it. "Don't think it could."

"Steve may just have the last laugh after all. At least he'll walk away with something."

"Unless he reneges," murmured Dan Walsh. "Maybe they haven't sealed the deal."

"Oh, the contract's signed!" Cotter smiled broadly at Max, as though he were Cotter's favorite person in the whole world. "Steve gets paid when he resigns. And there's not much chance he'll change his mind now. So, Dennis! No point in putting it off. I move we start foreclosure. What'll that take, Dan?"

Max closed his eyes as Walsh replied, "We give formal notice of default and intent to foreclose. They have thirty days to respond."

"What can they respond with?"

"It's a formality. Gives them an opportunity to dispute our finding or cure the default. We'll base the finding on the generator not working. We don't actually have a deal with the City as yet, but we can refer to the offer. Assuming the City is serious, by the time the thirty days are up it should be cut and dried. They'll have no reasonable expectation of ever servicing their debt."

"Spoken like a true lawyer! Okay, let's get on with it. I move we start foreclosure."

Amalia nodded vigorously. "I second."

Dennis rumbled. "Anything you want to say, Max?"

"Who cares?" Cotter practically bubbled. "He can't vote on this."

"Max?" repeated Dennis, with something like compassion in his voice.

"Yeah. Yeah, give me a couple of days. Before you hold this vote. Let me talk to her. Let her hear it from me. I owe her that much."

Cotter threw up his hands in mock despair.

"What's the friggin' point? She'll be hearing it from *us* soon enough."

Unexpectedly, Sandy McCane raised his hand. "I move we defer."

Dennis raised his hand. "I second. All in favor?"

Walsh held up his hand, and Cotter sighed noisily.

"Oh, all right. Two days. No more."

Slowly, Amalia raised her hand.

"Unanimous," Dennis announced. "You have two days, my friend."

"Let me have the letter."

"Take it."

Amalia watched him fold the paper.

"I don't envy you, Max Wyse. Not one little bit."

Dennis tapped the table.

"Meeting adjourned."

44

Max and Agnes sat on rickety stools at a workbench cobbled out of lumber salvaged from the house that burned, a small lamp flickering, the letter laid out between them, the barn that was still AP&L deep in shadow.

"*Jesus,*" she breathed. "I'm almost glad I never got the thing to work."

"You okay?"

"Yeah . . . yeah. I'll be okay. You want some wine?"

"Sure. Where is it?"

"I hid the last bottle from Steve. By the washbasin. Over there . . ." She waved toward it without looking away from the letter.

He returned with the bottle and a pair of small tumblers, poured, and pushed a glass in front of her.

"Thanks . . . God, they really don't want us in business, do they? When did Dennis say he got this?"

"He didn't."

"I wonder if he had it when we talked to him about buying Steve out."

"Wouldn't be a bit surprised."

"Wow. You really can't trust anyone, can you?"

"Well, I don't suppose you can blame a father for helping his son out of a tough spot."

"No, and there's been no love lost between Dennis and me. Dennis and Bill are probably both—"

"Forget that, Agnes."

She looked up.

"Good God, Max! What about you? What are you going to do? You paid Steve an awful lot of money."

He managed to smile. "Not much I *can* do. We signed a contract."

She nodded, and stared down at the letter. After a while, a cricket chirped somewhere in the shadows. Absently, she pushed her glass toward him. He refilled it, while she tapped the paper.

"How're they going to deliver it?"

"What do you mean?"

"They'll need wires. A transmission line. We already have a feeder down the main road, and twenty farms connected."

"How much wire do you have left?"

"A lot. Steve bought everything he could lay his hands on."

"That's good to know."

"You know, there could still be a business here. This offer is so cheap, I think AP&L could buy power, resell it, maintain the lines, and still make money. Enough to hire help, keep wiring farms, and keep growing."

"Seriously?"

"Well . . . not with the damn loan hanging over us. We'll never meet the payment schedule. And there's no chance the Committee would agree to change it. Not with Bill Cotter on it."

"Don't be too sure."

"You think? How would we sell it to him?"

"You mean, how do *you* sell it. I have to keep out of this. Amalia's already raked me over the coals for buying out Steve. Claims it's a conflict of interest. And she's probably right. You won't stand a chance if she sees me involved. Listen, if you think you could make this work, you have one day to figure it out. They vote day after tomorrow. Monday. Sure, Bill Cotter's nursing a grudge, but he's not a fanatic. And don't underestimate Sandy. He doesn't say much, but he doesn't miss much, either."

"One day? Not going to be so easy. Any advice?"

"Don't let them get under your skin. Don't let it get personal."

"That's your advice? That's it?"

"That's it."

The following day, Sunday, Max got his horse and rode out to Walsh Stables. He arrived as the sun rose, Johnny and Pete out front, saddling horses.

Pete grinned.

"Hiya, Max."

"Mornin', Pete, Johnny. The boss around?"

Johnny swore suddenly, sucking a bleeding knuckle.

"How'n hell you saddle a horse with one arm?"

"I can't."

From a far tree line, a pair of riders emerged, and Pete nodded toward them.

"Here they come now."

One was unmistakably the tall, balding Walsh. The other was a woman, nearly as tall, and as they neared he made out short waves of dark, almost black hair over a high forehead and high cheeks, and clear, widely-spaced eyes. The straight shoulders had a relaxed poise, the reins in her hand almost forgotten. She rode effortlessly.

Max stared.

Pete chuckled.

"Yeah."

The pair rode up and halted, and Walsh nodded, a little curtly.

"Mornin', Max." There was a question in the tilt of his head, but he went on. "Marta, this is Max Wyse, Andersonville's president."

"Pleased to meet you, Mr. Wyse. Daniel's told me a great deal about you."

"Max. Nice meeting you. So you're the mystery woman."

She laughed.

"Mystery woman?"

"Everyone's noticed the change in Dan, but no one knows anything about you. You're the mystery."

"I see. I wasn't aware I had such a profound influence on him."

"No kidding. He was getting to be a real sourpuss. Now he's all sunshine and daisies."

The City bus came bumping and swaying through the trees on its first run of the day, and Marta dismounted.

"Daniel, m'love, I'm off."

"Friday?"

"Without fail." She handed the reins to Pete, pursed her lips at Walsh in a brief imitation of a kiss, and walked to the bus, shoulders straight, arms swinging languidly, the men watching in silence.

"Wow, Dan."

"Okay, Max. What's up? You talk with Agnes?"

"I did. Last night."

"How'd she take it?"

"Surprisingly well."

"Yeah? Why's that?"

"She has some ideas the Committee might want to consider."

Walsh sucked his teeth.

"You know, you're walking a pretty fine line here. You better watch your step."

"Hell, I'm staying out of it. I told her that."

"That might be a little hard for some people to swallow."

"I just have a few questions about the loan."

"You call that staying out of it?"

"Look, I just want to make sure of a couple of things. Is that a crime?"

"Might depend on what you decide to do with the information."

"Is it a crime for Agnes to bounce some ideas off me, as a director, before bringing them to the Committee?"

"Look, I'm not trying to be an asshole about it. I'm just warning you. Maybe your heart's in the right place, but that's not always good enough. Especially if things go south. You want to be above reproach."

"They've already gone south. I don't see how it can get much worse."

"Well, don't say I didn't warn you."

45

Monday evening.

Dennis Foster slapped the table.

"Okay, folks. This here's a special meeting. We have two items on the agenda."

"Two?" Bill Cotter looked up. "I can think of one."

"Two," affirmed Dennis. "The question of foreclosure. And Agnes here wants to talk."

"Well, hell, let her talk."

"Anyone have any objections? All right, young lady. The floor is yours. Until I take it back."

Agnes stood up. She was ready. But then Amalia Hanover seemed to come awake.

"Now wait just a damned minute! Maybe I *do* have an objection."

Dennis sighed.

"All right. What's on your mind?"

"Is Max here as Town President? Or director of AP&L? Or maybe something else, hm?"

"Like what?"

"Oh, I don't know. I heard she paid a late night visit to his room a little while ago."

"That true, Max?"

"Well . . . in a way."

"Well *damn,* son! What do you expect people to think?"

"See my problem?"

"Look, Amalia, I don't have a vote and I have nothing to say. I'm just here to listen."

"Well, honey-doll, maybe you shouldn't be here at all!"

Shaking his head, Max got up and left. The windows rattled as the front door slammed, and Dennis glanced at Amalia.

"Satisfied?" He didn't wait for an answer. "Miss Agnes has the floor!"

She took a long breath.

"All right. I've seen the City's offer. It's unbelievable, but obviously they can afford it. I have no idea what they're really after, since it doesn't seem to be money. But I'll leave that to you. You'll have to negotiate a contract, and then you'll find out what they're really willing to commit to. So I'm in full agreement that you should take them up on it. They have the generating capacity. At least for now."

"What's that?" Dennis interrupted. "What do you mean, for now?"

"They have one generator working at the plant north of the City. They've been cannibalizing the others for years. You know how Robert Larsen used to say they were living on borrowed time. That's one reason. They can't cannibalize forever. So by all means, get what you can get while the getting's good. "

"Well, come on now, honey," drawled Amalia. "Surely they know all about their own generators. Don't you think?"

"You'd think."

"Well then, I think we can count on them to watch out for their own interests, and that would include keeping that plant operating."

"Amalia, last year they let a huge tank of gasoline drain right into the ground. Seven hundred thousand gallons. They practically had a revolution over it."

Bill Cotter frowned. Sandy McCane scratched his chin.

Dennis rumbled. "Yeah, okay. You made your point. That it?"

"No. That's not it."

"Well, get on with it, woman."

She looked down, counted to five . . .

"All right. We know the City can generate power. What they can't do is deliver it. Not until someone builds a line. We already have one. We have twenty farms wired. We need to wire more. We need to wire places like this one, the Town Office.

"Now, maybe the City will offer to do it all. Question is, do you want City crews out here doing what our own people could be doing? This town has a growing population. There aren't enough farms for everyone, and there's only so much farming we all need anyway. Andersonville's going to need new businesses."

Cotter yawned.

"Yeah, well, AP&L's a *failed* business. It's not a factor in any of this."

Dennis looked at him sideways. "You ever run a business, Bill?"

"No—"

"Thought not. You have anything else to say, young lady?"

"I do. We have the feeder and a large stock of wire. I'm proposing that AP&L resell City power at a suitable markup, and use that markup to hire our own people, maintain the lines, and grow the system.

"And that's not all. Our first generator almost worked. We still have the turbine and spillway. I'm proposing to invest some of the money we make to design and prove out a generator that *does* work. Then Andersonville will have alternatives. We'll have our own know-how. If the City fails us, or reneges, or refuses to renew a contract, we won't be completely at their mercy."

Cotter exploded. "What the hell do we need AP&L for? You already *proved* you don't know how to run a business!"

"Look—" Dan Walsh started, but Agnes cut him off.

"Bill, I deserve that. I didn't pay you much respect before. That was poor judgment, on my part. You don't have to like me. But I've learned a few things, and I can work with you."

Cotter stared at her, his mouth hanging open.

Amalia whistled softly.

"Well, honey, that's about as neat an apology as *I* ever heard."

"I've learned a lot about this business. I know I need help. Steve's good at what he does. Really good. I don't know if he'll do it, but I'd like him to work for me."

"Well, now, missy." Dennis coughed. "That might just be a long shot. I don't know Steve will ever show his face around your place again."

"Time will tell."

"Yup, it will. So what do you want from us?"

"Work with me. Give me a chance to make AP&L something we can be proud of—and something we can rely on."

"You looking for money?"

"Not necessarily."

"Good."

"Depends on what the City agrees to. And when."

"What else?"

"AP&L needs to *make* money. So I need your agreement that we can set our price close to what we originally planned."

"Now hold on a minute!" Amalia rose half out of her chair. "Why shouldn't we *all* get the benefit of cheap power?"

"Amalia, if we're going to have our own distribution system, build our own know-how, get our own generator, then we have to be willing to invest in it. With all the risks and all the uncertainly, this has got to be the best way. Everyone who uses electricity will be investing in it, a little at a time."

"Without being given a choice!"

"You all represent them, Amalia. It's not like they don't have a voice in it."

"You know, you're just like your damned boyfriend! You know that? Got a damned pat answer for everything!"

Quietly: "He's not my boyfriend."

"No?"

"No."

"Well, you two are pretty damned tight, if you ask me. You ever sleep with him?"

"Amalia, that's nobody's business but my own."

"Well it's *my* goddamned business if he can't do his job the way he's supposed to!"

"I think he has. But that's just my opinion."

Dennis slapped the table. "Okay! I think we've heard enough. Sit down. Item two. We're voting on a motion to start foreclosure against Anderson Power and Light. All in favor?"

Bill Cotter raised his hand.

Looking at Dennis, eyes narrowed in a kind of sneer, Amalia put her hand up.

Dan Walsh looked at Sandy McCane.

Sandy McCane looked at Dan Walsh.

Dennis Foster folded his arms.

They sat that way, no one moving, for the better part of a minute. Then Dennis cocked an eye at Amalia.

She lowered her hand.

He slammed the table.

"Motion fails!"

46

From all reports, the Church of the Word was living up to Marco's promises. And Elizabeth White read the reports.

So far she had allowed three missions to open in parts of the City that were supposed to be off-limits, sealed long ago as harbors of Cargo Flu. Apparently they were not so abandoned as once thought. People were living there. And while the missions served a few directly, they heard of many more, possibly hundreds, people living where people had no business living. All of them endangering public health. Some had been terminated over the years, without any thought given to where they might end up. Many more still had Corporate jobs. And the most important thing the missions were learning, so far as Elizabeth White was concerned, was that the biggest reason for this was *rope.*

Rope. Designed to pacify manual labor, smuggled under an elaborate scheme to conceal its origin, *rope* was indiscriminate, ensnaring the weak and disaffected alike. And it seemed there might be considerable disaffection, bubbling beneath the City's placid surface.

The notion that someone outside Medical Services might learn to make the stuff was an alarming one, and when she had stepped up to the position of CEO a year ago, Elizabeth had made certain that her Director of Intelligence, Mr. Dan Carter, understood very clearly that his continued employment depended on his successfully detecting and stopping such a thing, before it could spread. And she had no doubt that Mr. Carter understood just as clearly how he would fare personally, should he fail. But the secret seemed safe, so far.

The possible role of Marco's church in keeping a certain element of society in line, without impairing minds or wrecking lives, appealed strongly to Elizabeth's sense of economy. It also troubled her. Disaffection came in many forms, self-righteousness high among them, and she kept the Church on a very short leash. One of Marco's lieutenants, a rather flamboyant Brother Jim, met with her people monthly. Brother Jim was required to submit reports in writing, then submit himself for questioning, which he endured with indefatigable good humor.

But she met with Marco herself. Marco was dangerous, perceptive and manipulative, and she did not trust him with anyone else.

At odd moments, she wondered about Marco's assistant, that quiet, slender young man with dark eyes and long hair who seemed to follow him everywhere. There was something disturbing about that one. Unsettling. He was much too quiet, and much too wide-eyed, to be entirely believable.

47

The Anderson ranch began at the top of a large, rounded hill, where a broad dirt road climbed the steep northern face to a bare yard separating house and barn. Behind the house spread an acre of weeds, what remained of a large vegetable patch.

Overgrown pasturage, formerly used for sheep, undulated down the gentle southern slope, toward fields once filled with hay and oats, now choked with brambles, spreading out from the foot of the hill. To the west, an apple orchard grew wild, the ground carpeted with decomposing fruit.

Inside the house were crooked floors and crooked rooms, all under a fragile patchwork of roof. In the barn was a tractor that no longer ran. But on the other side of the barn, away from the house, was a new structure, a rude clapboard dormitory built to accommodate a half-dozen men. Just beyond it, at the brow of the hill, a small area had been cleared and set with rough wooden benches for meditation.

The men were a variety of ages, all unattached, all used to shifting for themselves, previously as hired hands, boarding where they could and sleeping rough when they must. The experience of being a part of something new, something higher than the grinding struggle to exist, was manna from heaven, and they went about their work with the grim devotion of crusaders.

In the old house, Marco took up residence, to personally oversee what was now Thomas Abbey. Raul was assigned the rectory and required to keep it in order.

Brother Jim was tasked with supervising the missions in the City, and Marco kept a close eye on Brother Jim. Between weekly service, the work of the Abbey, and trips to the City, Marco had become a very busy man.

But not too busy to notice, one afternoon, the brief look that passed between Raul and one of the athletic, young security guards in the conference room, when they arrived for a meeting with Elizabeth White.

He did not break stride. He did not look twice. But one Saturday evening he was waiting in the empty rectory when Raul crept back inside.

"I missed you today, Little One. Where have you been, this afternoon?"

The young man froze like a deer, casting brown eyes downward in abject submission.

"Please . . . forgive me . . ."

"Why? Have you done anything wrong?"

"Oh, no . . ."

"Of course not. I believe you. You are a good boy, Raul."

Raul nodded hopefully.

"Tell me his name."

This was paralyzing. But Marco smiled his kindliest smile, gently urging, and eventually Raul managed to answer.

"Tony."

"I see. Tony. Well . . . tell me about him."

The young man stammered, shrugging awkwardly, and Marco prodded again.

"Are you ashamed of him?"

"Oh, no!"

"So?"

"He loves me."

"I hope that is true. You are such a beautiful boy. I hope he does not hurt you."

"No! He would never do that."

"That is good to hear. Love is such a fickle thing."

"Don't . . ."

"Oh, Raul, don't be bothered by me. I am just an old man. Who has seen a little too much of life, perhaps. But I understand completely. I hope you are happy. But do be careful. I don't mean to speak ill of your lover—"

Raul looked down again, blushing incredibly.

Marco laughed.

"Such an innocent! Well, be careful. Young love is fragile. And most painful when hurt."

When Raul managed to look up again, the old man was gone, only the dread sound of that hated laughter echoing in his ears.

48

In some ways, Bert Morrow was an odd choice for Chief of Police. He did not have the swagger of an enforcer. In fact, his presence in a room full of people might easily be overlooked, and often was. But he was not incurious, and he was not stupid. He did not miss much, and this went a long way toward making up for the lack of swagger. His young deputies looked up to him, called him 'sir', and did as they were told. They also told him everything they heard, which was why he threatened a farmer one day that he would build a jail cell, just for him, if he did not stop knocking around his wife.

The farmer spat an obscenity, informed the Chief what he could do with his jail cell, and tried to slam the door.

The door caught on Bert's foot planted against it.

"I mean it. There is no one in this town who'll tolerate it. You will go to jail."

"Yeah? And who's gonna put me there?"

"We all will," Bert had informed him.

"So who's gonna feed the kid and old lady, with me in jail? Huh? *You?*"

"We *all* will," Bert repeated, then removed his foot and walked away. There was another obscenity, and the door slammed. But there were no more reports of Jack Harper beating his wife.

Bert made a point of listening to his deputies, even when he didn't seem to, and one afternoon, as two of them were gossiping in the Town Office, something caught his ear.

"What's that?"

"Ah . . . I said I was talkin' to Pete Sawyer. His sister was at the Abbey yesterday, and she asked about Brother Tom. Where he went."

"So? Where'd he go?"

"Dunno, Chief. No one would say."

"What was she doing at the Abbey?"

"Lookin' to hire some help."

"And no one knows where he went?"

"Guess not."

"Or they didn't want to say."

"Dunno. You should ask Pete."

"Maybe I will. You let me know if you hear anything else."

In the afternoon he rode out to the Stables, ostensibly to call on Dan Walsh. The two young men out front informed him that Walsh wasn't around, so he asked how business was. Then, casually, "Whatever happened to that preacher? Brother Tom. Haven't seen him in a while."

Johnny Gelpin grunted something.

Pete Sawyer shrugged.

Bert frowned. "What'd you say, Johnny?"

"I said he's gone, man."

"I know he's gone. I just never thought he'd leave. Thought he'd settled in here, with the church and all."

"Heard a rumor something funny was going on. That he left all of a sudden."

"Who told you that?"

"Jen heard it."

"From where?"

"Someone she was talking to. She's been going to Service Hill."

"You don't go with her?"

"Nah."

"You should."

"Why?"

"She's your wife. You should do things together."

"C'mon, Bert. You're not even married."

"Think I'm happy about that? Ask her who told her."

The intelligence that 'something was going on' did not sit well. Brother Tom's reputation was almost sainted, and if the man had failed that reputation, if the Abbey, or the Church, or whatever it was, had sent him on his way, it did not seem right the whole thing should be kept quiet. If Tom had done something criminal, he could just as well do it somewhere else. Justice was not served by secrecy.

So ran Bert Morrow thoughts.

Also, he was naturally inquisitive. He wanted to know, and the next day he rode out to Thomas Abbey.

Brother Jim met him on the porch and invited him in. Bert had not been inside the old house since the Andersons died. He followed Jim into the kitchen, and looked around carefully. Everything seemed clean, tidy.

"Well, Brother Bert! What can I do for you?"

Jim was about Bert's age, but with a gangly build, a thin beard, and a twinkling, intelligent humor in his eyes. But the humor felt jarring inside this house, the place so full of ghosts.

"Well, I want to talk to Brother Tom."

"I wish I could help you."

"You don't know where he is?"

"I don't. Of course, he left before I joined. But I'm not sure anyone else knows, either."

"That's strange. He must've told someone."

"Well, if you were talking about anyone else . . . but Brother Tom was intensely religious, I understand. Sometimes he went where the spirit moved."

"Was?"

"Sorry?"

"You said he *was* religious."

"When he was here."

"Uh-huh."

"You might want to ask Brother Marco."

"Where can I find him?"

"In the City today. He has a lot to do. But he still delivers the sermon on Sunday."

"Service Hill?"

"While the weather holds."

"You tell him to expect me."

"Is there anything else I can tell him?"

"Like what?"

"Well, can I tell him why you want to talk to Brother Tom?"

"Oh, I think not."

That Sunday, when Marco returned to the rectory after service, Bert was waiting.

Marco came in through the front door and stopped short. Raul, a step behind him, stumbled and froze, staring in awe at the Chief of Police.

Bert stood up from where he had been sitting.

"Brother Marco."

The old man managed a smile.

"I had expected to be honored with your presence at service, Chief Morrow. Sadly, I was misinformed."

"Yeah, I'm here on business."

"Business? You mean police business? Is there a problem?"

"I don't know the answer to that. What I came to ask is where I might find Brother Tom."

Bert had time to notice Raul cringe like a frightened animal, before a look of pain passed over Marco's face, and he placed a hand on the young man's shoulder.

"Go, Raul. There is nothing to fear. You have done no wrong."

Raul turned quickly and left.

Marco closed the door and nodded at the chair.

"Please sit down, Brother Bert."

"Why don't you tell me what happened?"

The old man sighed and shook his head.

"It is over."

"What's over?"

"Please, my friend. Try to understand. The boy has been hurt, seriously. Emotionally. He is recovering, but if it all were to be dredged up again . . ."

"Recovering? From what?"

"From Brother Tom's peculiar . . . ah . . . weakness."

As meaning of this sank in, Marco nodded. "Now, you understand."

"Christ! What about his grandparents? Do they know?"

"Unfortunately."

"Why unfortunately?"

"Because they have suffered a great deal. Sometimes I think it would have been better had they never learned the truth." The old man shrugged. "Now you understand? Why we keep it to ourselves. It would be best if the truth went no further. The boy is fragile. The family has suffered enough."

Chief Morrow nodded. He had his answer.

49

Dan Walsh knew there was more to Marta than met the eye.

This did not bother him. She might have been sent by the Corporation, but this did not bother him either. Whatever had brought her here did not matter. Only that she was here, with him.

But they were not children, and Walsh was careful. He seldom talked about the Town or its business, and then only in generalities. And she seldom asked. But once in a while, curiosity seemed to get the better of her.

"So tell me, m'love. What is it I hear about your local utility, Anderson Light and Power?"

"Power and Light. You tell me. What do you hear?"

"Well, they haven't been able to generate any power, have they? Is it a state secret?"

"It's a private business. You'll have to ask them."

"Seriously? You mean to say everyone in Andersonville doesn't know?"

"I don't know what everyone knows. Why don't you tell me how cheap the Corporation is willing to sell power?"

"Maybe I would, lover. If I knew."

He chuckled.

"I doubt *that* very much."

She ran a hand through his thinning hair. "What a suspicious mind you have!"

"Face it, Marta. You're too good to be true. What man of my age, in my position, would not be suspicious?"

"Don't underestimate yourself, Daniel. And don't put me on a pedestal. I'm no spring chicken."

He had laughed at that.

"I thought you were a City girl! Where did you learn that expression?"

"Wouldn't you like to know?"

She had told him she worked in a planning department, and he had to admit that might explain the curiosity. Professional interest. Still, she had her secrets, like her life in the City. He would ask about it, but she was evasive, looking uncomfortable, and he did not press it. Maybe she was married.

But he did not want to think about it. When they were together, it was as the first afternoon, when they rode from the Stables together. They kept the world at arm's length and concentrated on each other.

Except when her damned curiosity got the better of her.

That summer, Walsh Stables was busy, and especially busy on Sundays. The City added to the bus schedule, and Johnny and Pete opened the Stables right at sunrise, to accommodate people wanting an early start on the trails, before the day grew hot. Walsh gave lessons from morning to dusk.

And he wasn't alone. There was a new instructor at the Stables, taking on extra clients and causing no small sensation among the men, especially the older, settled ones, whose wives were not always so enchanted.

Marta had insisted, and Walsh had gone along, thinking she would tire of it. But she didn't. It became a familiar routine. Not so familiar, though, that he did not still appreciate the sight of her easy grace in the saddle, or the faint smile and shake of her head, more eloquent than words, when a client asked if she would meet him for a drink later.

But on a Sunday in the middle of August, when they arrived at the Stables, they found Johnny and Pete lounging on a bench by the barn, not a customer in sight.

"Ain't seen the bus yet," Pete informed them.

"Just a few horses out with some of our people," Johnny added.

" 'Our' people?" echoed Marta.

"I mean, folks from around here. No offense, ma'am."

"None taken."

Walsh sighed, looking at a dozen horses saddled and idle, and two able young men with nothing to do.

"Well, maybe something broke down and we all got up early for nothing. Can't say I mind the break. But they'd better fix it soon, or you boys may be out of a job."

"Hell," muttered Johnny, "I'll fix it for 'em. Or we can haul 'em out here in a hay cart. I need the work."

"And how is Jenny?" inquired Marta.

"Really showing."

"Well, that's wonderful. Is she feeling well?"

"So far. She doesn't have to do much, with her mother practically moved in."

Walsh laughed.

"Getting a little crowded around the Gelpin house, Johnny?"

"You could say that."

"Get used to it. You're a family man now."

"I'm not complaining."

Pete stood up. "Guess it's time to get to work."

A cloud of dust was drifting up over the distant trees. Presently, the City bus emerged, gears whining, and bounced along the rough ground before lurching to a stop. The door opened, and people began climbing out, more than usual, and Johnny and Pete hurried to get them in line and sort out the tangle of appointments.

When the last passenger stepped off, Walsh put a hand against the door before the driver could shut it.

"Good to see you! We were beginning to think you were giving us the day off."

"Well, there's a new schedule."

"What do you mean?"

"Gotta do a coupla runs first over to Service Hill, on Sundays."

"Service Hill?"

"Yeah. It's that new church. Church of the Word. Wanted to try it myself, but I gotta work."

"I'll be damned."

Walsh took his hand from the door. The door closed, and the bus pulled away.

"Daniel?" Marta called.

He walked over to a small crowd of people as someone loudly complained, "Look here, what're you going to do about this?"

"What's the trouble?"

"What's the trouble? I have an appointment!"

"Okay. How many of you have appointments for a lesson?"

Hands went up, and Walsh counted.

"Okay, this is what I can do. Anybody who came out for trail-riding, we'll draw lots to see who goes out first. We'll take the lessons in order. If we can't accommodate you today, or you don't want to wait, we'll take your name and you can come back another day and ride for an hour at half price. That all right with everyone? I don't know what else I can do. The bus driver just told me this is the new schedule, so we're going to have to cut back on Sundays."

A few people continued grumbling. Walsh added, irritably, "There's nothing I can do. The City runs the buses. Take it up with them."

The sun was setting when Walsh finished with his last student and turned the horses over to Johnny. Marta was waiting for him by the barn door.

"I'm off, m'love."

"Yeah, okay."

"What is it? Are you upset?"

"Oh . . . I just don't get it."

"We had a good day's business, Daniel. And we have plenty booked for next weekend. Are you really bothered by a little money?"

"It isn't the money. I just don't get this damn church thing."

"Oh? What confuses you?"

"Marco must filling those people up with all the old stories. I really thought we were past that. You just can't ignore reality. Christ, you'd think we'd have learned that by now."

Marta looked at him coolly. "Oh, you can ignore it when it doesn't matter."

"You're an intelligent woman. How can you say something like that?"

"Because, m'love, reality doesn't always matter."

"Oh, for God's sake! Don't talk nonsense. We *live* in reality."

"People don't live in reality, lover. They live in stories."

"And which people are these? Because if I ignored reality I'd be dead now."

"Then that was a reality you couldn't ignore. I'm not being argumentative, Daniel. I'm trying to help you understand something."

"A reality?"

"Don't be cute. Have you ever stopped to think why you dream?"

"What?"

"Why do you dream?"

"I don't know. People used to think it was wish fulfillment. What does that have to do with anything?"

"You dream because it's what the mind does. It makes a story. You walk down the street and you see a complete scene in your mind, but your eye only registers a fraction of what you think you see. You look at a page in a newspaper—if you're lucky enough to have one! —and you think you see a page full of words. But your eye can only see the few you look at directly. Your mind fills in the rest, automatically."

"So my brain adds some intelligence. What of it?"

"It does more. It spins the thread and weaves the fabric of your entire world, moment to moment. What happens when you fall asleep? You lie there in the dark, and you still have enough sensation of what's around you that your mind spins the scene of you in bed. But then things shut down. Your muscles are paralyzed, your senses disconnect. Your mind is cut loose from its moorings and does what it does. It creates a world. As fast as you experience it."

"Now don't start talking like this is all a dream."

"Not a dream. More a fabric, supported at a few key points by what you experience. But still a fabric created by your mind."

"That's crazy. There's an objective reality. Which you of all people should know. You can take an elevator to the fiftieth floor of one of your buildings in the City, and live to tell about it, because someone figured out the objective reality and built it right. If he got it wrong, it wouldn't stand, no matter what his mind created."

"Sure, lover. There's a real world out there. But you'll never directly perceive more than a small fraction of it. At any one time, a minuscule fraction. Just a few key points. Your mind fills in the rest. You'd be lost without it."

"But nobody has the right to ignore facts! You don't have a *right* to look out a window on the fiftieth floor and deny the facts of structural engineering!"

"Well, you don't have a right to be taken seriously if you do."

"Then how can you defend these people?"

"I'm not defending them. I'm explaining them, and how religion is part of a larger reality. An objective one."

"Which reality?"

"Your mind creates the fabric of your existence, because it has to and because you need it to. Yours has done an admirable job. You're a man of the world, what's left of it, and you've found answers to questions that many people go through life without ever thinking about. Why?"

"I don't get it. Where are you going with this?"

"Humor me. Why have you asked all those big questions? Why do you care?"

"I suppose, ultimately, because I want to live."

"There are lots of ways to live. You needed something more."

"What?"

"Explanations. We all do. It's part of filling in the gaps. We need a story that explains who we are, what's going on, where it all came from. It's the price we pay for being endowed with imagination."

"Then I'd think you'd want a *real* explanation, not some phony myth."

"Lover, what's the difference?" She smiled that wry smile of hers, the fine wrinkles at the corners of her eyes and the silver at her temples giving her an air of worldly wisdom at once intimidating and yet enormously seductive. He knew she was baiting him, and for a moment stayed quiet, thrilled with the fact that she enjoyed doing it.

"Like everyone else, you want something that satisfies. And what satisfies *you* is not necessarily what satisfies your minister friend. Or his flock. And why should it be?"

"Because we all live in the same world. Like it or not."

"But we all live in different parts of it."

"Look, Marta. Either the world is six thousand years old, or it's billions. It doesn't matter which part you live in."

"And why is that?"

"Why? Because the *evidence* is there. I don't see how you can ignore that."

"You'd be surprised at what you can ignore. But tell me, what geological evidence are your religious friends ever going to encounter, personally?"

"Probably none. They'll never look for it. But it's out there."

"And how would they know that?"

"Because the people who *did* encounter it wrote books and papers so the rest of us would know!"

"Of course they did. But so what?"

"Come on!"

"Lover, the geological record will never have a tangible effect on those people's lives. And so the geologists who wrote the papers can be safely ignored."

"But that's just . . . perverted!"

"No, it's what defines a lack of authority."

"Even if it's wrong."

"But it works. Religion is a system of thought like any other. It meets a need. It explains. It also promises, and it makes some compelling promises that comport with its explanations. People believe it because it has authority. They don't feel they can safely ignore it, because so many other people believe. That's somewhat circular, but think of it as self-reinforcing. That's more authority than geology will ever have with them. And that, m'love, is the larger reality you don't seem to grasp."

"Then why do I believe geology?"

"Because science has authority with you. You don't feel safe ignoring it. It's part of what makes you, you." She placed a hand on his cheek and grinned. "You must have had a simply *awful* childhood."

He smiled back, answering in a low voice:

"Because you weren't in it."
She slipped her arms around his neck.
"Always save the best for last."
The words hit like cold water, and he held her.
"Thank God you came."
Behind them, the last bus bounced to a stop with a rattle and the metallic screech of the door opening.
She laughed.
"And now I have to leave!"

50

"You know, y'all don't have to come along to these things, if it's too much trouble. Dan and I know our own way now. You can stay home."
Max did not look at her.
"Not on your life, Amalia."
They were riding home from the City, after two hours of negotiating with Bill Baird over electric power. Walsh was carrying a draft contract and pages of notes to review with the rest of the Committee. Amalia had argued over payment terms, Walsh over the City's right to shut off service without notice, while Baird had insisted that Andersonville's wiring meet City standards. Max had said nothing.
He knew he had to be there. And he knew her jab was a warning.
The summer dragged. The routine business of Andersonville took care of itself, needing only an occasional nudge from time to time. Like the time Joe Dryden was laid up sick and the road crew thought they would take a few days off and go fishing, and Max was there to make sure they stayed on the job. Times like that. He knew how lucky he was to get paid to do the nudging. He had no right to complain. And he didn't. Not out loud.
Instead, he visited AP&L.
He had spent most of his savings buying out Steve, and he knew it would be a very long time before he would see a return. If he ever did. But it was the one bright spot.
He would ride out three or four times a week, bringing sandwiches from the pub. The barn was always crowded with workbenches littered with tools. There were big spools of wire and boxes of hardware stacked high, but never any sign of food. He wondered how she lived. If she wasn't there, he would leave a package on a stool and put it right by the side door, so she would find it and eat.
He even offered to help with the generator.
"Look, why not? I'm not completely crippled. There must be something I can do."

"And let you see how lost I am? No thanks, Max."

But one day in August, she told him, "I know what the problem is."

She sat on a workbench, one foot swinging back and forth, hair tied back, shoulders slumping. She looked exhausted. But there was a palpable tension in the swing of that foot.

"Yeah? You think so?"

"Yep," she answered. "Got it all worked out." She accepted a sandwich. "So tell me what's going on with the Committee."

"Agnes, I don't know what I can talk about. I have to be pretty careful."

"Amalia keeping her eye on you?"

"On you, too."

"Well, you're a big boy. You don't have to tell me anything you shouldn't."

"I suppose you want to know about the negotiations."

"Of course."

"Well, you'll find out soon enough. The City wants to send someone out to examine your wiring."

"Not that much to see, but why not?"

"Including the wiring inside the farmhouses."

"They don't trust me to do it?"

"Apparently not, but maybe that'll come later. They haven't backed away from their price, which is good."

"Uh-huh."

"That's about it."

"Doesn't seem like anything that'll get you into trouble with Amalia."

"Probably not. Tell me about the generator."

"Oh, yes. The generator. I don't suppose anyone ever asks about it, do they?"

"Bill Cotter asked, but I didn't know what to tell him."

"Surprised no one ever comes out to talk about it. No one from the Committee. And I haven't seen *you* in almost a week."

"Well . . . what'd you find out?"

"It's subtle. It wasn't easy to prove, but I'm convinced. You see, the greater the electrical load, the greater the torque on the stator. When the frame gets wet, it gives a little. It twists. It isn't much, but when it twists it opens the gap between stator and armature, in between the support points. Enough to let flux escape, which makes the voltage drop. What do you think of that?"

"Sounds good. Can you fix it?"

"I can do more than fix it. I can make it better. I want to rebuild the whole damn thing, maybe with the stator on a hinge so I can fine-tune the voltage. I might even be able to automate it, if I can find the right motor, so it controls itself."

"Sounds like you've been busy."

"Well, I don't have much else to do . . ."

"Something wrong?"

"Oh, just a little cabin fever. I've spent the whole damn summer here, when I wasn't climbing around the dam."

"Well . . . why don't we go out for a ride?"

"What?"

"You know, on our horses. Get out of the barn. Forget about the generator. Forget all of it, for a little while."

She seemed to hesitate, running a hand through her hair.

"No . . . it won't change anything. I'll still have to come back to it."

"Agnes, you need a break."

She grinned.

"Are you going to start throwing things?"

He laughed. "No, I don't suppose so."

She eyed him a moment. "Too bad. I could use some excitement."

"Want me to throw something?"

"No, Max. Go home. But thanks for the offer."

51

On a warm afternoon a few days later, someone started pounding on the barn's big sliding door.

Finishing her lunch—a slice of bread with a thick layer of butter and honey—Agnes called, "Just a minute!", rinsed her hands, then went out the side door and around the corner.

In the yard out front were two men. She walked up to them. "Yes?"

"Is this supposed to be the light company?"

"That's right."

"You work here?"

"At the moment. What can I do for you?"

"We're from the Corporation. We're here to look at your lines."

She extended a hand.

"I've been expecting you. I'm Agnes, President of AP&L."

"Pleased to meet you, Ms. . . . ah . . ."

"Just Agnes."

"I see. Do you have someone who can show us around?"

"I'll show you. Where's your car?"

"Back on the dirt road. Was afraid we'd get stuck in here."

The path to the main road had been thoroughly beaten down by horse and foot traffic, but the ground was soft and not well drained, and they had to pick their way along the shoulder to reach the car.

They drove up and down the main road.

The two men took turns climbing poles. They made notes. They frowned a lot.

"What about lightning arrestors?" one asked.

"Uh . . . we don't have any."

"You need them."

"Okay."

"What about circuit breakers? Disconnect switches?"

"Look, we're just trying to light a few homes. I know it's not very elaborate, but we'll improve it as we go."

"Look, Ms. . . . Agnes."

The older of the two, round and balding, was sweating under the afternoon sun.

"We can put an arrestor on the line we bring down here. We'll install a breaker to protect your feeder. But look at what you have. Just a single phase of . . . what is that, six-gauge?"

"Four."

"Okay, four. At a hundred and twenty volts, how much do you realistically think you can do?"

"Like I said, we're just trying to light a few homes. Just a few lights. That's all."

"And what keeps people from plugging in whatever they have? Like a power saw."

"They'll just have to understand we're not ready for that."

"Well, they're your people. I guess they have to take what you give them. But the first time someone plugs in something they're not supposed to . . . Look, that wire won't handle much, so our breaker'll have to be a small one. When it goes, everybody loses service, until we can send someone out to clear the problem and reset the breaker. And that won't happen until one of your people get to the City to let us know. I don't see your customers putting up with *that* for long."

"Like I said . . ."

He was looking up at the wire, scratching his neck.

"I don't see why you don't just do it right."

"Look, we're doing what we can. We don't have a lot to work with. I mean, look around! This isn't the City."

"Okay, okay. But here's the bottom line. I won't recommend going ahead with this unless it's safe. And what you have is not safe."

The younger man spoke up.

"Maybe we could help. We could—"

"Don't make promises you can't keep," growled the first. "We'll make our report. Maybe they'll want us to help. Maybe they won't. It's not our decision."

She was trembling. She knew they could see it, and she held herself stiffly erect, trying to make it stop.

The older man shook his head.

"Look, miss. I'm not trying to be hard-nosed. I just don't want anyone to get hurt. That's my job. We'll find out what the higher-ups want to do. But you have to understand, it's not our decision."

"I understand."

"Well . . . come on. We'll drive you back."

"No. I want to walk."

"It's no trouble."

"Thanks. I'll walk."

––––––––––

Bill and Mike were relaxing over a quick beer in the lull before dinner, when Agnes walked into the pub.

She stopped and stood there, saying nothing, her face flushed, clothes dusty and stained.

Bill came to his feet.

"Agnes—what's wrong?"

She looked at him as though having trouble remembering who he was.

"Agnes . . . want a beer? A glass of wine?"

"Don't you have anything stronger?"

Watching her, he answered carefully. "Sure. Sit. I'll bring it."

She walked to the far end of the room. He moved toward the bar, jerking his thumb in the direction of the back, and Mike collected the two beers and left. Then he went to her table with a dark green bottle, two empty glasses, and a small glass of water and tiny spoon.

"Mind if I join you?"

"I'm okay, Bill."

"Sure." He pulled out a chair and sat down.

"Really. I am."

"Agnes, I've seen you when the world came down around your ears. I've seen you when you lost your best friend. And I have *never* seen you drink anything stronger than a glass of wine."

She wiped her eyes, her cheeks red over dark hollows.

"I know, Bill. You're a dear friend. But there's nothing anyone can do."

"Want to talk about it?"

She shook her head. He broke the seal, twisted out the cork, and poured a finger of clear amber liquid for each of them.

"Okay, then. I hope you're ready for this."

She held up her glass.

"To your health, Bill."

"Agnes, wait—"

But she tossed the thing back and exploded in a fit of coughing, tears streaming.

"Holy *shit*. How do you drink that?"

"Like this." And he raised his glass, breathed, sipped, rolled it in his mouth, and swallowed.

"Really?"

"You think I'd give you rotgut? This is special. I saved it from the old days."

"You're always so good to me. I feel like a heel."

"Must be pretty bad, if you're talking like that. Here, try it again. But take your time."

He poured. She sipped, coughed, and nodded, hoarsely whispering, "I see what you mean."

"Now . . . try this." He tapped a couple of drops of water into her glass from the tiny spoon, and she sipped again.

"Oh, *wow*. I could drink *that* all night."

Swirling his glass, he breathed it in, then finished it off.

"Damned good stuff. It'll be a sad day when it's gone."

"How much do you have?"

He tapped the bottle, and she stared at it.

"Jesus . . . if you're trying to make me feel like the lowest person in the world, Bill, you're doing a damned good job."

"Forget it." He poured again. "Do you want to tell me what happened?"

"Oh God, is that your way with women? Get 'em drunk, and they do what you want?"

"Worked better when I was a young tiger. Now I just like hearing people talk."

"Ah . . . talk. Well, we're drinking like this because I'm scared."

"You? Of what?"

"Of the Committee. Of the mess I've gotten myself into. But most of all, I think I'm afraid of Max."

"Afraid of Max!" He snorted. "That makes no sense. The man worships the ground you walk on. Although that might be just my personal opinion."

"I'm afraid of what I have to tell him."

"What do you think he'll do?"

"Oh, he won't do anything. It's what he'll think."

"What's he going to think?"

"I don't know."

"Agnes . . . what are you afraid of?"

"Failure, Bill. I'm afraid of failure."

"Oh. That. Well, I suppose that *is* something to be afraid of. Tell me what happened."

"Ohhh, hell. The City sent someone out to look at the lines. They're no good. All that work, and they're not safe! The generator's no good. Even if I fix it, it won't be enough. What if someone plugs in a power saw?"

"What?"

"A power saw! I never thought of that. He turns on his saw, or whatever else he has, and everyone's lights go out! And what if there was a problem with someone's wiring and there was a fire? Good God Bill! What if someone's house burned down? What if someone was killed? I don't know what to do! All that time wasted! And all that money. All that goddamned money! What are people going to think?"

He nodded sagely while she leaned on her elbows and put her face in her hands.

"Max believed in me. Can you imagine? I think I want to hate him for it. Because I can't live up to it. I don't know how he came back from Barbara's and did what he did. He thinks I'm like that. But I'm not. I'm not."

"Well, if you were just like everyone else, you'd still be in the City."

She sat back. "Maybe that's where I belong."

"You can always go back, can't you?"

"If only I could."

"Why not?"

"Couldn't face it."

"What do you mean? Face what?"

"Going back . . . to that. Going back like this. A flop. That's what Bill Cotter called me. A flop. And God he's so right. Going back would be like . . . like dying . . . only worse . . ."

They talked, and drank, and talked, until she passed out.

Then he put her to bed, and helped Mike get ready for dinner.

In the morning, after Max had finished eating and was lingering over coffee, Agnes shuffled out of the back of the pub, into the dining room. He waved and kicked out a chair and waited while she shuffled over and sat down.

"Rough night?" he asked.

"What'd Bill tell you?"

"That you had a rough night."

She helped herself to a taste of his coffee. "Liar."

"Well, he told me." He waved to Mike, and shortly there was a steaming mug in front of her, and some toast.

She chewed a little toast, sipped a little coffee, and rubbed her face.

"What? No pep talk? No lectures?"

"Wouldn't want to bore you."

"Oh, come *on!* What do you want from me?"

"Agnes . . . I didn't mean it that way. I don't want anything."

"Then I really *am* a failure. That's the *worst* thing you could say."

He wanted to reach for her hand.

"Look, I'm sorry. I didn't mean anything. I know you've been through hell. Right now all I want is for you to eat something and get over being hung over. Which, by the look of you, won't be until tomorrow."

"And then what? Go back and make it work?"

"Can you?"

"I don't know."

She put down her coffee.

"Listen to me, Max. Just listen. I know what you're thinking. You think I'm going to find a way. But maybe I can't. Maybe there isn't a way. You have to understand that."

"Look, I don't want to be dependent on the City. You *know* that. That's why—"

"*Max*. There may be nothing we can *do* about that. Nothing *I* can do. You have to be ready for that. You *have* to."

He looked away, across the room. But after a moment, nodded.

52

The warm weather lingered even as the days grew shorter, until late September when a cold wind whipped out of the north and drove slate-gray skies and a chill rain that drizzled and showered, washing away dry, dusty grime, the memory of summer, and leaving the City cold and damp and dark under a heavy overcast days after the rain finally ended.

Craig Olsen strode through the evening dusk, hands in his coat pockets, collar turned up, the clip of his heels echoing from empty store fronts. Just ahead was the island of light that he passed each evening, the mission, and he went by glancing enviously through the clean plate glass at three people in shirtsleeves, sweeping the floor.

Light and heat. Apparently the City thought pretty highly of them.

He thought about spending another winter at the hotel. He could easily afford rent now, but the habit of frugal living would die hard, and he had done nothing all summer about finding another place to live. Now, as he turned onto his street, the too-familiar canyon empty and silent as always, he realized it was time he got out of here.

A shadow flitted across an alley.

Craig stopped. People just did not *sneak* around here. There was no one to sneak from. But then, the light wasn't very good. It might have been anything, maybe nothing at all.

The following evening, he saw it again.

He crossed the street and peered down the alley. It was dark, too dark to see, and he had no interest in cornering someone desperate enough to hide from drunks and junkies. He turned away and continued walking to the hotel. When he was back in his own room, he made sure to dead-bolt the door.

People who live rough have a routine, to survive, to find a measure of comfort. It's an existential routine having to do with the cycle of day and night, the seasons, the forces of nature—something Craig Olsen was more than familiar with. These days he might be the only human being within blocks of here whose routine depended on something as abstract as the clock and the days of the week.

And today was Saturday.

He could see the street from the windows of his room, and late in the afternoon, as the shadows grew long, he pulled a chair to the window and settled in to watch.

The sun went down. A lone hooker crossed the street, the first sign of evening. She teetered on wobbly heels, an old coat held tight around her shoulders, bare legs a bluish chalk color in the cold, and disappeared into a building.

Out of the shadows, something dashed across the street and melted into the alley.

Craig got up and left the hotel.

He walked to the mouth of the alley, and placed a paper bag on the pavement.

"It's food, man," he called quietly. "If you want it."

He went back to the hotel and stayed out of sight.

The next evening, he returned. Again he called out.

"I have more. That's a hotel across the street. I live there. There are other rooms. You don't have to sleep in an alley. No one will bother you."

He heard something scrape, but saw nothing.

Monday evening, he left work a little early, was waiting near the alley when the ghost appeared. It froze in the street, filthy and emaciated, in dark, shapeless rags, eyes wide and burning.

Craig said nothing. He raised an arm and pointed toward the hotel, placed another bag of food on the pavement, then turned, walked along the sidewalk until he was opposite the hotel, then crossed the street and went inside.

A while later, when the ghost entered the lobby, clutching the paper bag, Craig was waiting. He pointed to an open door, a large storeroom. Then he went up the stairs to his own room.

For several days, he saw nothing of the ghost, but left a sandwich every evening by the storeroom.

Then, as he came down one morning on his way to work, the ghost appeared.

The man's eyes seemed to bulge. His chin thrust forward. His mouth worked, but no sound came out. He held up a hand, as though grasping something, and tilted it toward his mouth.

Craig jogged upstairs and returned with one of his plastic bottles of water.

The ghost took it and guzzled, coughed, and guzzled again. Some of the burning seemed to ebb from the eyes, and he extended the bottle back to Craig, still half full, returning it to its owner.

Craig shook his head. The man nodded, and turned back to the storeroom.

That was when Craig saw wide, inverted vees stitched to the man's sleeve just below the shoulder.

53

Pounding. Shouting. Then a long, howling scream, abruptly cut off.

Craig rolled out of bed and stumbled to his feet. Lights from the street flashed rhythmically across the ceiling, an icy, pulsing blue.

He listened at the door. Then opened it. Saw light flickering on the hallway wall, and followed it down the stairwell.

In the lobby, a chaos of uniformed men, police or soldiers, silhouetted black against brilliant electric lights. He shielded his eyes against the glare, and saw the ghost being carried across the lobby, struggling like an animal, overpowered by four men.

"*What the fuck!*" Craig shouted.

A light swung around, stabbing and blinding.

"No damned business of yours! Get your ass back upstairs!"

"What did he do?"

But it was lost in the confusion of shouted orders. Figures moved in and out of the storeroom, and buckets and mops and bottles were tossed in a pile.

One man nearby, watching the scene with a hand resting on his sidearm, spoke without turning his head.

"Got mixed up with the wrong junk."

"Junk? I've never seen anyone on *rope* like that."

Craig thought he heard a snort.

"Not *rope. Wire.*"

"Hey!" a voice bellowed. "Git yer dumb ass upstairs!"

Wire.

He had heard it right. Of that he was certain.

He asked Dave Barton.

"Don't know. Don't want to know. And you better not be mixed up in it. I'd hate to cut you, but I wouldn't have much choice."

"It wasn't me, Dave. Poor bastard who moved into the hotel."

"You still living there? What's the matter with you?"

"Yeah, I was going to move out."

"What's stopping you?"

"Habit, I guess."

"Some habits kill you, Craggy. Remember that. Get the fuck out of that hotel. Find a place to live. You're not in the gutter anymore."

That evening, Craig stood outside on the empty sidewalk, feeling night gather around him, hearing the distant sounds of the City echo from empty buildings lining the street. But really hearing the echoes of that scream.

Who had he screamed for? The answer was here, in the darkness with him.

Dave had told him to forget it. Forget the ghost. Forget he ever saw it.

But that scream . . . he could not forget.

He walked to the alley, stood at the mouth while his eyes adjusted, until he could see a little ways in, see a narrow strip of black pavement, and dirty brick walls. He took a few, tentative steps, and the sounds of the street were cut off. Water dripped. Stars appeared in the slice of sky between rooftops, thirty, forty feet above, and in puddles on the pavement.

He walked into the darkness.

Crooked, dulled edges of brick and the dark outlines of strange, angular shapes went by. He passed empty windows and came to the grated landing of a fire escape. Faintly visible was something rolled up and wedged against the wall.

A blanket.

There were two iron steps, and he climbed them, stopping on the landing. Sticking out from under the blanket was a paper bag, folded flat.

He sat down on the landing. The narrow pavement leading back to the street behind him was the only link to the larger world, of men and women, and the City. Here, a long ladder extended upward, toward the stars. Promising the only escape.

He sat on the landing, on a cold hard grate of iron, sick with something he had never felt before. At least not like this.

Why does it have to be this way?

He did not remember reaching for it, but his hand was on the blanket, damp and rough, and he looked up at the sky now blended with the rooftops, and tasted salt.

What is wrong with the world? What the hell is wrong with it?

Somewhere back there, beyond the end of the alley, was the street and the hookers and the junkies, and farther the Dave Bartons and the clean, bright places, the elect living in comfort high above these streets, surrounded by friends and by family, by maids and servants, by people who kept their world warm and bright, and uplifted.

Not like here. Where there was only one way out.

Why does it have to be like this?

He gripped the iron railing, pulling himself to his feet, gripped the cold metal, hard, trying to grasp the reality of it.

Then he walked out of the alley.

He walked three blocks.

The island of light was up ahead, and he slowed. A handful of people were inside, he could see them through the cheerful glass frontage as he got closer. He put his hand to the door, but hesitated, looking at his hand and feeling as though belonged to someone else.

Then he pushed the door open.

Faces turned as he stepped inside and shut the door behind him.

One was Misty's.

"Craig . . . honey . . . what happened?"

"I'm okay. I . . . just need to talk to someone."

54

The Town Committee received a letter from the City describing "substandard engineering", and stating in no uncertain terms that power could not possibly be delivered until all wiring met standards. Final negotiations over the contract were officially on hold.

But by the time the letter arrived, Agnes was ready with her plan.

She had ventured into the City and found the electric utility department, and found Ed, the older of the two engineers who had inspected the lines. She had begged him to delay the report. Then, with Ed's help, she had worked out a list of improvements, sketched drawings and diagrams, wrote out specifications and bills of material, and convinced Dan Walsh to help draw up terms of service that customers would have to agree to.

Some of the improvements would have to be completed before power could be turned on, like disconnect switches to isolate subcircuits. Others could wait until money started coming in. But now she had plans, real ones, ones she believed in and could defend. Like the one for a three-phase high voltage system that would run along the same poles, but extend farther, and serve more homes with heavier loads. Maybe even power saws.

She spent very little, conserving the company's cash to get through another winter and be ready for spring, when there would be the disconnects to install, wiring to inspect, and useless electronic power meters to be replaced with old-fashioned electromechanical ones, which Ed found in a City storage building and sold to AP&L for a song, and on credit. And she would have to hire at least one permanent technician, someone she could train to help maintain the system. As Ed told her repeatedly, the utility business ran twenty-four hours a day, seven days a week. No time off for holidays.

Max would come out to visit every few days, and she always looked forward to it, because he always brought something she needed, like hard bread, cured meat, goat's milk. She would have given anything for vegetables, but she asked for nothing. She accepted the things be brought, but would not ask for favors. Not from Max Wyse.

On a cold, damp Saturday afternoon, the weekly Committee meeting finally over, Max climbed on his horse and rode away thoroughly disgusted.

He went to the meetings because he was afraid of what might be said, unchallenged, about AP&L. But these days his presence always seemed to sour Amalia, not to mention Bill Cotter, even though Cotter was still a director.

He kicked the horse to a gallop.

When he arrived at the barn, Agnes let him in, and he immediately apologized.

"Christ, I didn't bring anything! Came right from the town office."

"Oh, don't worry about it. You look cold. Have some coffee. I just made it."

"Yeah, thanks."

"Any news?"

"Hell, no. Just a waste of time, with Amalia and Bill pissing on everything . . . sorry. You have your own problems. Don't mind me."

"It's okay."

For a few moments, he tried to concentrate on the warm mug, on the rough workbench, on the musty quiet of the barn, forcing himself to relax.

"What about you? Anything new?"

She shrugged.

"Not really. Working on the plans. Talking with a few people about coming back to work for me, come spring. That's about it."

"What about your generator?"

She seemed to hesitated.

"I . . . well, I have to scrap it. The whole thing."

"Why? I thought you knew how to fix it."

"Max, listen to me. Just listen. The City is going to electrify this town like it was in the old days. There is no way anything I can build with permanent magnets in a wooden frame will ever generate that kind of power."

"What about as a supplement? You know, generate some power to reduce what we have to buy from them."

"I know, and I hear you, but it's much harder than it sounds. And it would be pathetically small. In a year or two, if things work out, we'll be putting up a four-hundred-eighty-volt line. Max, I know you don't want to hear this, but they're going to make us even more dependent on them than ever."

"There *has* to be a way."

"Even you can't change the laws of physics."

"What does that mean?"

"I mean, there's not enough hydro power available from the river. It's pretty small as it is, and there just isn't enough natural head. And we can't raise it behind a dam without flooding property."

"Where else can we get power?"

"Well, even if we had some kind of fuel to burn, we don't have anything to burn it in. You'd want a steam turbine, but that's so far beyond our capability it might as well be on the moon. Look, I know what you want, Max. I just don't know how to get there."

"You could've done it, though. Before the City got involved. Before they came along to make it like it was in the old days."

"You can't deny people what's being offered."

"But it's setting us up for failure."

"Maybe you're wrong. Maybe this is the way it has to be."

He shook his head.

"No. Robert was right. They're living on borrowed time."

They were sitting atop one of the workbenches. In the shadows on the other side of the barn were large spools of wire, and he pointed at them.

"Look, twenty years ago all this seemed inexhaustible. We were lucky just to make it from one day to the next. But for twenty years now they've been eating through everything like rats in a grain silo. It's going to run out. It *has* to run out. And when it does, we'll all go down together. Unless we find a way to something sustainable."

"Well, maybe they are. Maybe they're working on it. How do we know?"

He stared at the wire.

"I wonder what they're doing about their gasoline problem?"

"Beats me, Max."

"They still drive cars. They still run buses. So they're still running out. Right?"

"I don't know. I just don't know."

Max thought he had a pretty good idea who would know, and he waited until the City approved Agnes's plans and there was another contract meeting. At the end of it, as Amalia and Walsh were leaving the conference room with a final draft for the Committee, Max held Bill Baird behind with idle talk about the weather.

But when they were alone, he said, "Bill, I'm worried."

"Oh? What about?"

"Gasoline. What's the Corporation doing about that?"

Baird glanced at the doorway, then lowered his voice.

"We're trading for it."

"Trading! Trading what?"

"Well, Max, I'm not at liberty to divulge terms."

"Who's supplying it? Aren't you dependent on them?"

"Now, that's just a little naive. This is simple economics. The law of comparative advantage. It's to our mutual advantage to trade."

"For something as crucial as gasoline? What's to stop them from using it against you?"

"You have a pretty unsophisticated view of trade! They need what we have as well."

"What could you possibly have that they need as much as you need gasoline? And that they can't get anywhere else?"

"Sorry, Max. Can't talk about it."

"What could you have? Besides . . . *rope.* Or—*wire?*"

"No comment."

But Max had seen the fear in his eyes at the word *wire.*

At their next meeting, after the Committee voted to approve the contract, Bill Cotter leaned back, stretched luxuriously, and drawled, "Now, let's just hope AP&L doesn't screw this up."

Max stood up and slammed his chair against the table.

"Bill, you'd better hope the fucking *City* doesn't screw it up!"

"Why should they?"

"Because they've already screwed up their gasoline supply!"

"Says who?"

"Says the fact that now they have to *buy* it. Think about that."

"So they're buying gasoline. So what?"

"So what? Last year they lost most of what they had! Millions of gallons! What's left has to run out, probably sooner than we think. So either they have to learn to make it themselves, or else they have learn to do without it. But they're not doing either."

"Oh." Cotter smirked. "Sounds to me like they've solved *that* problem."

"How? How have they solved anything?"

"Max," Walsh interrupted. "Are you just saying the gasoline has to run out, no matter where they get it? Is that what you're trying to say?"

"Exactly!"

"But you don't actually know that."

"What?"

"You don't know it for a fact. Maybe they're buying from someone who knows how to manufacture it, or has a virtually unlimited reserve somewhere. I'll grant you it seems unlikely. It's much more plausible that everyone else is running out, too. Given what we know. But it's still just a guess."

"Look, folks," Cotter intoned. "As long as they're buying at a reasonable price, then there's no crisis! If supplies get tight, the price'll go up. Simple economics."

Amalia nodded. "Sounds logical to me."

"Well, it has. Gone up."

"What?" asked Amalia. "How do you know? Do *you* know what they're paying?"

"They're paying with drugs. Their military drug. *Wire.*"

For a few seconds, the entire Committee watched him in silence.

"Son!" Dennis leaned forward. "Do you know that for a *fact?*"

"I picked it up talking with Bill Baird."

"What did he say?"

"He said he can't talk about it. 'No comment' is what he actually said."

Amalia sighed noisily and pushed back her chair.

"Well, hon, you find out something for a *fact,* you be sure and let us know. Okay?"

She stood up, and Dennis ended the meeting.

Max rode to the pub. He intended to buy sandwiches to bring to Agnes, but he found her there, sitting at a table, alone.

She grinned as he walked over to her. "My turn!"

"For what?"

"To buy."

He managed to laugh a little, running his hand across his face. "Max . . . are you okay?"

He sat down.

"Listen, Agnes. I don't know how you're going to do it. But find a way. Find a generator, buy one, invent one, build your system so you can scale it back if you need to. But find a way to build some independence into it. Because I know what they're doing."

"What're you talking about?"

"The Corporation. They're buying gasoline with drugs."

"What drugs?"

"What else? *Wire.*"

"Seriously? How do you know this?"

"Never mind how. And don't repeat it. It's a big secret."

"It's insane. But how does it affect us?"

"It affects us because it *is* insane. Maybe they're trying to buy time. Maybe they're working on a solution. But they're selling something that's truly dangerous, that can be used against them. I think it shows how desperate they are. Agnes—I don't think they know what to do."

———

The rectory yard that Sunday was gray with frost. A forest of naked branches that began a little way from the rectory, just visible in the early light, swayed monotonously, back and forth, in a steady wind that was a biting reminder of coming winter.

The rectory door opened, and a hooded figure emerged, walked to a simple podium, and threw back the hood, and Brother Marco gave his familiar blessing, to open Sunday service.

The crowd was arrayed in a long half-circle before the podium. Max stood behind it and listened to Marco relate news about Thomas Abbey, about an old man who had thrown away the bottle and taken vows. There was a short talk about a church building that would stand one day on the main road, so the rest of Andersonville would know the People as a vital force in the community. Marco urged generosity with the tithes.

He went on to talk of the missions to the City, and of one Craig Olsen, a witness to the hopelessness and inhumanity of a world without Brotherhood, profoundly changed by the Word, who would come one day soon and tell his story.

Then came the sermon, and as Marco spoke the light grew, the sky delicate blue with scattered puffs of white. The wind died, and a ray of sun broke over the clearing.

"Now, bring light to those in darkness!"

"Amen!" the crowd answered.

The circle broke, and people mingled, rubbing their hands for warmth, giving tight smiles and quick handshakes and hugs, dispersing even as the ceremonial bread was handed out.

It had been a cold hour.

"Brother Max!"

Marco walked over to him, smiling broadly.

"What a pleasant surprise!"

"Hope you don't mind. Wanted to see it for myself."

"But of course, of course. I am so glad you came." The crystal eyes seemed to glow. "So, tell me, how did you find it? Did anything interest you, in particular?"

"Well, I suppose the part about building a church."

"Oh? Is that all? Well, a bit of a disappointment. But then, my rhetorical skills are not those of Brother Tom."

"Whatever happened to him?"

"I wish I could say. He left us, and we miss him. He was an inspiration."

"You'd think if he started preaching somewhere, we'd hear about it."

"My thoughts exactly."

"Well, sorry to crash your party."

Marco placed a friendly hand on his shoulder.

"Brother Max. You are always welcome here. I hope you realize that."

"All right, Marco."

"Well, take care. Please return, any time."

Very late that night, Max sat alone in the pub's dining room, still awake.

Maybe I should quit.

And do what?

He kept thinking about the service that morning.

Marco is building something.

Shadows moved on the walls, cast by the lamp flickering.

55

A narrow, radiant bar of iron slipped through the hole he had laboriously drilled, and sparks shot from under the hammer as he pounded the end of the finger-sized rivet, its color dimming with each strike, until it was round and gray and inert, shrinking as it cooled and clamping the mouldboard against the beam.

Steve Foster tilted the assembly side to side, eyeing the alignment, then let it drop on the anvil.

The sound was clean.

He had spent a week on the plow, while also doing most of the winter repair work. It had kept him busy. Kept him from having to think too much.

Two more rivets to go. Tomorrow he would shape and file a rounded edge to the ploughshare. Then it would be ready to try.

A half-hour later, he set the plow aside and cooled the fire, then picked his way through the dark to the house. Yellow light flickered through the windows as he tromped across the porch, knocking mud from his shoes, then kicked them off and let himself inside.

They were in the living room, sitting together by the fire and reading old books borrowed from the town library.

His mother looked up and smiled.

"Wash up, dear. Supper's still warm."

"Dad, we can try it tomorrow. It's solid."

"How're your hands?"

"Better."

"Make sure to clean 'em good. Use soap and water. Even if it hurts."

"Yeah, I know."

"I know you know. Makes me feel better to remind you."

"Tomorrow's Sunday . . ." ventured Diane.

"I'll have breakfast ready when you and Dad get back."

She said nothing more, and he took a candle and padded to the bathroom, a thin trail of sooty smoke wafting behind.

Clenching his teeth, he scrubbed grime from a blister that had formed on the heel of his hammer-hand, despite the frayed work glove, scrubbed until it was pink and raw. He didn't need another lecture on infections.

He ate dinner in the kitchen, a plate of beans, corn, bread, and warmed-up beef. The kitchen was cold, and he washed the plate and returned to the living room and the quietly crackling fire.

Dennis put down his book. "Let's see."

Steve showed his hands, and his father nodded. "Mm. Okay."

He dropped into a chair and stretched out, watching the fire and sinking deeper into the chair as the tension drained from his muscles . . .

"Been meaning to ask you, son. You going to be around here, come spring?"

He blinked away sleep. "What?"

"Are you going to be around here this spring?"

"You want help with the planting?"

"Just asking. If not, I'll start thinking about hiring somebody. Del and I can't keep up the way we used to, and I have some ideas about growing tomatoes. Never done that."

"Maybe, Dad. I don't know."

"Just asking. Think about it, and let me know."

He knew what was on his father's mind. He had to earn a living. It was why he had taken over so much of the winter work, and why he had made the plow. To earn his keep.

But damn. What a way to make a living. What a *slow* way.

And he could hear the scorn dripping from *that* voice.

Steve Foster. Andersonville Blacksmith.

—————

Late Sunday morning, breakfast finished, Steve cleared away and rinsed the dishes.

His mother drifted into the living room.

Dennis stayed behind.

"Son, sit down a minute."

He dried his hands. "What's up, Dad?"

"Have a seat. Want to talk to you about something. We're going to have a visitor today. And I want you to listen to him with an open mind."

"Oh God, Dad. Not the church!"

"No, not the church."

"Then who?"

"Max Wyse."

"*What?* Jesus! What the hell—"

"Get over it, son!"

"What does *he* want here? Got another scheme to sell? The goddamned politician!"

"You got it exactly. He's got another scheme. He's been talking about it to the Committee, and I got to tell you, he's making some sense."

"So you want me out of the way?"

"No, I don't want you out of the way. He's coming to talk to you."

"Not interested. Don't want any part of it. Can't trust him."

"That's about what I expected. But I want you to hear him out. You don't have to do anything. If you think it's crazy, then forget it. But you got to do something, come spring. Another month hammering plows and no one will be able to live with you."

"Dad! Come on. Have I complained?"

"You don't have to! Your mother walks around here like she's on eggshells, when you're in the house. You're not happy here. And I don't expect you'll be able to take it a whole lot longer."

"Then I'll move out. I'll get a job somewhere."

"Well, maybe you will. But give the man a hearing. Maybe you'll be able to make your own job."

—————

Three men sat around the breakfast table, Steve looking down at his hands and not much inclined to help things along.

"What have you told him?" said Max.

Dennis rumbled. "Nothing much. Was leaving it to you."

"All right. Steve, look. I know AP&L is a painful subject. It didn't work out the way we all wanted. Maybe it has a chance as a power distribution business, but it used up pretty much all the money Barbara left behind. And most of that ended up back in the City. And there just aren't that many people around, like Agnes, and like you, Steve, who have skills, but who won't, or can't, work at farming. And we need more of everything. Roads. Power. Running water. Telephones. Whatever we can get. And we can't just sit around and wait for it to happen."

"You in a hurry?" He said it without interest, staring at the door to the living room.

"I am. I think the City is going to fall apart. I just don't know when. Could be this year. Could be five years. It's a matter of time. We have to protect Andersonville, and the best way to do that is to stand on our own, as much as we possibly can."

"How? You said it yourself, there's no money. And damn sure not enough people."

"That's exactly right. We need to get people to come out here. We need them to bring their skills *and* their money."

"Christ. Why in hell would anyone come here?"

"To *make* money."

"Come on!"

"Steve, we need *everything*. That means business opportunities. And if new businesses start up, there will be new jobs for people to do. Jobs that aren't Corporate jobs."

"I don't see it."

"You will. We're going to recruit people to come out and live here and be their own bosses. Think about it. In the City, there is only the Corporation. You work for them or you starve. We can offer alternatives."

"I still don't see it. Where would they even live?"

"Exactly!"

"What?"

"The first step is housing, housing we can rent to newcomers as cheap as possible. There's acres of land along the main road that no one will ever farm. Too damned rocky. But we can put up houses on it."

"And who's going to do it?"

"Maybe you."

"Me? With what? *I* don't have any money! Not *that* kind."

"You have some. And the Committee's going to parcel out land along the main road to anyone with a credible plan to develop it. You'll have a year to do something with it. If you do, then it's yours. You'll get clear title."

"I still don't have the money—"

"*Son!*" Dennis slammed the table. "Go out and *raise* it! Get investors! Work out a financial plan! That's how business is *done*."

"It's a good opportunity, Steve. The town's making the land available. We'll be doing the recruiting. All you have to do is build."

56

Raul looked across the table at Brother Marco. They were in the rectory, eating lunch. It was Tuesday, and Marco had come from the Abbey.

Raul knew it was one of his inspections. Brother Marco did not really trust him. But this time, he had a way to distract the old man.

"Brother?" he ventured. "Do you know about *wire?*"

The old man sat up.

"Wire? Where did you hear about *wire,* Little One?"

"Tony told me."

"Well, yes. I know something about it. A very dangerous thing."

"Tony said that, too. He's afraid."

"Why?"

"Because they're selling it."

"Who? The Corporation?"

"That's what he said. And he should know. He's in Security." He said this with a touch of pride. "He hears everything."

"And he heard they are selling *wire?* To whom?"

"I think another city."

"But . . . why?"

"For gasoline."

The big jaw dropped, and Raul quickly looked down, frightened of those crystal eyes that seemed to see everything, but thrilled to know something the old man didn't, and something so important. Important enough that he might forget the inspection.

"That's what he heard."

"Good God, if this is true . . ."

"It must be."

"Would Tony talk to me?"

"No—I . . ." Raul sank in his chair. "I wasn't supposed to say anything. I don't want to get him in trouble."

"No, of course not."

"Please, don't tell anyone."

"No. No, I won't."

On a Saturday in December, as pale sunlight grew in the trees outside his window at the back of the pub, Max dragged himself out of bed and pulled on yesterday's clothes. There was a mirror in his room, and he tried to push some the tangled mess of his hair into some kind of order, but he still looked as ragged as he felt.

In the dining room, as he slumped in a chair, Mike came over, grinning cheerfully.

"Mornin', Max! What'll it be?"

"Coffee."

"That all?"

"Uh . . . eggs. Fried. Toast. And coffee."

"Couldn't sleep, huh?"

"Now what makes you say that?"

"You read the notice?"

"What notice?"

Mike pointed. Across the room, on a piece of paper tacked up over the bar, dark block letters announced the new price for a cup of coffee.

"Does that say what I think it does?"

" 'Fraid so."

"What the hell? You just tripled the price?"

"Sorry about that. It may go higher."

"Why?"

"It's not just coffee, and it's not just us. Dad knows people in the City. Yesterday he went in to see what he could buy to tide us over. It wasn't much. There's a shortage there, too. Prices are high. And a lot higher for us."

"Who's your supplier?"

"It's a big family from way down south. They kind of caravan stuff up here."

"Sounds like a dangerous business."

"I guess so. Maybe it's getting more dangerous."

"Yeah, well, how about bringing me a cup of your very expensive coffee, so I can try and think?"

He made his cup of coffee last, nursing it while he ate, and thinking about fifty thousand people waiting on a caravan bringing supplies from God knew where. He was still pondering this when Bill appeared and set down a fresh cup in front of him.

"Ah . . . no thanks, Bill. Don't think I can afford it."

"This one's on the house." Bill sat down, leaning forward and lowering his voice. "Mike talk to you?"

"Yeah."

"Well there's something else you should know. I haven't told him, so keep it to yourself. There's a rumor going around the City, about fighting."

"Fighting? What do you mean?"

"Troops."

"Christ! In the City?"

"No, not in the City. Somewhere south."

"Jesus. Who was fighting?"

"No idea. Only that there were troops involved, and that no one has been able to move in or out of the area, wherever it is. That's why the shortages."

"Christ."

"Thought you should know."

At the Committee meeting that afternoon, he found that Marco and Brother Jim had arrived before him and were already seated in the chairs kept along one wall of the meeting room for members of the public.

It was Jim who got to his feet when Dennis opened the floor for questions.

"Folks, there's only so much land along the main road. So we'd like to stake our claim before you hand it all out."

Amalia glanced at Dennis and burst out laughing.

Dennis swore. "Shut it, Amalia."

"Don't tell me to shut it, sweetie. You should've seen your face, just then."

"I don't get it, Brother Jim. What's your claim?"

"We have a plan to submit."

"A plan? For what?"

"Why, a church, of course."

"Who said anything about churches?"

"Brother Dennis! You don't mean to say you're just giving away land to your friends, do you?"

"We are *not* giving away land to our friends! We are developing the road!"

"Exactly. That's what we understood. And a church should be part of it."

"Says who?"

"There's a good sixty of your fellow citizens who could come here today and tell you. A convenient place to gather is what they want. On the main road. And with newcomers from the City, why, I can tell you, you'll want a church."

"And why is that?"

"Come see our missions in the City! We've helped a lot of desperate people learn to lead decent, useful lives."

"Well, we're not about to invite a bunch of criminals in here."

"Be serious, my friend. If you're successful—and we have every reason to believe you will be—you'll be bringing in all kinds of people. Many will be in need of a good influence. Our little Church has salvaged some very desperate people, some who might have go on to *become* criminals. Come to the Abbey and meet them."

Dan Walsh spoke up.

"Much as I hate to say this, folks, I don't see how we can refuse. As long as it's a legitimate plan."

"Well, good *God,* man!" Dennis threw up his hands. "How're are we supposed to do this? There won't be enough land for *everybody.*"

"First come, first served. It's the only fair way."

The plan was accepted for consideration. Dennis slapped the table, the town secretary gathered her notes, and everyone filed out of the room.

Everyone but Max.

He remained at the big table, staring out a window, telling himself that he really did care, that he was just tired.

"You do not look well, my friend."

"Marco! Something on your mind? You got what you wanted, didn't you?"

"Brother Maximillian, I am not your enemy."

"No? Well, I don't think we're on the same side."

"We do have our differences. That is true." Marco pulled out a chair and sat down beside him. "But we have so much in common."

There was something fascinating about Marco, this close. The crystal eyes set back in their bony sockets seemed like windows opening onto distant places, and distant times.

"Marco, what could we possibly have in common?"

"We should be allies, you and I."

"I don't think so. Is that all you wanted?"

"Also, to share a bit of information. As a token of friendship."

"What information?"

"I have it on good authority that the City is selling *wire* to someone outside." Marco nodded appreciatively as Max sat upright. "Yes. I thought that might interest you."

"Where did you hear this?"

"A little spy told me."

"Well, I already knew that." He pushed himself to his feet. "And I don't see us as allies."

Marco stood up as well.

"Then you do not see very far. A word of advice, my friend. There is no one else who will give it to you." He leaned closer and spoke in a guttural whisper. *"Civilization means fighting."*

The words hung like dark clouds gathering, and Max stepped back from this man who seemed a throwback to forgotten eras, moldering cities, and fields of dead.

"I don't believe that, Marco. Civilization is about building. Creating."

"You should listen. Better men than you have understood this."

"You're wrong. If that's what you really think. I refuse to believe it."

Strangely, the deep-set eyes held a trace of sadness. Again came the whisper, inside a long sigh: *"Then you will lose."*

Seconds ticked by, like cold, hard drops of time rolling down to him from something unimaginably distant, yet close and inescapable.

"Why? Why tell it to me?"

"You are old enough to do your own riddles, no? I leave it with you."

Marco walked away.

57

That winter was a cold one. Thick, dry snow pushed by nights of howling wind piled high against farmhouses, followed by spreading clouds of wood-smoke enveloping tree and field as people burned through cords of timber.

Del Flores developed a nagging, hacking cough that seemed to get better, then grew worse, week by week, his face flushed with fever as he dozed in a chair by the fireplace under blankets piled high. Rosa fed him warm milk and hot soup, quietly praying more and more as he took less and less. Steve and Dennis drove a crude sledge under gray skies into the woods each day, scavenging dead limbs and trunks still upright, anything dry enough to burn, hauling it back to chop and split and take to Rosa.

Yet, despite the long, frozen nights and overcast days, and worry over Del, the Foster house felt warmer than it had in a very long time.

Steve talked about building, about how big the houses should be, how many rooms, how it would make sense to build a row of them as a single structure to save material. He and Dennis sketched plans together and made a list of potential investors. Diane would bring them tea and cookies, and sometimes stand alone in the kitchen, weeping quietly in a kind of helpless gratitude. Months ago she had returned to the bed once shared with Dennis, sleeping peacefully at his side. Maria's room stayed closed.

They went to service each Sunday, which Marco for now held at noon, and a cold, white glow from behind the sea of heavy cloud reminded them there was a sun somewhere, that it would return.

Toward the end of February, it did return, a pale yellow disk glimpsed through veils of white. The eaves of houses, rounded with snow, began to drip, and overhead streaks of blue appeared. Del's fever broke, and he began a slow recovery, resting comfortably, Rosa's prayers no longer dark with silent acceptance, but warm with hope.

The snow melted rapidly as the days grew longer.

On the first Sunday in March, sometime after midnight, Dennis awoke suddenly, holding his breath.

The room was silent.

After a moment, he whispered.

"Mother?"

Her face was turned toward him. He could see it in the silvery moonlight coming through the curtains, her eyes closed, and at peace.

"Mother?"

He raised his hand and gently touched her cheek. Then, painfully, exhaled. He propped himself up, leaned over, and held his lips against the cold forehead, hot tears dripping as he stroked the familiar hair in a long, hopeless, goodbye.

———————

Steve and Dennis walked back to the house from the far side of the pine grove.

Dennis looked up, saw the window as he had seen it so many years ago, remembered the boyish silhouette, recalled the stab of hope he had felt then, and he staggered, sobbing openly, Steve's hand on his shoulder, rubbing gently.

"Dad . . ."

He put his arms around his son, holding on, trying to hold on to everything, until the tears finally ended and he was simply empty, shivering with cold.

"Dad . . . come on. Let's get inside."

Dennis presided over one final Committee meeting.

When the meeting ended and people got up to file through the door, he drew a breath and cleared his throat.

"Max. Son. You got a minute?"

"Yeah, sure, Dennis."

Max sat down across from him. He waited for the front door to slam and the silence indicating the office outside the meeting room was empty.

"Son, I got something to say to you. I don't like sayin' it, but you need to know. So just listen to me.

"You remember Brother Tom. Well, I don't know whether Tom is dead or alive somewhere. But I know what happened. I was there. And I wish to God I had been miles away.

"It was up on Service Hill, after Tom's Renewal Day, the day the eclipse was supposed to happen. But it didn't. It happened the next day. A bunch of us had stayed up there after service, for some reason. I don't remember why. I think there were about twenty of us left. People were leaving, so maybe it was less.

"Well, the eclipse came on, all of a sudden. Threw a hell of a scare into the Flores boy. And then things came out. Things that shouldn't have, at least not like that, right in front of everyone. But Marco confronted them. Raul and Tom."

"Raul . . . and Tom?"

"Yeah. Turns out there was something . . . ah, *Jesus* . . . there was something going on. You know, man and boy. Shocked hell out of us, the way it came out.

"Max . . . this is hard, son. The way it came out sounded like Tom had forced the boy. And the whole thing turned ugly, pretty fast. Fact is . . . fact is, a bunch of us *stoned* him. Brother Tom. Knocked him down . . . *oh, Jesus . . .*"

He closed his eyes a moment, then slammed the table.

"Fact is . . . *I threw the first stone!*

"So now you know. We may have killed him. I don't know. He disappeared, and no one asked any questions."

"Who else was there?" whispered Max.

"Can't say."

"Then . . . why now, Dennis?"

His throat was closing up painfully.

"Because everything's changed! Listen to me, son. Steve wasn't there. He never went. Had no use for it. Never knew what happened."

"What do you want me to do?"

"Whatever you have to. I'm going to resign. I can't do this anymore."

"You said it sounded like Tom forced him."

"That's just the way it came out. But I don't know. We didn't give him much of a chance to explain himself."

"Jesus, Dennis."

"I know."

The sun was warm on their small porch, where Del and Rosa sat together.

There was a blanket over Del's lap, and Rosie held his hand. In spite of his own grief over Diane, Del smiled when he saw the familiar figure trudging along the path towards them.

Rosie got up and waved.

"Mr. Dennis! A cup of tea?"

Dennis Foster stopped before the porch.

His face was gray, and haggard, and in shock Del stood up beside Rosie, the blanket falling away.

"I want you two to know something." The voice was steady, but flat and hopeless. "I told them. About Tom. I told them what happened. And that I was part of it. Nothing else. I didn't tell them who was there."

A chill gust of wind whipped across the porch.

"I had to do it. Maybe they'll arrest me. I hope they leave you two alone. I think they will. Del . . . if anything happens to me . . ." The old man swallowed visibly. "Well, what's mine is yours. Yours and Steve's. You know that. You two work it out."

"Dennis . . . what do you expect to happen?"

"I don't know, Del. But somebody has to pay."

PART III

THE LAWYER

58

Elizabeth White had never expected to be Chief Executive.

Of course she knew how to delegate, how to listen, how to make decisions, and had long ago outgrown any need to prove she belonged in the executive suite. She could lead. But while James Dornan had been alive, it had been impossible to imagine anyone in his place.

Jim Dornan *was* the Corporation, building it over the ashes of Armageddon. And Elizabeth had been right there with him. She had followed him, had slaved for him, had supported him through it all. After her husband had died, she had even bedded him, briefly. But both had pulled back, ending the affair before it could endanger the company. Because both had understood without question that the Corporation was their hope of civilized life.

Sometimes she wondered whether he had ever anticipated what might happen. He had trusted her implicitly, of course. But Jim Dornan had been old-school. He had had his thing about *balls.*

She smiled whenever she thought of that.

Oh, Jim. Those days are so gone.

One of her first accomplishments had been to stabilize the gasoline supply, after the debacle with the storage tank. Now she was dealing with the problem of homeless people risking public health by living in unsanctioned parts of the City. And she would soon resolve the crisis blocking the flow of southern trade, so essential for things the City could not produce.

No balls required.

At her daily shortage briefing, her VP of Plant Operations reported on the improving gasoline situation.

"Good news is that Security just shut down a petty smuggling operation. We were losing at least fifty gallons a week. But the leak's plugged. People are getting used to Stage 3 bus schedules. Not so good news about the buses themselves, though."

"How's that?" she inquired.

"Air filters," replied Manny Romero, Director of Transportation.

"What about them?"

"We don't have any. Not new ones. We salvaged what we can from idle vehicles, but we're going to have to start pulling them off when they get clogged, and just run without them. Otherwise, fuel efficiency'll go down the toilet."

"What's the downside?"

"Engine wear."

"Gasoline is the immediate problem. When do we have to worry about engine wear?"

"Maybe a year."

"Then there's no question. Pull off the filters."

"Right-o."

Bill Baird reported on the favorable prospects of restarting the southern trade route.

She nodded. "Very good. When was the last tanker truck?"

"Um . . . came in Tuesday, Elizabeth."

"No trouble?"

"None at all. From all reports, things are quiet out west."

"Is the next one scheduled?"

"We're still negotiating."

Business routine. Nothing difficult.

An hour for lunch in her office, and she was ready for her intelligence briefing.

"Talk to me, Mr. Carter."

Dan Carter was smart and capable. A little too smart. Snidely arrogant. But impossible to do without, at least for now.

"We are watching events in the south. It seems there were one or two setbacks, but we still believe New Brighton is the side to back."

"New Brighton?"

"It's what they're calling themselves."

"I see. So they're still expected to win."

"That's correct."

"Are they using the *wire* yet?"

"Sparingly, as far as we know."

"Do our western partners know they have it?"

"We don't believe so."

"Does anyone else?"

"If you are referring to the army . . . ? No. I have no reason to believe so."

"How good are the chances New Brighton will use up what we've sent them?"

"The better question is, how much have they decided they'll hold back in reserve."

"Well? Do you have an answer?"

"The tides of war are not easy to predict. According to reports, the insurgents display an unusual willingness to fight against heavy odds. The hope is this will force New Brighton to use up more of it."

"Why do you use the word war? Isn't this more in the nature of a pacification? A police action?"

"War is war, Ms. White. This one just happens to be a little one-sided."

"I won't argue with you. But I would prefer you not to use that word outside this room. Do I make myself clear?"

"Perfectly."

"Just make sure nothing stands in the way of reopening that trade route."

"Understood."

"All right, is there anything I should know about Andersonville?"

Carter smirked in his usual way, which she found especially irritating.

"The locals are doing about what we expect, more or less. Is there anything in particular?"

"I don't want to make a study of them. That's your job. I want to be informed of any developments that might affect our policies or goals."

"And so you shall. At the moment, our assets are telling us what we expect to hear."

"Be very careful, Mr. Carter, they're not telling you what they think you *want* to hear. That would be a very serious error, on your part."

"Of course. You may rest assured."

"I'll be the judge of that."

Carter left, and she waited for her briefing with the company commanders, army captains whose jobs were evidently necessary, if she believed people like Carter.

Dornan had kept the army fragmented, five companies reporting individually to civilian management. She was inclined to follow the practice, until someone could explain to her why it was a good idea to consolidate so much power under a unified staff. Historically, armies often became much more interested in themselves than in their assigned roles, and she did not intend to let this one forget its place.

The captains arrived and reported, while she maintained a look of studious interest, asking a few questions, nodding at the answers. She did not like these people. But since she had to have them, she would not let them see that.

"Ma'am, there's one more thing we need to talk about."

"And what is that, Captain?"

"*Wire.* The men are jittery about it. They all know about Lansing."

The others were watching her. Obviously they had been discussing this among themselves.

"And how is Corporal Lansing?"

"Not so good. The doctors don't know if he'll ever speak again."

"I am sorry to hear that."

Another interrupted. "Yeah, we're all sorry. But that doesn't help Lansing. And it doesn't make the men any more willing to use that shit in training."

"I understand, Captain . . ." — She read the name on his badge — "Raddick. What would you suggest?"

"Stop selling it! I don't want to have to worry about meeting up with it in the field."

"I wish I could do that. But until we find another way to get gasoline—for army trucks as well as civilian vehicles—I'm afraid I don't have much choice."

Raddick glanced at the others, but they remained silent, poker-faced.

"Then give *us* the job. *We'll* get the gas."

"And how do you propose to do that? Start a war?"

"It's already started! How much longer before someone out west comes for us? Armed with the *wire* we've been selling them?"

"They have no reason to come for us, Captain. Now, I don't like selling *wire* any more than you do. But, trust me, we're being very, very judicious with it.

"Now listen to me, Captain. No one here is interested in war. And we're not going to do anything to invite it. I hope I've made that clear."

She glanced at her watch and folded her hands, ending the meeting.

The officers stood up. Four left the room. One remained. She looked up at him with a sting of resentment—and making a warning of it by letting it show.

"Captain Vick. Is there something else?"

"Ms. White. Many years ago, there was an old revolutionary who said, 'You may not be interested in war, but war is interested in you.' He knew what he was talking about."

She said nothing. She watched him coldly. And after a moment, he turned and left the room.

It was exactly the kind of thing she detested, a stupid slogan posing as something profound. These people playing soldier had no idea what she was doing for them. No idea how the world really works.

59

Andersonville was quite an interesting assignment.

This was a surprise. One thought of hard-scrabble farmers clinging tenuously to the land, each jealously guarding a patch of crops and perhaps a cow or two. Or eking out subsistence in a kind of commune, duties and roles and shares parceled out by a committee of elders. Either way, hopeless. And therefore uninteresting.

But it wasn't like that at all. The town was a laboratory, a ferment of ideas, all ignored by the City. Part of the assignment—the unspoken, personal part—was to make sense of it, and to document it, so that someone within Corporate leadership might one day learn from it. Even if the present leadership seemed so . . . in-curious. Surely that could not last.

It was fascinating to watch the whole counterpoint of mysticism and rationalism play out, each side goading the other, each now an indispensable part of the town's dynamic. And the tension between individual personalities and the nascent rule of law! Which would win out? Much too early to tell.

And there was even a mystery, the strange disappearance of the prophet Brother Tom. And another puzzle: the local Chief of Police. A man of unrelenting curiosity, if nothing else, he seemed to ignore it. Did he know something? Possibly. It could not be ruled out. Although the truth might be very hard to decipher from second-hand information.

But then, that was the challenge of intelligence work.

60

Dennis Foster's resignation did not come as a surprise, and at the next meeting, the remaining Committee members voted Dan Walsh chairman.

Then Steve Foster presented his plan for a ten-unit row-house and a claim for four acres along the main road. He talked about how he would build just a few units at first, then more as tenants moved in. He said the Town had to develop running water and sanitation, and he would then erect new housing with built-in pipes and wires, and eventually replace the original units. He told them he needed a large enough claim now for investors to back him.

Presiding over his first meeting, Walsh asked for a motion.

Cotter shrugged.

"*I'm* convinced. Let's vote."

Amalia and Sandy McCane nodded.

Walsh quietly slapped the table.

"Motion to vote carries. All in favor to approve Steve's plan? . . . Plan approved, three ayes and one abstention. The Town Secretary will so record."

Amalia blinked. "Who the hell abstained?"

"I did," said Walsh. "I recused myself."

"You what?"

"I can't vote on this."

"And why'n hell not!"

"Because I'm financing it. At least the first project."

"Well, for the love of—" She sputtered, eyes bulging. "Doesn't *anyone* around here understand what a goddamn conflict of inter-est is?" She threw her hands up. "And *you* a lawyer!"

"Why do you think I'm not voting?"

"*Well that ain't good enough!*"

"Amalia!" Max spoke up. "If we can't have anyone on the Committee with an investment of some kind, or who could gain or lose due to some law the Committee might write, then we won't have a Committee. It's that simple. He's doing the right thing. He hasn't said a word in favor or against, and he's not voting. What else do you want him to do?"

"Keep the hell out of it altogether! How do you expect the rest of the town to trust us if we've got our fingers in the cookie jar?"

"Look, we're *all* trying to get ahead, and everyone in town understands that. And everyone should understand the steps we take to avoid conflicts. Maybe it would've been better if Dan had left the room. And maybe the Committee should step up and write some rules about that."

"Well, maybe we should," she muttered darkly. "Because most of us here have a pretty good idea what happens when people lose trust, when they think their elected leaders are only in it for themselves. And I can tell you, sonny-boy, it ain't pretty."

61

A cold day in March.

Dazzling rays of white sun flickered through bare branches, the forest floor overlaid with a sparse layer of dirty snow, daily and leaving large circles of mud and last year's leaves around the wet, dark trunks of trees.

In no hurry to get anywhere, Max Wyse let his horse pick its own way along a backwoods trail. It was an hour after breakfast, and there was no one he wanted to see.

A low *thump-thump* startled him—a stag bounding through the woods, its huge crown slipping incredibly between trees as though they were parting to let it pass. It disappeared, and Max looked around, wondering just where he was.

Ahead was a dirt road and the foot of a long hill. A rough stone wall followed the road, and he recognized the way up to the Anderson place. He stopped by the wall, gazing up the hill for a minute, until he noticed a sign, a neatly lettered wooden panel propped against the wall.

Thomas Abbey.

He stared at it, then kicked the horse and wheeled, heading back to the pub at a fast canter.

Christ. I have to stop doing this.

At the pub, he turned the panting animal over to Mike, went in through the back door to wash up, then sat in his room, trying to think. But he succeeded only in growing drowsy, and he got up, kicked the chair back, and went out to the dining area, thinking to get a beer and talk with Mike.

But the big room was empty except for Bert Morrow, seated at a table by himself, right in the middle, a half-empty glass of beer on the table beside him. Max had no chance. Bert spotted him at once, and waved.

"How're you doing, buddy?"

He walked over and sat down.

"Okay, I guess. What's up?"

"Haven't seen you in a while."

"No?"

"Not since the last officers' meeting. And that's been a month."

"Yeah. Sorry about that."

"You losing interest?"

"What?"

"Losing interest. In your job."

"I've just been a little out of it, that's all. I'll see Ali and get her to set up the next meeting."

"You're not sick, are you?"

"Nope."

"Yeah?"

"I'm okay, Bert."

Mike deposited a beer in front of him, and went back somewhere behind the bar. When he was out of sight, Bert drained his glass and carefully set it down on the table.

"Buddy, you're going to tell me it's none of my business."

"Then it probably isn't." He sipped a little beer.

"You in love with her?"

He thumped the glass down, his face suddenly hot.

"Bert, what the hell are you talking about?"

"Agnes."

"Ah . . .*shit.*"

Bert watched him a moment.

"What're you going to do?"

"What am I going to do? Not a goddamned thing."

"Does *she* know?"

"Hell, probably."

"Don't be a martyr, buddy. A woman like that is not interested in a suffering hero."

"Listen to me, Bert. Just listen. I don't need advice, okay? I just need to get it the hell out of my system."

"Well, do it then. Do *something.* That's my advice. Man, everyone's looking ahead, but *you* wander around like you're at a funeral. You depress people."

"Yeah, thanks."

"Well, what do you want? Someone to commiserate with you over your sad life? *Do* something."

He rode out to AP&L.

The barn was freezing, and as the sun went down he drove AP&L's cart back to the pub, paid Mike for a half-cord of firewood and help loading the cart, then returned to the barn, where Agnes helped him unload and carry the wood inside, stacking it by the stove.

She lit a lamp, and he got a fire going.

"How in hell did you survive the winter?"

"I just ran out." She handed him a small glass of wine.

"Uh-huh. What were you waiting for?"

"Oh, I usually pay the kids to take care of it. But I keep forgetting."

The kids were the teenagers who still worked for her, on and off.

"Like hell. You were too cheap to pay them."

"Well, money's tight."

She sipped her wine placidly, watching firelight grow in the stove.

"Agnes, you can always ask for help. You *know* that."

"I know, and you're sweet to do it. But I don't like to bother you."

"Why not?"

She put her glass down.

"Because, Max. I don't want to take advantage of our friendship."

After a painful moment, he raised his glass.

"To friendship."

Her glass clinked against his.

62

The weather was warming, and Max began avoiding the barn that was AP&L, dividing his time between his room at the pub and the Town Office.

And a trip to Service Hill.

The hill stood out from woods and rolling meadows that descended south and east toward the river hidden in the trees. The sides of the hill were steep and covered in long grass, except for a broad path worn into the easiest part of the southern slope, where Marco's followers climbed each Sunday.

Max led his horse up the path one afternoon, climbing toward a place he had never seen before. He walked carefully, studying the terrain, the folds and clefts that wrinkled the hillside, wondering whether Brother Tom's remains might have been quickly disposed of here. It seemed possible, especially in the darkness of an eclipse. But risky. Animals could get to a partially covered body, and a shallow grave might wash down the hillside.

He went on climbing, reached the top, and wandered across rock and matted grass and patches of loose gravel and stones, maybe dislodged and scattered by worshippers tramping back and forth, or by rains and winds lashing the exposed summit. At the eastern edge, where the ground was worn bare, he stopped and closed his eyes, listening to the wind and feeling the distance, the isolation, feeling as though this were a different world, one answering only to itself.

He shivered.

What the hell happened up here?

Monday morning, Max waited for Bert Morrow to arrive at the office, then dragged the Chief into the meeting room and shut the door.

Bert sat down. "Okay, buddy. What's on your mind?"

In a low voice, he related Dennis Foster's story.

Bert listened without moving. Then he blew out his cheeks.

"Christ, Marco left out that part."

"What? Which part?"

"The stoning."

"You knew about the rest? About Raul?"

"The way Marco told it, Tom was caught out and left."

"And you didn't say anything!"

"Marco said he was worried about Raul. Said he was fragile. He did seem jumpy. But I guess that could mean anything."

"Did you talk to him?"

"Who? Raul? Nope. Marco sent him away. Seemed to be protecting him."

"I wonder who else knows."

"His grandparents know."

"The Flores?"

"Yup. According to Marco."

"Jesus. They must have been up there. Dennis must be protecting them. Christ—"

"Slow down. We don't know anything for sure about Tom. If they ran him out of town, why, that's one thing. But if they actually *killed* him, we'd have to do something about that."

"Dennis threw the first stone."

"So he says."

"I think he was telling the truth. Or what he thinks is the truth. You should have seen him, Bert. It's eating him alive."

"You think that's why he's just now getting around to telling someone?"

"Oh, Christ! Because Diane was there. She had to be."

"That'd be why he never said anything before."

"Bert, I'd do almost anything to protect these people. But we can't cover up a killing. Where would it stop?"

"Yup, you already know how *I* feel. But we don't know for sure yet anyone was killed."

"We have to find out."

"Yeah. I think we do."

63

On the first anniversary of the eclipse, Marco proclaimed Renewal Day and opened Service Hill for sunrise worship. But still it was a long, cold hike, and he looked forward to the day when he could preach indoors, in his own church, on the main road.

At least sixty people shivered on benches of rough boards, in the gray before dawn, listening as he related news about the City missions, about classes for children, and about plans for the new church building.

He paused, waiting in the cool breeze as Craig Olsen got up and stood before the crowd.

The horizon brightening behind him, Craig told his story, of how he had found the Word. He told of his ghost, how he had reached out and earned the trust of a pitiable creature who had shown human dignity by asking for help, for water, in the only way he could, then returning what he did not need. He told of the night City troops had stormed the hotel and dragged the creature away, sacrificing a fellow soldier to their own degradation. He said he had learned the meaning of Brotherhood that night, from people who had none.

Then Brother Jim got up and delivered a brief, rousing sermon, coming to its usual climax as the first rays broke over the horizon, and then it was fellowship time, and Raul handed out the ceremonial bread, and people crowded around Brother Craig, shaking hands enthusiastically, offering congratulations.

Raul was awestruck.

Craig was invited to breakfast, and after fellowship, the four, Marco, Craig, Raul, and Jim, walked down the hillside together and followed the long path through the trees, Raul stumbling and chattering in excitement, until they reached the rectory and went inside—and stopped short, as Max Wyse and Bert Morrow stood up and faced them.

Raul stared like a cornered animal, instinctively edging toward Craig.

Brother Jim looked at Marco.

Marco was shaking, his lips white, his crystal eyes like blue fire.

"What, may I ask, is the meaning of this?"

Bert cleared his throat.

"We have some questions."

"And you think it proper to barge in here uninvited?"

"Well, I *am* Chief of Police!"

"And do police have no respect for private property? If the door had been locked, would you have broken it down?"

"Well, you're a hard man to find."

"Not so hard, it seems!"

"Look, Marco—"

"Chief Morrow, I will not speak with you now. I will come to your town office tomorrow, in the morning. You may ask your questions then."

"Ah . . . all right."

"Bring Raul," Max added.

Marco did not answer. He held the door, until the two men left.

———————

Bert was waiting in the meeting room with Max, when Ali Knight opened the door and showed Marco in. Marco sat down without a word. Ali glanced at Bert, one eyebrow raised, shook her head slightly in warning, then left the room, closing the door behind her.

Marco sat in silence, acknowledging no one. The dark, heavy jaw and steady, cavernous eyes under the white mat of hair had a strange effect. The room seemed meaner, smaller, a little shabbier, and the man more like a judge than witness. Or suspect.

Bert began.

"Did you bring Raul?"

"The boy is terrified. He will not come."

"He's not exactly a boy. He must be eighteen now."

"I can not answer for his age. He is traumatized."

"Yeah?" drawled Max. "What's he so terrified of?"

"You, I think."

"Because *I* think he was there."

"Chief Morrow, is this an official inquisition?"

"I suppose it is. Of course it is."

"Is the town president deputized as an officer of police?"

"Well, no."

"Then I do not understand why a politician, or anyone else who is not an officer of the law, is present at an official inquisition."

"He knows what I know."

But Max got up and strode out, slamming the door, and Bert rounded on Marco.

"Enough! That's enough! I'm going to ask you some questions, and you're going to answer them. Got that?"

The old man waited. There was no change in his bearing.

Bert controlled himself.

"Where's Brother Tom?"

"I do not know."

"What happened to him?"

"I told you before what happened."

"Well, you didn't tell it all! I want the rest."

"Do you? I wouldn't be so sure."

"That's why I'm asking, goddammit!"

"Then I will satisfy your curiosity. Your fine townspeople at-tacked him. Gentle Brother Tom. With stones. They didn't ask him to explain. They didn't hold an inquisition. They took matters into their own hands, and they *stoned* him."

"And you tried to hide it! Then what?"

"Then they panicked. They ran away."

"What did *you* do?"

"Raul was in shock. I took him home."

"And Tom? He was . . . alive?"

Marco exhaled.

"Chief Morrow, I was . . . I do not know. In shock, like Raul. Horrified. How could Tom do such a thing? I brought Raul down from the hill and left poor Tom behind."

"I don't believe it."

The crystal eyes shifted away, indifferent. "Believe what you will."

"So there was no one left on the hill, except Tom?"

"That is correct."

"Then he's alive!"

"Is he?"

"Well, he's not up on that hill now, is he?"

"That does not mean he is alive. Tom might have died later, if he were badly hurt."

"Christ . . ." Bert rubbed his face. "He could be anywhere. Why didn't you tell me this before?"

"Are you serious? Do you seriously think I would turn over to you fifteen or twenty people, some of whom lost their reason in a moment of passion? And some of whom may have done nothing at all? Suppose poor Tom is dead. What would you propose to do? Hang them all?"

Bert had no answer.

Instead, he sent four deputies to climb up and down the slopes of Service Hill, looking for clues. They found nothing. No trace of Tom, no sign of what happened.

He was almost glad, and he took Max aside at the town office the day after.

"Buddy, we can't keep making this up as we go along."

"What do you mean?"

"We need laws. Written laws. Ryan used to hang bandits, and not too many people objected. But what do you think will happen if we try to hang one of our own, without some sort of law that's been voted on?"

"Yeah. I know."

"Buddy, this is getting dangerous."

"I know."

64

Hitching a horse at just the right angle, then setting the lines just long enough to wrap around you to control the animal while you maneuver the handles of the plow, is a complicated business. At least for a beginner. But Steve had managed to break a straight furrow fifty feet long, before stopping for another adjustment.

Dennis stood off to one side, watching. From time to time he offered advice, but mostly he watched. He felt like he was watching from a distance. As though he weren't really there. He saw the land that belonged to him as surely as his hands did, even his skin, yet for some reason the strange feeling of being a distant observer, with no personal connection, did not bother him. He did not feel fear. Nor much of anything else. But he did want to watch his son.

When two riders approached over a rise, it was almost an effort before to recall who they were, and then the sight of them made him tired.

"Mornin', Dennis." Bert greeted him. "Can we talk? Alone?"

"Yeah, okay . . . Son, you can handle this a while, can't you?"

Max and Bert climbed down and hobbled their horses, and the three walked down the path toward the house.

They stopped on the porch.

"This won't take long," Bert told him. "I just figured it ought to be private. Look, we know about what happened on Service Hill. What I want to know is, who was there."

He shook his head and kept silent.

"Was Diane?"

"She had nothing to do with it."

"And Marco?"

"He started it."

"What's that?"

"He knew something. Tried to get it out of Raul. In front of everyone. Don't know if he got exactly what he expected."

"Okay . . . okay. And Mr. and Mrs. Flores?"

He met Bert's gaze, but said nothing, until the Chief flushed and angrily rubbed his face.

Then he asked, "What do you want to do, Bert?"

"I don't know! I don't have all the facts!"

"A lot of people were up there."

"That's just the kind of thing I have to find out! Who was there. What did they do. What really happened."

"Why not just take it out on me?"

"What?"

"Put me on trial. I'll confess. I'll leave town. Or go to jail, if that's what you want."

Bert was speechless. Dennis looked at Max, but the town's president seemed to be in some kind of paralysis. Over Bert's shoulder, he could see Steve's figure moving slowly across the field, and he let his eyes rest on that.

"What about it, Bert? Hold your trial, and put an end to it."

"We're going to do the *right thing*. The *right thing,* goddammit! Even if I don't know what that is yet."

Dennis nodded, still gazing at the figure in the distance.

"I know you will."

65

The first step in building anything is to find the right material.

Steve Foster hired two young men who had worked for him before at AP&L, to help dismantle an abandoned house. His idea was to salvage studs and joists, windows and doors, nails and other hardware.

But the house had not been built well to begin with, and the roof must have leaked for years. The studs were badly warped under moldy drywall, window-frames and doors rotted, hardware rusting away. And there was no flooring, just disintegrating carpet laid over a badly cracked slab of concrete. They spent hours trying to straighten the nails they salvaged. The wood that hadn't rotted was so hard that even a slightly bent nail would fold over when they tried to hammer it in.

He knew there were materials in the City, bags of cement, stacks of lumber, boxes of screws and nails. But there was only so much, and whenever City people found out he had a use for anything, the price automatically went up. And he could hear the old Max Wyse refrain. Be independent. Be self-sufficient. Stand on your own two feet. As much as he detested the man, he had a point.

There was nothing in the town library on building construction, although something did catch his eye one day, when he was digging through the shelves in the corner of the office that served as library. A book stamped, "Withdrawn from Circulation" —from the *City* Library.

Now, that could be a mother lode. But how to find it? He could think of only one person to ask

"She'll talk to you," Dennis told him over supper. "Just tell her you need help. Believe it or not, that's one of the best ways there is to break down walls between people. And if she unloads on you, just take it like a man and let it go. You'll be better off for it."

———————

The next day, he rode to the barn and knocked on the side door.

She let him in.

"Hello, Steve."

"Hi, Agnes."

"I didn't think I'd ever see *you* here again."

"Well, it wasn't easy to come." He glanced around the barn. "So. AP&L lives. I suppose if anyone can make it work, you can."

"What do you want, Steve?"

"Look, I'm sorry I let you down. I'm sorry—"

"Steve. What. Do. You. Want."

"Well . . . I need some help."

"What kind of help?"

"I need to find the City Library."

"And?"

"And, I don't know where it is."

"Wait—that's it? *That's* what you want? You came all the way over here to ask directions?"

"Well . . . yeah . . . I guess so."

"You're some piece of work, you know that? After everything that happened . . . it's been months . . . You never even checked to see how I was doing . . . "

"Well, it hasn't been easy for me, either."

"No? What have you been doing all this time?"

"I kept to myself a while. Then Mom died, and it was pretty hard on Dad."

"I heard about that. I was sorry for you."

"Agnes, there are things that I regret. I can't change any of it, but I don't want us to be enemies."

"That's big of you."

"Well, okay, if you don't want to help, I get it. I won't bother you."

"Steve, wait. You're right. We shouldn't have to be enemies. Give me a minute."

She went to a corner of the barn and rummaged, and returned with a sheet of paper, then sketched a crude map, labeled a few streets, and explained it to him, their heads close together over a workbench.

Then she straightened and handed him the map, and for a moment, as they both held the paper, he felt a connection.

Then she released it.

Her eyes were on him as he looked down and folded the paper.

"Thanks, Agnes."

The City was every bit as enormous as she had warned. Hundreds of buildings. Hundreds of streets. And people . . . people walking the sidewalks, people in cars and buses and trucks crawling along the streets.

It was Saturday. He had taken the swaying, bumping bus from Walsh Stables. He got off at the stop she had written on the map and started walking, clutching the map and turning round from time to time, making damned sure he would recognize the way back to that bus stop.

But he found it, just as she said. A three-story building extending half a city block, the words "Free Public Library" engraven high over its massive entrance, and he stood across the street and gazed up at that long stone façade, wondering at the race of beings who could erect such a monument to knowledge.

Then he crossed the street and went inside.

His footsteps echoed through a towering atrium as he walked toward a line of desks. A large, red-headed woman with sparkling blue eyes and freckled cheeks looked up and grinned.

"Why, hello! I'm Sue. How can I help you?"

66

Shortages were easing in the City. And the price of a cup of coffee at the Andersonville pub was back to normal. The southern trade route was open again. But at what cost . . . this was not widely known.

Mr. Dan Carter had a policy of keeping his agents compartmentalized. Which was understandable, if tiresome. But what was the point of being in intelligence, if you didn't know how to obtain information? And Mr. Dan Carter himself was not entirely to be trusted.

The real story, once unearthed, was illuminating, and disturbing: The Corporation selling *wire* to something calling itself New Brighton, who had then supposedly put down an insurgency—although it might be difficult to know for certain which side had actually been blocking trade. But one thing was clear. There were now *two* places outside the City that possessed a very dangerous weapon: the so-called 'western partners' supplying gasoline, and whoever these people were calling themselves New Brighton.

It was pure extortion, and the Corporation had caved to it, paying ransom rather than doing its own fighting. If the army knew— but this did not seem possible. It was the army that would experience the brunt of *wire,* and Elizabeth White did not exactly enjoy their implicit trust. ?So they must be in the dark.

But how long could that last? Especially since the truth had not been so hard to come by. The Corporation had its leaks. Certain secretarial desks were not kept as tidy as they should have been, and some people in Security talked a little too much.

Not such a challenge after all, for a good intelligence agent.

67

It was early morning, on a Saturday in April.

Craig Olsen stared through the hazy window of his hotel room at the street below, thinking about Andersonville. He had seen little more than Service Hill, had met but a handful of people, but it had stayed with him. A world he had never imagined. And somewhere in that Arcadia was a place called Walsh Stables. And today he was going there, to Walsh Stables, on his own—to see about riding lessons.

He left the hotel and walked ten blocks north, into the real City, took an east-bound bus across town, then waited at a stop with a small crowd of people for the next bus to the Stables.

It arrived with passengers already aboard. Young men and young women. Families with small children. A couple with a picnic basket. An old man with a fishing pole propped against the window next to him. Craig found a seat as the bus pulled away and accelerated, heading south and swaying through the narrow streets, passing deserted sidewalks, and then a mission, one small storefront with a sign in the window and a number of people inside.

Here the City looked truly abandoned, the buildings lifeless and crumbling, everything seeming to merge into a single smear of brown, the color of decay. Even the children on the bus watched in silence, until an overpass marked the outskirts of the City and the canyon of ruin was behind them.

The bus accelerated. In a few minutes, trees appeared. Not long after, a dirt road. The bus slowed and eased onto it. Twenty minutes later, it bounced to a stop, the door screeched open, and for the second time in his life, Craig Olsen stepped onto the soil of that other world.

It was a different sun on his face. Different, clean air filled his lungs, and he savored it, savored the yielding earth, the trees and grass and the smell of life. He could almost forget why he had come.

Two young men appeared, assistants of some kind separating the passengers into groups. Another group who had been waiting when they arrived climbed aboard, and the bus left on its run back to the City.

Now riders were mounting up and moving off. A group of students followed a lanky, balding man, who, with the help of one of the young assistants, began showing his charges how to mount a horse.

But there was another instructor.

Dark-haired, with fine eyes and a profile at once intelligent, worldly, and alluring, she sat atop her mount erect and yet with a relaxed grace, the reins held negligently in one hand while she watched another group of students mount up. Her level gaze flickered, and for an instant met his, and in that instant Craig Olsen thought he understood the word 'goddess'.

Then she wheeled her horse, and the group followed her onto the practice field.

He heard a laugh behind him. "Yeah, she has that effect."

He turned to see a young man grinning at him.

"Who *is* she?"

"That's Marta. The old guy, that was Dan Walsh, the owner."

They watched for a while as Marta and her students cantered in a line across the field.

"So, mister, you must be new. Haven't seen you around before."

"This is my first time. I'm not sure, but I think I'd like to learn to ride."

"You think?"

"Well, I've never tried it. Those are big animals."

"Look, the name's Pete. Pete Sawyer." Pete stuck out his hand.

"Craig Olsen."

"Okay, Craig. Suppose I take you around the field once or twice, maybe a little ways out on a trail."

"On a horse?"

"Of course on a horse! There's a couple of mares here that're real gentle. You can see what it's like. If you decide you want lessons, we'll find a way to fit you in."

An hour later, as they rode along a broad trail under huge oaks, Pete asked, "So, Craig, what kinda riding you want to do?"

"Well, what I really want to do is ride around on my own. I want to learn about Andersonville."

"You want to learn about Andersonville? Best way to do that, if you ask me, is spend some time at the pub. If you want to meet people. The rest is just farms."

"Where are the pubs?"

"Just one pub, man. This ain't the City."

"So where is it?"

"A good ways from here. Seven, eight miles. Probably further."

"How long would it take to ride that far?"

"Too long for me to take you there today!"

"Sure, but riding would have to be faster than walking. I have to work with the bus schedule."

"Well, riding like this'd take you a good two hours each way. If it were me, I'd go at a trot or a canter. That horse you're on, give her a few breaks, you could make it in an hour or less. Some of the horses here could do it in a lot less."

"Sounds like I need some lessons."

"Yeah, you'll need a few. You'll have to convince Dan that you know what you're doing, before he'll let you take one of his horses as far as the pub."

"Fair enough. When can I start?"

At the end of the day, as Pete was helping Johnny air out saddle blankets, he heard Marta calling to him.

"Say, Pete! Who was that gorgeous creature?"

Grinning at Dan Walsh a few yards behind her, he shot back, "Name's Craig Olsen! New guy. Want him?"

Marta turned as Walsh walked up behind her.

"Daniel, m'love. You don't worry about me, do you?"

Walsh shrugged. "I should. But for some reason, I don't."

"No. We're both too wise for that. That's why I love you, you know."

68

That Sunday evening, Max rode out to the Stables just as the last bus left, carrying Marta back to the City. He waited around as the horses were brushed and fed and watered, until Pete and Johnny were headed home.

Dan Walsh walked over.

"Okay, Max. What's on your mind?"

"You know, Dan, I really didn't think she'd stick around this long. I wonder what she sees in you?"

Walsh kicked at a fence post, knocking clumps of dirt from his shoes.

"That all you wanted?"

"I wish it was."

"Well?"

"Did you know that Bert is investigating Brother Tom's disappearance?"

"No. I didn't know there was anything to investigate. What's he looking for?"

"An explanation. He wants to know what happened."

"Okay. So?"

"Well, what if somebody committed a crime?"

"Like what?"

"Well, let's just say, hypothetically, that Tom was murdered."

"Murdered! Where in hell'd you get *that* idea?"

"Let's just suppose. And suppose Bert finds some kind of proof. What's he supposed to do?"

"Arrest the culprit. Assuming he knows who it is."

"Then what?"

"Put 'em on trial."

"Suppose he gets a conviction. What's the punishment?"

"That's what judges are for."

"That's what I thought you'd say. But if someone like Tom was murdered, and someone we all know is convicted for it, and a court that's never done this before decides he's going to hang, there

might be some pretty strong feelings about it. Especially if whoever did it thought he had a reason."

"Yeah, there might."

"That's just one example. Everyone in this town knows everyone else. You remember when Bert leaned on old Jack Harper to
stop beating up his wife? I think we were lucky that time. Jack
has a few friends, and it could've turned ugly. A lot of people
might've said it's none of our business. They might not even believe it was all that bad, considering she never complained."

Walsh frowned. "Yeah, okay. I see that."

"I think Bert took a big chance, and I think he was damned
lucky."

"So?"

"Well, think about it. What makes this so hard?"

"You tell me."

"It's because we're making it up as we go along. If we try to pun-
ish a crime that we've just made up, people will question it. They
may take sides. Then we can't bring it to an end. And that's a
problem, because we can't just let these things go. Right? I don't
want to live in a town where a guy can get away with beating the
crap out of his wife, or killing someone, just because a few people
think it's none of our business. Do you?"

"Of course not. But you didn't come out here to talk philosophy,
did you?"

"We need laws, Dan. Written laws. Laws that are voted on."

"That's one helluvalot easier said than done."

"I know."

"Just trying to vote on laws like that, with teeth, could tear this
place apart."

"Yeah, I know. But think about it. Before you vote on something, you have to talk about it. And if people talk about it, and
then you vote on it after everyone's had his say, at least they'll
know what to expect. The more I think about it, the more I think
that will change the way people react. People may still get riled
up, but they'll be getting riled over something that's already settled, instead of something that takes them by surprise, where they
think they can still fight it. I've got to believe that will take some
of the steam out of it, and give us a chance to make it stick."

"You should've been a lawyer."

"That's why we have you."

"Yeah, I suppose I should have seen that coming."

"You've got to start it, Dan. With the rest of the Committee. It's
going to be hard, and it's going to take time. But we can't afford to
wait."

"Why not? What do you know?"

"Nothing. Not enough, anyway. I'm afraid of what we're going
to find out."

69

Horses and pavement do not mix, and horses were not welcome on City streets. But there was a vacant lot not far from the commercial center, where for a nominal fee one might leave a horse tied up for the day.

Steve rode in every day for a week, walked from the 'horse park' to the library, spent the day reading, then retrieved his horse and rode home in time to make dinner.

Dennis told him not to bother. Steve was afraid the old man would not eat.

The librarian Sue seemed genuinely intrigued with his problem. She would pile books on his table, and sometimes sit with him, for hours at a time.

By Tuesday it was clear that he must build with logs, and he began making sketches for an adze.

By Wednesday, he resolved to explore for brick that could be salvaged to make piers to hold a floor off the ground.

By Friday he was planning experiments to make lime for mortar by burning limestone in his forge, and identifying limestone with strong vinegar.

Sue watched him with frank interest.

"You know, you're just the opposite of Father Tom."

"Who's Father Tom?"

"Cute guy who used to come in here and read history."

"Well, I'm trying to work my way *back* through history. I need to be able to build with what I can find."

"Yeah, you're trying to make something. The Father was preaching. He didn't care too much about science or anything. But he did like astronomy."

"Astronomy, huh?"

"He was interested in that eclipse that happened. I found the tables for him."

"So he could observe it?"

"He was going to make a festival out of it. Called it Renewal Day."

"Oh! You mean *Brother* Tom."

"That's right. I always called him Father, for some reason. I haven't seen him in such a long time. I liked him. He was a good sport. Does he still preach?"

"He's gone, Sue."

"What happened?"

"No one knows. He just disappeared."

"Aw, what a shame. He didn't even say good-bye."

An adze would be as challenging as the plow. Steve envisioned the head formed of a single piece of steel, one end shaped into a blade, the other formed into a collar that would securely grip a long, wooden handle. But it was no easy thing, and after days of it he stood scowling at a pile of scrap, all failed ideas, wondering if he could find a way to cast metal into the basic shape, maybe find a way to make a crucible out of something refractory, find a way to make his fire burn hotter—

But then he laughed.

Saturday morning, he rode out to Anderson Market. Two things were strapped to the back of his horse. The first was a two-foot-wide board painted white with black lettering. The board was screwed to a narrow post, and this he drove into the ground. The second item was a folding chair.

He sat down by his sign to wait.

By noon, he had purchased two pickaxes.

Over the next two weeks, Steve shortened the arms of each pickaxe, so that one arm became a narrow stub like a chisel, while the other was flattened and widened, and squared off, with a cutting edge filed at the end. He fitted each with a stout, three-foot handle. Then he spent hours practicing on pine logs, until he was proficient with axe and adze at skinning bark, shaping surfaces, and cutting wide grooves lengthwise to hold one log atop another.

In early May he incorporated, capitalizing his four-acre claim and money from Dan Walsh. He then hired three husky young men to help fell straight pine, chop limbs, and skin bark, and as May passed into June a row of naked white logs began growing by the side of the main road, raw material to be cut and notched and shaped into the walls and roof of Foster Building's first project.

70

On a hot Saturday afternoon, Steve counted logs, stepped off lengths, and scribbled a calculation on a folded sheet of paper. His crew was resting in the shade of a tool shed, the first structure to stand on the company's claim.

"All right, boys. I think this is it. This is what we need to get started."

"What now, boss?"

He glanced at the sun.

"I say we knock off and go to the pub. You game? The company's buying."

"You bet!"

Tools and water jugs were stacked and locked in the shed, and a half hour later Mike looked up from chatting with a lone customer as the four walked into the pub.

Steve led the way to a far corner.

"Hey, Mike! We'll sit over here. We're a little ripe."

Mike got up and followed, waving at the air.

"Yeah, appreciate that. You guys going to eat?"

"Yeah . . . say, who's the new guy?"

Mike glanced over his shoulder.

"Him? He's from the City."

"From the City?" Steve scratched his jaw. "What's he looking for out here?"

"Says he's exploring."

"Way out here? Well, maybe Dad was right."

"Right about what?"

"About City people coming here and starting businesses, looking for places to live."

"Maybe so."

Mike brought beers and plates of beef and potatoes, and the four talked about the work coming up, about building a pair of gin poles for hoisting logs to erect walls, about the problems of placing a roof on top.

"Mind if I buy a round?"

Steve looked up, at the man from the City, and shut his mouth.

The man smiled.

"Name's Craig Olsen."

He stood up and shook hands. "Sit down, Craig."

They sat. Steve made introductions, then asked, "What brings you way out here?"

"Well, I joined the Church of the Word a while ago—oh, don't worry! I don't want to talk religion. No, they brought me out to Service Hill to tell my story, and I liked what I saw. The country. The people. And I wanted to learn more. So I've been taking riding lessons over at Walsh Stables. And today I got the go-ahead to ride out here and spend the night."

"No kidding. What's so interesting about Andersonville?"

Olsen laughed.

"It's different! A different world. Maybe I'm naïve, and I know you people must have your own problems. But in some ways the City just seems hopeless. And the last thing anyone would say about *this* place is that it's hopeless."

"So how'd you get involved with that church?"

"It's a long story, but I'll tell you the part that everyone seems interested in."

He started telling the story of the ghost. Mike arrived with a round of beer, and stopped to listen.

"I wonder if the poor bastard was using *wire*."

Olsen went suddenly quiet. His looked up at Mike.

"What do you know about *wire?*"

Mike pulled out a chair and sat down.

"Well, I know that the commandos who tore this place apart a couple years ago were using it. I saw what it did to them."

"Commandos?"

"That's what I said. You may not know this, but commandos were sent out here to track down James Dornan. They used *wire* too long. It turned them into animals. Couldn't talk. Couldn't sleep. I think it killed them."

"This fellow wasn't that bad, but . . . where do they get it? And why is it called *wire?*"

"I suppose they get it from the army."

"But why? What is it for?"

"You're asking the wrong guy. I don't know much more than what I saw."

"Who would know?"

"My dad might know something. But I know him, and he won't talk. Max probably knows."

"Who's Max?"

"Max Wyse. President of Andersonville."

"Could I meet him?"

Mike stood up and started gathering empty glasses.

"Stick around. He lives here."

———

It was a dark night, clear and moonless. Above glittered an ocean of stars.

Sometimes, when riding home after a long meeting, Max would doze in the saddle, trusting the horse to keep to the road. But not tonight. Tonight they had argued. And the more they had argued, the more a criminal code, as Walsh called it, looked out of reach. Sandy McCane seemed to get it, but Bill Cotter shot down every idea for how to begin. And Walsh was for some reason flummoxed by Cotter.

Amalia was no help.

"Max, honey," she had coolly informed him tonight, "I'm not about to shove my opinion down the throat of every hard-working sonofabitch in this town who's smart enough to keep himself and his family alive without any help from me. Don't you *dare* try to shove your opinion down mine."

His body swayed with the easy rhythm of the horse, the night punctuated by the soft thuds of hooves. At length, he saw the faint glow ahead.

Mike was still up. Good old Mike.

He reached the pub and led the horse around back. Mike joined him in the stable, and together they unsaddled the horse by the light of a lamp perched on a rail, the quiet clink of fittings and rustle of the blanket being shaken out muffled by stacks of hay.

The horse safely in a stall, they closed up and walked to the building. There was the rattle of the latch as Mike felt for the door.

But he paused.

"Say, Max. There's a guy here says he wants to talk to you. But it's pretty late. Want me to tell him to wait till morning?"

"What guy? What's he want?"

"Guy from the City. He's in that church. We all got to talking about those commandos two-three years ago, and . . . well, better let him explain what he wants."

"Yeah, why not. I don't think I can sleep."

Mike led the way inside and down a short hallway, to the dining room, where, by the light of a candle, a figure sat reading a book.

He stood up as they entered.

"Say, Craig. This is Max Wyse."

The man from the City hesitated, but Max was used to this kind of reaction, and held out his hand.

Craig shook it.

Mike moved away. "Goin' to bed, folks. Gotta get up early."

Max sat down.

Craig followed. "Thanks for seeing me. I know it's late."

"Mike says you've got something on your mind."

"You're president of this town?"

"That's right."

"And you were involved with those commandos, the ones Mike told me about."

Slowly, he nodded. "Yeah. I was almost killed by them."

"Mike said they came from the City."

"That's right."

"Mr. Wyse, this is all new to me. I've been hearing about something called *wire*."

"What about it?"

"Look, I live in a rough part of town. Never mind why. But there aren't many people there. Prostitutes, junkies, people with nowhere else to go. A few weeks ago, I tried to help some bum who was sleeping in an alley. It wasn't easy. He was afraid of his own shadow. But I got him to move indoors, gave him some food and a room to stay in. And I know he was grateful.

"But, you see, he couldn't talk. He tried. He tried very hard. So at one time I'm sure he *could* talk.

"Mr. Wyse, I think this man was a soldier. And I think he had been using *wire*."

"The hell you say."

"Mike said the commandos couldn't talk, either."

"What makes you think he was a soldier?"

"The stripes on his sleeves. It was a uniform. But not Security."

"How's he doing now?"

"I don't know. A few days after I got him inside, the place was raided. They dragged him away."

"Not real gentle when they do that, are they."

"You've seen them do it?"

"You could say that."

"Where?"

"Let's just say we both have things we don't like to talk about."

"Sure. I understand. Look, Mr. Wyse. I want to find out where *wire* comes from. Mike thought you might know something about it."

"I do. Same place *rope* comes from."

"You know about *rope?*"

"I know about it."

Craig exhaled. "I didn't know it was out here. No one said anything."

"It isn't out here. Not yet anyway. Only in the City."

"Well, do you know where it comes from? I see *rope* destroying people all around me. And now *wire*. Where's it coming from?"

"Straight from Corporate Medical Services."

"What? That makes no sense! Why would they?"

"You really don't know?"

"What's your theory?"

"Listen to me, Craig. This isn't theory. I knew the man responsible."

"Who?"

"Paul Stevens. Doctor Paul Stevens."

"I think I've heard that name."

"He was a senior vice president."

"Okay, maybe he was. What do you know about it?"

"Are you sure you want to hear this? Have you thought about what might happen if they find out?"

"Are you trying to scare me? They haven't done anything to you, have they?"

"I helped them, Craig. Not with their drugs. I helped Dornan. I know people you'll probably never meet."

"Look, I need to know. I can't just forget about it. So I'd be grateful for anything you can tell me."

"All right. Here it is. *Rope* is used to keep people in line. People take it because it's an aphrodisiac. Then it goes to work on their memories, enough to keep them from organizing, enough to keep workers from planning anything against their Corporate masters."

Craig sat back. The man looked as though he had been struck.

"*Wire* is different—You sure you want to hear this? *Wire* can make a man impervious to pain. He's aggressive, he's totally focused, and he'll fight like a fanatic until he's told to stop, or his body collapses. High doses will turn a man into a machine. They don't sleep, don't get tired, don't care about anything. Those commandos Mike told you about? They tortured and killed everyone they found. Everyone. The only thing that stopped them was Cargo Flu. I suppose a bullet could have stopped them, but you'd have to find them before they found you."

Craig ran a hand through his short hair.

"If this is true—"

"It's true."

"Then it has to stop!"

Max stood up.
"Yeah. Good luck with that."

71

The next morning, Craig was on the first bus back to the City.

He stared through the windows at fields and streams passing by, at the rustic innocence of Andersonville receding behind him.

The bus rattled along nearly empty. The driver had tried conversation, glancing in the mirror over his head at his silent passenger. But there was no response, and he shrugged and turned his attention to avoiding the holes in the dirt road.

Now the bus bumped onto pavement, the ride smoothed out, and the bus accelerated.

A short while later, they entered the ruin.

This was home. The world he belonged to. What was behind him, the Arcadia he had stumbled upon when he found the Church, he did not deserve. No one deserved it, whose home was the City. He could almost hate the Church for this.

Skyscrapers towered ahead, man-made structures cutting hundreds of feet into thin summer air, gleaming and monumental. Yet with a poison seeping within.

He slouched against his seat, drained after a sleepless night. The things he had learned did not seem possible. The people who had suffered . . . Misty . . . Patti . . . the ghost dumbly pleading for water, his eyes bulging . . . It did not seem possible that human beings could do such things. But he was not surprised. And that was what had tormented him, all last night, keeping him awake until the smell of coffee had reached him in a corner of the big, silent dining area: That he was not surprised.

The streets were growing wider. People were about, early risers strolling the sidewalks. They looked innocent. But not in the way of the people of Andersonville. Rather, like children, trusting their elders, trusting the forces watching over them. Unaware they were being cultivated, as a means to an end.

But an end kept in shadow by those who held the trust.

72

That man Craig Olsen had found something.

Olsen had stayed the night at the pub and returned on the first bus, very early Sunday. He had looked preoccupied. Distant. Angry, even. Almost as though he had been slighted somehow, or maybe robbed. And in anyone else, this would be the reasonable conclusion. But not Craig Olsen.

The man had a certain magnetism. Even the little hermaphrodite Raul Flores was affected by it, if certain gossip was to be believed. It was his imperturbability, the innocent strength. From all reports, the only time anyone had ever seen him emotional was on Service Hill, when he told the story of his ghost.

Whatever had upset Craig Olsen, it surely was not be the loss of a little money.

But his ghost! Could he have discovered something to do with his ghost?

Out here?

73

Craig Olsen began preaching.

There was no point at which he decided. He didn't plan on it. It started at the nearby mission, the week following his night in Andersonville. He stood up one evening, in the middle of a discussion, and he began speaking about *rope,* about what it did to marriages and families. What it did to minds.

Heads nodded as he spoke. No one disagreed.

A few nights later, he started talking about *wire,* and about his ghost, the Corporation's ghost, the soldier who could not be allowed the freedom to exist.

People shifted in their seats. Some were riveted. A few frowned.

He told the story of the company's original CEO, James Dornan, hunted down and murdered by City commandos taking *wire* and following without hesitation orders to torture and kill innocent men and women.

"Now hold on, Brother!" someone objected. "That's some wild story there!"

"You think that's wild? Do you have any idea where *rope* comes from? I don't mean the dealers. I mean the *real* source." The man shrugged. "Why do you think these drugs are here? It's because they come from the Corporation itself! The *Corporation* manufactures it, all of it, and uses it to control *us.*"

"Prove it."

Craig laughed.

"Go to Andersonville! Tell me if you see families destroyed because people take pills, fuck anything that moves, and can't remember what they did the next day. Tell me if people are hauled off in the middle of the night, so no one learns what they're not supposed to know!"

People looked at one another. Some shook their heads and left.

But night after night, Craig persisted, talking and arguing, and night after night, as word spread, more people showed up, crowding into the mission to listen to Craig talk about how their masters were poisoning their minds.

Brother Jim was alarmed.

He tried to persuade Craig, gently, that the mission was to salvage the lost. Not challenge Corporate authority.

Craig was unmoved.

"What good is the Word, if it is silent?"

"I know, Brother. I know. But what if it is silenced because we offend the people who give us permission to be here?"

"You know, everyone in the City is hostage to the people who run it, because they depend on them. *You're* a hostage. *You* depend on them. Well—*I* don't."

"But you do, Brother. If you are part of this mission."

Craig relented. A little.

But even Marco was losing patience. People who came from the City for dawn worship atop Service Hill surrounded Craig at fellowship time, to talk about drugs, about ruined families, about the high-level conspiracy to keep them in their places.

A certain person in the crowd was especially wide-eyed and rapt, and Marco warned him one day in the rectory.

"Be careful, Little One."

"Of what?"

"You admire Brother Craig."

Raul looked down, blushing like a guilty child. "He's such a brave man."

"Perhaps braver than you can imagine. He says very dangerous things."

Raul nodded.

"I know."

"Do you? Do you remember what happened to his ghost? This is why I tell you to have a care. I would not want to see anything happen to you." Marco watched for a sign of agreement, or at least comprehension. But Raul just stared at the floor.

He tried a different tack.

"How is Tony?"

"Oh . . . I don't know. I haven't seen him in a while."

"Why? Is anything wrong?"

"Oh, no . . . I just haven't seen him."

"Well, be careful, Little One. In case something should happen."

Privately, Marco wondered why it hadn't already.

74

It was raining outside his windows on the tenth floor.

Dan Carter leaned back in his chair, propped a foot on his desk, and watched sheets of water cascade down the glass.

It had been a very quiet week. Dangerously quiet. All week, Elizabeth had canceled his intelligence briefings, with no explanation.

But she had summoned him this morning.

"Talk to me, Mr. Carter."

"Well, Elizabeth, there isn't that much to report at this time."

"You mean, now that things are quiet and trade restored."

"More or less. We are, of course, still watching—"

"What about Andersonville?"

"Ah, the usual. Everything as we expect. Nothing out of the ordinary."

Elizabeth would have replaced him long ago if she could have. Of that he was certain. She regarded him with such poorly-concealed contempt. But this morning . . . this morning she had positively smirked. Gloated.

He got up and walked to the window. Ten stories down, wind and rain lashed the streets and a few lonely pedestrians, a blustery summer squall that would most likely end by evening.

Elizabeth was playing a very dangerous game. But maybe unwittingly. This business of trading *wire* . . . it was bad enough she used it to buy gasoline, to sweeten the deal. But at least anyone could understand that the alternative, of running out altogether, was a very, very stark one.

New Brighton, on the other hand . . . Most people would consider what the trade caravans brought to be small luxuries. Not worth going to war over, much less arming a potential opponent.

Caving to New Brighton's blackmail had been her decision. She had even forbidden him from using the word. But blackmail was blackmail, and he was certain that New Brighton, or whoever they were, had used only a portion of what they had received. Enough to test it with actual troops and learn to use it in combat.

So now there was a second stockpile outside the City, quite a bit closer than the western partners, and controlled by people who knew how to use it.

Elizabeth could have sent the army to protect the caravans, but that might have made an enemy of New Brighton, and then she might have had to raise additional companies, maybe even put in a general staff, in order to prevent war by being very well-prepared to fight one. Which would have offended Elizabeth White's sense of economy.

Carter shook his head. The price they would pay if *wire* were used against the City—the price the *army* would pay—that would be considerably higher.

He turned away from the window and paced about his office.

It was simply not possible to prevent the company commanders from learning what she had done. Not indefinitely. It was a matter of time. And when they learned of it, they would turn on her. It was inconceivable that men like Raddick would allow the army, not to mention the City, to be exposed to surprise attack carried out with *wire*.

He stopped by the window again. The rain seemed to be subsiding, and in the distance a streak of pale blue appeared through ragged clouds.

It was astounding to him that Elizabeth could fail to see this, fail to see her own jeopardy.

But, then, not very surprising.

75

It was still dark on a Sunday morning, and Tony Schaub sat in a huddle on the bus to Service Hill.

He had never come out on a Sunday before. He always met his friend on Saturday, when Marco wasn't around. But something had changed. Raul was never there, and Tony wanted to know why.

He had a brown paper bag in his lap. This was not unusual, and did not attract attention. People from the City often brought along something to eat later in the day. But there was no sandwich in Tony Schaub's paper bag.

The bus stopped and let out a dozen passengers, and he walked with them to the foot of Service Hill, and they climbed the slope as the world was turning gray.

Standing in the back of the flock, he listened to the long service, watching the outline of Raul's slender form as the light grew.

Then the sun broke over the horizon, and fellowship began, and people shared bread and shook hands and joined together in small groups. From a little distance, he followed Raul to a group forming around someone named Brother Craig.

The sun rose higher, the group broke up, and Raul turned. The glowing smile in his beautiful young face, the smile that Tony thought reserved especially for him, turned to shock, and Tony froze, sinking under the weight of that shock, the forgotten bag dangling from his hand.

Raul ran away.

Marco opened the rectory door.

"Come in. You must be Raul's friend, yes?"

Tony nodded.

"Raul!" called Marco, and the young man appeared. "Here is your friend. I will leave you two to talk. I'm off to the Abbey. It was nice to meet you, Tony."

Marco left, closing the door, and Raul stood looking at the floor.

"Are you seeing him?" Tony asked.

Raul shook his head, without looking up.

"Are you mad at me?"

Raul shook his head again.

"I've missed you."

"I missed you, too."

"But you're never here! I thought you didn't want to see me any-more."

Raul giggled. "I . . . I had a crush."

"I thought you loved me."

"But I do! I don't know why . . . I don't know what happened to me. Brother Craig is so handsome—you saw him—and so brave. He's not afraid of the Corporation. But when I saw you, I remembered."

"Then why did you run away?"

"I was so ashamed! I thought you'd hate me."

"You are very foolish, Raul. Like a frightened deer. Do you know that?"

"I know." He put a hand on his hip and slouched. "But a pretty deer, yes?"

"Yes," Tony answered, breathing a little faster.

Raul glanced at the bag.

"Is that for me?"

Tony tossed it aside. "Later."

But Raul grinned and stuck out his tongue. "Show it to me!"

Tony retrieved the bag and pulled out some papers. Raul moved closer.

"What is it?"

"It's about *wire,*" Tony whispered. "I found it in a conference room. Someone left it behind."

"What does it say?"

"It says that they sent *wire* to a city called New Brighton, so New Brighton would do something for them. It says they're worried about how much New Brighton still has. I wanted to show it to you, so you'd know I was telling the truth."

Raul stared at the tight blocks of print. But he wasn't thinking about *wire,* or New Brighton. He was thinking that this was something that would interest Craig Olsen.

He bumped Tony with his hip, lowering his eyes.

"I thought you missed me."

Tony grabbed him, hands sliding greedily over his buttocks, and Raul laughed, pushing against the beefy chest.

"Be careful! Be gentle with your little deer—!"

76

The City's electric department eventually found a disused distribution transformer. They installed it on a pole by the North Road and connected it to AP&L's main line, but with the power off. Agnes and two men she hired spent a month installing disconnect switches and wiring subcircuits. Ed came out personally to inspect and approve the work. When it was complete, he set a date with her, in June, to throw the switch.

They agreed on a simple plan. When the time came on the appointed day, City technicians would drive out to the transformer. At exactly noon, if they had not heard from her, they would close the switch, energizing the line.

Agnes was leaving nothing to chance. She hired and trained extra hands, appointing the two experienced men foremen. The crews would spend the final hours before noon inspecting the line up and down the main road, every connection and every branch, verify all disconnects were open, and check each customer's breaker box to ensure all circuits were off. All this had to be accomplished with enough time to send a rider up the road and stop the City, if necessary.

When the power was finally on, there would be time enough to turn up a section at a time, then each house, then test each circuit. Systematically. Deliberately. One circuit at a time. Ed had lectured her at length about the hazards of old wiring neglected for so many years inside combustible wood-frame houses.

At dawn on the appointed day, men gathered in AP&L's yard to go over final instructions.

Max arrived.

He tied up his horse and waited, watching the men gathered around her, listening and asking questions, nodding at her answers.

When the crowd broke up, he walked over to her.

"Agnes, let me help. Tell me what I can do."

She laughed.

"Max, you're sweet! But you have no training. What could you do?"

"I wish you'd stop calling me that. Look, I'll do whatever you want. I'll be your messenger boy. You can't be everywhere at once, right? How about it?"

"Well . . . okay. But why the sudden interest?"

"Are you kidding? I've been watching this since your first generator. When Barbara was alive. It's been a long time coming. Today's the big day. You think I'd miss it?"

She looked away a moment, and his brief glimpse of her face made him regret mentioning Barbara.

But then she smiled.

"All right. You're my messenger. But stick close."

"Okay, boss."

The crews instructed and ready, everyone mounted up and set off. At the main road, the two foremen took their respective crews in opposite directions. Poles would be climbed, connections checked, and lines followed to farmhouse and ranch.

Together, Agnes and Max watched as the teams moved farther and farther apart.

"Well, Max, cross your fingers. Only a few hours to go."

"Nervous?"

"I am. I wish Barbara could see it."

"Yeah. So do I."

"Even though it's not exactly like having our own generator."

"Well, don't give up on that. I haven't."

"No? I haven't seen much of you lately. But I do hear things. Trouble with the Committee?"

He laughed.

"No, no trouble at all! They just don't want to do anything."

"Someone told me you were thinking of quitting."

"Ah, yeah, well . . . I've thought about it."

"What would you do?"

"No idea. That's the problem." He shrugged his mutilated shoulder. "I'm not much good for anything."

"Well, I don't see you climbing poles or plowing fields."

"Not much chance of that."

"There are almost certainly jobs in the City you could do. But I don't think you'd want that. Would you?"

"I don't know, Agnes. I just don't know. If I give up here—"

She reined in, hard.

"You know—those are words I never thought I'd hear! Not from *you.*"

"I'm sorry. Forget I said it. I'm just tired. I'll get over it."

"Well, you'd damn well better! I don't know what I'd do—what we'd *all* do—if you weren't around." She laughed, brushing something from her cheek.

"Well, I'm still a director of AP&L. So you'd better keep on doing what you're doing."

"Okay. Listen, I think we'd better split up. You go west and follow that crew. But stay on the road. If anything comes up, anything at all, come get me. I'll be with the other crew. When yours is done, meet up with me. Okay?"

"Got it."

They separated, and he his horse and caught up with his crew. As the morning wore on, he watched and stayed out of the way. The foreman assigned tasks, marked his map, and sometimes rode out to a farmhouse to double-check or answer a question.

Everyone was conscious of the sun. At the foot of each pole, hour by hour, its shadow shortened.

When the last house was checked, the crew regrouped and started eastward, dropping off a man every half mile or so, to monitor the line and watch for signs of smoke.

Max spurred his horse and left them behind.

Presently, he made out Agnes coming toward him. She halted as he reached her, her horse prancing nervously while she looked up and down the road.

"Okay. Follow me."

They galloped west again, to where the foreman waited by a pole where a line was strung south, to a farmhouse somewhere on the other side of a tree line.

"Ready, Josh?" she asked.

"Yep. All set."

"Okay. Switch it on."

Josh went up the pole and cranked the lever of a bar that engaged a contact above. Then he waited, watching down the wire toward the farmhouse, the spikes on his boots dug in, a woven-rope strap around the pole secured to his waist.

Max looked at her. "Now what?"

"Now we wait."

She got down from her horse, and he followed. The sun seemed directly overhead, but the pole's shadow, only inches long now, was still pointed west.

They waited. Minute by minute, the shadow shrank, turning inexorably northward.

He watched Agnes, the hollows under her cheekbones, the narrow rectangles of her eyes looking up at Josh, who was shaking his head.

He watched her, forgetting the shadow and the wire, seeing only this woman whose every nerve was tensed, sunlight glinting from her pale hair tied back, completely unaware of him.

Suddenly Josh leaned forward, peering toward the tree line. "He's coming."

"Well?"

"Can't tell yet."

Max called up, "You don't see any smoke, do you?"

"Sure don't!"

He and Agnes stood looking at one another, listening, waiting, almost reduced to that one sense.

Then a shout from overhead.

"It's on!"

There was a moment, a brilliant second or two, when it felt like it was just the two of them, standing in sunlight together, as though the first two people on earth.

"Lights on!" They heard the man yelling, hooves pounding. *"Lights on!"*

She laughed and threw her arms around him, until he heard Josh on the ground and the snort of his man's horse, and she released him.

"And no smoke!" She laughed again.

"Hell, no!"

"Well done, boss." Josh stuck out his hand. She shook it, they shook hands all around, and stood there a while, at a loss for words, grinning awkwardly, but unashamedly.

Then she pushed back hair that had fallen loose.

"Okay! We'll test as much as possible before dark. Every house we check can have one circuit tonight. Just one! We don't have time today to test any more. Tell 'em we'll be back tomorrow."

Josh clapped his hands and rubbed them together. "Right, boss!"

"Max, stay with Josh, will you? Same as before. Come get me if anything goes wrong."

"Okay . . . Good luck!" But she was on her horse, galloping eastward to join the other crew, and he turned in time to see the foreman smirking at him.

"Damn, Josh! Don't you have work to do?"

As the sun went down, the crews regrouped in front of AP&L, and she checked off names and handed out pay to those hired for the day. Max watched her, watched the sharp, sure movements, the outline of her face, her eyes intent, yet serene. He knew what she was feeling. He could see the profound joy that might be hidden to others. He could feel it too.

Dusk was settling, and the men laughed when someone muttered, "Don't that beat all. A power company with no lights."

Then the last man took his pay and waved it in the air like a trophy.

"I'm for a beer!"

The yard erupted in cheers. Max shouted, "Okay! But it's every man for himself. I've seen this woman's books, and she's not spending a nickel."

Horses flew through the hot evening, chased by shouts and laughter. And as they flew, from time to time a gleam of light, distant but steady, pierced the gathering darkness.

Then they were stomping into the pub, calling for beer, jostling each other and shoving together tables, and chiding the few who sat down prematurely, until all were standing with glasses raised in the air.

"To AP&L! And the best-looker of a president a power company ever had!"

They cheered and drank, but mostly drank, then dropped into their seats, and for three hours Bill and Mike were kept busy with food and drink and trying to keep some semblance of order in their dining room.

Max laughed at wild stories, deflected the occasional question, and watched the glowing woman across from him, watched her laugh with abandon—and grinned whenever she caught him watching.

It's a beginning, he thought. *For all of us, but for her most of all.*

Finally, Josh banged down an empty glass and got to his feet.

"Okay, gents! AP&L is in business, and some of us got to work in the morning."

They drained glasses and ambled to the bar to settle up. Max stayed behind. Agnes leaned on her elbow, her chin cupped in her hand, and idly turned a half-empty wine glass.

"What a day! And, Max—thank you. For being there. It meant a lot."

"You know I wouldn't have missed it."

"I know. And I'm sorry I gave you a hard time about it."

"Well, you had a lot on your mind."

"I did. I was scared to death."

"Well, now you can start bringing in money. You're on your way, Agnes."

"Looks that way, doesn't it? Look, there's Bill, wondering when we're going to leave and let him clean up."

"Let him wait. He's had a good night, too."

"Mm, so he has."

"Want anything? More wine?"

"No, I'm just going to finish this."

"Well, take your time. I'll get the bill."

"No, wait! I can pay my own way!"

"Not on your life! Not tonight."

He got up and walked to the bar, waiting while a few stragglers paid and left, until the front door closed and the room was suddenly quiet

Mike grinned at him.

"So they did it, huh?"

"*She* did it."

"Yeah, listen to you! If she walked across the street, you'd rope it off and call it holy. Don't look at me like that. Everyone sees it."

"Yeah, well, it's nobody's damned business. So why don't you stuff it and tell me what I owe? For both of us."

"Oh, *her* tab's taken care of. On the house tonight. Here's yours."

He paid, and turned to see her walking toward him, with Bill descending on the dishes behind.

She smiled.

"All set?"

"All set."

Voices and tromping hoofs were receding down the road as they came out the front door, and soon there was only the rhythmic trill of a nearby cricket. A quarter moon was sinking in the western sky, and for a long minute she gazed at it.

He stood near, and could hear her quiet sigh.

"Such a beautiful night."

"Well . . . come on. I'll ride back with you, make sure you get in okay."

In the pale light filtering through the trees, he saw her head shake.

"I don't want to go to the barn tonight."

"Uh, well, okay. Do you want me to get Bill—?"

"Max." She took his hand. "Max, I want to stay tonight. Here. With you. In your bed. If you'll have me."

"I . . ." His voice cracked. "Why?"

"Because . . . well, damn it, because I love you."

He was not sure if he answered, but his face was in her hair, against her neck, the scent of her in his nostrils, and she was laughing quietly.

He whispered, "How do we get back in?"

"Through the door?"

"How do we get past Bill and Mike?"

"I don't care. Do you?"

"No. No, I don't."

They went in and walked across the dining room, his arm about her shoulders, her arms about his waist, Bill and Mike staring as they passed into the back.

He watched in disbelief as she walked across his room, drawing the curtains. A candle flickered on a small table. He reached down to snuff it out.

She stopped him with a hand on his wrist.

"I want to see you."

She undid the buttons of his shirt, and he shrugged out of it. She rested her hands on his shoulders and slid them down, wincing a little as she crossed the stump of his arm. Then, lightly dragging her lips down his chest and belly, she knelt and unfastened his trousers.

He kicked his clothes away, and she pushed him toward the bed, pushed him down, then stood before him, undressing, watching him watch her.

Then was on him, the length of her body against his, kissing his face, until he pushed her over and she lay with her arms flung out, her head back and her mouth tilted up to him.

Yellow light flickered on the rough ceiling. The candle was beginning to sputter.

"Mm . . ." Her soft voice came to him, and he turned to look at her.

"I thought you were asleep."

She pushed herself up and leaned over, her face flushed in the candlelight, and brushed her lips across his, breathing softly over his face. Then she propped herself on one elbow, a hand flat on his chest.

They were atop the bed, the night too warm for covers, and he looked down the length of her body, at the pale hair loose about her neck and shoulders, at the trim breasts, the sharp concavity of her back.

"My God, you're beautiful."

"Hmpf. Does that mean you'll leave me when I'm old?"

"Not if I'm too decrepit to go."

"That's flattering."

"You know . . . something in me still can't believe you're here."

"Are you asking what changed my mind?"

"I suppose I am."

"Max, I've known a few men in my time. Sorry if that makes you uncomfortable. I want to be honest with you. But I've never known anyone as strong as you are, as good as you are, who looks at me the way you do. It took me a while to see it. But on the road today, when you talked about leaving and going to the City . . . well, that's when it hit me. I was afraid I'd lose you, forever."

"I think you're stuck with me."

"That's the nicest thing you've said."

The candle finally sputtered and died, and the room disappeared, leaving the image of her smile in his mind.

From the darkness came her whisper.

"Make love to me."

The room gray with dawn not far off, he awoke suddenly, conscious that she was not at his side.

But she was there, sitting on the edge of the bed, dressed and smiling down at him.

"Go back to sleep. I have to start early."

"But you haven't eaten."

"I have. Mike is up."

"Christ, I forgot! You have to test the wiring today."

"That's right. Join us later, if you like. But I think the hard part is behind us."

"I will."

She ran a hand through his hair.

"Dearest Max. See you soon."

The air was cool, the sky brightening, and she posted to trot along the main road, poles passing by, and two black lines rising and falling over the road in a long, easy sweep.

She reached the trail to AP&L, worn wide with the passage of carts and horses over two long years, but rough and rutted, and she brought the horse to a walk and let it pick its own way. It was early, there was no need to hurry. No one would arrive before eight o'clock. She had all the time in the world, and she savored the smells of earth, then turned her mind to business, to her plan for the coming days, reviewing the steps and tasks, gauging the time for each.

She came out of the trees—and dropped the reins. The horse carried her steadily forward, nearer and nearer the charred wreckage that was Anderson Power and Light.

Gasping, her lungs struggling for air, she stood in the stirrups, until her scream shattered the dawn.

77

People drink coffee even in summer, and one of the first things Ali Knight had done, after being elected Town Secretary, was to install a small wood stove under a window in an alcove in the front of the Town Office, where she could boil coffee without resorting to the hearth. Even Amalia had finally given in to her haranguing that the town pay for coffee and sugar, and her secret ingredient.

Since the coffee was free, the office was generally the first stop of the day for anyone on the job. Which in the case of Bert Morrow and Joe Dryden was daily. Dryden was in charge of road maintenance, and when he wasn't meeting with a crew to go over instructions, he was reviewing the survey, writing reports, or planning expenses.

Ali had just pushed the coffee off the stove, and Dryden was seated at a desk going over some half-crumpled notes. The front door burst open, slamming against the wall, and a raw voice cut across the room.

"Where is he?"

Dryden looked up as Agnes strode inside, several men right behind her.

She was shaking. The hollows under her cheekbones looked as though some force were squeezing the life from her. The men were silent, and their silence demanded an answer.

Dryden got to his feet, and she looked at him, then through him, then at Ali.

"Where is he?"

Then the men turned and stepped back, making a path. Framed in the open doorway was Bert Morrow, and Agnes raised a stiff arm and pointed to him.

"You!"

"What?"

"You are Chief of Police! *It's time to do your god-damned job!"*

"Ah . . . okay. Why don't you tell me what happened?"

"My place was burned! Anderson Power and Light! And you're going to find the sons of bitches who did it! *So I can nail their fucking hides to the wall!"*

Ali started to speak, but Dryden waved her still.

Bert glanced at the men. Their grim silence backed up the charge.

"Show me."

Without a word, she stalked past him, and the men followed her outside.

Bert caught Ali's eye.

"The first two deputies that show up, send 'em out to AP&L. Fast as they can get there."

He left without waiting for her reply.

Outside, Agnes and her men were already mounted and waiting, and he untied his horse, climbed into the saddle, and looked at her.

"Well?"

Savagely, she kicked her horse. The animal bolted.

It was a wild, reckless flight over three miles of road, and Bert cowered low, gripping desperately with his ankles. Perhaps because of her slight body that looked too insubstantial for the violence within, Agnes led the way, moving farther and farther ahead. He was forced to slow down at the deeply rutted trail to AP&L, but Agnes kicked her horse on, and pulled up in front of what was left of the barn before the rest straggled in.

He stopped beside her. She spoke coldly over the panting animals.

"There."

The barn's roof was gone. Three walls were partly burned down, the fourth completely. Inside were piles of black rubble.

"Anyone touch anything?"

She shook her head, her eyes on the wreckage.

He looked behind him, and shouted, "Keep those horses back!" Then he climbed down. "Come on. We're going to take a look. Just don't disturb anything."

She got down slowly, and he led her to the right, to the eastern side of the barn, where, except at the corners, the wall was burned to the ground.

"What was over here?"

"Nothing."

"Was anything stored here?"

"No. That was the side door."

"Where's the stove?"

"Bert! You think the stove was lit last night?"

"Just humor me."

She pointed at the opposite side, where much of the wall was intact.

"There. See it?"

"Yeah . . . okay. Was anything stored over here that could be fuel?"

"God damn it, Bert! What are you saying?" She was flushed, her eyes dangerous.

Forcing all the calm he could muster into his voice, he said, "Listen to me, Agnes. Just listen. You're going to have to work with me. It's not going to be enough for me to be convinced. This is deadly serious. You might have been killed. I have to be able to convince everybody in this town, beyond a shadow of a doubt, that this fire was deliberately set. Do you understand?"

She raised a hand over her mouth. The hand was shaking.

"Are you all right? Do you want to sit down?"

"No. I want you to do your job."

"Okay. Just answer the question. What else was stored here?"

"Ahh . . . tools. Wire, over there. I had a lamp, Bert. And some old kerosene."

"How much kerosene?"

"I'm not sure. Maybe a quart. Maybe a little more."

"Where was it?"

"Way in back."

"Okay. Follow me." She hesitated, and he took her arm and led her along a line where the wall had been, moving toward the back of the barn.

"Can you see it? Can you see the lamp or the kerosene?" She shook her head. "Look, all that burnt stuff in there is mostly roof. See? So we're going to walk in there and find the lamp. Okay?"

"Okay."

"Ready?"

"I'm ready."

"Hang on to me, and try to step where I step."

He picked his way through debris and around workbenches covered with charred wood. On one was the lamp, half-buried, but intact.

"This the only one?"

"Yes. I broke the other."

"When?"

"Long time ago."

"Okay. What was the kerosene in?"

"A metal can. An old gas can."

"Do you see it?"

She looked around, shaking her head.

"Where did you keep it?"

"Over there. Where the stove is. Well, not right by the stove. By the wood pile."

"It's not there."

"No."

"And you're sure you didn't move it?"

"I'm sure. I keep it over there so it's out of the way. It's just for the lamp."

"I wonder where the hell it is."

They turned around worked their way out again. Then he led her around to the front. Two deputies had arrived, and were now waiting with the crew.

He strode toward the deputies.

"Jim, get that crowd back and keep 'em back. Kevin, get down here. Come with me."

He brought Kevin to where the side door had been.

"You start searching, from right here on out into the trees. Follow any trails, any broken brush. You're looking for a metal can, might smell of kerosene. Or anything else that doesn't belong. I don't care if it takes all day, and tomorrow too. I'll get you some help, soon as I can. But you're either going to find that can, or you're going to know for *goddamn* sure it's not here. Got that?" Kevin nodded, wide-eyed. "All right. And listen, you find anything, *don't touch it.* Don't let anyone *else* touch it. You just come get me. Got it?"

"Right, boss."

Bert slapped his back and started for the front of the barn.

"Say . . . boss?"

He stopped, and looked back, and Kevin asked, "Was anyone hurt?"

For a moment, he was sick, and shut his eyes. Then he shook his head.

"No. Everyone's going to be all right."

He came around to the front again, and found Agnes leaning against Josh, her arms folded across her body, her eyes still on the barn.

Josh spoke.

"Bert, you need her for anything?"

"No. Where're you taking her?"

"The pub. Bill will put her up. Hell, I'll pay him myself, if I have to."

"Don't be stupid," she muttered. "I can take care of myself."

"Well, you got nothing to take care of right now. We'll get those circuits tested, me and Carl. You don't need to be here."

There was a sudden pounding of hooves, followed by frantic shouts from Jim — "Keep back!" — then Max Wyse bawling, *"Get the hell out of my way!"*

Horses side-stepped as he forced his way through. He took one look at the barn, leaped to the ground, and sprinted toward Bert.

"What the holy fuck happened!"

But Josh grabbed his arm, pushing Agnes against him.

"Here, pardner. She needs you. Get her outta here. We'll fill you in later."

78

Five people sat along the wall in the meeting room, sat quietly through a half-hour discussion of the state of the roads and trails,

followed by an argument over the town budget, followed by a vote
on hiring another deputy.

The vote failed.

Dan Walsh looked up from his notes.

"Ah, okay. That's that. Floor's open."

No one answered.

"Weeell?" drawled Amalia. "Anyone come here to talk? Or can
we go home now?"

Max Wyse stood up.

"I didn't hear anything about a legal code."

"No, hon. I don't guess you did."

"That's too bad. Because we now have two serious crimes to deal
with."

"Says who?" Cotter yawned. "I'm not convinced we even have
one."

Steve Foster got up.

"My property was vandalized, same night AP&L was burned.
Tools stolen. Shed knocked down. They tried to burn the logs, too,
but it'd take a helluva bigger fire to light up those. At any rate,
we're stopped until I can replace the tools."

"Sounds like a problem for the police. Catch anyone, Bert?"

Bert Morrow hefted himself to his feet.

"I will. Question is, what do I do with them."

"Why ask us?"

Walsh interrupted. "Bill, you know goddamned well why!"

"Seems to me," Bert went on, "you folks have a problem."

The four Committee members just looked at him.

"You don't want to ask me what that is. Fine. I'll tell you.
There's a damn good chance the same party's behind both crimes.
They both have to do with the City, and we know there's been a lot
of ugly talk about that, up on Service Hill. It may be turn out to be
one person. It may be more. But when I find them and hold a trial,
I'm going to be able to prove what they did. And if we don't know
what to do with them by then, it may end in a lynching."

"Suits me." Cotter flicked an imaginary speck of dust from his
shirt. "Serves 'em right."

"Really? Because it may not stop there. What if they were kids?
People will fight over it. Someone might get killed. Then what?"

"What makes you think kids were involved?"

"Because they weren't too smart about it."

"You have any evidence?"

"You could say that."

"Well? What've you got?"

"Investigation's not over. You'll find out later, when I put 'em on
trial."

Cotter sat back.

Amalia rolled her eyes.

Walsh exploded. "He's exactly right! He's doing exactly what he
should be doing. He can't let anything taint his investigation, or

alert his suspects. He has to build a case step by step, so it's air-tight and no one can question the verdict. That, and a sentence, is the only way to get closure."

"Well, hell," drawled Amalia. "How does *that* solve anything? Man still won't know what to do with 'em. Like you and Maxie keep sayin', we can't make this up as we go along, or people won't buy it. So where the hell do we go from here? Write a thousand laws in a week?"

"Restitution," said Bert.

"What?"

"We've been lucky so far. No one's been hurt. It's all been property. Fine. Enact a law providing for restitution. Whether the guilty have to pay for it, or rebuild it, or give up their own. It's fair, and we don't have to worry about keeping people in jail. Or hanging them. At least not until something more serious happens. Which it will, eventually."

McCane spoke.

"I'd imagine it'd be pretty hard for a couple of kids to replace a barn."

"If they're kids, the parents are responsible."

"Oh my," breathed Amalia. "I can just see how *that* will go over."

"They'd better get used to it," rumbled Dennis Foster, seated next to Agnes. "People live here, they got to be responsible."

"Well, Dennis, honey, we might just have a civil war over *that* little detail. Hm? Isn't that what you're trying to avoid?"

"Honey." Dennis winked at her. "You can't keep backing down and avoid it forever. Might as well have it out now. Like Bert says, eventually we'll be faced with something more serious. Although," he glanced sideways at Agnes. "Someone pretty nearly got herself killed this time. You're chairman, Dan. And you're trained. You got to drive this. Make it happen."

"I agree. Anything else?"

"Nope. That's all."

79

Each morning, Steve made breakfast, for himself and for Dennis. It was a routine that he kept to religiously, making sure the old man ate and also making the house feel a bit less empty. Especially on Sundays.

On this Sunday, Dennis was actually cheerful.

"That's damn good coffee, son. How'd you do that?"

"Ali, at the town office, showed me her secret."

"And what's that?"

"There's an egg in it."

"An egg! No sh—No kidding."

"Yeah. Makes a difference."

"It does. You spending time with her?"

"Not really. She's a little young."

"Pretty grown up, if you ask me. Seems like good people."

"Yeah . . . You going somewhere?"

"Goin' to church, son."

"What? Seriously?"

"Seriously. Today, anyway. See you later."

Dennis rode out to the rectory.

He tied his horse and walked to the door, rapped at it, then rapped again, until the door opened and Raul appeared, looking up at him.

"Yes?"

"I want to see Marco."

"Brother Marco?"

"Get him."

Raul disappeared, and Marco came to the door.

"Brother Dennis! Come in, come in."

"Maybe it'd be better if you came out here."

Marco stepped outside.

"Close the door . . . Okay. Now, you listen to me. I don't put much stock in religion. Never did. But you probably knew that."

"But Sister Diane—"

"Leave Diane out of this."

Marco lowered his eyes, nodding respectfully.

"But no matter what I think about it, it looks like this church of yours is going to be part of the community."

"I think so. It is becoming an institution, don't you think?"

"I think it is. And I think it will be, even if you're not in it."

"And what do you mean by that, Brother Dennis?"

"I mean that I know you were the last one up there, on Service Hill, with Brother Tom."

"I don't see what—"

"You lied to Bert."

"Did I?"

"You told Bert you brought Raul down from the hill. That was a lie. Raul was already gone. I saw him run when the shit hit the fan."

"Well, I'm not so sure what you saw, Brother. It was dark. It was confusing."

"Not so dark we all couldn't get a good aim at poor old Tom. If'n it been pitch dark, he'd still be with us."

"I . . . suppose that's so."

"You were the last one. But the hell of it is, I haven't told any-one."

"And I'm not sure why you're telling me. It was a terrible thing. We all had a hand in it, to one degree or another. We all bear some responsibility. And we all have to live with our conscience. Is that not so?"

"Conscience is a funny thing, Marco. A man has to figure out what really matters to him, then stick to it. It ain't always easy."

"Was there anything else, Brother?"

"I'm not done. You're part of this community, you and your friends. Whether I like it or not. Personally, I don't think I care anymore. Some people seem to need what you have. So be it. But here's what I *do* care about. If you're going to be a part of this community, then you're going to by God *act* like part of it."

"Go on."

"Someone set fire to the barn belonging to Anderson Power and Light. Someone vandalized Steve's project. Bert's theory is it's someone who doesn't like our involvement with the City, someone who's fanatical enough to think that whatever he does is justified."

"I suppose it's possible."

"It's a good theory. And it involves you and your church. You and your preachers are telling people that the City is evil incarnate, that we all have some kind of higher duty. So maybe you're partly responsible."

"That is a serious charge."

"It's a serious business. Someone might have been killed."

The crystal eyes looked straight at him. "I won't argue with you."

"Good. And here's the thing. If you or your people have any reason to suspect one of your flock, then you have a responsibility to bring it to Bert."

"Now, that's a very fine line, my friend—"

"Yeah, life's tough! Ain't it."

Marco remained silent.

"Of course, maybe I should take my own advice. But I'm giving you a chance, to do the right thing. And one thing more." He stepped closer and lowered his voice. "No one can hurt Diane now. Steve wasn't there. And I don't care what happens to me. So maybe you better think about that."

80

About a week later, Brother Jim rode to the town office, a very troubled man.

They had argued about it violently the night before. He and Marco. Well, *he* had done the shouting. Marco had just stood there, the heavy jaw set like stone, the guttural voice adamant, while he had shouted and Raul hid somewhere in back.

In the end, it had come down to an ultimatum, and Marco delivered it with cold authority.

"Just *do* it. It has to be done. Accept it. She told *you*. No one else."

"She told me in confidence!"

"Then tell Chief Morrow in confidence! Let *him* wring the truth out of her! But *tell* him. The Church is *not* going to fall for the sake of one woman's guilty secret! I will not allow it!"

"Why should it fall?"

"For reasons that are beyond you."

It was early when he arrived at the old frame house, but three horses were already tied up outside, and his mouth turned down in disgust.

This is wrong. This is so wrong. Linda will never forgive me.

He got off his horse and tied it, walked to the door, and stood looking at it a moment.

Better hope she never finds out.

He took a breath and went inside, where he found Joe Dryden and Ben Keller sitting idly and drinking coffee.

"Mornin'," he mumbled.

Dryden nodded to him.

"Morning."

"Ah . . . Bert Morrow in?"

"Bert?" Keller looked up. "You been robbed, Brother?"

"Uh . . . no. Not exactly." He shoved his hands in his pockets, pulled them out again, scratched his head. "Just need to talk t'im."

"You might be a little early for Bert," chuckled Dryden.

Ali Knight came out from the alcove with a cup of coffee.

"Here you go, Brother. Have a seat. Bert should be along soon."

Jim nodded. He sat down away from the others and stared at the floor, the coffee growing cold beside him.

After a while, there were sounds of more horses outside. A handful of young men stomped noisily inside. Dryden went with them into the meeting room, carrying pages of notes.

Keller got up, stretched elaborately, sighed noisily, and went out.

Brother Jim waited.

A while later, Dryden and his crew reappeared. They went out the door, laughing, dust swirling outside as the front door closed behind them.

The office went quiet again. Ali came over and sat down beside him.

"Sorry, Brother. He should've been here by now."

"Well, not your fault, Miss Ali."

"You don't like coffee?"

"Ah . . . forgot about it."

"Want some hot?"

"Don't believe I do. Maybe I'd better come back."

But the front door opened and Bert stepped inside, and Ali jumped to her feet, Jim wincing as she loudly accosted the Chief of Police.

"Bert Morrow! Brother Jim's been waiting *all* morning for you!"

Jim slapped his knees and stood up.

"It's okay, Miss Ali. It's okay."

They sat in the meeting room with the door closed. Brother Jim was hunched over the table, staring in silence at a spot somewhere in front of him.

Bert waited a bit, then cleared his throat.

Jim spoke without moving.

"This isn't easy."

"Well, take your time."

"Uh . . ." he looked up at Bert. "You know Jack and Linda Harper, don't you?"

"I certainly do."

"Well, it's about their boy. Little John."

Bert settled back in his chair. If Jack Harper was beating his son . . .

"Chief Morrow . . . I . . . Linda told me something in confidence. She came to me for counseling. If there's any way you can look into this without telling her how you found out . . ."

"I can try. I can't promise anything."

"I know. But if you could try."

"Look, Brother. I can see something's eating you. Why don't you just tell me what it is?"

Jim closed his eyes.

"It's about the arson."

It felt like he had been punched. It was hard to breathe. "Go on."

"You have to realize . . . the Harpers are a troubled family. It's everything poor Linda can do to . . . well—"

"What about the goddamned arson!"

Brother Jim sank in his chair.

"She thinks . . . she thinks Little John may have . . . Little John and another boy, Ben Miller."

"Linda tell you this?" A bleak nod. "Why?"

"She doesn't know what to do! She hasn't told Jack. She's afraid to."

"She has reason. But how does she know? Did the boy tell her?"

"No. Maybe. I don't think so."

"So why does she think he's involved?"

"Well, Little John sneaks out at night a lot. She doesn't say anything, but she knows. Jack is usually drinking and falls asleep, and she lets him sleep. The boy goes with Ben Miller, and sometimes they get into a little trouble. They got caught peeping in a girl's window one night—"

"Yeah, I know. What about the arson?"

"The day after it happened, when she picked up his dirty clothes, they smelled of kerosene. She confronted him, asked him why they smelled like that. He said he couldn't smell it—probably couldn't, you know, if he'd been wearing them. But he got pretty surly. Called her some things I don't want to repeat. Jack heard it and beat him silly. The boy hasn't talked to her since."

"And you're sure about this? You're sure this is what she said?"

"Chief Morrow! I can't get it out of my head! Of course I'm sure!"

"All right, Brother. I won't mention you. But she'll probably guess."

"I know, I know. God help me."

81

Brother Craig was very, very interested in the papers Raul had to show him. Nothing came of it, so far as Raul was concerned. But that didn't matter. He hadn't expected anything. Not just yet. He still had Tony, and for the moment it was enough to sit so close to Brother Craig and be at the center of his attention.

Well, almost the center.

That was enough, for now.

It was ten blocks. That was the distance from the bus stop to the hotel. Just ten blocks of mostly empty pavement. Ten blocks from gardens and skyscrapers and reflecting pools, to an unheated room on a nameless street that was his real home, and the cold, hard reality of forgotten alleys and discarded people.

Someday, maybe someday soon, there would be a lot more.

They had sold *wire* to people outside the City. And not just once. Deadly in so many ways, now *wire* was spreading. And why? So people would not have to go without sugar and coffee. And gasoline.

He wasn't clear on who was responsible. But clearly they were amoral. And weak. And the result would be destruction. Because that was all *wire* was good for. It was only a matter of time, of how many people would be sacrificed. How many thousands.

Even in Andersonville. Andersonville was too close. He thought of the fields and the pub and the people he had met, and felt physically ill.

The storefront mission passed by. He recalled what Carol had told him, that the Word had opened her eyes. But still she did not see. They were hostages, everyone in that mission, the unthinking means towards an end they could not grasp.

He remembered telling Brother Jim that he, Craig Olsen, was not afraid of the truth, because he was not a hostage to the City. Jim should have laughed. The truth was far larger, far worse, than anything he had imagined.

If evil is a deadly worm coiled about the vital organs of a patient, then how do you remove the worm without killing the patient?

Maybe, thought Craig, you can't.

On Monday morning, he went to work as usual. He worked every day that week, as usual. He wanted to be sure.

But on Friday, after work ended and the shop cleared out, he went to Dave Barton's office.

Barton plopped in his chair, rummaged in a drawer, and produced a cigarette.

He held it up.

"You know, I think we're finally running out of these things. Imagine that."

He lit it, inhaled deeply, and blew a long gray jet at the ceiling.

Craig smiled.

"You've been a good friend, Dave. You saved my life."

Barton shook his head, waving smoke away.

"What's on your mind, Craggy?"

"I have to quit."

The cigarette stopped, in mid-air. Barton stared with his mouth open, as though unfamiliar with the word.

"I hate to do it, Dave. But you won't want me here. There'll be too much trouble."

"What in blue blazes're you talking about?"

"I'm going to preach. Full time. For as long as I can."

"Are you nuts?"

"I have to."

"Craggy, people don't just quit. Get fired, yeah. But no one quits."

"I know. And I know it will make trouble for you. But I can't live with what they're doing."

"I *told* you not to get mixed up with that bunch, didn't I? You're losing perspective! You think it's the end of the world, so nothing else matters. Well, let me tell you, the world's not going to end so easy. Whatever you think is going on, in a few months you're going to find out you still have to live. You'll come crawling back here, like before. But I won't be able to do anything for you. No one will. Not if you quit like this and make trouble."

"You're probably right. But I have to do it."

"Craggy, you don't have to do *nothin'*. Just climb down off that high-horse and be human! That's all."

"I wish it were that easy."

"Why not?"

"I can't explain it to you."

"No? Then how're you going to explain it to anyone else? Huh? Tell me that!"

"Do you know where *rope* comes from? Do you know about *wire?*"

"Shit, Craggy, no. And I don't want to."

"I don't have that choice. I know already. And I'm going to tell what I know."

Barton ground out his cigarette.

"Craggy, I'm begging you. Drop it. For all of us."

Olsen got to his feet.

"I'm sorry, Dave. Thanks. For all you've done. I'm going to miss it here."

82

"You want to know what evil is?"

The crowd huddled together in a morning breeze atop Service Hill, and awaited the answer.

"In the City we all smuggled *rope,* because we all used it. It's an aphrodisiac, and we used it a lot. What we didn't know, what no one told us, was that it was also affecting our minds, making us stupid, until we were too stupid to realize it. We didn't know it was *designed* that way, to *make* us stupid. And we didn't know it was designed by the same people who made it illegal, the same executives, so we wouldn't know *who* was making us stupid.

"They made it illegal, then put people in jail and ruined their lives for doing exactly what they wanted people to do in the first place. If that isn't evil, I don't know what is.

"But that wasn't enough! They couldn't stop there. They designed another drug, called *wire. Wire* is for war. It turns soldiers into machines. They fight until they collapse. Their bodies burn out, their minds are destroyed. That's what happened to the man you call my Ghost. He could no longer speak because he had been using *wire.* And it wasn't enough to take his power of speech. They came and took his freedom too.

"Was this evil enough?

"No! Because they started selling *wire* to other places run by people like them, people who wanted *wire* for war. People who *demanded* it. That's how the City buys gasoline—selling a deadly drug to replace the gasoline they lost through their own incompetence.

"Was *this* enough? No! Because then they sent *wire* to a city called New Brighton, to pay them to open a trade route. Because the City couldn't get coffee!

"So, these . . . these *executives,* who are supposed to know everything about business, who are responsible for thousands of lives, these people are not just ruining marriages and families, they're going to bring ruin down on the entire City itself! Because they think they can't be hurt.

"But sooner or later, this drug that was designed for war will lead to war. And when that happens, the armies that take it won't stop. No one will be able to stop them. Not until they destroy everything, including themselves. It will be Cargo Flu all over again.

"This is what's coming. You can't avoid it. You can't fight it. But some of you may survive it. *If you learn Brotherhood!* If you are self-sufficient.

"I expect them to come for me, like my ghost. To kill the truth. I can't stop them. And maybe nothing can save you. But at least the Word can open your eyes.

"It opened mine."

83

The trouble with working in intelligence is that you could spend months, even years, observing something like Andersonville, developing a routine, fitting in, getting to know people. Actually having a life. And then something happens to pull that life out from under you. And leave you with nothing. Because you forgot. You don't belong.

There was something not even the army knew. Which made it very, very dangerous. But that man Craig Olsen knew it. How he found out was unclear. But he was talking, and loudly, to anyone who would listen.

This would be a difficult report to file. Such a temptation to ignore it, to pretend one didn't know. But that would be quite a foolish thing to do, because it would be discovered by someone else and reported, and probably sooner rather than later.

So there was really no choice.

Dan Carter read the latest field reports with more than a little satisfaction.

The information had surfaced.

Now for the final step. To wave an unmistakable red flag over it, one that even the army would understand, and at the same time demonstrate to Elizabeth White—and to whomever came after her—that Dan Carter had but diligently and faithfully done his duty.

84

Early September. The days were shorter, dry, pleasantly mild. Sunrise came at a more reasonable hour.

She remembered as a girl thinking it was the best part of summer.

Now it was only part of the calculation.

People would climb Service Hill as it was just beginning to turn light. The sermon would end at sunrise. The mornings were still warm enough for fellowship time to go on at least an hour. Craig Olsen would probably have breakfast at the rectory, then leave for Walsh Stables to catch the bus to the City.

That seemed her best opportunity.

She had filed her report and received new orders. There were to be no witnesses. No surviving ones. The objective was Olsen. With proper planning and a bit of luck, she might have no one else to deal with. But she was prepared.

Saturday came. Throughout the day, hour by hour, the reality of it grew, until after dinner she had to run outside and into the trees, to vomit, then stand for long minutes, shaking, cold, and lightheaded.

She went to bed early, pleading illness, then lay awake staring into the dark. When sleep finally came, it brought suffocating dreams of death and loss and aloneness, and long before dawn her eyes snapped open, a heavy pressure throbbing painfully in the middle of her chest.

With trembling hands in the dark bedroom, she dressed in silence, hardly breathing. There was no need for light, she knew the place so well, and she made her way outside, closed the front door without a sound, and put on her shoes.

From the crook of a tree she retrieved a small bundle wrapped in a dark rag. Then, with the cool breeze in her hair, she began walking. When the trail came out in the open, she checked the stars she had memorized, and continued, knowing she was on the right path and would arrive at the rectory long before sunrise.

Dan Walsh got out of bed and peered out a window. And after a minute, turned away and dressed.

His robe fluttering in the breeze, Marco saw his People gathered in the gray light atop Service Hill. Brother Jim was in the City, which was unfortunate, because today there would be a very serious talk with Brother Craig. He would have preferred it with Jim present, to reinforce the ultimatum and help Craig see reason. But he would do it himself. Raul, of course, did not count.

He sent Raul to announce it was time, then began walking, hands folded, head bowed, toward the eastern brow of the hill, the distant rim of silver light promising a new day.

Sitting cross-legged in the gray light behind some thick brush at the edge of the yard, she could just see through it to the path that led to the rectory door.

The yard was larger than she had imagined, and this worried her. Olsen would be moving, and there could be no mistakes. She decided her best opportunity was to start walking toward him when he came out after breakfast. She would be exposed for a few seconds, but it could not be avoided.

She unwrapped the black semi-automatic pistol, every edge and curve as familiar to her as her own hands, checked the magazine and slide, and set the safety. The metal as cold and smooth and heavy in her hand. It was such a well-preserved relic, she thought, from a time when they really knew how to kill people.

Marco ended his sermon as long black shadows stretched across golden meadows far below, pointing towards the sun rising in its endless cycle of renewal.

"Now go, and bring light to those still in darkness!"

"Amen!" the crowd answered, rising with smiles and hand-shakes.

Raul passed out the ceremonial bread, and people formed into knots of conversation, and the knots coalesced into groups, and one group centered on Craig Olsen. Marco, quietly congratulating a couple on the birth of a child, frowned as he caught snatches of 'New Brighton', and 'war'.

There would have to be a very serious talk after breakfast. Very serious indeed.

She awoke suddenly, her mouth dry, her legs stiff. The earth was awash with light, and she looked around, aghast, then glanced eastward. The sun was just rising in the trees.

She peered through the brush. The yard was empty.

Carefully, she shifted her position, uncramping her legs, and settled in to wait, the weight of the gun securely in her lap.

She clicked off the safety.

It would not be long now.

"I hope you will join us at breakfast this morning, Brother."

People were drifting away after fellowship, taking their leave and heading home.

Craig hesitated. He knew what Marco wanted.

But the old man smiled.

"Come now, brother. I think you owe me the courtesy."

"All right, Marco."

She stiffened. Was that a voice?

It came again, and her fingers wrapped around the grip of the pistol. Should she do it now? Or wait, and see if she could catch him alone as he left?

There was a movement through the trees, someone on the trail, and she leaned forward, peering intently through the brush.

Three figures emerged. Two she recognized instantly, Olsen and the little hermaphrodite. But the third . . .

The earth seemed to heave under her.

The three men entered the rectory, while she sat behind the brush, paralyzed, one hand on the gun, the other covering her mouth.

Raul was all smiles, sitting between Brother Marco and Brother Craig, oblivious to the strained small talk between the older men, blushing when Olsen complimented the food, pouting when they all left the table and Marco asked him to wait in another room.

In the small living area, Marco invited Craig to sit down.

He remained on his feet.

"I know what you want."

"Do you?"

"You want me to stop talking about the Corporation. About their drugs."

"It cannot continue."

"Well, I knew you would try to stop me sooner or later. I understand your position."

"Then you agree."

"No. I don't agree. But we each have to follow our own conscience."

Marco remained silent.

"I won't stop, Brother. If you want me out, I'll go. But I won't stop."

"I see. Do you understand how dangerous this is?"

"Probably better than you."

"Then . . . why?"

"Someone has to."

"But, Brother! You cannot win if you are silenced. Surely you understand that."

"I don't expect to win. I can't stop them. But if I can help even one person see the light and maybe prepare himself, it will have been worth it."

"Will it? When you might help hundreds?"

"I have to speak the truth."

Marco replied slowly.

"The truth is a tool, Brother. A dangerous one. To be used with discretion."

"And that's where we disagree, you and I."

"I can see that. I am frightened for you."

"Well, don't be. I'm doing this with my eyes open."

"Perhaps."

Craig extended his hand. "Thanks, Brother. For all you've done."

"You are very welcome, Brother Craig."

They shook hands and moved toward the door, Marco calling to Raul to come drive Brother Craig to his bus.

The door opened.

Don't think. Just do it.

Olsen appeared, and she was on her feet, coming around the brush and striding toward him.

He looked up, startled, his step slowing as Marta raised the pistol and in mid-stride squeezed the trigger. The recoil stopped her cold as the shot boomed across the yard, and a spasm contorted Olsen's face. He staggered back. His eyes rolled up, and he fell over.

Behind him stood Marco, transfixed.

She screamed:

"Father!"

Marco stared, sudden recognition lighting his eyes.

"Marta! My little Marta! You're alive! . . . My dearest, dearest little Marta—"

She shot him. For a long moment, nothing happened. The wonder in his eyes did not change. Then his face went slack, the great jaw fell, and he collapsed in a heap, a bright red stain spreading across the white robe.

Something crashed through the trees, and she spun around.

"Oh my God! *No, Daniel! No!*"

"Marta! Sweet Jesus, what have you done?"

"Stay back!" she screamed, and he stopped, still yards away, staring at the gun in her hand.

"Turn around, Daniel. Turn around, m'love."

"My God! What are you doing?"

"Please, please, m'love. Turn around."

"No, Marta!"

"Then, lover, I'm afraid you'll have to watch."

She raised the gun to her head.

He sprinted for her.

She stood straight, and closed her eyes.

85

There was a window. Some sort of gauzy curtain. Rectangles of light on the floor, and specks of dust drifting through the light. A floor of dull boards worn dark, little black holes where the nails were.

There was a door, with a kind of crude latch. Voices on the other side.

It looked like a small room in the rectory.

Then there was a quiet sound, and a pressure on his shoulder.

"Dan."

Walsh looked up at Dennis Foster.

"Dan, can you hear me?"

"Yeah, I can hear you."

"That's good, son."

He looked across the room, expecting to see through the open doorway. But it was closed, and he sat back and rubbed his face.

"What do you want, Dennis?"

"Son, you need to bury her. Soon. You understand that, don't you?"

He put a hand over his eyes. He could not answer.

"Listen to me, son. I made them cover her. No one can see her."

"Okay. Thanks."

"And they're making a shroud, so we can move her. Okay?"

"Yeah . . . okay. How did you get here?"

"Del came and got me. Dan, listen to me. Aren't many people around here who truly understand what you're going through. Listen to me. Don't bury her alone."

Walsh looked up, and saw pain in Dennis Foster's eyes. An old pain.

"Are you offering?"

"I am."

"All right, Dennis. But just you. No one else."

"And Steve."

"And Steve."

When Dennis left him, he was beginning to understand the word brotherhood.

———————————

They buried her the next day, at sunset, in the trees behind Walsh's home.

Dennis and Steve lowered the body wrapped in its white shroud, and waited in silence for Walsh to bend down and toss in a spade of dirt. Then the Foster men joined, and daylight faded to the rustling fall of earth.

———————————

Early Tuesday morning, Johnny Gelpin arrived at the Stables and found Walsh at the barn.

"Say, boss," Johnny ventured, climbing off his horse. "You okay? We can handle this, Pete and I."

Walsh had unlocked the door, but he stopped.

"You listen to me, Johnny. Listen. The last thing I want from you, or from anyone else, is your pity. Got that?"

"Uh . . . yeah. Okay, boss."

There was a long, awkward silence. Then Walsh nodded, and opened the door.

86

The last Saturday in September, late in a gray afternoon, as Walsh opened the weekly Committee meeting, a steady autumn rain came down outside the windows.

There was routine business, which he presided over with a kind of quiet dignity, while the other members watched him and tried to hide it, as though expecting something to happen.

Nothing did.

When the meeting broke up, Max waited behind while the others left. Walsh got to his feet, gathered his notes, and glanced at Max.

"Well?"

"Dan, there's nothing I can possibly say."

"No, there isn't."

Walsh stood a moment looking at the papers in his hand, then tossed them on the table.

"Well, I suppose you should know. I'm going to resign."

"Yeah. I was afraid of that."

Moving to the window behind him, Walsh leaned against the sill and peered outside. Rain drummed gently against the glass.

"I don't think I care anymore."

"Dan, what are you going to do?"

"Does it matter?"

"Yeah. Yeah, I think it does."

Outside the meeting room, in the front office, they could hear Ali humming, a simple progression of sound with a quiet reason of its own. An answer, maybe, to the steady rain.

"Well, I'm not going to kill myself, if that's what you're thinking."

"That's good."

"I thought you'd try to talk me out of it. Resigning."

"If I could think of a way, I would."

Walsh nodded, still peering out the window.

"Dan . . . a couple of years ago, I was ready to give up. And I was going to do something . . . well, something pretty bad. Hell, I'd already done some pretty bad things. But this was different. Because I just couldn't go on. I thought the world was going to hell, I couldn't understand why, and I wanted it to go on without me. But something happened, out there in Westboro. I learned something."

"Yeah?" Walsh muttered, still gazing outside. "What was that?"

"I'm probably not saying this right. I've never tried to explain it before. But I learned—I learned that the only world that really matters, is the one you make for yourself."

There was no answer.

Max took a breath.

"I knew I wouldn't say it right. Sure, a tree might fall on you, or a horse might kick you, and there's nothing you can do about it. There's a real world. But there's more to it. You're alone. And things don't just happen. You make choices along the way. Sometimes because you're reacting, without thinking. And sometimes because you *see* something, and bring it to life. You know what I mean? You build your own world. Like weaving a fabric, thread by thread. Whether it ends up what you wanted, or not. What I learned is, *that's* what matters. That's what you work for. Your own world."

Walsh seemed not to have heard. Now he turned and looked across the room, as though at someone entering.

"I'm really sorry, Dan. I know I'm not making any sense. I'll shut up now."

"No . . . it's not that. I was remembering something Marta said."

The rain drummed against the window, a steady, monotonous sound, of waiting. Of anticipation.

Walsh seemed to come back to himself. He looked at Max.

"Thanks. Thank you for that. You're a good man."

87

Mitch Miller had the reputation of a dour man.

A few years back he lost his wife to pneumonia, and started drinking. The drinking turned hard. Thirteen-year-old Ben, searching for him one morning, had discovered his father in the stable behind the pub, asleep with the horses and reeking of vomit and manure. Miller had staggered to his feet and swore to the boy that not another drop would ever pass his lips.

He had kept his word, and Bert Morrow could respect that.

But Bert was more interested in Ben, who must be seventeen now or thereabouts, and whom he had not seen since the wife passed.

Early on a frosty Sunday in October, Bert climbed Service Hill in the dark. He nodded to the astonished Del and Rosie Flores, and looked around at dozens of barely-visible gray figures. One pair standing apart caught his eye, and he recognized the stiffly straight back and squared shoulders of Mitch Miller. Next to him was someone just as tall, and of similar bearing, but considerably leaner.

Yup. Chip off the old block. That must be Ben.

Service began. The horizon slowly brightened. Bert stayed at the back of the crowd and watched Mitch, and especially Ben, watched them sit and kneel and stand at the appropriate times—and noted the way Ben knelt, hands clasped tight, head bowed as though in pain. When the first rays of sunlight struck the hill and Brother Jim finished, for long seconds Ben remained on his knees, gazing at the rising sun, as though alone with it.

Then it was fellowship time.

Bert waited by himself, and continued watching. When Ben Miller caught his steady gaze, the young man froze, eyes wide, then turned abruptly, his back even straighter, his head a little higher. Little John Harper came up to him, but Ben angrily shook his head and walked off.

A short distance away, Linda Harper looked at Bert, a quiet desperation in her eyes.

It was enough.

Bert spent a number of days thinking. Then he talked with Dan Walsh, and thought some more. He said nothing to anyone else, until he was ready.

He rode out to the Harper place, accompanied by three deputies. He pounded the door, and told Linda he wanted to speak with Little John. Alone.

Red-eyed and pasty-faced, Jack Harper came stomping to the door from somewhere in back, shoved Linda aside, and demanded, "What d'*you* want? What's he done?"

"I need to speak to him."

"Well, you can speak to me!"

"Are you taking responsibility?"

"For what?"

"For whatever he's done."

"Well, you tell me what you think he's done!"

Bert shook his head.

"This is serious, Jack. I'm trying to help, all I can. But I have to question him. Either here, or I can take him to the Town Office."

"Like hell!"

"Either I talk to him here, or I have to arrest him."

"Like *hell!*"

"I have to, Jack. I can't let him run away."

"Why should he run?"

"He's afraid. And he has reason. This is serious."

It was only then that Jack Harper seemed to take in the two deputies standing behind Bert, armed with rifles. Glaring, flushed red from the neck up, he stepped back.

When Bert walked into his room, Little John was sitting on his bed, staring at the deputy plainly visible outside through the window.

Bert shut the door and leaned against it, arms folded.

"I know what happened, son."

The boy seemed to stop breathing.

Bert shifted his position, bending a little closer to the shrinking huddle that was Little John Harper.

"Ben told us."

"He—No! I want my dad!"

"I came here to help, son. Your friend confessed. He told us everything. But I think he lied about something." Bert paused to let this sink in. "He said it was your idea."

"*No!*"

"Well, that's what I thought. He's older than you."

"He wouldn't say that!"

"He's pretty scared, son. I feel sorry for him. But he's in an awful lot of trouble, and he's scared."

"I want my dad!"

"Your dad can't help. But maybe I can."

"What're you going to do?"

"I don't think it was your idea. I think it was Ben's."

Little John was shaking.

"Are you willing to stand up for yourself, tell us it wasn't your idea?"

"It wasn't my idea!"

"You know who Dan Walsh is, don't you? He's head of the Town. He's also a lawyer. I want you to tell it to him." Bert opened the door a crack and called, "Send in Dan Walsh."

Little John gaped, eyes round, maybe terrified at hearing someone else give orders inside the Harper house. Or maybe it was being confronted by two strange men in his own room. But bit by bit, the boy stammered out the story.

Walsh wrote it down, asked him to read it, and then sign it.

The boy complied, shaking badly.

Bert put a friendly hand on his shoulder.

"You did the right thing. Now don't go and do anything stupid, like run away. You know you did something wrong. But maybe we can sort it out. Okay? I'm going to leave one of my deputies here. If you have any questions, you ask him. All right?"

The two men left the house, ignoring Jack Harper's sullen questions.

Outside, as they untied their horses, Walsh asked, "Now Ben Miller?"

"Now Ben Miller."

The Miller place was a ways south of the main road, tucked into the rolling hills east of Thomas Abbey. Two sprawling ranches occupied nearly all of a vale maybe a half-mile across at its widest, while the Millers managed on a few acres at the far end, growing hay and vegetables.

Bert, Dan Walsh, and two deputies rode the length of the vale, passing by pastures dotted with sheep and cows chewing idly near a rail fence. An unpainted barn rose up ahead, big wooden doors now swung open, and a long hay cart.

A small, bare house stood behind the barn.

Mitch Miller came out as the party rode into the yard. He squinted, scratching at his short, gray hair.

"Bert Morrow. What can I do for you?"

"Hello, Mitch."

"Dan Walsh, too. This a social call?"

"You don't know why we're here? Ben here hasn't told you?"

Miller turned around. His son was standing a few feet behind and glaring at the Chief with undisguised contempt.

"Ben?"

The boy remained silent.

Bert watched him complacently. "You know why we're here, don't you. Well, we've heard Little John's side of it. Want to tell us yours?"

Miller chewed his lip. "Side of what?"

"The arson, Mitch."

The word fell like a knife. Mitch Miller took a step toward his son.

"What's he talking about?" Ben shrugged, and Miller raised his voice. "Well, they didn't come all the way out here for *nothing,* did they?"

"Maybe they did."

Leather creaked as Bert eased forward on the horn of his saddle, peering intently at Ben.

"Don't have the courage I thought you had." The boy's head seemed turn against his will, until he was looking straight at Bert and sneering hatred. "I thought conviction had something to do with it. Guess I was wrong."

Warily, Miller asked, "You guessing about this, Bert?"

"Afraid not. I told Little John that Ben here confessed. That he told us it was Little John's idea. That scared him, shook him up pretty bad. Enough to spill the story. But I'm willing to listen to Ben's side of it."

Miller closed his eyes.

Ben sprinted for the barn.

The deputies leaped down with their rifles, but Miller held up his hands.

"Bert! Bert! He's my son! God help me. Let me handle this."

Miller walked to the barn. Inside, Ben whirled to face him, a badly-rusted rifle in his hands.

"Put it down, son."

Ben raised the weapon across his chest, as though it might shield him.

"Put it down."

Eyes wild, Ben Miller shook his head, backing away as Miller walked steadily toward him. When just a few steps remained, and with his back against a wall, Ben threw down the weapon.

Miller put his arms around him.

They sat around the Miller's kitchen table, except for the two deputies stationed outside the house. Everyone seemed to face Bert unconsciously, as though in the presence of a presiding judge.

Miller asked, "What are you going to do?"

"Well, we're mighty lucky, Mitch. No one was hurt."

"Amen to that."

"Dan and I think we might be able to settle it, if the Millers and Harpers are willing to replace what was destroyed and stolen."

Miller blew out his cheeks.

"That'll be a burden, I can tell you. No two ways about it. We don't have much in the way of money."

"You have two strong backs. That ought to be worth something."

"I suppose that's true, although the farm here takes just about everything we have."

"Well, Mitch, I'm willing to listen. You know this has to be paid for."

"I know."

Walsh drummed his fingers.

"You know, Ben could help by taking a job over the winter. I'll bet Max could arrange one in the City. He has contacts. A little City money could go a long way here."

Ben looked stricken. "But they're *evil!*"

Suddenly, Mitch Miller shouted, "*Son!* They're *people!* People! Like us! Some do evil. Most don't. Just like us!"

"Come out to the Stables, Ben. You'll see a lot of City people there, and you might be surprised. In fact, you can work for me next summer, if Mitch can get by on weekends."

"I'll get by."

"That's slavery!"

"It's *punishment,*" intoned Bert. "And it could be a lot worse. You'll probably have to do a lot of work you don't want to for a couple of years. But in the old days they would have locked you up in a cage they called a jail for a whole lot longer. Maybe until you were an old man."

Looking at his son, Miller replied, "We'll do what we have to. And consider ourselves lucky."

Bert gently slapped the kitchen table and stood up.

"I'll take that as a promise. I can't guarantee anything. It's going to be tough for some people to swallow. Steve Foster's plans may be ruined. And Agnes might have been killed. But the way I see it, we all don't have a lot of good options."

————————————

Outside the Millers' house, Walsh waited while Bert instructed his deputies to relieve the other at the Harper place. The two mounted up and galloped north, the way they had come.

Bert watched as they rode off, his shoulders slumping.

Walsh walked up to him and slapped his back.

"You okay? You pulled it off, man! You got to the bottom of it! I had no idea you were this devious."

"I don't like to be."

They mounted up and headed north, passing through the vale at a trot, until they were in the trees and forced into single file along the winding trail, Bert leading the way in silence.

At the main road, they turned west, and Walsh caught up and rode alongside him.

"You know, Bert, I should feel relieved. And I do. But this whole thing scares hell out of me."

"Why's that?"

"Well, think about it. If the barn had been completely destroyed, it might have looked more like an accident. Or Ben Miller could have done it on his own, without Little John. Then we might never have learned the truth. And it's still not over."

"Nope. It's not over. But we do have the truth."

"We've been damned lucky."

"We have. And—don't take this the wrong way, Dan, but I have to say it—I've done my job. I think we can work out a settlement. But I still don't have a way to charge those boys with a crime. I don't have the authority. It's between the Harpers and the Millers and AP&L. Like you say, it looks like we're lucky this time. But what about next time? And there *will* be a next time. You know that."

"I know, I know. Max started in on me weeks ago. I can get somewhere with Sandy. I just can't get Amalia or Bill on board. Amalia especially. She's afraid the town will blow up if we vote more laws."

"I don't see what choice there is."

"I hear you. But she's pretty stubborn."

"Well, there's one way to deal with that."

"Yeah? How?"

"Get her off the Committee."

"Um, yeah. Might be easier said than done."

"Well, you know what Dennis says."

"No. What does Dennis say?

"Life's tough, ain't it."

Walsh laughed.

He pulled in his reins and laughed until tears rolled down his face, and Bert urged his horse closer.

"Buddy . . . Christ, you okay?"

"Yeah." Walsh wiped his eyes. "Oh, Jesus. I haven't had a laugh like that since . . . well, since Marta."

"Sorry. Didn't mean to bring that up."

"No, it's all right—Bert?"

But then Walsh heard it too. A distant shout.

Bert kicked his horse and the animal bolted toward the trail that led to the Harper place. Another shout, the words more distinct, and Walsh spurred his own animal.

Bert stopped for his deputy racing to meet them, but Walsh surged past them and onto the trail, shouting and kicking his horse into a frenzy, branches lashing as he bent low, the single word *No!* echoing through his brain as they burst from the trees with the Harper house dead ahead.

He jerked the terrified animal to a halt, leaped to the ground, and sprinted—but something dragged at him—two deputies holding him back. He wrestled with them, trying to free himself, until he grasped what they were saying.

"He's armed! He's armed!"

Walsh stopped struggling.

His throat rasped. "What happened?"

Cautiously, they let go, watching him, still alert. One answered.

"Jack started in on Little John. Knocked him down. Linda got in the way and he just went wild. Knocked her out cold. Might have killed her."

"Then what? What's he doing now?"

"Don't know. He's got Little John, and he's got a gun. He threatened to shoot, and I got out while I could."

Walsh glanced at the rifle in his hand.

"That loaded?"

The deputy's eyes flickered down to his weapon, and in one irresistible motion Walsh seized it and sprinted for the house. The door jumped from its latch at the impact of his foot, and then he was inside, bellowing, *"No!"*

The first image to enter his awareness was Linda Harper sprawled out on the floor.

The next was Little John, cowering in a corner.

Then Jack Harper. And a rifle swinging up.

But Walsh's rifle was at his shoulder, and he emptied it, the trigger rattling uselessly after the crash of shots died away.

Only then did the body of Jack Harper slide to the floor.

Little John screamed, and screamed again.

Walsh stood in a cloudy haze. Out of it, the homely figure of Bert Morrow moved to Linda, crouching by her. Someone else was pulling the screaming boy from the room.

He turned. He walked through the open door, out into blinding sunlight. He felt soft earth beneath his feet, and stopped.

His throat was on fire. His ears rang. He saw the rifle in his hand, saw something falling through the air, glittering like crystals and leaving dark streaks on the barrel.

Then a movement, a deputy nearby, standing there with fear in his eyes, but standing there nonetheless, one hand extended in silence.

Dan Walsh lifted the rifle.

The young man nodded, as the weight of the rifle passed from one to the other.

88

It was a few days later.

At the sound of the door closing firmly from the outside, the meeting room grew very quiet, and Chairman Dan Walsh gravely considered the seven people sitting along one side of the meeting table across from the Committee.

To his left were Steve and Agnes, to his right the Millers and the Harpers. Between them sat Ali Knight, looking more than a little nervous.

Which was, thought Walsh, as it should be.

He let the silence draw out. No one moved, except Little John Harper, confused and frightened, looking up from time to time at Ben Miller beside him, as if at an unexpected stranger.

Linda Harper stared at her hands. She was pale, vacant, and had not uttered a word since arriving with Little John. Walsh wondered if whatever was left of her was capable of comprehending what was about to take place. It was a dimension to the problem he had not considered. In the end, Linda didn't matter. That was the cold truth. But he needed her.

"All right." He looked from face to face. "Everyone understands why we're here."

Mitch Miller swallowed. Linda seemed to nod, a little.

"The Compact of the Town of Andersonville vests the power to create courts of law with the Town Committee. We have not done so." Walsh looked briefly at Cotter, McCane, and Hanover beside him. Amalia returned his gaze, her eyes steady and level as if with a challenge. But she remained silent.

"Now we have a problem before us, one we can not allow to go unanswered. There has been injury, and it must be redressed. Each of us on the Committee has taken an oath, to fulfill duties of care and loyalty to this town, under the law and the Compact. We have neglected our duty of care, which can not be denied. We are obliged now to rectify this neglect. And we will do so, beginning with the case before us.

"Lacking a court of law, it falls to the Committee to right the wrong by seeing to it the injury is redressed. And while I can promise you that I personally will not rest until a court of law *is* finally established in Andersonville, I can in no way guarantee when it will be.

"But the injured parties are entitled to more than promises.

"As well, our town! Our *town* is entitled to more. We lack a specific law dealing with the crime of arson, but it is clear that arson, and destruction of property, and recklessly endangering lives, threaten the town far beyond any individual injury so caused. This is *not* a private matter. It affects us all. The town as a whole has a legitimate interest. And rightfully it was our town police who obtained evidence, and ultimately confessions, and brought these before the Committee."

Ben Miller had entered the room with an Olympian scowl, head high, but as Walsh spoke had begun to look as though the air were leaking out of him.

Little John appeared in a state of shock, from time to time turning to gape at his mother.

Strangely, Linda was beginning to look a little more *present*, her eyes now focused on Walsh.

"Therefore," Walsh continued, "this is what we propose to do. We will hold a hearing on the facts of this case. The Committee will then order defendants and plaintiffs to adjourn to reach an agreement for restitution. If they are unable to do so, the Committee will reach its own decision on the matter. Either way, the Committee will then vote formally on whether to accept the resolution, free defendants from further liability, and stop plaintiffs from further claims arising from the immediate facts. If the vote carries, the resolution will have the force of law throughout the Town of Andersonville, and will be enforced by its officers. But if the vote fails, we will start over. And we *will* continue, until we *reach* a resolution."

He paused. He could feel Agnes watching him, her eyes intent and shining in a way that left him distinctly uncomfortable, and he looked away from her, trying to dismiss it.

"I said to you that this is what we propose. Because before proceeding, we require the agreement of plaintiffs and defendants. They must agree that what we are about to do is in the interest of justice. That they will abide by the final outcome, whatever it is."

Immediately Linda nodded.

"Yes. I do."

Glancing at Agnes, Steve murmured, *"I* do."

"I agree," she answered.

Mitch Miller nodded.

Ben Miller said nothing. Little John looked up at him, his young face ashen. Mitch put a hand on Ben's shoulder, but Ben shrugged it off, roughly.

Walsh considered him.

"Son, if you can think of a better alternative, then tell us. Because I can't."

Still Ben said nothing.

"What should we *do?*" Transfixed on Ben hunkered down and silent, Little John moaned. "Why did you tell them *I* thought of it? I didn't!"

Then Ben looked at him.

"Oh, you little dope! That's how they tricked you."

"They . . ." Little John swallowed. "They killed Dad. They *killed* him! I don't know what to do . . ."

"Well, Ben?" Walsh spoke evenly. "It looks like it's up to you. Your decision."

Red patches rose in Ben Miller's face. Little John, sitting beside him, was slowly falling to pieces. Tears were dripping from his face.

"You made a mistake, son. But you have a chance to make it right. Give yourself that chance. You can still have a life."

Abruptly, the Olympian scowl returned, and Ben Miller laughed.

"You call *this* a life? *This?*" He waved vaguely at the room.

"Son, everyone in this room started with nothing. You're coming to be a man. You're strong, you're intelligent. You'll be able to *make* a life, trust me. And if you don't like Andersonville, after you're released you can go where you please. No one will stand in your way."

"And go where? The *City?* That cesspool?"

"The point is, you'll be a free man. *A free man.* Free to go or to stay. You'll be a citizen of Andersonville. That won't change."

Little John sobbed, sinking lower in his chair, and Ben watched the boy dissolve into silent weeping, head down, his shoulders jerking spasmodically. Linda reached to stroke her son's hair, looking up at Ben with a helpless, silent plea.

And Ben Miller put an arm around Little John's shoulders.

"Ah, Johnny, Johnny, Johnny . . . don't worry, Johnny. It wasn't your fault."

To Walsh, "Let him go. I'll do whatever you want, but let Johnny go. He didn't know any better."

Walsh answered carefully. "That is something you will all decide together . . . Ali."

She looked at him and blinked, then remembered, grabbed the papers in front of her, and stood up, and went from defendants to plaintiffs, handing out pages.

"You sign two copies and keep one . . . Agnes, Steve, you each sign for yourselves and for your companies."

Pens were passed around. Linda helped Little John, pointing to where he should sign, all the while stroking his hair. Ali collected the copies and sat down again.

"Everyone accounted for?" asked Walsh, and she nodded. "All right! Now listen to me. This coming Saturday, at eight o'clock in the morning, in this room, we will hold a hearing. We will take evidence and testimony. You are each commanded to appear. The

Town Secretary will record the proceeding, the evidence, and the testimony. You will each receive copies. On Saturday, two weeks hence, you will again appear in this room and together present your proposed restitution. Is that clear? Do you understand, each of you, that you are legally bound to appear as ordered?"

He lifted a hand, paused a moment, then smacked it down.

"We are adjourned."

Agnes rode to the pub.

Max was eating dinner, and she walked to his table and sat down.

There was an odd light in her eyes, and he asked, "Everything okay?"

"I . . . well . . . oh God! Dan was magnificent!"

"Oh? How did it go?"

"Everyone signed."

"Well, that's good. But no one really had much choice, did they? When you come down to it."

"No, but . . . it almost blew up. But it didn't. And you know, they didn't sign just because there wasn't much choice."

"No?"

"No. Something happened today. I think everyone realized they're living in a new world. And Dan is the reason. They *listened* to him. They really *listened*. He was amazing. I wish . . . I wish Marta . . . I just wish she could have seen it."

"Yeah?" Max smiled. "You're not falling for him, are you?"

"What? Oh, don't talk nonsense! I've already fallen for someone."

"Yeah. I have that same problem."

89

Elizabeth White sat in a large conference room, scanning through the latest farm production figures. She glanced at her watch, and frowned.

Those damned army people were late.

Her two security men stood at ease at one end of the room, gazing straight ahead, respectfully, not glancing at her. But she felt the question in the glance that wasn't there, and decided she was not going to be embarrassed in front of her own guards. In another minute, she would leave. The minute passed, she heard footsteps enter the room, and presently looked up at four of the company captains standing across the table from her.

She composed herself into the proper expression of impatience, tapping the table with her pen, a not-too-subtle command to sit down and get on with it.

They remained standing.

It was Raddick who spoke.

"Ms. White."

"I would like an explanation, Captain."

Slowly, he smiled, and in a way she found patronizing and offensive. Insolent. She gathered her notes. She would not tolerate this. She would deal with them later.

"Ms. White, this is not the meeting you were expecting. This is *our* meeting."

"Oh, *is* it." She rose to her feet.

"We're here to ask you, very politely, to step down."

"You . . . what? Step down—from what?"

"From your job. Your position. CEO."

"Captain, have you lost your mind?"

"I'm trying to make this as easy as possible. But we can do it any way you like."

"Captain! I will deal with you later."

She picked up her things, just as a half-dozen soldiers entered the room.

Her bodyguards blinked.

Raddick pointed to them.

"*You two,* stand down. Get out. Now."

The guards looked at each other. They looked at the soldiers, one of whom, older than the others, cocked an eye at them.

They got out.

"Captain! Do you understand what you are doing?"

"That I do."

"You cannot do this."

"We're doing it."

"You cannot! You must listen to reason."

She jerked back as Raddick slammed the table.

"*You* listen! You're *finished!* I *knew* it was a mistake to let you buy gas with *wire.* Because you sure as shit couldn't stop there, *could* you?"

"Captain, you have no idea how complicated this is."

"And you have no idea what you're doing! You think it's crazy you're being tossed out by the military? How about the whole City being overrun by somebody *else's* military? Using our *wire?* Before we even know what's hit us? That's what *you've* done!"

She looked from one to the other, searching for an uncertain face.

"Where is Captain Vick?"

"Resigned."

She sneered, because now she was frightened.

"Well, at least *one* of you has retained his sanity!"

"He's resigned, because he's going to be the new CEO."

90

Marco lived.

Raul, silent and terrified, nursed him for weeks, never leaving the rectory. Brother Jim brought supplies every few days, and watched in disbelief as the old man regained consciousness, then was able to sit up, then began moving about with Raul to assist him.

And one frozen Sunday in January, after Brother Jim concluded service in the yard outside, Marco made an appearance, leaning on Raul, waving and smiling as the crowd applauded.

Jim kept him up to date, bringing news regularly.

"There's a new CEO in the City."

"Oh?"

"Someone named Vick. Gregory Vick."

"Have you met him?"

"I have, and he's got me worried. I don't think he's in favor of the missions."

"What did you tell him?"

"The usual things. Salvaging the lost. Having a presence. Keeping watch. He said he would 'take it under advisement'. I suppose that means he'll let us know what he decides."

Marco sighed.

"All right. How is attendance?"

"Some of our City brothers and sisters are coming back, but they're scared. I try to reassure them. I tell them how we're working with the City, trying to meet the Corporation halfway. Hopefully, the word will spread."

"Yes. Hopefully."

"What about you, Brother? How's your strength?"

The old man grimaced. "It may be a while before I climb Service Hill again."

"Well, don't you worry about a thing. There are some very promising brothers at the Abbey. Very promising. We'll keep it going."

"I know you will."

Max Wyse rode a bus for the first time in his life. Or at least, that he could remember.

He had been to the City before, of course, and he thought of that during the short trip from Walsh Stables, of how much closer the City was now, how much it was becoming a part of life in Andersonville. Maybe it was appropriate he was taking his first bus ride to meet with a new generation of Corporate leadership.

He got off in front of the headquarters tower and checked in at the security desk.

Bill Baird came down to meet him.

"Well, well! Max! How are you? Any trouble with the buses?"

"None at all. Felt a little different, that's all."

"I'll bet it did. Can I get you anything? Coffee? No? Are you ready?"

"Ready as I'll ever be."

Baird led him to an elevator. Max winced as the door slid shut, but found himself completely at ease as the floor smoothly accelerated under his feet. He looked up and watched the numbers rapidly changing.

They got off. Baird led him to the boardroom, showed him in, and left, closing the door behind.

There was only Vick, standing by the windows, and Max walked to him. They shook hands, and Vick nodded at the view outside.

"It's a big place."

Max looked down, at buildings that marched into the distance, block after city block. He thought of the thousands of inhabitants, of the organization that bound them all together, and he thought back to the dark night he had met Vick for the first time, in that forgotten outpost where he had been hiding James Dornan.

"It's a long way from Westboro, Captain."

"It's not 'Captain' anymore. I resigned my commission to take this job. It's just Vick now. Or Greg."

"Okay . . . Greg."

"Shall we sit?"

They sat by the table, their chairs swiveled to let them watch the horizon.

"You know, Max, we're going to be making some changes."

"Sure. Which ones do I have to worry about?"

"I don't have a list, as yet. Although I'm thinking about closing those church missions."

"Oh?"

"What's your opinion?"

"I'm not religious. Never had much to do with them."

"Does that mean you have no opinion?"

"Well . . . you know, sometimes I just wish people would give up the old superstitions. Or whatever it is. But they don't. Maybe they can't."

"I suppose it's a comfort to some."

"Or maybe life makes more sense to them when they imagine it to be so." But he thought of Dennis Foster, and Dan Walsh, and others he had known.

"The trouble is," Vick went on, "it was getting out of hand. I know what happened in Andersonville. The arson. That kind of fanaticism is dangerous. You found them, didn't you?"

"Right. Two teenaged boys."

"I understand there was almost a riot when they confessed."

"No, nothing like that. It got a little ugly, but they're working it out."

"It's the sort of thing I want to avoid."

"Well, Capt— Greg. Keep in mind, the church helped us find them."

"Something to think about, I suppose. So, tell me what you'd want to see from me. What changes do *you* think are needed?"

"Me? *I* don't know anything about the City! I have my hands full in Andersonville."

"Well, if you could ask for any one thing, what would you want to see from Dornan?"

"Dornan?"

"The City. We had a public ceremony and announced a new name when we announced the change in leadership. Tried to reassure people."

"Sorry I missed it."

"Sorry I didn't invite you. What's your answer?"

"You really want to know?"

"That's why I'm asking."

"Get it together. Get the City, get Dornan, standing on its own. Because if you go down, you'll take the rest of us down with you."

"That's my mission."

"And one more thing." He paused, searching for the words, while Vick watched him. "We're not just a bunch of homesteaders now. We have laws. And even if we're still finding our way, everyone has to abide by them. Including people from the City. Including your security agents, if you send them. If someone breaks a law in Andersonville, they'll answer to Andersonville."

Vick nodded.

"Understood."

91

That winter, people found old electric heaters and tried to use them on AP&L power, but the system wouldn't hold. Lights dimmed and went out up and down the line. Agnes and her part-time 'engineers' had to go out each day to check meters and track down illicit heaters. People grumbled, but she and Josh and Carl explained, patiently but firmly, that service was for lights only, until the company could upgrade its lines and its contract with Dornan.

The company was storing tools and materials in a temporary shelter rigged up with lumber from the barn, but with spring approaching and with money coming in, Agnes signed a contract with Foster Building for a log structure, for offices and storage, and by the end of April, trees were being felled.

One night, there was a clunk at Max's door at the back of the pub.

"Come in!"

He had been expecting Agnes, and heard her voice— "I *can't!*"
—and went to the door.

It opened easily.

She stood there with a glass of wine in each hand, and he laughed and pulled her inside, kissing her as she held the glasses out of the way.

"What's the occasion?"

She handed him a glass. "Happy birthday."

"How do *you* know when my birthday is? *I* don't know when it is."

"From now on it's today. For two reasons. Number one, today is my birthday, and from now on we're going to celebrate birthdays together."

"That's a good reason. Happy birthday."

"Thank you. And two, I have a surprise for you."

"What?"

"It's a surprise. You can't see it yet."

"Why not?"

"Because you're going to have to do a little riding. Tomorrow."

———

In the morning, they rode from the pub together, taking a long trail deep into the woods. Eventually, he caught sight of the river through the trees, and began to hear the fall, where the old generator had been, and the channel was cut.

The channel was flowing.

She reined in.

"We walk from here."

They tied the horses, and he followed her along a path from the gate at the head of the channel, now partly raised, down an incline to a small clearing, where a wide, rust-colored metal box was four or five off the ground, on heavy posts. Wires ran from the top, through the trees, and back toward the channel. The sides of the box had rough slots cut top and bottom. Heat seemed to radiate from it.

The front of the box was hinged at one side, and had a handle at the other, and she turned the handle and swung open the door.

He stepped back as heat struck his face. Inside was an array of white rectangles, each wrapped in wire glowing red.

"What *is* it?"

"A test. What you're looking at are old toaster cores. This is a load box. You're looking at around ten kilowatts."

"Sounds like a lot."

"It's a step. Now, come on."

She shut the door and took his hand, and they walked together toward the channel, the roar of water now thundering, until they reached the edge where the channel ended and water arced onto Steve's old cross-flow turbine below.

Bolted to the turbine was a large cubical frame of blackened wood, coils of wire inside, and a big spinning wheel.

He yelled over the noise of the water.

"Is that what I think it is?"

"If you're thinking it's a new generator!"

He gaped, trying to follow her shouted explanation.

"It has a hybrid armature. Permanent magnets augmented with electromagnets. That means light weight and a lot of flux, but controllable, so the output can be regulated, within certain limits. I found asphalt in the City and coated the frame and joints. The joints are reinforced with plywood webbing—see? I had some trouble with the brushes—"

His arm had slipped about her waist, and now he pulled her against him, his mouth on hers, as the water slid past and crashed through the machine.

She pushed away, laughing.

"Remember, darling, it's a test! A prototype. It doesn't mean I'm ready to supply power."

But he was laughing. He threw his head back, and the sound of his laughter mingled with the roar of the fall.

92

The trail was unfamiliar, narrow and overgrown, barely a foot-path in places, that wound through the woods two or three miles from Service Hill.

He had never been this way before.

The horse balking at the dense trees, Max tied it and continued on foot, deeper inside the wood, silent rays of sunlight penetrating tangles of branches and new green leaves, the air warm and dry and quiet.

The path descended, and the wood changed. The trees became older, heavier, spaced farther apart, the forest floor carpeted with decomposing leaves.

Then a clearing, a kind of shallow bowl maybe thirty yards across.

At the far side, where the ground rose a little, stood a shack. Near it, a ring of stones encircled a small fire, with a pot balanced precariously between stones.

There was a single, battered chair.

Marco stepped out of the shack, leaning on a gnarled walking-stick.

He stopped.

"Come to gloat, boy?"

Max stopped as well, in the middle of the clearing, listening to the faint crackle of the fire.

"Gloat? No. Why would I?"

"I can think of one or two reasons." Marco studied him, the sunken eyes gray in the muted light. "But, no matter."

Max waited, unwilling to move closer without a sign, feeling somehow that it was trespass.

"So? Why are you here?"

He hesitated, looking at the shack and the small fire.

"Is this where you live?"

"It is where have I lived for many years."

"It's very . . . secluded."

"It suits me."

He smiled, in spite of himself. "I suppose it does."

"Well? Why are you here?"

"I'm not sure."

Seconds ticked by, like drops of time rolling down from ages past.

Marco nodded.

"I can offer you some tea."

Max walked across the clearing.

"There is, sadly, but one chair, and I am afraid I must lay claim to it. I am not as strong as I was."

"Of course, Brother Marco."

"Just Marco, if you please. There is no need for pretense here. There is another cup inside, if you don't mind fetching it."

Max stepped inside the shack, squeezing through the narrow space between the cot and small table beneath a long shelf burdened with books, cloth spines worn and faded. He found the cup and brought it outside.

Supporting himself with his stick, Marco carefully poured tea from the metal pan, handed a cup to Max, then lowered himself into his chair.

Max sat on a rock nearby.

"Brother Jim told me you'd left the church."

"There wasn't much point in remaining. I leave it in good hands, I think."

"I was surprised. I didn't think you'd ever leave it."

"Nor I. But there it is. I am an old man. I would only be in the way."

"Why do you say that?"

"Too much pain. I don't think I'll ever be free of it." He sipped a little tea. "I find I am not surprised to see you."

"No?"

"I think I've been expecting you."

"Why is that?"

For a moment, the old man looked at him, and the crystal eyes seemed to laugh.

"Perhaps because we are so much alike."

"Seriously? I don't think we're at all alike."

"Granted, it may be hard to see. But we're both religious men."

"You're too right. I don't see it at all."

"Well, perhaps you might, one day."

———————————

Max visited once or twice a week. Sometimes he brought the old man tea leaves and sugar. They talked, and Marco would make tea and shuffle about the clearing with his walking-stick, the knob of it worn smooth and fitted to his hand.

Sometimes Max would arrive to find the old man with one of his ancient books open in his lap, turning the pages with tender care. Other times he would find him gazing into the trees, deep in some kind of contemplation. But of what he thought about, he never spoke. He would just smile quietly when Max walked into the clearing.

They talked about many things. But one subject still preyed on him, and on a warm spring day Max spoke of it.

"Tell me something, Marco. Where is Brother Tom? What happened to him?"

Marco was bending over the fire, stirring the water.

"Why do you ask?"

"Some people think you killed him. You, or someone in your church."

The old man continued stirring, the water beginning to steam in the damp that lingered in the clearing.

"I arranged for his disgrace."

"You what?"

"I exposed him. I made Raul confess to their strange relationship. In front of the flock. A few of them."

"But . . . if you didn't approve . . . if it offended you . . . couldn't you have found a better way to deal with it?"

"Well, my boy, whether I approved or not had nothing to do with it. Tom had to go."

"So you could replace him."

"Someone had to."

"Why? Was he harming anyone?"

The water was steaming thickly now, the metal pan pinging.

"He was harming the church." Marco glanced at him. "You see? Tom had a gift. A vision, of something mighty. And the words to go with it. But when he began sleeping with the boy, the vision left him. He no longer cared. No longer cared about the one thing he had ever done in his miserable life that mattered."

"What about Renewal Day? I thought he cared about that."

"Only after I frightened him."

The water was boiling now, and Marco pulled the pan from the fire. He stirred in a little tea, watched the leaves swell, waited for them to settle, then poured into the old mugs.

Max carefully sipped a little of the scalding liquid.

"So you were his judge."

"His people judged him. Rather more harshly than I expected, but that is what comes of keeping secrets. People find out, and feel betrayed."

"What about Raul? How did you get him to confess?"

"Raul is a simple lad. The eclipse frightened him."

"Seriously? I thought the festival was planned around that. Doesn't he know what an eclipse is? Didn't anyone explain it?"

"You misunderstand. Of course Renewal Day was planned for the eclipse. But the eclipse did not occur on the appointed day. It happened the next day. A frightening slip in the cosmic gears, no? Why do you suppose it was? Was it a sign? Of divine displeasure? An accusing finger pointing down from the heavens at the corrupt author of Renewal Day and his unnatural lover?"

"That's ridiculous! Someone made a mistake."

"Of course someone made a mistake. Last year was a leap year."

Max lowered his tea and stared at Marco, who was smiling faintly, as if to himself.

"Such a simple thing. I looked at the town calendar. No February 29th. Someone forgot. A day was lost, and Tom never noticed. But then, he had much to distract him."

"And you let him pay for that mistake!"

"I had expected him to simply leave, and take his young plaything with him. Of course, the younger would have tired of the older, probably sooner rather than later, and there's no telling what Raul might have done then. The boy is not normal."

"So now you have your church. Was it worth it?"

"I think so. It will become an institution. It should outlive us all. But that will be for Brother Jim and the others. Not for me."

"You're not going back to it?"

Marco lowered himself into his chair, spilling a little tea, and leaned forward, cupping the mug in his hands, staring into the trees.

"I'm afraid little Marta has seen to that." He exhaled, a long deep sigh. *"I wish . . ."*

"What?"

But Marco just stared into the trees.

They argued often, the old man holding forth like an ancient philosopher or a deposed prince.

"The rule of law? You don't know the meaning of it! Until your courts in their hoary dignity and magisterial indifference lay waste to lives and seize property and commit the most awful injustice without violating a single procedure or neglecting a single precedent—you don't know what the rule of law is! You are amateurs. You do not even fear your own police. One day you will learn to dread your courts, and then you'll know."

"You're a cynic, Marco."

"Am I?"

Max shrugged. "Well, what do you expect me to think?"

"As I told you once, civilization means fighting. Or have you forgotten? Do you still deny it?"

"Paul Stevens told me it meant organization."

"And he was right."

"But you have people preaching that organization is slavery!"

"And so it has been."

"Then what's the answer?"

"Answer?"

"The solution!"

"What makes you think there is one? I know of no solution. Ten thousand years of civilization have not produced one. Ten thousand years is not enough. The race is still adapting."

"Adapting! To what?"

"To itself."

The old man looked up at the tops of trees surrounding the small glade. The sky was clear, and the air above seemed to shimmer with a kind of energy thrown back from the earth.

"To its intelligence. Its imagination."

For a moment, Max felt a sudden connection, as though he had looked into the old man's soul.

Then he remembered.

"But religion! Religion is such a giant leap backward! What does religion have to do with intelligence?"

"It has to do with imagination. What you object to, I think, is *organized* religion. Which is just a way to *use* imagination. The imagination was already there, already at work, but unharnessed. I merely harnessed it."

"But for what purpose?"

"For what purpose is any organization? To create an institution. To be a power. To rise above helplessness."

"By making other people *intellectually* helpless!"

"By changing their helplessness into strength. Their imagination already runs far ahead of their perception."

"Why not teach them? Wouldn't that be better, in the long run, than feeding them stories?"

"Teaching feeds the intelligence. Stories feed the imagination. And imagination is the mortar of organization."

The old man smiled, a knowing smile that slowly reached the crystal eyes laughing in their dark sockets.

"You don't like my methods, my friend. Then come up with your own."

One day in early summer, when Max walked across the clearing and looked around, he found the fire ring cold, the ashes scattered. And the walking stick was missing.

He stood by the shack and looked up at light filtering through the trees, at sparks of dust drifting through the light, dust, it seemed, drifting down to him from something that might once have been, centuries ago. A battle, perhaps. Or a city. Something that had changed the world.

He entered the shack, studied the shelf of books, pulled one down, and took it outside.

Settling into the old man's chair, he opened the book and began reading.

93

It is a good day.

Boiling surf roars up the beach, hisses in the sand, then retreats, spent, then roars again.

Sunlight falls through towering clouds of summer, falls splashing like liquid fire across heaving blue water rolling in from the horizon. Surf thunders and gulls scream and the beach seems to quiver underfoot, a shifting anvil for the pounding of the waves.

A head bobs in the water offshore, crowned with short white hair, followed by shoulders now surging with an easy stroke, a slow pace set for distance, moving seaward.

In the afternoon, a breeze comes up, whipping at the tattered white cloth hanging from a gnarled black stick stuck upright in the sand. The breeze freshens and the stick tilts, then falls to its side.

Freed, the cloth flies in the wind. It touches the sand, dancing, and flies on.

About the Author

D. M. Smith was born in Boston and has lived in New England, California, and Texas. Educated as an engineer, he started two technology companies and has since embarked on a second career in writing, sometimes pursued while driving around the American Southwest.